# THE SEVENTH PROTECTOR

DILARA KAYMAK

To mom,
who taught me that imagination is limitless and dreams are endless.

Thank you for your unconditional love and support.

# CHAPTER 1

The gray clouds staining the crimson sky shifted with the strong wind as they blocked the sun, preventing its light from touching the ground. The plants had yielded to the breeze that was strong enough to snatch them off their roots, and the trees had fallen in silence as their branches interlaced with each other. It was as if nature had lost all its vitality. The birds did not sing, nor did the earth breathe. There was no trace of the magic that ruled over everything.

Lying in a meadow surrounded by mountains, the man coughed harshly as his broad chest heaved with every breath he took. As blood seeped from the open wounds beneath his gold-colored steel armor and met the earth, he heard footsteps beating down on the ground. Before long, the dark figure returned. The wounded man put both of his hands on his sides as he tried to straighten up, but his body was in pain, making it impossible for him to move.

"You won't succeed," he said through his wheezing breath as he fixed his amber eyes on the stranger standing before him. "You're not powerful enough."

"Power?"

He witnessed the evil glitter in the gray eyes of the man in black as one side of his lip curled up. "I have the power of the gods."

Then the man leaned over and grabbed him by the cape. "One more gone," he said in a hiss. The hatred in his eyes was even more evident now.

As his other hand rose slowly, the wounded man could just barely open his eyes. The light emitting from the stranger's palm caused him to shiver.

"Five more . . ." said the stranger, and his smile broadened even more.

"Just five more to go."

# CHAPTER 2

*Two days later*

As the buzz rising from the town square grew fainter with each step I took, my eyes caught a glimpse of the wooden hut at the end of the road. I pressed the plants and the herbs I had bought to my chest so that they wouldn't fall as I climbed the broken steps. I pushed the wooden door with my shoulder to walk into the small house. The smell of dust filled my nose as soon as I stepped in, and I coughed roughly.

"I'm home!" I called out as I left the things I had bought on the wooden table in the kitchen. I half-opened the thick curtains, which could only manage to conceal part of the broken window behind the counter, to invite the sunlight in, while glancing at the dirty dishes and glasses lined up at the side.

"In here!"

I smiled as I turned around. My little sister was sitting at the other side of the counter. She began swinging her feet, which she had slid down from the wooden stool where she was perched, and waved at me. I walked over to her and pushed her golden hair to the back of her shoulder. My lips found her forehead.

"Hi, honey," I said as I put my hands on her shoulders and caressed her back. "What are you doing?"

Sarah was seven years younger than me. We both had the same golden hair and brown eyes but she was much more beautiful than I was. The smile spreading over her face brought the two large dimples in her cheeks into focus as her eyes turned to the paper in front of her.

"I'm drawing," she said, pointing at the almost-empty ink bottle she had left next to the paper. Her brushes were scattered on the counter, painting the wood black, as usual. "How does it look?"

I turned my eyes from the brushes to the torn paper in front of her and leaned forward to better see the figures she had drawn.

"This is what I drew," said Sarah, with a big smile on her face. "This is you."

Her index finger hovered over the still-wet ink and pointed at a vague figure with long hair. Then her finger traced the shorter figure standing beside the first one. "That's me," she said, then pointed at the other two. "And these are mom and dad."

My gaze shifted to the figure at the far end. Sarah had drawn him wearing the old hat that he always used to wear, and under the cloth cap were his rectangular-framed glasses. I leaned forward and embraced my sister with a bitter smile covering my face. "Is it done?" I asked.

When she nodded, I took the paper and walked to the back of the small room. I took a brush from the drawer, dipped it into the can of glue standing at the side, and pasted the picture on the wall. The paper took its place among the other pictures she had drawn over the years.

"This is nice," I said as I touched the smooth texture of the paper hanging on the wall. It was different from the ones she normally used. "Where did you get it?"

When she didn't answer, I folded my arms and turned to her. "Sarah?"

"I bought it." She wasn't looking at me. "I found some coins left on the counter."

I shut my eyes tightly. "Sarah," I breathed again.

Her brown eyes, full of guilt, found mine. She frowned. "Will you tell mom?"

I walked back toward her and kneeled in front of the wooden stool she sat on as I held her hands. "Of course not. But next time you need something, just tell me."

We didn't have many coins left until the end of the month, and I still had to buy a bunch of stuff. The paper, just like the paints and ink she was using, was expensive, and I wasn't able to buy it very often.

"I like drawing," I heard her murmur.

My fingertips gently went through her blonde hair. "I know."

"I want to be a painter." She still wasn't looking at me. "I will go to a rich city where nobles will pay for me to paint."

"You still have time to decide that," I said as I got up. "Don't worry about it now, you are still young."

It was really hard to survive but I didn't have the courage to tell my sister that it wouldn't work out for people like us. Nobles were out of our league and she should feel lucky if she ever had enough money to even leave the village.

Her curious gaze suddenly found mine. "And what do you want to be when you grow up?"

A smile formed on my lips, and I laughed at her question. "I am grown up."

"So, what do you want?"

I hesitated. It was odd to think that my little sister was the one asking this. But I didn't know what I wanted to do—I didn't have a single idea. I only wanted to survive, maybe not go to bed hungry or cold. But those weren't dreams, not in the way Sarah was so passionate about.

"You're home early."

My mother was standing at the kitchen door. When our eyes met, she left her cloth gloves on the counter and wiped her sweaty forehead as her hazel eyes looked around. I pointed at the herbs on the counter.

"I got what you asked," I said as I handed her the last remaining coins in my pocket.

My mother nodded slowly. "We don't have any water or rice left," she whispered. She looked at Sarah out of the corner of her eye to make sure she didn't hear us. "We're out of medicine, too."

"Is that what the herbs are for?"

I locked my hands on the back of my neck when my mother gave me a nod.

"I can go and bring water from the well in the evening," I said while I took off my partly tattered boots. Then I walked out of the kitchen and went to the bedroom. I sat on one of the stools by the window and extended my legs forward while my mother followed me inside. I stretched.

"What about meat?" I asked as she turned to me.

"What about it?"

"Sarah hasn't been eating properly," I said, trying to whisper. I knew she was still in the kitchen, drawing again, but I wasn't going to take any chances.

4

Mother shook her head before taking a deep breath. "We can't afford it, not for the next few weeks at least."

"I could help, you know."

Her eyes found mine; her face was unreadable. "You don't know how to hunt."

"I wasn't talking about hunting, mom."

As she looked at me, she realized what I meant and her eyes grew bigger. "No stealing," she said with anger. "We talked about it, Anna. You can't keep doing that."

I had to try hard not to roll my eyes. She was too proud, and I wondered if she knew other things I had stolen over the years. I knew she would never accept them once she knew, but I wasn't bothered with the idea. I was only trying to survive, and keeping my little family alive was my priority.

"I actually want to talk to you about something," she said, watching me with her bright eyes. I turned to her, questioning, and almost at the same time, we heard the sound of the bell chiming at the town square, just as we had been hearing it for the last two days.

"Long live the king," murmured mother, the same way she did every single time she heard the bells. Then she brought her hand slowly over her heart to pay her respects. This time, I rolled my eyes. None of them in the capital deserved our respect, yet there were people like her whom I could never understand.

When she was done, she turned back to me. She looked nervous, and I was curious enough to listen.

"Anna," my mother said, and rubbed her hands as she perched on the stool next to me. "You know that a new Protector has to be assigned to Aerlion after the death of our realm's previous Protector."

I nodded. "So?"

"The Selection Ceremony for the new Protector will be in three days . . . I heard that the families of contestants would be given money."

I quickly covered my face with my hands. "Mom," I said, protesting.

"Listen to me."

She quickly took my hands and held them away from my face. "You getting up there means that we will get paid by the kingdom. And it is an amount that would last us a few days at least."

5

Despite all the riches that the kingdom had, the people of my realm were very poor, and the fistful of money that would be given during the Selections was considered a large amount in where I lived. I could understand why my mother was being so insistent, but I didn't want to get on that platform, nor did I want to do anything in the name of the kingdom that had pauperized us to the point that we had become in need of the money they would give.

I abruptly withdrew my hands from her. "Then you can participate," I said harshly.

"That's why I ask this of you. I won't be in the village for a couple of days," she murmured. "There are wounded people in the neighboring villages. Rumors say that animal attacks have increased recently."

"Can't someone else go?"

"Everyone's going," she said. "That's the problem. It's more than one person can handle."

"Is it a bear attack?"

It was normal for the predatory animals I saw in the woods to attack humans. If you went far enough from the village, nature was never hospitable. We all knew that.

"I don't know. They say that those who went to the forest came back with deep wounds. I have to go, and I don't think I will be back for a few days."

"And you are telling me this now?" I said, protesting. "I can't get everything needed for the house and take care of Sarah at the same time." I frowned. "And I can't take her along, either. You know that!"

My mother leaned forward and held my hands again. She said nothing, but she didn't have to speak anyway. Her begging eyes were telling me enough.

I averted my gaze from her and looked around our old house. Most of the wooden parts of the hut had withered, and the wind blew in from the broken windows. Our pantry was almost empty and we were out of medicine for the next winter. I was forced to walk an hour to the nearest well because the flasks of water at the village stalls were more expensive than we could afford.

Through the half-open door, my eyes caught a glimpse of my sister sitting at the counter. Sarah was still drawing. But the ink in the bottle was gradually disappearing with every dip of her pen. And buying a new one for her could take longer than I thought.

I exhaled in defeat and said, "I'll never get chosen."

Mom only nodded. "I don't have such expectation, anyway."

Then she held my hands even tighter. "Anna, it's not your destiny to become a Protector. I know the Goddess won't choose you. But I don't want you to stay in the village, either. Only if we had some extra money . . ."

She couldn't finish. She didn't have to, anyway. By now, I had memorized the words that she had been saying for the past few years. The only goal of my parents was to have more money and to leave this village behind. They wanted to go to the capital city, which was full of riches and where people never went to bed hungry, so they could give a better future to Sarah and me. They were sure they could find a job as healers, a job they had been doing in our village over the years. But all our dreams had ended with my father's sudden death. I didn't even remember my mother talking about this since then.

"Fine," I said, nodding with my eyes shut tightly. "I'll do it."

I heard my mother breathe a sigh of relief. She pressed her dry lips to my forehead and drew back. Then she stood up and took silent steps out of the room toward the counter. She glanced at Sarah before beginning to sort out the herbs I had left.

I got up and walked to the armchair in the corner of the room. I sat at the edge of the cushion and pulled out the box from under the mattress. Opening the lid, I took out my father's dusty, rectangular-framed glasses.

"For our future," I murmured, trying to be silent. My eyes filled with tears. "For Sarah."

# CHAPTER 3

As I was passing through the crowd in the town square, I rose up on my tiptoes to check the direction I was headed. I could see the high platform on the other side of the human flood.

I jerked back in order not to hit an old woman who had just appeared in front of me, as if I had to be reminded how crowded the village was today. From where I was, I could see the line moving toward the platform. I directed my steps to that side, and at the same time, I saw a group of royal guards standing next to the wooden platform. It was hard not to notice them. Today, they were everywhere.

The gaze of one of the guards was on a boy standing in front of the group. I knit my eyebrows and moved closer to hear them better. I could hear the conversation rising from the group. Just then, one of them pushed the little boy back. His thrust wasn't a light one. The boy stumbled but he didn't seem to be bothered at all—he was trying to explain something to them with a desperate expression on his face. I breathed harshly.

The royal guards of the capital represented the kingdom, and that was the only reason I needed to hate them. Royal guards provided security in the capital city, and there were only a few of them staying in the village to prevent any possible unrest. But I had never seen such a crowd before today. As their voices rose once again, I took a hesitant step toward them.

The little boy was between the stall behind him and the guards in the front and I noticed he was trembling. From what I could understand, the guards hadn't allowed the boy to sell whatever he had for safety reasons, and they were doing everything they could to make him go away. But they weren't allowing enough time for the kid to gather his stuff and leave.

I looked at the boy. He seemed around the same age as Sarah. With that, I exhaled angrily. I didn't know what I could do but I wanted to intervene. I clenched my fists but before I could move again, I was swiftly drawn to the other side of the crowd by the hand that had grabbed me by my wrist.

"Anna, come here, darling. I can't let you get in trouble, especially when your mother isn't around."

I faced two blue eyes as soon as I turned my head. Agatha was our only friend in the small village. Although she was a few years older than my mother, she always wanted us to call her by her first name. She was cheery, full of life, and—in the words of the villagers—a bit crazy.

"Come now," she said, and pulled me in front of one of the shops.

Agatha and her husband, Mr. Albert Whitby, had settled in my village about five years ago. She always said that, although they weren't as influential as the leading noble families that ruled the capital city, they once used to have as much power as the lesser nobles. When her merchant husband lost all his possessions, they had been forced to move to our humble village.

"I hope your mother will be back in a few days," she said. "I heard the news. It's terrible."

I eyed her from head to toe while she started to swing the feather-covered fan that she always carried around. I had heard that Mr. Whitby had sold Agatha's jewelry to pay for his debts, but she had somehow managed to hold on to her clothes. She always walked around the village in the fine dresses, which I thought she once wore in her mansion. Now, as I gazed at her, I could see that she had no interest in the affairs of the village despite the many years that had passed. Today she was wearing a sky-blue dress with a huge bow, and she seemed not to care about the fact that her hem was getting muddier with each step she took. Apparently, some habits were very difficult to get rid of.

"She's supposed to return today," I murmured, but my eyes kept turning toward the group. The little boy was already gone and the guards weren't allowing anyone to get close to them. I knew that he would have made some sales if he could have remained at the village square for a few more hours. We were all hungry and in need of money. But none of the people from the capital cared.

Agatha followed my gaze. "The strong will always stomp on the weak. This was the first thing I learned while living in the capital. You can't change the system, my dear."

Then she folded her fan and walked in front of me. My eyes focused on her messy hair, which she had tied at the top of her head with a few old hair clips.

"Where's your sister? It's been days since I've seen Sarah! I always tell her she can drop by anytime she wants, but she's always too shy when you're not around!"

Ever since mom had gone, I had been forced to take care of my sister in addition to doing the housework. But at this hour Sarah was at school, as were most of the children in the village, and I had one less problem on my mind for a few hours.

"You know she's at school," I said as I took a step back.

Despite all the time that had passed, I still hadn't gotten used to how warm Agatha was toward us. This was the reason why the Whitby couple were the only people I spent time with, other than my mother and my sister, but it still felt weird. I was too feral for the rest of the villagers. The only thing I had been trying to do since my father's death was to make sure my family got through the winter comfortably. It had been years since I'd had time to sit and chat with other people.

I raised an eyebrow and asked, "So, where's Mr. Whitby?"

She laughed aloud. "The best part of being married to a merchant is that he is rarely at home."

I followed her gaze, which turned to the platform. "Don't tell me you're here for the Selection," I said. The Whitby ranch was at the far end of the village, and Agatha didn't like the villagers. I couldn't believe she came all that way just for this.

She opened her fan once again and began swinging with slow motions of her wrist. "Of course, I'm here for it! I can buy a new pair of earrings with the money that the kingdom will pay to the contestants."

Mr. Whitby was the most cautious man I had ever seen when it came to money. He had become even stricter, after some years in the village, realizing the fact that they would never return to their old life in the capital. He would absolutely have stopped his wife if he had known what she intended to do with the money, but he was out of town. There couldn't have been better timing for Agatha.

"When is he coming back?"

"Ah," she said with a grin on her face. "I hope not for a long time."

Then she reached for my hand in excitement. "Did you see the guardsmen? There are so many of them. I'd like to see those pretty faces under the helmets. You can't imagine how charming they can be!"

I rolled my eyes as the smile on her face broadened with her own words. No matter how friendly Agatha was with me and my family, she was born a noblewoman and she had lived in luxury for many years. I was repeatedly reminded of this with every word that came out of her mouth.

"Probably, they all have the same arrogant expression," I murmured.

"There is nothing more than arrogance at the capital city," she said, and continued in the same breath. "That much money and power will mislead anyone."

From the corner of her eye, she looked at the guards standing by the boy's stall. "Even them."

Even if you were just one of the thousands of guards at the palace, you could have a wonderful life just because you lived in the capital. But I couldn't even imagine such a life. I had never been there in my life and I never intended to.

"Imagine if you were chosen!" she added with excitement. "Ah, the royal palace is beautiful! And you have no idea how attractive the king is!"

When she giggled, I grimaced. Unlike her, I wasn't so thrilled to see the palace or the king. He was only one of the hundreds of arrogant nobles in the capital.

"I am only here for the money," I reminded her.

As the crowd in front of the platform grew, I realized that more people than I had expected had come to take their chances.

"We'd better get in line." She turned to me quickly as if she had just remembered something. "Come to my house with your sister this evening, even if your mother doesn't come back. We'll have a feast for ourselves while Albert isn't around, with a part of the money they give."

It was touching that she was willing to spend part of her money on us. My mouth watered with just the thought of the foods that could be bought. But before I could say anything, she winked at me and pulled me toward the line in front of the platform. The fact that this place was so crowded clearly showed all of us how much the people living in my realm were dependent on the kingdom.

I was living in one of the Seven Realms under the rule of the capital city, Ardria, and my realm Aerlion, where hunger and poverty reigned, was the smallest and the most destitute compared to the others. We were called the Seventh Realm.

All the realms were connected through gates to the capital to the lands where the king and the nobles lived, and the Protectors existed to ensure the balance in the Seven Realms between the poor and the rich, the people and the nobles, and between those with or without magical powers. Five days had passed since the death of the Protector of Aerlion, and during this time, the king's royal guards had visited the villages in my realm one by one, unceasingly searching for the new Protector of the gates. And now, it was the turn of this tiny village where I had spent my whole life.

My gaze wandered around the crowd once again. Only one Protector from each realm could be chosen, and according to what people said, the search for the Protector could last for days, even weeks. It was for this very reason that the kingdom was giving money to the poor people to increase the number of participants. And this was also the reason for the crowd gathered here today. Everyone would take his or her chances if it meant getting out of this place and earning more money than we could even dream of.

I stood waiting in line behind a middle-aged man, and Agatha was right behind me. It took only a few seconds to arrive at the front of the line. As the guard eyed me with her cold gaze, the guard sitting at the other side of the desk asked my name.

"Anna Clayton," I said.

The woman's gaze turned to Agatha, and I noticed her noting down yet another name on the list in front of her. "Next."

Before I walked away from the desk, I took the pouch filled with money given to me and couldn't help but smile. Mother was right; we didn't have to worry for a few days at least.

I headed to the wooden stairs on the right side and blended in with other people standing side by side. One of the royal guards came over.

"Open your hand."

I turned my palm to the guard and watched as he left a leaf there. Then, he did the same to Agatha, who was standing next to me now. While I curiously stared at my hand, I couldn't help but notice the effect it had on me. When I looked at the participants around me, I saw that they were all looking down, focused on their palms. I looked at the leaf, trying to figure out what it had to do with the ceremony.

The sound of ground-shaking footsteps ended the buzzing in the air and caused me to turn toward them. The steps belonged to a big group of people. I looked at the stairs that led to the platform and saw the group that was walking in the direction opposite from where we were gathered. And from the increasing whispers, I realized that I wasn't the only one who had noticed them.

The group stood across from us and I found enough time to examine them before a bell was rung to silence the crowd. They wore the same silver armor as the royal guards, but their blue capes, hanging down over their shoulders, separated them from the rest. The long swords on their waists caught my attention.

I leaned forward. "Who are they?" I asked in curiosity. "They are not royal guards, are they?"

Agatha turned her gaze to me. "Oh, them? They are the Phoenixes," she said as her eyes fixed on the group. "They are special, dear."

"Special?"

She nodded. "They are the guards of the Protectors. Contrary to the kingdom's royal guards, they have magical powers just like the Protectors. That's what makes them special," she said. "The Phoenixes are given to the kingdom at a young age to be raised once the magic they carry is discovered, and they get training in Ardria. When a new Protector is needed, they are the first ones to be tried out. And then, they join the army of the newly selected Protector to serve the kingdom."

She was smiling as her eyes wandered over them. From her past life in the capital, she knew a lot about the kingdom. "They are specially trained, and very skilled soldiers."

"Is that the same for the other realms, too?" I asked, still curious.

Agatha leaned her weight on one of her legs and wiped a drop of sweat on her forehead. "There are Phoenixes in each of the Seven Realms.

I used to see them in the capital, but not during the time I spent in the palace. They were not allowed to go in freely there."

At those words, I glanced at her. "Why not?"

She was whispering now. "When I was still living in the capital, I heard something. Some of the nobles were talking—they said that the Phoenixes had rebelled against the kingdom some centuries ago." She looked back at me. "And that they tried to take control of the Seven Realms. It wasn't a topic that was discussed freely, so that is all I know. They work for the kingdom, but they take orders from their Protectors. That is why the nobles never liked them."

"And what about you?" I asked her.

Agatha only shrugged. "They are all right, I guess, but I wasn't as powerful as the other nobles in the capital. So, I don't know the details . . . all I know is that the king had taken the Phoenixes out of his staff and that he put them under the command of the Protectors. No one wants to deal with them anymore. That's why they belong to the Protectors."

"So why are they here?" I asked as I continued to stare at them. I guessed they had probably been to other villages in my realm and taken part in dozens of ceremonies before arriving where I lived. Aerlion was big enough to have hundreds of villages. "If they've taken part in the Selections at other villages, isn't it meaningless for them to try again with us here? To continue traveling?"

Agatha shook her head in disagreement. "They can't serve anyone until a Protector is chosen. They have to be here. Besides . . ." she paused and turned her head over to the group as she pointed at the leaves that the Phoenixes were holding in their hands. They were the same as the ones we had been given. "Imagine that you trained all your life for the skills a Protector needs to have only to serve someone else. Isn't that humiliating?"

She continued after a short break. "The reason why they are here is . . . well, the Protector is still not chosen, right? Who knows how many more villages they have to go to! I guess they continue to try out, no matter how degrading it is. Maybe they are trying to prove that all those years of training haven't been in vain."

I faced forward and said nothing as I watched the group. Just then, the chimes of the bell rang out. The buzzing of the crowd was cut like a sharp knife at the same time a guard put the last leaf into the hands of a child at the end of the line. I could see that everyone was standing upright, staring at the leaves in their hands. We were all waiting in deep silence, tension rising. Soon after, I heard the sound of strong steps climbing to the platform, and I raised my head.

I saw an old man who had tied his gray hair, streaked with white strands, at the back of his head. In contrast to the others, he was wearing a red cape over his silver armor. His sword was hanging from his waist and he looked more splendid with each step he took. Although I had no idea who he was, it didn't take long for me to realize he was a man of high rank. Perhaps the real reason for the silence was having someone like him in our tiny village; I didn't think that anyone here had ever seen a nobleman in their lives.

The old man turned around when he reached the middle of the platform and took a short glance at the side where the group of Phoenixes stood. Then he turned to us. Now he was an equal distance from both groups. We were all watching him carefully while he slowly reached for the sword at his waist. The old man held the sword with both hands, lowered its tip down on the wooden platform, and stood straight as if he was leaning onto a stick. I couldn't hide my disappointment. I was expecting something different, perhaps something *magical*.

"Focus down on your hands."

As everyone lowered their gaze, the first thing that came to my mind was how his voice was even colder than his appearance. The platform and the rest of the town square had fallen into a deep silence with his words. The stranger was standing as still as a statue, and his eyes were fixed on the sky. I followed his gaze and looked back over my shoulder to see that the sky had been painted crimson. And the sun was about to set.

I shut my eyes as the others did. I had a lot on my mind. I would have to pick Sarah up from school after I was finished here. Then we would go home, or maybe we could stop by Agatha's first, as she had offered. I was surprised that my stomach didn't grumble at the thought of this. Although the Whitby couple were not so financially different from the rest of us in the village, Agatha would have her way when it came to spending for pleasure. She was still holding on to habits she had from her old, noble life. I tried to think about how Sarah's eyes would grow wide when she saw the food, but then . . .

The platform began to tremble.

I opened my eyes in fear and noticed the cracks forming on the wooden platform under us. With each second, they were getting bigger. A few heads turned down to the wooden platform and I heard someone taking a sharp breath in fear. I wanted to shout and tell everyone to run. I wanted to leave. But I was lost for words as a sharp feeling suddenly stabbed me in the chest.

My gaze was drawn to my palm as I blinked at the creepy feeling that spread from my fingertips to my back, and from there to all over my body. The leaf in my hand suddenly started to float into the sky in bright light. A shocked breath escaped my lips and then I involuntarily let out a small shriek. The spreading light became even brighter.

"My dear . . . you . . ."

The leaf Agatha was holding glided in the air and found the wooden surface of the platform. Her astonished voice must have drawn attention since the eyes of almost everyone in the crowd were turned to me within a few seconds.

I saw that the old man at the middle of the platform had half-opened his eyes, which he had shut a few minutes ago. And it didn't take long before I became the point of his cold gaze. He straightened up, picked up the sword, and began walking over to me with steps that shook the floor. I moved back in bafflement while the crowd parted to both sides, giving him enough space to walk through. The leaf fell from my hand but the white light continued to spread from the spot where it had once been.

The man stood right before me and lowered his dark eyes from my face to my palms. I immediately became more tense, with his tough gaze focused there. The light was still spreading. I gasped.

As he faced the crowd, I barely heard the words coming out of his lips. "The Goddess has made her choice!"

I watched him raise his sword and stick it into the floor right in front of me, harsher this time, before kneeling. As if it was a signal, everyone else followed him. There were no more whispers or humming anymore. People began to bow one by one, and I looked at the floor, searching for the leaf that had dropped from my hand a moment ago. But it had already flown away.

I turned to Agatha, in need of help, but she wasn't any different from the rest. And it wasn't only the villagers, either. I could see that the royal guards waiting below the platform, and the Phoenixes standing across, were all on one knee.

I wanted to beg the people to stand up. I was confused and I felt helpless. But then. . . I took a sharp breath.

I was now the Seventh Protector.

# CHAPTER 4

I took a big step while trying to get rid of the odd feeling in my stomach. I blinked a couple of times, trying to forget how nervous I was. It felt hard to breathe. I wiped my sweaty palms on my pants and continued to look around, just as I had been doing for the last few minutes.

Giant chandeliers were placed on both sides of the walls that were full of paintings, and their light saved the hallway from drowning in darkness. The wide windows were partially covered with velvet curtains, and a cool breeze was coming in from somewhere, causing me to shiver. The servants, who were running around with silver trays in their hands, paused for a moment to peek at me before they went on their way, disappearing in the hallway in both directions.

All I could think about, as we continued to walk, was that everything had happened so quickly. And there was only one question on my mind: Why me? When I remembered the shocked gazes of the people focused on me, I brought my hands to my chest and looked for the white light that had spread from my palms only a few hours ago. But nothing happened; whatever that was, it had disappeared without a trace.

My eyes wandered over the portraits that almost seemed to be alive on the walls. I was fascinated by these after having seen the pictures Sarah drew. We didn't have the means to pay for paints or canvasses, and after the figures my sister drew with ink, this place was evidence of why the capital was so unreachable for people like me. With this thought, I kept looking at the big sconces hanging next to each other along the way.

"Are these made of real gold?"

I wasn't aware that I had been thinking out loud until I noticed that the guard on my left had turned his gaze to me. He nodded and said, "Yes, my lady."

Just then, both the escorting guards slowed down. I took my gaze away from the marble floor and focused on the big door in front of us. We had arrived.

The doors opened even more slowly than I had expected under the watchful eyes of the guards standing at both sides of the marble door. Time seemed to have slowed down. I didn't even notice that the other guards by my side had withdrawn to the corners. The light coming out of the open door glared in my eyes as I tried to make out the figures that had appeared inside the big room.

I brought both of my hands to my sides and held my breath. At the rear of the room, there were nobles lined up on both sides of the throne room in their elegant clothes, and with jewelry that was too much for me to ever afford. They all turned and looked at me as I walked by.

While their sharp gazes never left me along the way, I heard a few people murmur. I lowered my head and took a look at my old clothes. I was wearing the same leather boots that I had been wearing for many years, fabric trousers, and a white shirt. I felt crushed under these people's stares. The wall between the nobles and people like me became thicker. I couldn't help but question what I was doing in the capital. I didn't belong here. I really wanted all of this to be a nightmare.

I stopped for a second at the smell, surprised that my stomach didn't growl. My eyes caught two tables behind the nobles gathered on the opposite side of the throne room. Meats, fruits, and more. The wine bottles were placed on the tables and most of the lords and ladies were carrying crystal glasses filled with red wine. They were having a *feast*. My eyes grew wide at the amount of food left on the table. Never, even during special occasions, had I seen this amount of food at home. So, this was their life in the capital while people where I lived suffered to find something to eat?

It was impossible not to be fascinated by the opulence of the interior. The stone walls, just as those in the hallway that I had just passed, were covered with paintings of a similar style. There were marble statues in front of the tall columns. The curved walls joined at the top and there was a giant crystal chandelier hanging from the dome.

The whispers started once again, this time more quietly. I fixed my gaze on the people, realizing that it wasn't just the lords and ladies lined up at the rear who were watching me.

19

On the left side of the room, there were four men and a woman wearing robe-like black jackets. The golden royal standard was embossed on their jackets, at the arm. I didn't know if it was because of his old age or because he was squinting his eyes as he examined me, but the face of the old man at the front of the group was in wrinkles. This made it almost impossible for me to guess how old he was. I fidgeted uneasily and looked at the others next to him.

One of the men had tied his thick hair, which had white strands here and there, at the back, and his dark eyes were buried under his thick eyebrows. The black jacket he was wearing was able to cover only a part of his long body, and the steel armor he wore under the dark-colored fabric was almost shining under the jacket. Then, behind him, I noticed the young man who was hiding like a shadow. His gaze was fixed on the ground, examining the marble floor with uncaring eyes.

Right next to him was another man, dark-haired and quite young. His eyes were scanning the throne room, and he was smiling at the nobles behind as if he had found something more amusing to do. Lastly, I turned to look at the woman standing at the side. She was very tall and had a slim body. Her pitch-black hair fell over her shoulders, bringing her long neck to the forefront, and she was studying me curiously with her large green eyes. A warm smile appeared when our eyes met, and I quickly turned away to look at the group on my right.

The other group consisted of six people. Two of them were women, and their golden armor wrapped their bodies like a second skin. The proudly puffed chests of the four men next to them were covered with bright steel. The royal symbol, which was embossed on the flags and the jackets of the other group, was also woven on the group's black capes, which hung over their broad shoulders.

While I continued to examine them, I felt the weight of a pair of eyes that had focused on me. I turned my head to the dark eyes that had been following me ever since I entered the room, and when I caught a glimpse of the marble stairs, I saw the man sitting on the iron throne. A pair of black eyes eyed me from head to toe.

The pressure on me began showing its effect once again. I began looking at him just as he had been doing, whereas I probably should have bowed. It was difficult to find even a single person in the Seven Realms who didn't know who he was. But Agatha was right—he was indeed handsome, and his appearance before me had left me breathless.

His back, which was set in a way that made him appear to be carrying the weight of the world on his shoulders, was upright and drawn like a bow, as if it refused to lean on the throne. The new growth of stubbly beard on his warm-toned skin made his face appear tougher. And his black hair, as dark as his eyes, stretched from his ears to his neck. His thick curved eyebrows cast shadows over his eyes that looked cold as ice, and for a second, I thought I was going to shiver under his gaze.

He was much younger than I expected him to be, maybe in his early twenties. He was one of the most beautiful men I'd ever seen and looked much healthier than all the starving or ill boys in my village.

As I continued to examine his face with great curiosity, I thought he was in mourning. I didn't know how I knew that but I could distinguish sorrow behind his tough expression. I had seen the same expression on the villagers each time sickness or hunger took one of us. Sadness had spread over his face like a mask. Just like everyone at the palace, I thought he too was probably in mourning. And deep inside, I felt that this was because of the death of the Protector before me.

I bowed very slowly and with hesitation, and the whispers finally ceased one by one. The person who cleared his throat loudly was no one other than King Warren, who was sitting on the big iron throne.

"Welcome to Ardria, *Protector*."

*Protector*. I thought I would never get used to this title. I had gotten out of the village where I had been raised, and I had come to the lands of the king. And now, I was in the royal palace. I was surrounded by nobles, and the ruler of the Seven Realms was sitting right in front of me. All of this felt so strange that I wanted to run back to the village and never leave it again.

Ardria, the capital city of the Seven Realms, had always been full of safety and wealth. While my realm, Aerlion, and the others were in poverty and fighting for survival, this place had always been unreachable. And no one had ever lent a hand. Even the previous Protector of Aerlion, my predecessor, had turned his back on us. But it wasn't just him or the king to blame. The system that had spread from the capital to the other

Seven Realms had been in place since the first rulers, and as it was getting worse each passing day, thousands of people like me were suffering from it ever since.

"Upon the death of the previous Protector of Aerlion, the crystals have chosen you," he said, but the expression on his face made me think that he didn't want to believe that. After a moment's pause, he pulled his gaze away from me and turned to the people in the throne room. "You must take his place and assume his duties to continue from where he left."

When King Warren paused once again, it appeared as if he didn't know what to say next. When he stood up and raised his hand slowly in the meantime, the lords and ladies behind us bowed to him and started to leave the room. No one spoke for some time. The only thing that could be heard in the room was the sounds of steps hurrying out.

When one of the guards closed the door from the outside, the gaze of the king and those in the two groups standing at his sides found me. They all looked ready to speak. The stable and calm expressions, which they had worn like masks on their faces while the lords and ladies were in the room, quickly disappeared as whispers grew louder in the throne room once again.

"You," said the old man in a black cape, standing in the group at the king's right side. He took a step forward. His face was wrinkled with age and the deep lines were buried under his gray beard. The thick mesh of his cape was having difficulty covering his belly. I witnessed the cruel expression on his face as the golden bracelets that he had lined up on his right arm rattled when he threateningly swung his hand toward me.

He disappointedly eyed me from head to toe. "You're just a child! Look at her! There must be a huge mistake."

I narrowed my gaze at his words, forcing myself not to open my mouth and respond. I knew that everyone in the room, including King Warren, was watching me. Now I better understood why the king had let the nobles out of the room.

"The crystals have chosen the wrong one!"

"The crystals are never wrong."

The voice that rose from behind the giant pillars caused me to turn in that direction to see a man stepping out from the shadows into the light. It didn't take long for me to realize that he was the man I had seen at the platform today. He was still wearing the silver armor that he had been wearing before. The red cape over his shoulders swayed with each long step he took toward us. His dark eyes alternated between King Warren and the old man.

I immediately turned to the king. I could hear the old man laugh as I said, "There has to be a mistake."

"As I told you," murmured the old man under his breath.

I paid no attention and went on without taking my gaze away from the king. "I just participated for the money. I'm not a Protector! Please believe me."

The king remained silent for a while as his gaze slowly wandered over me. His expression was harsh, though I could see the way his eyes softened. "This is your destiny."

"You're making a mistake!" I snapped in response.

My knit eyebrows loosened up as I saw the king become serious in contrast. He tilted his head to the side and rested his arms on both sides of the throne. "And what makes you think the crystals were wrong?"

I didn't even know what the crystals were. I was a total stranger to the magic in the Seven Realms. My lips parted but I couldn't speak. I didn't know how to answer. The king continued.

"Magic responds to the one who truly possesses it. The guards have visited many villages in the last few days but we got no results from anyone. All until it was your turn."

"I don't want to be a Protector," I finally said. "I just want to go back home."

I thought of my mother, to whom I could say goodbye only briefly because she had come home late after the ceremony, and of Sarah, who was afraid after being picked up from school by the royal guards while I was trying to reach out to her. I couldn't believe that I had been in the village only a couple of hours ago until the guards took me away from the only people I cared for.

"So, we have to trust this child to take care of the people of the Seven Realms, huh?" The voice of the old man in the black cape filled the room once again as he went on. "Disappointing."

The king looked irritated. But before he could speak, the man in the red cape, who was still standing next to me, suddenly turned to him and said, "Careful, Lord Cheng." The man's lips formed a straight line when their eyes met.

"Your duty is to talk *only* during the King's Council. You will not dare to protest the decision of the Goddess in front of King Warren himself."

The man's words caused the throne room to fall into a deep silence. I noticed that the lord was looking at me with a grimace. But he bowed to the king and moved back to his place with slow steps as I glanced at the two groups. The man right next to me had mentioned the King's Council. So, did that mean that the people in the other group were the rest of the Protectors?

I turned my gaze back at the group of council members wearing capes and caught a glimpse of the tall man standing next to the old lord. The corners of the middle-aged lord's lips had curved upward under his thick beard. He looked at the red-caped man next to me and grinned vaguely. At that moment, I realized how similar they looked; their faces were almost identical.

The red-caped man turned to me again. As he leaned forward, a few tufts of his tied hair, with white strands among them, came loose and shadowed his long face.

"You will protect Aerlion from now on," he said. Then, he did something I never thought he would do. He placed a warm smile on his face, making him appear a few years younger. I was taken aback when he held my hands and pulled my palms to himself. He looked at the spot where the light had spread a few hours ago. "You are ready for this. There could be no mistake that the crystals chose you . . . I can feel the magic you carry."

He looked at the grimacing Lord Cheng and at King Warren, who was still watching us indecisively. I tried not to think about his gaze on me.

"And a voice inside me says that you will soon prove this to all of us."

When he turned back to me, I saw that his eyes were shining with excitement.

"Welcome to Ardria, Protector Anna."

# CHAPTER 5

"One more time."

The tall and skinny body of the middle-aged man standing in front of me was covered with a dark green cape, and the silver armor he wore revealed itself through the wide green fabric as he harshly threw his tied gray hair over his shoulder and crossed his arms.

"Again!"

"I *am* trying!" I snapped at him. I wiped my sweaty forehead on my arm and tried to stay balanced under the weight of the heavy armor I was wearing.

The commander shook his head.

"Stop whining like a child and do what you're told."

I only sighed. In a corner of the big palace courtyard, I was continuing the training that I had begun on the day I arrived here. And in the meantime, I was trying to fulfill all of Commander Balfour's orders.

I was told that each Protector's army had a commander who was directly under the command of the Protector. Commander Balfour was born in my realm, Aerlion. He was quite strict when it came to my training, and he had been the right hand of my predecessor. With his death, Balfour was forced to leave his desk duty and come over to train the new Protector of Aerlion. But I couldn't say that I was in any kind of shape, despite our days of training.

Hours had followed days, days had chased weeks, and I had completely lost track of time. When night came, I would go to my room and try to stay as far away from the others in the palace as I possibly could. My new room was almost as big as my house, and it had been enough to make my head spin. I spent all my free time in it, and I tried my best to remain out of sight.

The King's Council hadn't convened since I had stepped into the palace, nor had King Warren called the Protectors to his presence. I didn't know if I was the cause of the problem, but I wasn't complaining, either. The more distance I put between them and myself, the less I would see the disappointment in their faces when they looked at me. Some of them were better at acting, but their eyes said a lot. I wasn't wanted here.

I lost my breath with the blow I received to my abdomen and found myself on the ground. I opened my eyes wide with fury and turned to the commander. He only shrugged.

"You are not focusing."

"Because I can't do it!"

I threw my wooden sword harshly to the ground. The sword slid across the courtyard and stopped next to the commander's feet. He stepped on it with his leather boots.

I extended my arms to the sides and pointed at myself. My hair was messy and I was soaked by sweat and covered with dirt. "What do you think I've been doing all these days? Don't you have more important things to do? Can't you just leave me alone?"

I exhaled, let myself back on the ground, and turned my head to lean my cheek onto the cold stone floor of the courtyard. I focused my eyes on the garden behind the courtyard and on the cloudless blue sky that was visible through the thick trees. I could hear the birds chirping. As I felt the breeze brushing my hair, I closed my eyes.

Then the footsteps approached. "I can't. The king pays me to train you."

I raised an eyebrow and opened my eyes to see the smirk on Commander Balfour's face. And in the blink of an eye, with agility un-expected from one his age, he took the wooden sword from the ground and tossed it over to me. I caught it by the hilt as I sat up. My bewildered eyes met his.

"Are you trying to kill me?"

"Your reflexes are improving . . . although slowly, very slowly."

"Great! I can do *this* after all those days."

I kept staring at him as he straightened his dark green cape. The color of the Phoenixes' capes was blue and the Protectors' was black. The old man who had brought me to the capital after the ceremony in Aerlion was the only person in the palace to wear red, as far as I could see. I made a note to ask Balfour about him. And this was how we were separated from each other in the palace.

"Your opinion will change completely once you realize how honorable your duty here is. You are special, Anna."

Commander Balfour sat down next to me.

I thought I should be thankful for having him here instead of one of the commanders of the other six realms. I had seen them only once. All seven commanders had been waiting for their Protectors while I walked out of the throne room on the day I had arrived. I remembered Balfour dragging me to my quarters under their sharp gazes. Compared to them, and despite all my complaints, even the strict Balfour was much friendlier.

"I don't understand why I work so much. I don't even get out of the palace!"

Balfour turned to look at me. "You are getting ready to be a Protector. You need to possess all the fundamental skills."

"And for what? To carry my sword as adornment and live in luxury for the rest of my life?"

I straightened my back and sat like him. "Look at me," I said. "I can never be like the Protector before me. I have no experience; I don't know how to fight. I cannot protect the people of the Seven Realms. There has to be a big mistake."

"The crystals are never wrong."

I covered my face with my hands. "Crystals!" I frowned. "Everyone keeps saying that! What are the crystals?"

The commander stared at me for a while. "You don't know the story?"

When I shook my head, he exhaled and laid his sword down next to mine. "Do you remember the leaves given to the candidates during the Selection?"

I nodded and he went on. "They are leaves from the Vitae, the Tree of Life. Each of them bears magic much greater than you could imagine."

I turned my head to the commander with the story I was hearing for the first time. He had managed to attract my attention. He placed a victorious smile on his face and turned his eyes to the sky. "The Tree of Life is in Ardria, the capital, which is at the center of the Seven Realms, and where all the realms are connected with magic since the beginning of time."

His interest in history was all too evident. And now I could see how eager he was to enlighten a stranger who knew nothing about the past of our world.

"It is said that this tree bears the powers of the Goddess Vitae. The name comes from there. According to popular belief, the Goddess divided the world into eight realms and chose seven people to protect the realms surrounding Ardria. And she gave each of them a dragon. Their duty was to provide security for the hundreds of gates that connected the realms to each other."

My eyes found the white stone walls at the far end of the courtyard. The palace that was surrounded by trees looked quite plain but was majestic from the outside. I could have thought differently if I hadn't known the lushness of the inside. But even the harmony of the velvet and gold that dominated the interior was enough reason for me to hate this place.

"Seasons and days had begun to form and after the first winter, the tree gave seven buds and they all had seven different crystals inside. These crystals carried the magic of the Seven Realms. Some believe that the crystals were the heart of the Goddess, which she divided into seven different pieces against evil, and they were all left for the Protectors."

I turned my gaze back to Balfour and saw him loosening the ties of his green cape. "Vitae is the source of the magic in the realms. And the leaf given to you on Selection Day was just one of those that had fallen from it. They carry the magic from the tree—that's why they are given during the Selection ceremonies. They form a chain between the creatures of magic."

"So, is this true then? The story, I mean?"

Balfour nodded slowly. "The Tree of Life is majestic. And so are the main gates in the palace."

He looked at me and went on, "Perhaps we should take a break from the training. I can take you to the main gate of Aerlion. I bet you want to see it."

He suddenly rose without waiting for me and took his sword from the ground before walking away. I got up quickly. I realized that I would be doing something significant for the first time since I had come here, and it brought a smile to my face. I left my wooden sword on the ground and followed him. After walking around the wide courtyard, we passed through the forest, which was in the opposite direction from the palace. The terrain became steeper as we walked and I felt weeds brushing against my skin with each step I took.

"I thought we were going to the main gate."

Balfour didn't even turn around to look at me. He was easily striding along the path that he had memorized over the years. "The gate of Aerlion is this way. The seven main gates are scattered around the palace. And this is why this spot in Ardria was chosen thousands of years ago for building the royal palace—it is in the center of the gates. The forest is the shortest path from the palace to yours."

He picked up speed after his words. I took another big step as I tugged at my black cape, which had been given for me to wear over my gold-colored armor, so that it would not get caught in the bushes.

"Tell me," I said to Balfour who was walking in front of me. "What was the Protector before me like?"

I noticed him throw a glance over his shoulder as he slowly let out his breath. "Why do you ask?"

I shrugged. "Even if I'm from the same realm as him, no one in my village has any idea about the previous Protector of Aerlion. No one has ever seen him."

Balfour cleared his throat noisily and faced forward. His steps were slower now. "He was my friend," he said softly. I couldn't see his face, but I could hear the sadness in his voice. "I was a young Phoenix back then, came here a month after he was chosen."

He smiled, fixing his eyes on the ground. "Breccan was strong but affectionate at the same time. He was the only Protector I knew who wasn't afraid to stand up to King Warren. He was stubborn and he never gave up. Everyone loved him."

Protector Breccan . . . he was the Protector of Aerlion before me. His name had become taboo for everyone in the palace, and his death had deeply saddened the people of the capital. The fact that I was his successor was enough reason for them to hate me. Yet, I could understand why they all loved him. He was one of them. People from Aerlion had never seen him over the years. He turned into one of the high-ranking people who stayed loyal to the king, but not to his people. While we suffered, he turned his back on us as much as everyone in the capital.

"I'm sorry," I said in a near whisper. I really *was* sorry. I wouldn't have been here if he was still alive. I would never have been chosen and I wouldn't have left my miserable life in Aerlion.

"You know what, you remind me of him in many ways . . . Maybe it's a common trait for the Protectors of Aerlion to be so stubborn."

My lips curved up but I kept my eyes on the ground. We didn't talk for the rest of the way.

The forest was silent. The sky above, woven with dense and dark tree leaves, was hardly visible through the branches. The warm breeze that blew once in a while licked my face as it passed by. The air was dreary, preventing the sunlight from touching my skin. Balfour slowed and waited for me to catch up. I looked in the direction he was pointing.

"This leads to the main gate of Aerlion," said Balfour, still pointing at the stone stairs surrounded by ivy. The stairway curved like a snake along part of the mountain in front of us.

"You first."

I began climbing with slow steps. I kept one hand on the rock wall where the ivy tickled my skin. I could hear footsteps following me so I didn't turn back. My hesitation had long been replaced by curiosity.

The stairs ended and the first thing I felt was the strong wind. I held my blowing hair with one hand and tucked it under my cape with a broad smile on my face. Ardria, the capital city, was clearly visible from where I stood. I first looked closely at the big royal palace and the line of houses that began just after the palace gates.

The mountain seemed to be carved in such a way that its top had become flat, and right behind me was a rather large cave. The stairs that led up from the other side of the cave were made from marble that was the same color as those at the palace, and they seemed to reach another structure behind the dense trees.

My gaze slid toward the hollow between the rocks and I narrowed my eyes in an attempt to see the inside. But the area around the hollow shadowed with huge boulders was as dark as the inside. I took a step in that direction and felt movement in the cave. Only then did I realize that there was something inside. As I skimmed the darkness, my urge to go in that direction got the better of me and I took another step toward the cave. It was Balfour's voice that drowned out the humming from the cave.

30

"Dragons are proud creatures, and vindictive. Don't go near. He'll come to you."

*Dragon.* That single word made my heart skip a beat. I had never seen a real dragon before. Where I lived, there was no sign of the magic that ruled over the Seven Realms. Even though I felt a strong urge to go there, I only nodded.

I remembered Balfour's previous words. *Every Protector had a dragon.* Although I tried to deny it, I could already feel the bond between us.

"Come," said Balfour, to draw my attention elsewhere. He stepped between the cave and me. "I'll take you to your post. Don't you wonder about the place you'll be spending the rest of your days?"

Then he started walking. I took one last look at the dark cave and went after him. We started climbing the stairs again and reached the mountain peak after a few big steps. I straightened my heavy and creased clothes. Contrary to the opinion of the people at the palace, Protector's clothing wasn't practical at all. And since I had just started my training, my body was crushed under the weight of the steel.

"The main gate of Aerlion," said Balfour.

With his words, I took another step to the side and looked at the enormous gate before me. The first thing I noticed was how huge it was. The oval gate was surrounded by a white light that resembled the one emitted from my palm on Selection Day. Its surface was transparent but it was wavy like water. The city under us could be seen clearly below it. Magic was moving around us in thin lines like a spider web, patterns appearing and then disappearing. Even from where I stood, I could feel it. The mountain was surrounded by magic, and this was the source. It was a strange but also a familiar feeling that I couldn't describe.

"There are six more gates like this one in the palace, and they all draw their power from the Vitae. Fascinating, isn't it?"

The white marble stairs in front of the gate led to another marble structure that was a bit higher above. The front of the temple was open and I could see the big throne behind the pillars.

"The temple was built to show the bond between the Goddess and the Protectors. It is yours."

I turned my face to Balfour. He had a friendly smile on his face as he said, "Everything is ready for the new Protector of Aerlion. Now the only thing we need is for the Protector to be ready as well."

My gaze wandered. So, was this how I would spend my days from now on? Was I going to fight for the kingdom as I lived in a luxury that I had never had before? The more time I spent here, the more I was able to convince myself that everything going on was real. But on the other hand, I still didn't want this. I would rather run away and return home. It wasn't fair. My life had completely changed over the days since I was chosen. Now I had all the luxury I needed to live just like a noble. While people from my realm were suffering from hunger, the servants were bringing me more food than I could ever eat. And it was all because someone said I was *special*.

Balfour's eyes, as well as mine, turned to the stairs at the sound of footsteps, and I noticed the approaching crowd. The group walking toward us was wearing silver armor and blue capes, with long, sharp swords at their waists. The blond boy walking in the front, seemingly around my age, raised his head when he noticed our gaze on him. It didn't take long for his eyes to narrow with anger. I shrugged my shoulders as Balfour regarded me.

I thought I remembered some of them from Selection Day. The group approaching me was the Phoenixes of Aerlion. I exhaled slowly as I recalled them bowing before me reluctantly when I was chosen. They had trained all their lives to become the next Protector, or to serve him. Many of them had taken part in the Selections upon the death of Protector Breccan. But the crystals had chosen an inexperienced person, someone who had no idea about this kind of life.

The blond Phoenix walked over with thunderous steps and the group followed him. They didn't stop until there were only a few feet between us. When the group had approached, they all bowed in front of Balfour.

"Hello, Commander Balfour."

Then the boy's green eyes slowly turned to me. I tried to smile against his cold attitude, but my lips only trembled.

"Hello. I'm Anna. I'm from Aerlion and . . ."

"Yes," said the blond boy as he interrupted my words harshly. "We know."

Balfour didn't make a sound as his gaze alternated between the two of us. I knew I had to face them, now that we were together, but the way they looked at me didn't help at all.

I cleared my throat softly. "I'm very sorry for Protector Breccan."

The boy gritted his teeth as mutters rose from the group. "Don't talk about him. You didn't even know him."

I raised my eyebrows in surprise. "I know, but . . ."

I dashed back when the boy brought his hand to his sword in a rage. I noticed that his eyes had become wet with tears.

Balfour looked at the boy with warning eyes. "Hunter," he said.

But the boy ignored the commander completely. "I don't know why the crystals chose you!"

Hunter turned away and rushed to the stairs, completely ignoring me. The rest of the Phoenixes wasted no time in following him. I fixed my gaze at the point where they had disappeared and whispered to myself.

"Neither do I."

# CHAPTER 6

My eyes were fixed on my leather boots as I walked along the familiar stone road covered with tall grass. I was carrying two buckets of water, which I had taken from the well outside of the village. It was late at night. My body swayed to each side with the weight and I tried not to drop them. I was tired and all I wanted to do was crawl into my tiny bed.

The village square had fallen into night, and darkness covered everything. The bright crescent above was slightly illuminating the dark village. The candles in the houses had blown out hours ago and people had let themselves fall into the arms of deep sleep.

I picked up my speed as I approached the town square. Soon, the path that I had memorized over the years appeared before me. The small hut was at the end of the road.

As I took a big step, a few drops of water spilled from the buckets. I tried to stay still. I was crushed under the weight. I carefully put the buckets down. As I rubbed my aching neck, my gaze found the large pebbles among the wild plants. Something was shining there. I narrowed my eyes and walked over.

*Was it raining today?* I thought. But no, it was the opposite. The past weeks without rain pushed people to be careful with how much we took. That was why I left for the well after everyone fell asleep. Taking two buckets of water was unacceptable.

There was a big puddle on the side of the road. I knelt down next to it and touched the pebbles with my thumb and index fingers as I felt something sticky on my hand . . . but it wasn't water. It was a pool of blood.

My eyes grew wide with fear and I got up quickly, looking around. I began following the traces of blood on the grass. I had totally forgotten about the buckets by then. I began running when I realized where the traces were taking me. I turned the corner and climbed the stairs of the small house. My hand found the wooden door that was already ajar. I held my breath and pushed the rough surface that slid under my hand. The squeaking of the door was ear-piercing.

"Mom?"

There was no answer. The herbs she had placed on the counter were as she had left them. And my sister's brushes were still on the counter. But something was wrong.

"Sarah?"

The door squeaked. I let out a timid breath when I heard the footsteps coming from the outside. I slowly took a step back. A dark silhouette shadowed the windows. And there was more blood on the floor. Fear spread over my body. I took another step back and stepped into the old kitchen. The sounds ceased the moment I was inside the room. I could hear the bugs chirping outside and there was no sound other than the wind hitting the windows.

Just then, I felt a warm breath on my neck. I jumped and turned around to meet a devastated face.

"He's coming!"

The man's voice was no different from a croak. His long, once-gray hair had been painted red with the blood flowing from the open gash on his forehead. His black cape was torn and he was wounded all over his body. The stranger firmly grabbed my shoulders with his shaking hands and his warm breath licked my face. His amber eyes flew wide open.

"Darkness is coming!"

•

I woke up gasping.

My hands found the silky linens under me as I crawled on my back, pressing myself to the headboard. I pulled my legs into myself and took in deep breaths. I pushed my sweaty hair away from my forehead with one hand while slowly closing my eyes.

"Just a nightmare," I whispered. "It was only a nightmare."

I took a quick look around. I was in the room given to me at the palace. But even knowing that there were royal guards waiting outside didn't give me any feeling of security. I looked at the big engraved wooden door as if someone could come any second. The blood was too real and my heart was still beating fast with fear.

If I were at home, I would have crawled into Sarah's bed to sleep. But I wasn't home anymore and I didn't even know when I could go back there. I inhaled timidly as I realized I was completely alone.

The heavy quilt over me had fallen from the bed with my kicks. It was on the marble floor, right next to the wide couch. I dangled my feet from the side of the bed and let them meet the cold floor. Then I stood up and threw the thick quilt back onto the bed. I covered my eyes with my hands and paced in the big room.

"It wasn't real."

I took my hands away from my eyes and saw the sky through the velvet curtains. The darkest shade of the night ruled over Ardria, and a voice inside me said there was still time until the first light of day.

I put my robe on over my nightgown and walked to the entrance. I held the heavy handles and opened the door. The guards waiting on both sides of the door turned to me immediately. I ignored them and stepped into the wide hallway. They didn't make the slightest move to stop me. The rapid sounds of my bare feet on the marble floor could be heard clearly in the hall.

I passed through the halls dominated by gold and reached the stairway. The floor was illuminated by torches. I felt the warmth on my face as I passed under them. I made a turn in the hallway and reached the lower floors. I tried to remember the areas Balfour had shown me before and pushed the small wooden door at the end of the first floor.

The scents of various herbs filled my nose and I inhaled the familiar smell; it reminded me of home.

The shelves were full of lined-up jars and flowerpots with various plants in them. There were herbs left to dry on the wooden table. Just a bit farther in the room was a single bed placed in front of the door, which I assumed opened to another room inside. And on the other side of the bed were the stairs that went up to the books of various sizes, lined up behind the open balcony on the upper deck.

"Hello!"

I stopped examining the room and turned to the girl walking over with her big brown eyes fixed on me. She seemed a few years younger than I was, and she had a curvy figure. Her brown, almost red hair was braided tightly. She was wearing a long-sleeved dress. She never took her wide eyes off me as she stopped and swayed excitedly in her place.

"How may I help you?" she asked as she joined her hands behind her with a big smile.

"I want something to help me sleep."

The girl walked away over to the plants stacked on top of each other on the counter. She nodded. "Because of stress? An illness, perhaps?"

I turned my gaze to another corner of the room and murmured, "Nightmare." When she looked at me and frowned, I quickly added, "I haven't been able to sleep well for the past few days. Please, just prepare something for me to relax."

The girl nodded and faced forward. It was a stupid reason to come here. But after my endless training with Balfour and the stress of trying to avoid everyone in the palace for days, I felt tired. I really needed to sleep.

I heard the heavy footsteps when the door of the infirmary opened noisily. The girl turned her gaze behind me and ran past. "Welcome, King Warren."

My eyes opened wide at the name she called out, and I turned around only to see the king's gaze on me. It was obvious that he wasn't expecting to find me here. After a brief moment of surprise, he slowly tilted his head to greet me and I did the same. It was awkward, as this was only the second time we had met. Without the nobles surrounding us, it felt strange to stand this close to him.

"Protector Anna."

"King Warren."

The healer girl looked at me for a second before she went over to carry on with her work. When she came back, she was holding a small glass bottle.

"It's ready, Your Majesty."

King Warren took the bottle from the girl and glanced at me as he said, "Thank you, Paige."

And then he closed the door from the outside. I could hear his footsteps as he walked away. After he left, I turned to the healer girl again only to see her watching me carefully. But she said nothing. She walked to the table, picked up more herbs, and looked at me over her shoulder. "I'll prepare a mixture for you. It'll make you sleep comfortably if you drink two drops of it before going to bed."

"What about my nightmare? Will it make it go away, too?"

The healer girl, Paige, turned to me and asked inquisitively, "What kind of nightmares are we talking about?"

I trembled as the stranger's face appeared before my eyes, and I remembered how he had held me by my shoulders. "The very realistic kind."

She reached for one of the top shelves and said, "I guess I could add a few more things. You'll sleep till the morning."

I watched her pick some herbs and put them into the cauldron. And then she used a big ladle to pour the hot liquid into the glass bottle. As she walked over, my eyes looked at the spot where King Warren had disappeared. "Why was King Warren here? I thought he had servants to fetch him anything he wanted."

"This is a very strong mixture but it will make you sleep easily," she warned as she handed me the glass bottle. Then she looked at me. "He likes walking around the palace at night. Personally, I think he looks more comfortable without all those nobles." She added, "He can't sleep as well. I prepare him a mixture similar to yours, but much stronger. He usually comes over a few times a week to pick it up."

I narrowed my eyes and put the bottle on the counter. I instantly felt more awake than ever. "Why?" I asked. Then I crossed my arms. "Is he ill?"

Paige shook her head. "Nightmare . . . because of what happened to his family, to the previous king and queen." Then she quickly changed the subject as if she didn't want me to ask any further questions.

"You know what— everyone's been talking about you. I heard some in the King's Council and nobles in the palace saying that it was a mistake for you to be chosen, but King Warren shut them up. For now, of course . . . Have you met the other Protectors? What about Commander Balfour? What do you think about the Phoenixes? I always find them rather rude and arrogant."

"Slow down," I said as I raised my hand to stop her endless questions.

Paige slowly let out her breath as she said, "I sometimes forget I shouldn't be jabbering."

Then she turned her wondering eyes back at me. "Tell me, how is it to live in Aerlion? I've always wanted to see the other realms but I've never left this place."

"Were you born in the capital?"

She nodded. "My father is from Carran. So was my mother, but I never knew her. They both came and settled in Ardria. My father became the palace healer after I was born, so we moved in here."

She looked over her shoulder at the mess inside and grimaced. "He's not here right now, as you can tell. He went to the countryside to collect some herbs, but he'll be back in a few days. I take care of this place while he's away."

I nodded and looked at the healer girl. "Did you say Carran?" I asked, trying to remember the names of the other realms.

"Yes." She stared at me with questioning eyes. "Don't tell me you've never heard of Carran."

"I know there are seven realms," I said as I looked away, feeling overly stupid. "I didn't continue my education. I know almost nothing about magic or the realms."

Sarah would go to the old hut that had been turned into a school by a few people from the village, and she tried to learn such things, despite everything. Whereas I would run away from school and fool around all day when I was her age. My village was a small one but it had plenty of places for those who knew how to hide.

After my father's death, I had been completely focused on making money. Most of the people had a single goal, and that was to survive. Our goal was to not be hungry when the sun went down, and we didn't care about the rest. Even the number of people that ever left the village was very few, other than the merchants.

Paige looked at me with her big, surprised eyes. Then she raised her hands and counted to seven with her fingers. "Carran, Orin, Belwald, Odeir, Demos, Nadeer, and Aerlion . . . the Seven Realms ruled by the capital realm of Ardria."

I repeated the names to myself as Paige went on, almost forgetting to breathe. "Each Protector is chosen from the realms and their duty is to ensure the people's safety."

I looked at her with a grimace and said, "I already know that . . ." but she didn't let me finish my words, waving her hands in a flurry.

"One day, I'm going to visit each realm. That's my dream!"

I leaned my hips to the counter and crossed my arms. I had been watching the healer girl as she started to clean up some of the herbs left on the counter. "Being a Protector doesn't seem like a difficult thing."

Paige's eyes widened with my words. "It's so important," she said and shook her head. "The crystals don't choose just anyone."

"But I guess they did this time," I whispered. Disturbing thoughts invaded my mind and I exhaled slowly when the reality hit me once again. I took the bottle I had left on the counter and waved it at Paige.

"I've got to go now," I said. I didn't want to continue this conversation, at least not tonight. It was already late and Balfour wouldn't be happy if I were to be late for training. "Thank you."

I held the bottle tight in my hand, pushed the wooden door open, and walked out. As soon as I turned the corner, I was faced with King Warren. He was standing next to the pillar a bit farther from the door, blending in with the shadows. We were both frozen. When I looked at him, very surprised, he took a step back. He was still holding the bottle Paige had given him.

"I . . ." he began, but then his gaze filled with panic. At that moment, I realized that he had been listening to us. He hadn't walked away as I had thought. Instead, he hid there and waited. I waited for him to say something, but all he did was to avoid my eyes.

"Good night, Your Highness," I said slowly. This was awkward, and I just wanted to return to my room. I turned and hurried as the sound from my bare feet echoed in the hallway. I walked away without ever looking back.

# CHAPTER 7

I held the heavy wooden bow tightly and pulled the string toward myself. My arms trembled with the tension as I pressed the arrow between two of my fingers. I tossed my head, trying to throw back the lock of hair that had fallen to my forehead. My arms ached with pain.

"Shoulders backward, keep your back straight. No, don't bend your arms."

Balfour narrowed his eyes while giving more instructions, as he had for the past few hours. I breathed out slowly and let the arrow go without letting him finish his words. I heard the commander exhale when the arrow got stuck in a tree behind the target.

I lowered the bow and began walking to get it but he stood in front of me. "No, no . . . leave it there. Try again please." And he passed me another arrow from the heap behind us.

"I don't understand why I can't do it," I said as I placed another arrow on the bow. "Maybe using a bow is not my thing. Can't I try the other weapons?"

"Using a bow is easier. You will have to learn all sorts of weapons, anyway." He pointed at my shoulders and I immediately straightened my back again. "Protectors may only begin their actual duties after completing their long-term training. Besides, you haven't had much progress on the matter of magic, either."

I drew circles with my shoulders in an attempt to relax my muscles. "I read the books you gave me. They are useless."

Balfour shook his head but said nothing. Instead, he pointed at the target board hanging on one of the branches ahead. "There's a lot you have to learn. Do you really think you could turn into a Protector with a few weeks of work?"

I shrugged. "Maybe?"

He looked at me, displeased, and scratched his beard. "You have much more to learn. Magic, the history of the realms, the noble families, battle strategies, your duties to the kingdom and your people . . ."

Then he suddenly directed his sharp gaze back. "Draw the bow."

I was so focused on what he was saying that I flinched with his sudden command. My hand relaxed and I turned in the direction of the target, but I was completely unaware that the arrow had already flown in the opposite direction.

"Hey!"

I turned quickly. There was a dark-tanned, young, and very handsome man standing under the trees at the other side of the courtyard. He was tall and muscular. His curly hair was short, and the golden armor he was wearing fit his body tightly. His dark eyes focused on me in bewilderment as he waved his hands. The arrow was hanging in the tree bark just above his head.

"I come in peace!"

I quickly dropped the wooden bow and raced over to the stranger.

"I'm so sorry! It was an accident! It's just that I've only recently started training and . . ."

I heard footsteps approaching from behind. Balfour stood next to me and bowed respectfully, causing me to forget what I was trying to say.

The commander murmured as he straightened up, "Welcome, Protector Darrell."

*Protector* . . . my lips turned into a straight line as I examined the man with my widened eyes. Of course, the black cape and gold-colored armor were only given to the Protectors. How could I not realize that?

Protector Darrell turned his gaze back at me and grinned. "You could kill someone with that thing in your hand."

My lips twitched upward unintentionally. "I'm sorry."

Balfour bowed one last time to Protector Darrell before he threw a glance at me and walked away to collect the arrows stuck in various places around the courtyard. I watched him from the corner of my eye. He was never like that with me.

"I thought Ardria hadn't given you a warm welcome, so I came over."

When he started walking on the stone path that circled the courtyard, I followed him. I could see Balfour's figure moving away in the opposite direction.

"It's so good to finally meet you, Protector Anna."

"Likewise."

Protector Darrell turned to me with a big smile on his face and said, "I've been to Aerlion only once, but I can say it's quite a nice place."

I shrugged as I focused my gaze on the ground. "It depends on where you've been. I had never been out of my village before."

Aerlion consisted of many small villages. There were no cities in my realm, only poor, small villages. And I had never left my hometown before. I hadn't seen a need to do so. Every place in my realm bore the traces of the same kind of misery.

Protector Darrell opened his mouth as if he was going to say something, but he didn't continue. We kept walking in silence. Then I felt the urge to bring up a topic. I cleared my throat and asked, "Which realm are you from?"

"Demos."

His face lightened up with that single word. He turned to me proudly and added, "You must visit someday. Demos consists of a single, big city. It has an endless sea view and the biggest harbor in the Seven Realms. The city is made out of glass and everything is covered in gold."

I smiled. "Sounds really . . . impressive."

I was soaked in sweat because of practicing since the first light of day, and the courtyard that was scorching under the hot sun hadn't been very helpful either. I used one hand to swing my sweaty hair behind my shoulder and said, "I guess King Warren will let me out of here to visit the realms when my training is done."

"You're not a prisoner here," he said as he smiled. "This is for your own good. You may not be aware of it but you've made some enemies by being chosen as the new Protector. Not everyone is fond of us."

"Do you mean the Phoenixes?" I asked as I recalled our latest encounter with them.

"What? No, they're just . . . *sad*."

And disappointed.

"They are your soldiers. They don't hate you. Every Phoenix swears to remain loyal to their Protector and to serve their realm. The danger I'm talking about is outside, on the other side of the capital's borders. And believe me, an angry group of people can cause a great deal of damage to the king."

He glanced at me and changed the subject. "How is your training going? You know you can also ask for help from your Phoenixes, right?"

Balfour had mentioned the same thing before. Phoenixes were elite soldiers and they were spending all their days training anyway. They could train me as well. But after what had happened, I was not eager to cross paths with them for a while.

I let out a soft breath and shook my head. "There has to be a book on how this is done. Or a magic spell to help me . . . I don't want to admit it, but I suck."

Protector Darrell laughed and brought his right hand to his chest. And just then, a light, similar to the one that had emitted from my palm on Selection Day, came to life.

"That's exactly what I'm talking about," I said as I breathed in disappointment.

He brought his hand back to the sword—which looked nothing like the piece of wood given to me—at his waist, and rested his fingers on the scabbard. "We are the Protectors, magical beings. Give yourself a chance and some time."

I imitated him and raised my right hand, but nothing happened. I heard him laugh as I stared at the lines on my palm.

"You're new at this. This is the result of years of training."

"*Great*," I murmured as I rolled my eyes. *Years?* Really? I studied him. "How many years did it take you?"

He smiled broadly, revealing his white teeth that looked like pearls. He had a charming smile. "Twenty minutes."

"You can't be serious."

"I had been raised here since birth. I used to be a Phoenix. When Demos's Protector died, the Goddess chose me."

Had another Protector died? I had never heard of it. Although we lived disconnected from other realms in my village in Aerlion, gossip would usually spread easily.

I asked, "How many years ago was that?"

"Quite a long time ago. It's probably been two centuries, at least."

I stopped walking and stared at him in confusion. I eyed Protector Darrell from head to toe and said, "That's impossible. How old are you?"

Protector Darrell stopped, too. He turned his gaze to the sky with a thoughtful expression. "I'll be two hundred and thirteen this year," he said.

"What?" I asked with a horrified expression. How could that be possible? I began examining his face to see how serious he was.

He shrugged. "We are magical beings. The royal family, the five noble houses, Phoenixes, and Protectors . . . everyone blessed with the powers of Goddess Vitae is bestowed with hundreds of years of life."

I felt like my whole world was crushing. I couldn't breathe.

My eyes grew in dismay and it was Sarah's eyes that first appeared before mine. Then I thought of my mother. I harshly gulped down a feeling that sat right in the middle of my chest as I thought of our little hut. I was here for my little sister, to provide a better future for her. And what place would I have in her life? Would I be a part of her life at all? And then what? She would age, days would pass, and . . .

"You knew that, right?" Protector Darrell saw my petrified face and leaned toward me as his lips formed a straight line. "I shouldn't have been the first one to tell you that. I'm—"

I interrupted abruptly. "I—I need to go."

Protector Darrell was still looking at me indecisively as I quickly turned around and began walking in the opposite direction. I was hurrying away so he wouldn't catch up with me. As I walked away, I tried to convince myself that his gaze focused on my back didn't matter. The weight on my chest had been enough to trivialize everything else.

•

The lights of the weak fires that reflected out through the houses' windows were illuminating the dark streets. The dark fumes from the chimneys blended into the night and the silhouettes of the royal guards roaming the streets were moving around like ghosts.

I pulled my legs toward myself and placed my chin on my hands that were resting on my knees. I didn't want to be here, but I had no other option. I wouldn't return to the palace, at least not now. I had been sitting for hours on the summit of one of the mountains that surrounded the capital. I had dived into the forest after my conversation with Protector Darrell, and I had found myself here after a while. All I wanted was to be away from everyone.

I harshly wiped my eyes as my sister's face filled my mind. I would not cry.

I let myself down onto the ground and lay on my back as I turned my gaze to the sky. The stars looked wonderful from the capital. Stars were visible in my small village in Aerlion, too, but not like this. I remembered the times I had gone to the forest at night with Sarah. We had fallen asleep many times under the dark sky.

I smiled vaguely, knowing that I could no longer hold back the tears piling up in my eyes. I could never return to that simple life . . . I covered my face with my forearm as sobs left my lips. I hadn't even noticed the shadow that flew just over me. I got up in fear with the sudden breeze, and after a couple of seconds, I heard someone approach.

"Finally," a voice said behind me. "I've found you. Everyone's been looking for you."

The woman fixed her dark eyes on me. Her brown skin was shining under the moonlight. She had a toned body and her muscular shape was clear despite the armor she wore. She glanced at my red eyes for a moment with a bittersweet smile on her face. Her black cape was big enough to hide her body. She came over and stood right next to me. She was still smiling as she sat on the ground, the same way I had.

"Protector Ramona of Odeir," said the woman slowly. "I'm happy to have finally met you, Protector Anna."

She put her hands on the grass and leaned back. "You've found a nice spot to be alone. The capital looks much more beautiful at night."

Then she turned to me and went on, "Darrell told me what happened. I'm so sorry you had to find out that way. He is feeling terrible."

I turned my eyes to the city under us. "I would have found out anyway."

"Perhaps. But it must have been too sudden. King Warren was planning to keep it a secret for a while longer because of the reaction you might have. Well . . . I guess he was right."

I could feel the weight of the Protector's dark eyes on me. But I said nothing.

"Do you have a family?" she asked suddenly.

"A mother and a sister...The only reason I took part in the Selection was to provide them a better future, but now . . ." I couldn't finish my words.

"They are already living better now, all because of you. You must know that King Warren gives money to the families of the Protectors."

I nodded. "That was the only reason I participated: *money*. But I won't be a part of their future. I have to be here and they will grow old in the meantime. Day by day, I will lose everyone around me. Two hundred years," I said in horror. "A person is not supposed to live that long."

Protector Ramona's dark eyes were still on the city below us. "Actually, it's much longer. The price of being a Protector."

I watched her as she pulled her legs to herself; she had a sad smile on her face now. "How old are you?"

"Eighteen."

She smiled. "You've only been living for eighteen years." A tired expression spread over her face. "You'll learn to look at life differently when you've passed three hundred years like me."

I gulped loudly and turned my eyes to her face. Magic was as scary as it was intriguing.

"No one told me the truth."

"Would it matter if they had?"

"Obviously," I said harshly. "If I knew, I would never have gone to the ceremony."

I heard her sigh. "Magic finds you, even when you don't want it. Believe me, I tried." She paused for a second. "If you weren't selected that day, the capital would have continued the search until your powers become apparent. It would only have taken a few more days or weeks for the royal guards to come and get you. When Breccan died, his powers passed on to you. You carry a greater amount of magic than you can imagine."

When I didn't reply to what she said, she took a deep breath.

"Contrary to most of the people here, I had an ordinary life back in Odeir. I didn't know much about magic and I became a Protector only by coincidence, just like you."

She let out her breath slowly and began tearing the grass from the ground. "I had a fiancée. We were in love and wanted to get married. But I had to come to the capital when I was chosen . . . It was awful."

Her gaze was still fixed on the city. I wiped my eyes as she went on, "When I arrived here, King Warren's father, King Alastair, was at the throne. He threatened me. He said he would exile my fiancée if I didn't accept what I was."

"Why didn't your fiancée come with you to the capital?"

She shook her head slowly. "The capital won't welcome you if you don't have enough money, or if you don't have any titles or influence.

Even if there is no official rule, we can never think of having a relationship. We are expected to devote our lives completely to our realms and the kingdom. Besides, she was a regular person; and I wasn't just a human anymore."

I embraced myself and murmured, "That's awful."

"But it makes sense, too."

She laid her hands on the grass behind her and extended her legs forward. "I am three hundred and thirty-eight years old. I did go to Odeir plenty of times, but I've never once returned to my village. There's no one left there, anyway."

"So, what happened to your fiancée?"

"She stayed in Odeir and had a long life."

"How long?" I asked in a breath.

"Sixty-seven years. Not too bad for a human, don't you think?"

My expression became gloomy once again as I thought about Sarah and my mother. I closed my eyes tightly while I surrendered to the feeling of longing. Sixty-seven years . . . would that have been enough for me?

"That day I realized it, that we could never be together. I had turned into a magical being when the crystals chose me. There were times I hated this but I wouldn't change it for anything else. I feel proud when I think of all the people I've saved. I witness them grow up and get married. Years pass by and their families continue for some generations. One reason they're alive is that I'm at the right place at the right time. As a Protector, I keep the people of Odeir safe."

Watching someone else live a life that you could never have seemed very painful. I knew I wasn't ready for this. "I don't want to lose my family," I whispered.

"You will not lose them. You will know that they go to bed in peace every day because of you. Your sister will grow up and maybe she'll marry someone she loves. She'll have a nice, long life. And you'll learn to let them go when the time comes."

My sister was the reason I had taken part in the Selection. So, would it be enough for me to know that she was safe? I would keep her and everyone else alive. As I learned new things about being a Protector, I was in fact realizing that the job wasn't actually what I thought it was. And now it didn't seem so appealing either.

"We have to get back to the palace now."

I exhaled loudly. Protector Ramona rose to her feet and extended her hand to me. I got up with her help, and followed her into the trees behind us. The sounds of our footsteps mixed into each other and other than my occasional sniffling, the forest was quite silent.

I stopped walking when I heard a rustling behind the trees. A strange feeling took over me. I slowly looked over my shoulder and gazed into the darkness. But I saw nothing. I hesitated with the feeling of being watched; it was as if someone was following us. A shiver went down my spine.

I had narrowed my eyes to see into the dense trees in the darkness when I heard Protector Ramona calling my name. I was quite behind. I continued walking with quick steps. Before long, I noticed the sky-blue dragon on the other side of the giant trees. Protector Ramona was standing close to it. The dragon had yellow eyes and its skin was covered with blue scales. It was shining under the moonlight.

"This . . ."

"Meet Etha."

When Protector Ramona walked closer to the dragon, she lowered her head as if this was a command. Her sharp yellow eyes were on me. I took a step toward them but the dragon hissed. "Hush, Etha," said Ramona. "Stop trying to scare her."

The dragon grunted and closed her eyes. Ramona turned to me. The admiring expression on my face must have told her a lot, as she added with a grin, "Wait till you meet your dragon." Then she made a signal for me to come over. "Let's get out of here."

Dragons had always been a legend to me. It was said that dragons once ruled the Seven Realms but no one had seen a single one of them during the last few centuries. So, their stories had turned into tales. As far as people knew, only the Protectors' dragons were still alive. And now, a dragon that proved the legends right was standing before me.

I walked over with timid steps. When my fingertips found the dragon's sky-blue scales, I gently rubbed her skin. Etha turned to me and puffed her warm breath at my face.

"You're not *that* scary," I whispered.

Protector Ramona climbed up easily and sat on the dragon before lending me her hand. I climbed on the giant dragon with her help. Etha began moving as I put my hand on her thick skin and pulled myself forward.

I turned my eyes to look at the dark forest behind us one last time. I still had that feeling of being watched. There was a tickling sensation on my skin, and it felt just like the time the guard put the leaf in my palm during Selection Day. It was magic. But unlike me, Protector Ramona didn't look suspicious at all.

"Hold on tight," she said, and then touched Etha's skin gently.

The dragon spread her sky-blue wings to both sides and we took off in seconds. I held on tight not to fall while I burst into laughter with the thrill. The wind hit my face fiercely and messed up my hair. I swayed every time she flapped her wings, smiling as I looked at the city shining under us.

Then the dragon rose higher into the clouds and blended into the darkness on our way back to the palace.

# CHAPTER 8

The huge doors of the throne room opened as the humming coming from the crowd gathered inside seemed to grow louder. The breeze flowing inside shook the crystal chandeliers hanging from the ceiling. As I walked, all gazes turned to me at once.

I took a few more steps as Protector Ramona passed by me to take her place among the others. I was by myself, and I knew no one was coming to save me from the angry nobles. I tried to look away from the tension, but knowing that they were all watching me just made it worse. I slowly raised my gaze to see leather boots hurrying toward me.

"Where have you been?" asked King Warren as he took a breath with rage.

He was now standing right in front of me. His dark eyes were wide open and they did not seem to let me out of their sight even for a moment. "How could you leave the palace without telling anyone?"

"Protector Darrell . . ."

"Darrell didn't know where you were going."

He ran his hands into his dark hair and I noticed the veins stretching on his neck. King Warren's anger was almost tangible. "You are here to do your job, *Protector*. You are behind in your training; you can't even use your magic. You need to stop acting like a child."

Apparently, Balfour was reporting directly to King Warren. I grimaced and hardly stopped myself from grunting. "It could have been different if you hadn't kept the truth from me," I said, but the king shook his head in response.

"As if your reaction would be different. Your actions only prove me right."

I knew that all the Protectors and the members of the council were watching us, watching *me*. I narrowed my eyes as his scolding continued.

"You have no idea how dangerous this was." He closed his eyes as if he was trying to calm himself. "Give me a reason not to punish you."

My eyes became even smaller with his words as I hissed in rage and took a step toward him. This made the guards on both sides of the king's throne take action. The guardswoman, who appeared next to me in no time, suddenly pointed her sword at my neck, and I didn't even have time to defend myself.

"Step away from the king. *Now.*"

I froze. I could feel the sharp tip of the sword on my neck. She was *so* serious. I looked around as I gulped slowly. The Protectors and the council members looked still as statues but they were all tense. Balfour, who was waiting behind the Protectors with the other commanders, had his lips in a straight line. My gaze met Ramona's and she slowly shook her head, telling me to move away. I looked at the council members waiting on the other side.

My eyes found the old lord from the day I had first come to the palace, smirking where he stood. The humiliation I felt suddenly vanished, I was now angry. Despite the cold metal pressing on my neck, even the slightest detail in the room would be enough to ignite the flame inside me. And that's what happened. I furiously turned to the guard as the king's words were still ringing in my ear.

There was not a single soul daring to move. I knew that the gazes fixed on me were expecting me to follow the guard's orders and draw back, but my hesitation completely disappeared as I turned my gaze to King Warren, who was standing behind the guard. He had already gotten rid of his confusion and now had that cold mask over his face; he was playing the role of Brutal King once again. I knew at that moment that he wasn't going to take a step back. He was waiting for me to give in.

I gritted my teeth when the woman pressed the blade further, as if she was trying to remind me of the existence of the sword on my neck once more. But rage took over—I couldn't draw back now. Not after being humiliated in front of everyone. Not in front of that old lord watching me with a pleased expression.

They didn't know how stubborn I could be, but they were going to see it . . . so be it.

With a sudden burst of courage, I went for the sword's hilt. But because I hadn't lost eye contact with the king, my bare hands landed a bit higher, on the sharp edge of the sword. The guard took a few steps back as a shocked gasp rose from the side where the council members were lined up next to each other. With the burning in my skin, I turned my hands into fists and tried to prevent the flow of blood coming from the open wound. My furious gaze was still upon King Warren. Apparently, my clumsiness had left an impression on them, though different from what I had expected.

"Because I know what freedom feels like," I answered what he had asked just before the guard stepped in. My eyes were already red with rage and pain. My hands were burning.

"I am not one of you. I didn't start training at a young age, like the other Protectors here. Nor was I burdened with heavy loads. I was *free* . . . and I was brought here against my will. So, I may now be a Protector that serves *you*, but you can never restrain me. You may try punishing me. Do whatever you want; you can never chain me."

The king's gaze was still focused on mine. I watched the anger fade away from his eyes slowly, but I quickly turned away. I opened my fists to show them, to show everyone, that I wasn't as weak as they thought. I felt the warm blood dripping from my fingertips that were numb with pain. I was thankful that my voice hadn't trembled while talking, nor had I burst into tears right after.

The throne room had fallen into complete silence as the gasps ended. I knew that the others wouldn't move before King Warren or I did.

As tears began to fill my eyes, I knew that I didn't want to cry in front of all these people. I was too proud. All that display of power couldn't be for nothing. But I was also relieved. Wasn't this what I had wanted to say ever since the day I came to the palace? Each time Balfour looked at me with disappointment or the nobles had a displeased expression on their faces, this was what I thought. I wasn't a noble, I wasn't like them. And I was never going to turn into one of them.

I lowered my head in order not to meet the shocked gazes. I turned around without another word and hurried away. The only sound that could be heard until I left the throne room was blood dripping from my open wound onto the marble floor. And I never looked back.

•

"Can you pass that over?" asked Paige as she pointed at the bandages on the wooden shelves that went along the walls of the infirmary. I stood up from where I sat and held the bandage with my fingertips to prevent it from getting soaked in blood. I looked at the green mixture that the healer girl was preparing in one of the metal bowls. She left the wooden spoon on the counter and came over. I extended my hands to her.

She had already begun grunting before her eyes turned to my palms. "I can't believe you."

"Me neither," I said as I remembered King Warren's shocked gaze. "I held a sword with my bare hands."

"You *held* it?" Paige murmured angrily. "If you'd pressed a bit further, you might have been left with no hands to hold with."

With her scolding tone, I raised my brows. I knew she was younger than me, but I felt like a child being reprimanded by her mother. Paige knit her thin eyebrows and roughly poured some of the mixture onto my palm. I pressed my lips together at the burning and squirmed in my seat. She held my hands with hers and didn't let me move away.

"You're the weirdest Protector I've ever seen."

I pursed my lips. "Thanks."

"I'm serious," she said, and went on in the same breath, "Even King Warren was probably shocked."

I straightened up when she brought up the topic of the king. "I don't know what his problem is with me, but . . ."

"His problem is that you don't follow the rules. King Warren is overly strict because of past events, and he's trying to rule the Seven Realms all by himself."

Paige shook her head and continued to take care of my hand. I raised an eyebrow and asked, "Past events?"

Curiosity had made me forget the pain spreading from my palms. Paige pressed her lips together and shook her head slowly. Her gaze was still on my hands. "Forget it."

"What happened?" I insisted. "What was that?"

The healer girl turned her eyes to mine. "I'm not supposed to talk about it," she said before turning her attention to my hands once again. "You should ask Balfour."

She applied the rest of the green mixture as I kept looking at her. We both knew I wasn't patient enough to wait. "The thing you were about to say; is it something everyone knows? I mean, do the people of Ardria know?"

She only nodded.

I went on, "Look, whatever happened, it was before I got here. Don't you think I should know it, as a Protector at least?"

Paige exhaled and shrugged her shoulders in surrender. "Very well. But promise me not to talk about it, especially not inside the palace."

When I nodded, she moved over to my side. Her eyes were on the candle burning on top of the round wooden table in front of us.

"This happened before King Warren sat on the throne." She exhaled once again before going on. "You first need to know about the system in Ardria before you can understand what happened . . . You have to know whom to befriend and whom to stay away from."

She pushed the mixture she had just left on the table away and rested her hip on the spot that opened up.

"There are five noble families. Montborne, the house of King Warren's father, King Alastair. Then there are the houses of Barrington, Lunavier, Tendros, and finally Ironlash, the house of Queen Isadore's family. These five families have been fighting for the throne for thousands of years. One member from each family is chosen as a member of the King's Council. Less powerful nobles are not chosen, only the heads of the five families. The king has to be neutral so there is also someone from his family in the council."

I nodded to show her that I was listening carefully. She continued.

"Montborne and Ironlash have been allies for a long time because of the previous king and queen. But King Warren tries to help all the noble families as much as he can, and he keeps them close by."

Then she paused and looked at me as if she had just remembered something. "Like the man who brought you here on Selection Day. Lord Cyril, the elder brother of Lord Raymond, the council member from the house of Ironlash. The Ironlash family has been responsible for the Selection of the Protectors and Phoenixes for many centuries. Although Lord Cyril is the elder one, he gave his place at the council to his younger brother."

Paige took a lock of her hair that had fallen away from the rest, which she had tied tightly, and tucked it behind her ear.

"These two families have a strong bond that wouldn't be easily broken because of the previous king and queen. The same goes for Lord Theon, the king's cousin and the representative of Montborne. I'd never think that he'd betray King Warren."

"On the other side," she said before pausing to catch her breath, "The Lunavier family is known for their independence. The only thing keeping them here is the oath of loyalty to the kingdom that they made many centuries ago. And they are loyal to their word. But I can't say the same for the houses of Barrington or Tendros. What they could do is . . . unknown."

I nodded as I thought of the old lord in the red cape whom I had seen on the platform on Selection Day. "Lord Cyril," I repeated. "He defended me against another council member on the day I got here."

"Lord Cheng. The representative of the Barrington family. He has no blood ties; he gained his power at the council by marrying someone from the family." Then she shook her head and said, "I don't like that man."

I remembered his unfriendly gaze that had been fixed on me as soon as I had entered the throne room and what he had told me at the time. His expression today, while the king was scolding me, was the same. I shrugged. I could agree.

"Like I said, the noble families were always in a fight for power. So, coming back to King Warren . . ." She stopped for a while and began nervously swaying her short legs as she went on. "The Phoenixes used to be directly under the king's command. It didn't matter which realm you came from; you would just be included in the king's army, just like the royal guards. Word is that—and everyone knows that these rumors are true—Lord Cheng provoked the Phoenixes a hundred years ago and promised them independence. What he wanted was to put an end to the dynasty of the Montborne family and to take the throne. And so, an uprising took place in Ardria. King Alastair and Queen Isadore were killed by the Phoenixes, and King Warren took the throne after he repressed the uprising."

I gulped harshly at her words and turned to her even more inquisitively to listen to the rest of the story. I remembered what Agatha had said when I asked her about the Phoenixes.

"And then what happened?"

"The Phoenixes responsible for the uprising were executed, and the rest were punished in other ways. The Phoenixes who didn't take part in the uprising, but also didn't do anything about it, were rejected by the king, and they were given under the command of the Protectors of the realm they came from. And this way, they have moved away from the palace completely. That's why we call them Phoenixes, you know. They were regular soldiers until they were separated from the rest of the guards. So, a new group of soldiers was born."

"And what about Lord Cheng?"

"He's *still* alive," Paige said with a grimace.

I shook my head in disbelief. "But how?"

"They couldn't find enough evidence. Even if they had, he's the head of the Barrington family. They can't do anything to him because it would mean disrupting the balance between the five families."

Then she fixed her gaze on me and went on, "That's why King Warren wants everything to go by the book; all the Protectors to be in their places, and the council members to stay at the palace . . . He thinks there will be chaos if the rules are not followed. He must be afraid that another uprising will take place and history will be repeated. That's why he was mad when you disappeared today; he is scared."

That explained the royal guard's reaction when I stepped toward the king. She wanted to protect him, to prevent what had happened in the past. And maybe she was also scared. Phoenixes had the power to kill royal members and they'd proved that before, during the uprising. A group of royal guards fighting with them would be no match against a Phoenix. And a Protector was even more powerful. We had the power to protect, help, or even destroy.

Regret had settled in the left side of my chest as my thoughts on King Warren began to change. He was only *scared*. I swallowed loudly before speaking. "I shouldn't have judged him so quickly. I was too harsh on him."

I remembered the time we had met in the infirmary, the time when he looked too tired and vulnerable. With everything going on, it must have been tough for him.

"Frankly," Paige said as she got up and reached over to the side to wrap the bandage over my hands, "King Warren's past is really sad but don't let my words affect you. I sometimes think he doesn't even have a heart."

She drew back after she was done with the bandages on both of my hands. "They should heal in a couple of hours."

She was right. Another thing I had learned about the Protectors was that our bodies healed very quickly. And that meant that there would be no trace of the split in my palms after a short time.

I placed my hands on my lap and watched the healer girl tidy up the counter. She had risen on her toes to put the bandage back in its place on one of the shelves when we heard a sharp sound. The bluster of a storm followed the thunderous sound and I saw the colorful glass jars shake on the shelves.

"What was that?"

Paige turned away when the sound of bells echoed from the high tower of the royal palace through all of Ardria. She dragged the wooden stool over to the counter adjacent to the wall and put her knees on it to rise high enough to look out the dusty window into the courtyard.

"The main gate of Belwald," she murmured without turning to me. "Something's not right."

As I took a step toward her, the wooden doors at the other side of the infirmary swung open and a royal guard in silver armor rushed in. I could see how nervous he was by the expression on his face. His eyes found me. "Protector Anna, you need to come with me."

He used the back of his hand to straighten his tilted helmet while I eyed him from head to toe. Paige came over and put her hand on my shoulder. "You'd better hurry."

I hesitantly turned to the guard and said, "I'm coming."

He nodded and hurried to the door as I ran out of the room behind him. Even though I didn't know why I had been summoned, I realized that something was wrong. I was asked to come, despite what had happened earlier today. My heart began pounding with thrill and fear. As our hurrying steps echoed in the empty hallway, the thunder could still be heard from beyond the thick walls of the palace.

# CHAPTER 9

I followed the guard in front of me and climbed the stairs quickly. I put my hand on the stone wall before stopping only for a second and looking back. From where I stood, I had a clear view of an Ardria that had surrendered to the night. Despite the sun that would rise in a couple of hours, the streets were still illuminated by bright torches. I held on to the piece of rock under my palm as I watched the scenery. I hadn't realized that we were so high up until I looked down. We had climbed much higher than the mountain where the main gate of Aerlion was.

The stone stairs, which had been carved into the mountain slope, led to another hill behind the palace. When the sound of footsteps ceased, I raised my head and noticed that the guard's armor was now shining with the light of the many torches ahead. Only then did I notice the humming of the crowd. I got to the final step and walked onto the area.

The top of the mountain was flat, just like the one with the Aerlion's main gate. There was a huge temple surrounded by white pillars, and I immediately noticed the two Protectors in their golden armor waiting at the wide area in the front. Farther ahead were two giant shadows. My eyes grew wider when I noticed the dragons and saw that they were much larger than Etha, Protector Ramona's dragon. They were fascinating.

My eyes immediately searched for Ramona or Darrell, but there was no sign of either of them. I noticed King Warren talking to one of the Protectors, whose shining golden armor could be seen from all the way over here, standing behind the guards and the two commanders. I tried to keep my face blank and walked over to them. Eyes turned to me as I approached the crowd, and the whispers grew louder with each step. I let out a breath; of course, word of what happened in the throne room must have spread quickly. By now, I had learned how much nobles liked to gossip.

King Warren fixed his dark, sharp eyes on me as I continued to approach. He straightened his back, and when I was close enough to hear them, he said, "Protector Anna, let me introduce you to Protector Edmond of Belwald."

I turned to the old man whose height only reached my shoulders and who was wearing armor even smaller than mine. He had a white beard that came down to his chest and long hair in the same color. I had heard the rumors of people from Belwald before; white hair as bright as snow and despite the freezing cold, skin as warm as the sun.

Protector Edmond narrowed his eyes. A displeased expression formed on his face as he asked, "Are you planning on sending an inexperienced Protector with me to Belwald, Warren?"

I ignored his tone and turned to the dark eyes that had been watching me. "What's happening?"

King Warren was serious as he said, "When there is a problem in the realms, the Phoenixes send us a signal. Their magic is connected to the gates, so the gates alert us." He added, "A message came from Belwald to Protector Edmond. I want you to go along to gain some experience. It's probably nothing serious."

Even though he had a calm expression, his eyes said the opposite. And then I realized he was really *wishing* that whatever had happened in Belwald wasn't serious.

I asked, "And why did you ask for me?"

He shrugged. "You wanted a way out of the palace, didn't you? Here is your chance."

"But why?" I insisted. It didn't make sense. Only an hour ago, our rage toward each other was so clear. The way he talked in the throne room and the way I reacted back . . . I hated him as much as he despised me. For the nobles, what had happened today was a scene worth watching. So, what had changed?

I watched him as he breathed out loudly. "Despite what I try to maintain here, I know how it feels to be stuck in the palace and to be controlled." He turned his gaze away and cleared his throat. "Besides, you can learn a lot from Edmond."

*He didn't have a choice,* I reminded myself. After his parents' death, he'd had to sit on the throne. And he was still afraid of the past, afraid of dying. Just like Paige had said, that's why he was so obsessed with the rules.

I didn't say anything back. When his gaze focused on a spot behind me, I heard footsteps coming from behind Protector Edmond.

"This is Protector Sam," King Warren said as he pointed his dark eyes toward someone else. "From Carran."

Protector Sam had a tall but shapely body with broad shoulders. I shot a glance at his short ginger hair. He appeared in his midtwenties but I had learned that no one was what they appeared to be.

"Hello."

Contrary to my expectation, Protector Sam had placed a simple but warm—considering the welcome I had just received—smile on his face. "I look forward to working with you, Protector Anna. From what I saw in the throne room, you are going to adapt to the capital very easily."

Then he laughed. "It's better to show some teeth to the nobles, and even the king." He looked over at King Warren. King Warren didn't react, only rolled his eyes, but he didn't look annoyed either. Protector Edmond smirked. I could see that they were friends, or at least acquaintances who had spent at least a hundred years together.

My gaze shifted to the two dragons behind him. Protector Sam realized what I was looking at and pointed at the dragon that was farther away. "That's Edmond's dragon, Zyna." Then he pointed at the closer one. "And that's Gryvyn," he said as his eyes shone. "Yours must be somewhere here, too."

I let out a short breath with the thrill of finally meeting my dragon. And I didn't have to wait long, either. A shadow passed over us. With the sudden breeze, I shielded my face with my hands and removed locks of hair from my face. The others seemed calmer; Protector Edmond didn't even look bothered. Protector Sam gently smiled and headed toward the group of guards together with Edmond. I stared at the dark shadow behind Zyna and Gryvyn.

One side of the king's lips was curved upward, but he didn't say a word. I left him and walked over to where the dragons were waiting. And before long, I was standing in front of the giant creature.

The dragon had black scales and his eyes were the color of fire. He slowly spread his wings when I came near, allowing me to see the blackness fading into gray at his wings. The dragon's fiery eyes were on me but he remained still as a statue. I didn't move either. My chest heaved with excitement as the dragon's eyes narrowed even further. I was so focused on him that I hadn't even turned to look at the two other breathtaking dragons to the side.

King Warren came over and stood next to me. "Protector Anna," he said calmly. The timbre of his admiration for the dragon was evident in his voice. "Meet Deegan."

From the corner of my eye, I saw the faint smile on the king's face. "You seem less angry than an hour ago."

I was expecting the king to scowl and tell me how irresponsible I had been, but instead, I heard his soft laughter. "I can't put up with a stubborn Protector. I leave that to Balfour." There was a sarcastic smile on his face now. "It's nice to see that your hands are still in place."

I didn't even know what to say against his altered mood. I gritted my teeth and turned to the dragon once again, ignoring him. I took a step toward Deegan.

"How much longer are you planning on watching him?"

I turned my head to see the owner of the grunting voice next to me—Protector Edmond. He gave me a short look and then easily climbed onto the huge, dark green dragon at my other side. Only then did I notice Protector Sam was already in his place on top of his brown-skinned dragon.

My hesitant gaze found Deegan once again. The dragon was still looking at me, and something inside me said that he had never taken his eyes off me the whole time. King Warren took a step toward Deegan and made a gesture with his hand for me to come over. I approached him with steps as light as a feather. I raised my hand without waiting for any sign from King Warren and my palm found its way onto the dragon. Deegan's warm breath hit my face and he bowed his head.

As soon as my hand touched Deegan's tough skin, my fingertips slid through the gap between his eyes and onto his nose. Deegan's eyes were closed as I continued to rub my hand along the gap between his eyes. And at that moment, a vision appeared between us like a curtain.

The place where I was standing began to shake. I was startled by the vision that had suddenly appeared and I noticed the gray sky was filled with bolts of lightning. I was blown back by the storm, and I shielded my face with my hands. I made out the black skin under me as soon as my eyes caught a glimpse of it. I was sitting on Deegan, and we were flying high above a valley. Deegan was trying to go higher with every flap of his giant wings. I raised my head and tried to look in the direction he was aiming. He was trying to fly above the clouds to escape the storm.

I held on tight and rested my forehead on his thick neck. As I lowered my head, the claws of the pitch-black dragon came into my view. I noticed the small figure between his claws. It didn't take long for me to realize that it was a man. When my eyes grew wider, the man raised his head with difficulty, as if he had felt that I was looking at him. He took a deep, painful breath. His amber eyes met mine, and at that moment, I realized that it was the same man from the nightmare I'd had a few days ago. He had warned me then.

His gray hair and beard were tangled into each other. His face was dirty and the blood coming down from the open wound on his face was covering his features. I bent down even farther. I saw the blood flowing in streams from under his golden armor and I breathed with fear. And without a second thought, I extended my hand to the stranger.

A bright light shone in the sky. And with that, the dragon suddenly convulsed and a painful cry rang in my ears. The voice belonged to the man.

As Deegan suddenly lost control and began falling, I held tightly onto the skin under me and looked at the man. But he wasn't there anymore.

I saw his weak body falling to the valley under us. The man held out his hand to me, although he knew I couldn't reach him.

There was pure fear in his amber eyes.

My hand left the dragon's skin. Then my eyes, wide with fear, quickly found the fiery eyes staring back at me. I looked around to see where I was and saw King Warren a bit farther away, talking to a guard. He had already left my side. The other Protectors were busy with their own dragons. I rubbed my hand over my face. A grunt-like sound came from Deegan as I looked into his big, red eyes.

"What are you trying to tell me?"

In response, Deegan just exhaled his warm breath to my face.

"Hey!"

Protector Edmond, the owner of the ill-tempered voice that called out to me once again, began waving his hand from on top of his dragon. "Are you coming or not? I won't wait for you like this every single time."

I gritted my teeth, turned my back to him, and moved over to my dragon's side with intentionally slow steps. I put my hand hesitantly on Deegan's body as I heard impatient sighs coming from behind. I tried to remember how I had climbed onto Ramona's dragon, Etha. I put one foot on the dragon's body and held on to the saddle to pull myself up. I fell onto Deegan's back.

As soon as I took my place, the dragons rose to their feet and began walking to the middle of the area. I pushed myself forward so I wouldn't fall, and I began watching my dragon in bewilderment as he followed the others. Apparently, he didn't need my guidance; the thousands-of-years-old dragon already knew what he was supposed to do.

Thunder roared over the capital city once again and I looked up to see the bright circle behind the dark clouds.

"The main gate of Belwald," I murmured. The light coming from the gate was moving around the transparent circle, and a thunder-like sound was echoing around. It was the alert the king had mentioned.

The dragons spread their wide wings when the torches in the courtyard, where the gate to Belwald was, lit up one by one. I looked at King Warren. His lips formed a straight line as the three dragons took off. I quickly turned and held on tighter to the reins in my hands as my eyes grew in wonder.

The three dragons instantly rose into the sky. I felt dizzy immediately after realizing how high we were. I clung to my seat in fear as we flew toward the bright ring. The dragons didn't slow down; they sped up. Protectors Sam and Edmond straightened up in their places and I shut my eyes in fear. As we flew through the gate, the gush of the wind paused only for a brief moment.

The cold passed through my clothes and made me shiver. I opened my eyes and saw a snow-covered valley below us that looked nothing at all like Ardria. The sky was light gray and I saw nothing other than the large snowflakes falling. We weren't in Ardria any longer; we had arrived in Belwald.

My hands relaxed when I realized that I was safe, but I was still cautious. I was thinking that the king should have provided training on how to ride a dragon before sending me here. I had never felt so unprepared for anything before. But at the same time, it felt just like an instinct.

I wrapped one arm around myself against the cold. I leaned forward and let out my breath to see the vapor coming out into the air.

"We'll meet the Phoenixes," shouted Protector Edmond so that we could hear him despite the storm. I saw Protector Sam nod vaguely to him, and when Edmond turned his eyes to me, I approved with a brave look on my face. Meanwhile, I was hoping that he hadn't noticed my body trembling with both cold and worry.

When he directed his dragon downward, Protector Sam and I followed nearby. The storm calmed down as we descended. As the snowflakes hitting my face became softer, I placed one bandaged hand onto my lap and closed my eyes for a short while, trying to enjoy it despite the extreme cold. I still couldn't believe I was riding an actual dragon. *My* dragon.

"Down there!"

My gaze shifted to where Edmond was pointing. I could see the flames of the torches shining through the mist. The Phoenixes who were waiting for us became visible as we reached toward the group. Behind them, I noticed a wooden hut that served as a shelter. A group in blue capes was waiting for us in front of it.

We landed the dragons onto the field in front of them. I let myself down from Deegan's back. My feet mired in the snow and I tried to hold on to my clothes. I was still shivering as the group rushed toward us. Protector Sam got down from his dragon and took a few steps toward me. I hesitated to approach. Our eyes met and he shook his head as he passed by. "Never show your feelings. You always need to appear strong in front of them."

His eyes found the Phoenixes and I understood what he meant. He was talking about what they had done to the royal family in the past. There was really no place for weakness. The wall between the nobles and the Phoenixes was valid between the Protectors and Phoenixes as well. Protector Sam's expression was cold and cautious.

"Protector Edmond," said someone from the group. "Protector Sam." Then he fixed his gaze on me and bowed just as he did for the others. "Protector Anna."

My lips curved up.

"What's the situation?"

We all turned to Edmond's commanding voice. The old Protector was walking with difficulty in the snow because of his short stature. He stopped in front of the Phoenix, who said, "We arrived here a few hours earlier upon the news of an attack on a nearby village. A few of the villages were evacuated because of it. There's quite a lot of damage, and King Warren sent word that help would be sent from the capital."

An *attack*? I remembered my mother going to another village in Aerlion because of injured people. She had said it was an animal attack, but if the same thing was happening here, there could be more than we knew. I gulped strongly with this thought. After being brought to Ardria following the Selection, my only wish had been for my family to be safe.

"Any casualties?"

The old man's cold tone caused me to look toward him. I knew he had been living this way for years, but even the possibility of someone dying was blood-chilling. And the thought of getting used to this was even worse.

"Two died after returning to their village to give the news. They had lost too much blood when they arrived."

I looked away. Protector Sam turned to me upon my sudden movement and watched my reaction carefully.

The Phoenix went on. "The Phoenixes have already started to help the rest of the village with the preparations. But . . ." The old Protector knit his brows as the Phoenix's face became tense. "Someone from the village is missing. And . . . there's something you need to see."

Edmond's face was extremely tense as he nodded. "Give me details on the attack."

They began walking to the wooden hut and Protector Sam, who had chosen to remain behind, came over to me with a faint smile on his face.

"How are you holding up?"

"Actually . . ." I began as I rubbed my hands. My tension had returned when there were now fewer people around. "I thought it would be an easy thing, like theft or a group of people attacking each other; at least that is what would happen in my village. I thought we would talk to the villagers, say a few words, and after showing up, we would let the Phoenixes handle the rest. I didn't think someone was actually dead."

He looked at me with sympathy. "You'll get used to it in time." When I grimaced, he added, "Believe me, there'll be worse times. This is not as bad as you think."

"We're talking about people dying. I thought it wasn't serious."

I couldn't stand the sight of blood. My mother—like my father before her—was the healer of my poor village, and they had been using our small house as an infirmary over the years. I used to learn things from them about healing or which herbs to use for different sicknesses, and I had focused on keeping people alive. I had seen people dying before— mostly from diseases—but it still felt awful.

I went in the opposite direction of the Phoenixes and leaned my back on the hut they used as shelter. Protector Sam stood in front of me. I crossed my arms as I let my gaze wander over the high mountains that were hardly visible through the storm.

"The Phoenixes used their powers, right? That's how the gate of Belwald warned us."

Protector Sam nodded before crossing his arms as I had done. "All seven realms and the capital are connected with magic, ever since the first times. You know the story of the Goddess, right?"

I nodded as I recalled the story Balfour had told me.

"Protectors, Phoenixes, gates, dragons, and the tree . . . we all are bonded by magic and the magic in our veins comes from the Goddess Vitae. Though we are not as powerful as the Protectors before us, we are still strong."

"If it's only to help people, why do we have magic then? Royal guards can do well even if they don't have any powers."

Protector Sam shook his head. "The Seven Realms haven't always been this way. The magic was first given to the Protectors to fight the dark magic in the realms."

I uncrossed my arms. "Dark magic?"

"There were creatures of magic that once roamed the Seven Realms and killed many. People used to call them the Old Ones. They were real, dark, and scary creatures, and even the dragons didn't seem scary at all when compared to them." He added, "With magic, we were supposed to hunt those things."

"Have you ever seen one?" I asked.

"Just once, many years ago. Before, the duty of the Protectors was to keep the dark magic away from the people by hunting the creatures. But as time passed, the dark magic in the realms became less, and now they are all extinct. So, in short, we can't say that the Protectors of our time do much. Most of us just like fooling around at the palace or training the newly chosen Phoenixes. Though the commanders usually take care of that now . . . We stay in the palace and go to our realms to patrol once a week. When there is a conflict among people, we usually send Phoenixes so that we won't be needed. I am surprised that they even called for us."

He laughed and leaned against the hut's wall behind us. "Protectors really don't do anything. You can even say it's kind of boring. But, well, we get paid for doing nothing."

"So," I said in an attempt to understand what he said, "is the dark magic also the reason why we have powers?"

"Power is a broad concept. The Phoenixes are also magical like us, but we are much stronger than they are. We fight better, heal faster, and can live longer. And then there's this."

He raised his hand and I looked at the shining light in his palm. I remembered Protector Darrell doing the same thing on the day we met.

"This is a power, a light that destroys the Old Ones and helps us fight the darkness."

"Is it only the Protectors that can kill those things?" I asked as I continued to stare at his palm.

"When you have magic, you can win a fight against an Old One faster than with other methods. I guess ordinary weapons could cause harm, but villagers fighting on their own has never ended well. It is better for people to wait for help from the Phoenixes or us."

He extended his hand once again. I watched with envy as he used his power easily. I was expecting to see the white light again, but this time it wasn't a gleam like before, but actual flames appeared. I flinched and he grinned.

"We can summon all kinds of light, flames included."

I was about to speak when I heard footsteps approaching. Two Phoenixes came and stopped right in front of us. "Protector Edmond awaits you," said one of them. Then he pointed at the big tent behind the hut. "They're at the back."

Protector Sam eyed me, and then we both walked around the hut toward the tent. Edmond was at the front of the tent, talking to the Phoenix who had greeted us when we arrived. The tent entrance was held open as we walked in. Edmond turned to us. I noticed the shadow on the ground behind the two men who were at the far end of the big tent. It smelled like something rotten inside, and I held my breath as we moved closer. At first, I thought it was a dead animal. When I squinted my eyes to examine the shadow, the guards moved away to give us more space to walk through.

The thing on the floor was not a wild animal. It was completely black. The figure, taller than a regular man, was slim; it had hands and feet just like ours, but it was taller and its body was covered in thick, dark feathers. I had never seen such a thing before.

"That's . . ."

The Phoenix next to us murmured as my eyes grew wider. "Dead. The other Phoenixes and I hunted it down this morning. It was responsible for the attacks on the villages."

The attack wasn't done by an animal. It was this . . . *thing*. That was why the Phoenixes had asked for the Protectors to come. I remembered when my mom said she didn't know what caused the attacks. But I knew now. I sighed in horror. "Dark magic."

Next to me, Protector Sam nodded.

Protector Edmond used his boots to turn the creature's face to us. Its gray eyes were open and extremely glassy. For a second, it reminded me of a person and I couldn't help myself to feel sick. I held my breath.

The old Protector winced at it in disgust and said, "A Dralein."

I knit my eyebrows but couldn't take my eyes away from it. "A what?"

"Dralein," repeated Protector Edmond. "They used to live on the frozen slopes of Belwald."

"And they should've been extinct years ago," added Protector Sam. I turned to him and saw his horrified expression. I remembered his words. Dark magic was the main reason why we were chosen and the Old Ones had gone extinct a long time ago. So, how was this thing lying in front of us now?

Protector Edmond drew back. I had realized that the situation wasn't good but the thing I couldn't figure out from the looks they gave each other was what it meant for this creature to return.

He exhaled slowly and looked at us. It was now impossible to see any signs of the sarcasm he had shown earlier. He grunted seriously. "We have to return to the palace . . . *Immediately.*"

# CHAPTER 10

Chaos was ruling inside as each furious word echoed over the throne room. The words rising from the council members were fueled by the Protectors' objections, while the commanders chose to stay behind, silently observing the commotion around them. Other lower-ranked nobles at the far end of the room were whispering among themselves without taking their eyes away from us.

I exhaled sharply and raised my head to look at everyone one by one. And finally, I turned to King Warren. He was sitting on his iron throne at the top of the steps. He had placed his hands on both sides of the throne, watching us restlessly. As if he had sensed I was watching him, his dark eyes found me. I raised my brows and turned my gaze to Protector Edmond and Lord Cheng, who were yelling at each other in rage. At the same moment, the king's harsh voice cut through all the humming sharply.

"Enough! Both of you."

King Warren straightened up on his throne and turned his dark eyes in the direction of the council members.

"Lord Cheng," he said as he fixed his gaze on the council member who hadn't been quiet even for a moment. "Speak. *Now.*"

Lord Cheng slowly cleared his throat and folded his hands. "After one of the missions which took place many years ago, we were told that the last of the Dralein was killed. We all believed we were safe. But now . . ."

He paused and raised his hand swiftly before waving it threateningly to Protector Edmond. "We hear that they are *still* not extinct. Besides, one of them attacked a village in Belwald and caused the death of two. Another person is missing! Imagine if they were here, attacking the people of the capital. This mistake is unforgivable."

Protector Edmond lunged forward. "Look at me, you little . . ."

The humming continued. The king angrily rose to his feet and came down the stairs from his throne. The stomp of his footsteps wasn't enough to silence the people this time.

"I told you to stop," said the king.

Protector Edmond's voice became more and more quiet as he turned his gaze to the king, who was alternating his angry gaze between him and Lord Cheng.

"It has been centuries since the last time someone saw a Dralein. We can't look for someone to blame."

Lord Cheng was quick to shake his head. "It is Protector Edmond's job to . . ."

The king turned to the council member. "Protector Edmond is aware of his duties and knows what he has to do. I advise you the same."

The nobles at the rear began whispering among themselves, loudly this time. The lord silently cleared his throat. His face was all red now. "Yes, Your Highness," he said.

"It's my fault." Protector Sam took a step toward King Warren.

"Protector Breccan and I had found the Dralein during a visit. It's been more than two hundred years; it was about the time I was chosen. We had hunted three of them from Carran to Belwald and kept searching all over Belwald for weeks, but we didn't find any trace of them. They have been gone for the past two hundred years. That was why we thought they had been the last of their kind. Apparently, we were wrong."

Lord Cheng exhaled loudly and I felt eyes from the crowd turning to me. They were reminded of the fact that I was there, just as every time Protector Breccan was mentioned.

Lord Cyril, who had been standing next to the king's throne since the beginning of the meeting, walked over to Protector Edmond and put his hand on his shoulder, causing the old Protector to go back to his place. Lord Raymond was standing next to the other members of the council. He fixed his eyes on his older brother as Lord Cyril walked around the throne room.

"We have to be careful."

As I watched him, I realized he was an advisor to the king. Even though he had the council members, King Warren still kept him close.

Maybe it was because Lord Cyril and Lord Raymond were his family, coming from the same house as his dead mother. The old lord was always around when needed.

Lord Cyril's eyes took a tour of the room. "No one can know what will happen next. But we also have to take lessons from the past. It is not a good sign that the creatures have returned. We can never allow something like Rogue to happen again."

The uneasiness reflecting from the faces of the Protectors and council members was obvious. King Warren walked back to his throne with big steps. No one said a word again. As I watched their reactions in confusion, I looked over my shoulder at Balfour, who was standing behind me. But his gaze was fixed forward and I realized I would have to wait for the right time to ask. Apparently, there were many more stories about the past of the Seven Realms that I needed to know.

•

As the sun disappeared behind the hills surrounding the capital, the light reflecting on the houses faded away slowly. The people were hurrying to get home, knowing that it would become dark soon. I could hear the laughter of small children along the streets I passed through. I passed the shop of the blacksmith, who was working in front of a bright fire and whose every hammer strike on the metal echoed along the street. I could see the palace from where I stood but I had no clue where I actually was.

I straightened my tangled cape and covered my chest with it. I wasn't wearing my armor. I wore my daily clothes and the only thing showing that I was a Protector was my cape. I had also covered it under another thick cape. I didn't want to be recognized. It was the first time that I had set foot out of the palace and blended in. Not being crushed under the gazes of the people of Ardria was unfamiliar to me. With every step I took outside the palace, I remembered what freedom was like and I realized why I didn't want to return. I felt alive.

I looked back over my shoulder to the palace once more. Balfour had said that he would cover for me for a few hours. It wasn't allowed for a Protector who hadn't completed her training to leave the palace yet. King Warren wanted to ensure our safety. But considering my non-developing skills, I could guess that the king was planning to keep me inside for a long while.

I moved aside to not collide with two men coming from the opposite side, carrying big heavy cases. I took a peek at my reflection in the window of the building next to me. A man was standing at the door, inviting people in. Our eyes met and he called out to me. I looked inside through the filthy windows. I could see the stools in the room; some people had passed out on the tables.

It didn't look like a place I would go. But then I remembered no one knew me, I was just an ordinary girl passing by. The man raised his voice upon my hesitation to get my attention again and courage filled me, so I timidly walked into the building. The roar of the crowd came out the moment I pushed the door in. I was among people for the first time in weeks and right then, I realized how much I had missed it. It was different from the nobles that I met during council meetings. The capital was so full of life.

Inside was a bar. There was a counter right across from the door and there were stools in front of it. All of the round wooden tables behind it were full, and the walls behind the tables were lit with bracket lamps. I slowly sat at one of the vacant stools in front of the counter. I noticed that people didn't even care about me and that they went on with their chattering. I was invisible to the people once again, just as I had been in my tiny village.

A man from the other side of the bar came over and began staring at me with expectation. I quickly looked around.

"I . . ." I began, looking at the colorful bottles behind the counter and then at the glasses on the tables, "I . . ."

"She'll have the same."

I immediately turned around to the deep voice coming from the other end of the bar. A man was sitting on one of the stools. His short beard was the only thing not hidden by the hood of his brown cape. The bartender nodded at him and began preparing another one of the yellow drinks that the stranger was having.

I turned to the stranger under the hood and said, "Thank you."

The man nodded and reached for his drink. "A token of my gratitude for the kingdom." Then he slightly raised his head and fixed his sharp gray eyes on me. "It's not every day that one sees a Protector."

My eyes grew wide and I leaned forward to wrap myself under my cape. "How did you know?" I whispered.

The man's eyes turned to my back and I did the same. The second cape I had put on had folded and the royal emblem on the fabric underneath was showing. I tidied myself up in a hurry and looked around. A group at the other end of the bar was looking at me with hostility. I tried to ignore them.

"I have never come to the city before."

The man nodded. His long fingers were tracing the glass. "The capital is appealing for many people. It's a shame that Protectors are tucked inside a cage like pets."

I knit my eyebrows with his words and reached for the glass when the drink, the same color as his, was put in front of me. I held the glass with both hands. "Only until I complete my training."

"One king dies, another takes the throne. But they are all the same." A grin had covered his face as he shook his head. "You should feel lucky just for being here right now. The king holds the nobles on a short leash."

"You must know the king well since you speak so comfortably about him."

The stranger's lips curved slightly. His hand went to his brown cape and he lowered his hood to reveal his dark, curly hair. By looking at his face, I could tell he was handsome, but his skin was too pale, as if he was ill. He looked young, maybe in his midtwenties. When he smiled, I saw the dimples appear on his cheeks. He had a charming smile.

"I used to work at the palace. I was a . . . researcher, until King Warren fired me."

"Aren't you a little young for that?" I asked as I looked at him. He was a human, not a magical being. King Warren should be at least a hundred years older than him. I thought someone who once worked at the palace must look like Balfour, old and very tough.

The stranger laughed as he picked up the glass. "Perhaps. But I was good at what I was doing. That's how I found my way to the palace."

I sat straight on the stool and left the drink on the counter without taking a single sip. "Why did he fire you, then?"

The stranger gulped down his full glass and left it on the counter before signaling for another one. The bartender behind the counter quickly appeared for a refill. "I had an interest in history and during my research, I came across some facts which the kingdom wanted to keep secret. As you can imagine, the king wasn't happy with this and I was fired from the palace. Either that or death; you see it wasn't a hard choice."

I took a deep breath and murmured. "It does sound like King Warren."

He glanced at me. "I'm sure they don't tell much to the Protectors. They still keep on fooling you with the same old information."

Although I had no idea what the stranger was talking about, I nodded while carefully watching him. The stranger took his newly filled glass to his lips before continuing. And with that, his cape—similar to mine—shifted. I caught a glimpse of the wide pocket at the chest of his shirt. I narrowed my eyes and tried to figure out what was inside the pocket, causing the bulge in the fabric. Suddenly, my ears began to ring and for a second, I thought something was shining behind the fabric. But the stranger cleared his throat and harshly pulled his cape over to cover his chest. I backed off when he turned back to me. He exhaled cynically as if nothing had happened, and he brought the glass to his lips once again. His drink was obviously burning his throat; he nodded.

"I'm not surprised. Warren was always like that, controlling. You can never change a person."

"So, were you two also friends?" I asked curiously after noticing he called the king by his name.

His lips curved. "Something like that."

The man looked around with his gray eyes and examined the people around. He looked a little drunk. I leaned forward and said, "What do you mean exactly by *the history of the kingdom?*"

He moved over slowly. "Do you know about the crystals?"

Hearing this from a stranger reminded me once again how I hadn't known anything until Balfour told me the story. Honestly, could I be the only one who knew nothing about the history of the Seven Realms?

"Do you mean the crystals that the Goddess gave to the first Protectors?"

He slowly shook his head. "They never belonged to the Protectors. The crystals were created for the peace and order of the realms, but the first Protectors got hold of them and they chose to use them for the kingdom only, not for the people." There was now great disappointment on his face. "Maybe they were afraid of the crystals' power . . . such a shame."

"Are the crystals as powerful as people say?"

The man turned his eyes to me once again. "They had infinite power. They brought *life*. The crystals could be used to destroy the dark magic in the Seven Realms, or they could be used to create it just the same. They could also be used to heal people, to end poverty. People could have become something other than the helpless creatures that they are today. Even . . ."

By now, his deep voice had lost all power. He fixed his gaze on his drink and exhaled. "The crystals could even be used to bring the dead back to life."

I was startled. The first thing I thought of, as I stared at him with my eyes wide, was Sarah. And her endless drawings . . . If the crystals were used for their intended purpose, *he* could still be alive. We could be a family. My heart sank with the pain. And it was once possible.

"When the first Protectors kept the crystals for themselves, some people protested, but they made sure that no one ever found them so they could maintain their power over the realms. The kingdom wanted to control, to keep people dependent. Imagine if the people didn't need the kingdom anymore—there would be chaos."

I took a sharp breath. The only thing that the people wanted was to survive, just as those in Ardria. We were all human. But the nobles only cared for the other nobles. The rest of us meant nothing.

"It's really a shame. The crystals that were intended to keep the Seven Realms in order aren't even used for the good of its people."

"And what happened next? Between you and the king, I mean?"

The man kept his eyes on his glass. "Did you see the tree?"

He went on when I shook my head. I remembered Balfour mentioning it, but I had no idea where it was hidden inside the palace. "Vitae is the source of the magic in the realms. The Protectors, like everything else, are connected to the tree by magic. I discovered how to find the hidden crystals by using the tree. I just needed the help of the Protectors . . . But Warren found out about my research and I was given the sack, without being able to proceed any further."

A bell from the city hall rang, showing it was almost nighttime. It was patrol time for the guards.

I began staring at the glass in front of me, I was so lost in my thoughts that I didn't even notice the stranger moving. I heard footsteps as the man took some coins from his pocket and gently left them on the counter. He suddenly came near me. I felt his fingers gently closing on my hand and his lips slowly touched my skin.

"It was nice talking to you. I'm glad to have met you, Protector. Especially because we were able to talk before the kingdom poisoned your thoughts."

I quickly raised my head and tried to go after him. "Wait!"

But the stranger left the bar and blended into the crowd on the street. My shoulders shrugged as I let out a deep breath. He was gone, but his words were still echoing in my head.

"So, it is true, then."

A crowded group was standing behind me, the same one that had been sitting at the other end of the bar. When the alcohol-infused breath of the man at the front reached my nose, I realized he was drunk. They all were. And the fact that they were talking loudly had caused everyone inside to fix their gazes on us.

"A *child* has indeed been chosen to protect us!"

I fidgeted uneasily when the laughter broke. I could see that they outnumbered me.

"This was not how I had imagined the people of Aerlion to be!" The man at the front continued to stare at me.

I let out a breath when the group laughed once again and I rose to my feet. I wasn't looking for trouble. I left the last coin in my pocket on the counter and headed for the door. But two men from the group cut me off. At the same time, I heard the harsh voice of the bartender behind the counter.

"You can't cause trouble in here. Get out!" Then he looked at me. "All of you. Out!"

But no one paid any attention. A woman came out of the group and walked over to me. She reached for my cape. "The kingdom probably has high-quality stuff for you," she said as she tugged at the fabric. "So, what are you, a pretty doll for the kingdom to dress up?"

I pushed her hand roughly and drew back. With that, she raised her eyes to my face and hissed with anger. I knew the problem wasn't the money; people from the capital were rich enough. The problem was me.

"Don't come any closer," I said, trying to stay calm, but my voice cracked.

78

When the woman lunged at me, I extended my arms to put some distance between us and closed my eyes. I felt a tingling at my fingertips. As I slowly opened my eyes, I saw the woman reel back by the force of the light coming out of my palms. The wooden table and chairs were knocked over and many of the lamps on the wall were broken. A few gasped. I opened my eyes wide in surprise and turned my palms to myself to see the magic.

The light blinked one last time. My feet were swept off the ground and I fell back on the counter. I was knocked down with an ache at the back of my head. I tried to rub my eyes but my head was spinning, and I could only see blurry shapes moving before my eyes.

The bell over the door chimed and I heard quick footsteps rushing in. Two big hands started shaking me. Only then was I able to make out the green eyes staring at me.

"Protector Anna!"

My head was still spinning as the stranger in front of me continued to talk, but I heard none of it. As the pain at the back of my head increased, I closed my eyes.

# CHAPTER 11

The flames rising from the fireplace were warming my face with a sweet sting as I listened to the crackling of the burning wood. My hair was messily tied under my neck, tickling me. I rubbed my fingers on the itchy cotton surface under me as I slowly opened my eyes.

The first thing that caught my eye was the plant-covered shelves along the walls that were full of glass jars and books. A very old chandelier was hanging down from the middle of the ceiling; some of its crystals had fallen with time and its iron was rusty. As I looked around, I noticed the man in front of the fire. I stood up slowly and let my feet down from the bed. The stranger heard me and quickly turned to me as his broad shoulders relaxed. When our eyes met, he walked over.

"I would advise you to sit," he said, and pressed down on my shoulders despite my efforts to get up. "You might get dizzy. You need to move slowly."

I made another attempt to get up despite his warning. The point at the back of my head hurt and there was an even greater pain down my spine. I closed my eyes and pressed my lips together in pain.

The man shook his head but instead of saying anything, he got up and fed the fire with the few pieces of wood that he took from the side. The fire flared up.

"Where am I?" I asked as I looked around. "What happened?"

I looked around only to realize I was in the infirmary. It felt much bigger than the last time I had been here. In the daytime, it looked different.

"You're at the palace," said the man while quickly gathering the pieces of paper scattered on the wooden table. The sound of papers rustling against each other mingled with the sound of the burning wood. "After what happened in the city, a Phoenix passing by found you and brought you back. You are lucky that your injuries aren't serious. You are almost healed."

I looked around once more as the man eyed me. Where was Paige?

"Do you remember what happened?"

My gaze moved to my hands resting on my lap and I turned my palms upward, waiting for the same white light to appear again. But nothing happened.

"I don't know what I did."

"You are a Protector," said the stranger as he bent over. His loose brown shirt was sliding over his frame with every move he made. "It's natural for your powers to wake up. They appear to protect you whenever you find yourself in danger."

I ignored what he had said and jumped in with, "Who are you?"

The man straightened his glasses that were sliding down from his nose and assessed me. He looked in his midforties. His curly hair probably looked livelier than it ever had under the light of the red flames.

"Gavin Whitlock, the healer of the palace," said the man, and unnecessarily bowed. "I'm also the king's private physician, and Paige's father."

I remembered Paige telling me that her father had gone to gather some herbs and that he would be back in a few days. Gavin continued.

"My daughter and I took care of you when you were first brought here. She went to the city before you woke up; you just missed her."

Gavin shuffled around with some glass jars and sniffed what was inside. He moved from one jar to another as if he was looking for something, shaking his head each time. "You've been here only for a couple of hours. The sun just came up and you're healing faster than I expected."

Then his eyes opened wide and he quickly reached for one of the jars on the upper shelf. "Ah! Here it is!"

The healer put some herbs into a pot and began crushing them. I looked at the green mixture with great disgust. Its strong smell had already reached me. The dusty shelves and the sultry air inside made me dizzy once again. I turned my back to him and rose slowly. I leaned on the wooden counter behind to reach for the window. Whatever the healer and his daughter had done to me, I was already feeling much better. The handle of the window moved with my touch as if it was not heavy at all, and I thought I should be grateful for Balfour's training. The window squeaked open and the warm air filled the room. I inhaled the clean air as I put my other knee on the counter before sticking my head out the window.

There was a clear view of the courtyard from the small rectangular window of the infirmary. My eyes caught a glimpse of a familiar face by the fountain on the other side of the stone path that was surrounded by huge trees. King Warren was walking on the path that connected the garden to the courtyard, and he was accompanied by a stranger. I scowled when I saw the king and I fixed my gaze on his back as he walked along. The memories of the stranger I had met at the bar were still fresh. What he had said about the crystals was the real reason behind my scowl, and the king's selfish interests were the reason for my anger. I kept my eyes on his broad back. As the time passed by, I felt like I could find several reasons to hate the king more.

Gavin suddenly appeared behind me. "You need to drink this," he said as he brought over the mixture with crushed green herbs and whatever else he had put inside. I moved away with a grimace, trying not to breathe too deep.

"What's that for?"

"Nausea."

I shook my head. "I feel perfectly fine."

"You won't in a few hours."

The smell reminded me of the mixture my mom used to make for the pregnant women in the village. She used to say the taste was worse than the smell. I tried hard not to gag.

"No, thank you," I said as I moved over to the bed and wasted no time putting on the black cape that was left next to it.

Gavin raised his eyebrows. My gaze only stayed on his face for a brief moment.

"Thank you for taking care of me but I have to go . . . maybe I'll come back later."

I pushed the wooden door with my shoulder and began walking in the hallway. The side of the hallway, which connected the two buildings, was surrounded by pillars of white marble. And the yellow-white tiles seemed to be gliding under me with each step I took. I walked out between the last two pillars and stepped out into the courtyard. The garden looked more fascinating from where I stood. I followed the sound of the water from the fountain in the middle, as the whooshing of the warm breeze accompanied the chiming of birds. My eyes immediately fixed on the king and I held my breath before directing my steps toward him.

Whatever they were talking about, I could hear the stranger's soft voice. It was King Warren who first noticed me and the sound of their footsteps ceased as they raised their heads.

"Protector Anna," said the king and fixed his dark eyes on me. I was looking for some hostility in his tone but I didn't find what I was looking for. "Glad to see you are okay. You worried us all."

I forced myself to smile; the king's warm attitude felt awkward. I replied, trying to be kind as possible, and turned my eyes to the man standing next to him. The man, whose face could be considered as handsome as the king's and who was wearing the black jacket of the council members, turned his dark eyes to me.

"Council member of the Montborne family, my cousin Lord Theon," said King Warren to introduce the stranger. I raised my eyebrows as he spoke and realized that this man's face did indeed seem familiar. His features resembled the king's. I had seen him at the council meetings before but I had never paid enough attention to the people around me during the times in the throne room. That was why I hadn't been able to recognize him immediately.

"Hello," said Lord Theon with a nod. Wrinkles formed under his eyes when he smiled. He looked more kind, the opposite of the king. "We're all glad you're fine," he said, almost repeating what the king had just said.

King Warren fixed his eyes back on me. "We took care of the situation. We'll make sure that the people who attacked you can never come near you again."

I nodded slowly but I felt embarrassed. I was not sure if the more important thing was the fact that they had attacked a Protector or if it was the fact that I hadn't been able to defend myself. Remembering how I had injured myself with my own powers made me feel worse. I could imagine what the nobles thought of me. I was a mistake from the beginning and this time, I had proved that very well.

The king didn't make any comments on the fact that I had snuck out of the palace. I hoped that he hadn't reprimanded Balfour because of me.

A shadow cast over my face. "Was anything done to them . . . by me or Protector Breccan? Is that why they hate me?"

The spot at the back of my head ached and I barely stopped myself from touching there. Maybe I really should have drunk the mixture Gavin had prepared for me.

The king and the council member looked at each other. Then Lord Theon placed a sincere smile on his face.

"The only person chosen from among the people was Protector Ramona. The others were already Phoenixes before they got here. The people, contrary to us, aren't magical. And since the Protectors were all been chosen long ago, none of them were alive at the time. The dark magic disappeared over the years and the people's need for you has become less. But now it's changing again. They are afraid. We all are . . . Breccan's death was so sudden. Their lives completely depend on you now and that's why they expect you to be strong. No one feels safe anymore."

He paused and broadened his smile as if he was trying to instill confidence. "They need time. Just like everyone else."

I tried to smile but my lips didn't even move. I could feel King Warren's steely gaze on me but I didn't turn to look at him.

Although I appreciated his efforts, I knew that he was born in luxury and he spent all his time at the palace. He was a nobleman *and* blood-related to the king, whereas I had spent all my life knowing what living in fear really meant. I had grown up with that knowledge from my village and others where death and hunger roamed freely. I knew how the people thought, because I, too, had lived in fear just like everyone else.

I shook my head. "Time won't be enough. They'll never stop, not until I get stronger and prove myself."

Lord Theon continued to smile, just as I had expected him to. But he also shot a glance at the king.

"I heard those words from someone else a long time ago," said the lord, squinting his eyes as if he was trying to remember the past. "The important thing is not to lose control of yourself with the power you could gain. People will see you, and they will trust you."

Just as I was about to reply, the king and the lord focused their gaze on a point behind me. I saw a royal guard rushing towards us.

"Your Majesty."

The woman was left breathless by the time she came over; still, she didn't break her stance and bowed to us properly. "Lord Cheng has called for a meeting. He is waiting for you in the throne room with the other members of the council."

When he heard the name, King Warren made a face as if he had eaten something sour. But it was Lord Theon who spoke. "What is it this time?"

His tone was extremely harsh and the guard stood frozen with his question, not knowing what to do. I could easily see that the lord disliked Lord Cheng. How could he like him, anyway? They both had the same reason to hate him.

"Due to Protector Edmond's news about the missing . . ."

The guard suddenly stopped talking and I saw that it was the king's piercing gaze that stopped her. My brows rose and the woman quickly fixed her gaze on the ground.

It was Lord Theon who turned to me first. "We'd like to continue chatting but my cousin has to get together with the council members for some tax issues."

*A lie,* I thought to myself, forcing myself to smile. What could they be hiding from me?

"I hope we can continue our conversation tomorrow evening," he added.

"Tomorrow evening?" I asked, not knowing what he meant.

He turned to the king and elbowed him mockingly in the ribs, trying to lighten the mood. But the king looked unfazed.

"It is Warren's one hundred and twenty-seventh birthday."

My knit eyebrows immediately relaxed as I looked at the king with a terrified look. He seemed to be amused by this. His expression also relaxed and a crooked smile formed on his face. I gulped harshly. It was really scary that people could live for so long. But they weren't human; they were blessed with the powers of the Goddess. And so was I . . . I couldn't help but think about my hundredth birthday.

"We'd better get going."

Lord Theon bowed his head and turned around to walk behind the guard. And King Warren didn't waste any time in following them. I fixed my eyes on his back as they walked away from me. But as I turned away,

I didn't miss King Warren stealing a glance at me over his shoulder before disappearing at the corner of the pillared path from where I had come into the courtyard.

# CHAPTER 12

I could hear the screams.

With each collision of newly sharpened swords, a metallic sound echoed in my ears. My bare feet touched the tall grass as I took a step. The plants reaching up to my waist brushed my naked arms. I walked toward the thick cloud of smoke in the valley. The sounds increased as I came closer.

An arrow shot from right across the area whizzed close above my head as I let out a breath in fear. A man passed me by, shouting cries of war, and I saw the bloodstains that had splashed over his armor. The armor he was wearing wasn't like that worn at the capital by the royal guards; it was plain and crude. I watched him as he blended into the cloud of smoke.

I turned around to get away but my foot hit a helmet on the ground. The piece of metal, which once belonged to a guard, had been bent out of shape as if it had been hit by a blunt object. I moved my eyes away with difficulty.

A roar echoed. I thought that it couldn't belong to a human, and I knew what that was . . . I turned my gaze to the dark figure in front of me. My eyes opened wide when I saw the shadow with vague lines standing right in the middle of the thick fog. My legs began to ache as I tried to gather strength, hopefully enough to get me out of there as soon as possible.

A Dralein . . . Its dark eyes suddenly turned to me while I was staring at its tall, crooked body. My mind was begging me to run away but my body couldn't move.

My hand went to my belt but there was nothing there that could protect me. I looked around hopelessly and noticed the shield a few feet away. The creature made its move at the same time as I did. It stretched its long legs and began running at me, waving its big claws. I hurried in the opposite direction. I threw myself to the ground and slid on the grass, feeling mud under my fingernails. I rolled and slowed down as I reached for the shield. When I held it tight and turned it to myself, the reflection I saw on it was not of myself, but of a stranger.

As the woman's blue eyes turned to her reflection on the shield—to me—the shadow behind her grew bigger. But this time, it wasn't the Old One. Seven different colors were emitting out of the shadow's palm standing right behind me.

•

The servants swiftly drew the thick curtains to the side, inviting the sunlight into the room as I slowly parted my eyes. I pushed the quilt down to my waist and straightened up before turning to the group standing at the other end of the big room. But they didn't even stop to look at me. One of them began shining the golden armor hanging at the side, while another one placed the sharp-looking sword, which was obviously new, onto the shelf hanging on the wall.

My brows rose. Was that a real sword? For me? Thinking that I could easily injure myself during training, I wondered to whom this absolutely unbrilliant idea belonged. I would place my bets on Balfour.

I sat at the edge of the bed. I was used to the servants doing their work in silence so I didn't try to talk to them. I could already guess the short, single-word answers they would give in response. I wrapped my arms around myself and moved over to the wide window to look at the tiny snowflakes pouring down from the sky. Ardria was already covered with a thin layer of snow, but I knew this was nothing compared to the cold of Belwald.

The heavy doors opened. A servant walked in carrying a gold-colored silk dress. Another man was holding a matching pair of earrings with yellow gemstones on them.

"What are those?" I asked with hopes of receiving an answer longer than usual.

The servant closest to me didn't raise her eyes from the floor as she said, "This is the dress you'll wear tonight, Protector Anna. King Warren requests the presence of all Protectors at the ball."

Of course, his birthday . . . how could I forget?

The servants hurried out when they were done and closed the door behind them. I moved over to the dress hanging on the rack as soon as they left.

The dress was sleeveless; it had thin straps and became looser from the waist down. It was beautiful. I had never had enough money to buy a dress before. Besides, it would be quite meaningless for me to wear something like this in the village. I remembered Agatha's dresses and smiled, trying to imagine what would she say if she were here.

I rubbed my fingers on the soft fabric, thinking how well my family could live if I sold this. I could easily earn a few coins from this dress. But my family was already living a comfortable life with the money sent by King Warren. They didn't need me anymore. I quickly took my hand away from the dress. My whole life was built on survival and I couldn't change my old habits. My sister's face busied my mind as I slowly exhaled with longing. I wondered what mom and Sarah were doing right now.

"Knock knock!"

I took a step back. Paige was standing right next to the door. She was wearing her usual work clothes. She took a long step into the room while her brown eyes focused on the dress.

"Wow," she said as she moved closer and took a tour around it. "This is definitely your color. Whoever sent it must have good taste."

"It's for the king's birthday," I said as I struggled not to grimace. But the healer girl had noticed my voice and her pink lips curved up in joy.

"I can see your enthusiasm."

She moved away from the dress, walked to the big bed on the other side of the room, and laid herself on it. The sheet wrinkled as her wavy hair spread over the thick blanket. "So, you still don't like the king, huh?"

"This is not about my feelings for him," I said as I crossed my arms. Then I moved over to the window and leaned my hips on the sill. "It's just . . ."

I weighed the words of the stranger I had met at the bar, about the kingdom and the Protectors. I realized I didn't want to discuss it with anyone else, including Paige. I just waved my hand to move on.

"Well, he's not so bad," she continued. "Have I told you that he took us into the palace and gave us a place to stay when my father and I first came to the capital? I've known him since I was a child."

I sighed. No one here could see the royals as I did, but I didn't blame them. Some had been here for years and some had probably been carried away by the glory of the capital. None of them cared about the others left behind. But I did. Paige had told me about King Warren's past, but no matter how much I tried to empathize with him, I still couldn't justify his harsh attitude.

Paige quickly got up and walked over to me. There was a broad smile on her face now. "You'll look so pretty when you meet the nobles tonight! Maybe you can even find a lord or a lady there!"

"What do you think about the ball?" she asked then, pointing at the silk dress. Her eyes were shining with excitement. "You can't look at that and say it's not beautiful.

The dress was probably one of the most beautiful things I had ever seen, but I wasn't going to tell her that.

"It's all right," I said as I sank into the armchair next to the big bed. "I thought they would make us wear our armor."

I didn't make any comment on the second part. I wasn't eager to find someone here tonight and looking pretty wasn't what I needed right now. I couldn't care less about the nobles. However, I couldn't help but think about the stranger I had met at the bar. If he were still here, working at the palace, he would probably have been joining us.

Paige pursed her lips. "It's all right! How hard did they hit your head?"

I rolled my eyes.

"The Phoenixes and the royal guards will continue their work. The only people allowed to join the ball with the nobles are the Protectors. You are required to join the council members and the other nobles."

Then she smiled in a way that displayed her white teeth. "Even if you're going there as a Protector, you will not be on duty. Don't you think it's better that you wear something nicer than those boring uniforms?"

She extended her arms to the sides and spun around twice. "Nobles, jewelry, dancing . . ." she said, and giggled.

I ignored her. "What if there's an attack? A . . . a Dralein, for example?"

My thoughts had drifted to the black figure that had appeared before me in my nightmare. Paige grimaced. Even though she was trying to look calm, the subject seemed to disturb her as well. I didn't know whether the things in Belwald and what was told during the council had to remain secret or not, but I could guess that rumors had already spread. That would explain why that group attacked me—they were scared and wanted to test me.

"Nothing will happen. The palace is the safest place in all the Seven Realms."

Silence filled the room. Neither of us attempted to talk for some time.

"I was told that those things were extinct," I said after a while.

Paige looked down at her shoes. "They were." Her tone indicated her thoughtful mood. Then she straightened her back. The tension followed her every step of the way to the door. "I have to go back and help my father."

Her tone was calm but she seemed happy about not being forced to talk about this any longer. She gave me a short glance.

"He told me you guys met," she added quickly. "See you tonight!"

Then she waved and walked to the door with steps lighter than a feather. She knocked once and the guards waiting outside opened it for her. She disappeared with the same light steps.

# CHAPTER 13

The hem of my silk dress brushed the marble floor with every step I took as I looked around the big ballroom. The room was illuminated by big sconces on the walls and I saw three big chandeliers hanging right above me. The diamonds on the chandeliers were shining under the light coming from the candles. There were embellishments on the wall of the ballroom and above them were a few big paintings with golden frames. Some parts of the ceiling were painted the color of the sky. I slowly exhaled. It was beautiful.

I couldn't deny the guilt. The only difference I had from the people where I came from was the fact that I was *special*, and most of them would never even come close to owning the things I had right now. This included my sister, my mother, and the rest of my village. I looked around; Sarah would have loved this ball, whereas we had never had an actual birthday celebration.

As I tried to move forward among the crowd, I could feel that there were fewer eyes fixed on me. Perhaps it was the fact that I had managed to look like them for the first time. But I didn't feel that way at all.

I noticed Protector Edmond eyeing people with his tough gaze. Our eyes met. The expression on his face became even grumpier. I took a step toward the old Protector and saw the two people standing next to him. I began walking over as soon as I noticed the woman in a dark blue dress with her dark, silky hair hanging down to her waist, and a man dressed in silver. The woman suddenly turned her black eyes to me.

"Protector Anna," she said as she curved her lips and took a step toward me. She had skin as white as snow and big, elongated eyes. She had a different accent. "You are everything they say about you! You look gorgeous. Tell me, how do you like the ball?"

My cheeks blushed with her compliment and I smiled. "Different than I had expected," I said softly. It wasn't exactly a lie. I had thought that the ballroom would be as pompous as the palace, but this place was more beautiful than any other room I had seen inside the royal palace.

The woman was the Protector of Orin. Although I had never spoken to her before, I had heard a lot about the rest of them. I tried to remember her name and thought about what Balfour had told me about her.

"Thalia," said the man next to her as he came over. He had light brown skin and pale green eyes. I was forced to raise my head because of his height. "Aren't you going to introduce us?"

Protector Thalia nodded with a smile that spread over her face. "Anna," she said as she turned slowly to me. "This is Protector Leon of Nadeer."

"It's a pleasure to meet you," I said with the same kind of smile.

"I heard great things about you. Commander Balfour said you've improved a lot."

I smiled in return. "I still have a lot to do."

As my eyes wandered around the ballroom I heard Protector Thalia's voice. "Don't look so stressed. Tonight will be fun. Even the king can't ruin your mood."

"I wasn't thinking . . ."

She didn't let me finish. "That was brave," she said as I watched Protector Leon nod in agreement. "What you did in the throne room. Warren sometimes can get on your nerves. But keep the king close. Believe me, the Montborne family is the best ally you can have in the palace."

My gaze shifted to King Warren, standing next to Lord Raymond. He was wearing dark clothes, matching his eyes and hair, making him look like a shadow in the gold-colored room. As I continued to watch him, I noticed the king's curved lips. He was having fun. He didn't look like the cold king in the throne room anymore.

As he was taking a sip from his drink, his pitch-black eyes suddenly found mine. His eyes widened. I watched him while his gaze wandered over me and finally went back to my eyes. I didn't dare to move and he didn't turn away.

Protector Thalia was watching us when she continued. "Protectors serve the kingdom but even *we* take sides. Montborne can give you power."

My eyes narrowed and I quickly turned to her, ignoring the king's gaze. "I am not interested in the fight between the noble families."

"But you live in Ardria now." This time, it was Protector Leon who was talking. His pale eyes found mine. "The capital changes people. You'll see that."

I noticed his hand slowly moving to Protector Thalia's waist. My eyes grew wide in bafflement. They turned to me and said, "It was a pleasure meeting you."

Then I saw them walk over to a young man who had chosen to wear his dark-colored cape to the ball. It was Lord Conrad, the head of the Tendros family.

"Nice ball, isn't it?"

I slowly turned and faced the man in his plain gray suit. It was Lord Cyril of the Ironlash family, the elder brother of Lord Raymond. I tensed as he came over. My gaze shifted to the stickpin on his chest, with the family emblem. And the red cloak he wore—the only one in the palace—was hanging from his shoulders.

"Indeed," I said as I looked around. "But it's the first time I have attended a ball, so I can't really compare."

He nodded slowly. "Look at you. It seems like there is no sign left of the girl I saw at the Selection. You've blended in with Ardria very well."

Although I didn't know what to make of his words, I shook my head. I wasn't going to change, nor let the city do it. "I am still the same person."

His lips curved upward as he fixed his gaze on me. "Good, then," he said. "We need the Protectors more than ever. You must remain the same. Power can bedazzle people."

I shivered as the crooked black figure in my dream appeared before my eyes, and I tried to move the vision of the Dralein out of my head.

"Are you talking about the reappearance of those things?"

"That and more. Dark days are coming. We have to be prepared for everything."

Dark days . . . I remembered the man in my dream. He had said something similar then. *Darkness is coming.* I turned to him.

"I've been having some strange dreams," I said slowly. "Weird dreams that I can't explain." I thought about the old man warning me and the battlefield in my dreams. "I know it sounds stupid but . . . But they don't seem to belong to me. It's as if . . . as if *someone* is trying to tell me something. Telling me to be prepared."

When I talked, I realized how stupid I sounded. Embarrassment filled me and I looked up. But not even a single muscle on his face moved.

"I advise you to pay attention to them. It could be a warning. And they could keep you alive, too."

"So, do you know what they could be about?"

"Anna!"

I heard Paige's excited voice first. She was walking over with hurried steps. I turned to Lord Cyril once again, only to see that he had left me there, walking away slowly. I wanted to go after him but Paige suddenly held my hands and forced me to whirl around. I had to take my eyes off the lord's back; apparently, our conversation was over.

Paige was wearing a short-sleeved green dress that was slightly loose. She had thrown her hair back with a golden circlet. "You look beautiful," she said with a broad smile. "More beautiful than all the ladies could be."

"So do you; look at that," I said as I pointed at her dress. Her smile broadened even further. Then she quickly held me by the wrist.

"Being at the ball means that I can finally do the thing I want the most."

I let her take me out of the crowd and into a corner. She turned to look at me over her shoulder as we walked. "Gossip! What do you think the nobles in the palace do all day?"

We moved in front of one of the big windows. My eyes involuntarily searched for King Warren one last time. When our eyes met, *again*, he quickly turned away. This time, he was next to Protector Darrell.

"First tell me about Protectors Thalia and Leon."

Although Paige was surprised at the fact that I knew something, the subject didn't seem to interest her much. "Everyone knows about them. Thalia has been here longer. People say they began dating after a few months they were chosen. They both could live for centuries, so it actually makes sense . . . Still, I don't think I could spend so much time with someone."

Her gaze found Protectors Thalia and Leon, who were talking to her father, Gavin. Then she took a deep breath as if trying to show that she wanted to move on to another topic. In just a short amount of time, while scanning the crowd with her eyes, she told me everything I needed to know about the nobles.

I looked at her with a scowl. "Is it really important that I know all this?"

Paige's lips curved as she nodded quickly. "Knowledge means power."

I giggled and then turned to look around the ballroom. I was examining the guests one by one when I saw the woman who was coming down the wide marble stairs.

"Who's that?" I asked curiously.

Compared to all the other nobles Paige had told me about, I had found someone who really attracted my attention. Paige sighed softly.

"Lady Bria, the council member from the house of Lunavier."

The woman's thick, pitch-black wavy hair ended around her waistline. She was greeting everyone while her green eyes, shadowed by her long eyelashes, wandered around the ballroom. She was wearing a dark red dress, in contrast with her porcelain-white skin, and her long hem swayed with her each step. I couldn't stop comparing myself to her, and a feeling of jealousy grew inside me. I knew people that would give everything to look like her.

"Very beautiful, isn't she? Some people really are born lucky," said Paige with envy flowing in her words. "Her father left his place at the council to her just before he died a few years ago."

Lady Bria moved among the guests, still smiling. Then she noticed the king with a crowd around him. As soon as King Warren's eyes caught a glimpse of her, he began looking at the council member with a . . . *different* expression on his face. Paige explained before I asked.

"King Warren's childhood crush," she said with a smile. "They grew up together. However, the Lunavier family is known for their obsession with their independence and the last thing they want is to follow the king's every step. Although they have sworn allegiance to the kingdom, it's hard to guess their moves."

"So," she went on as she turned her eyes to me, "even though King Warren chased after her for a century, they've never had a relationship as one would expect."

I grinned at this thought. Something the king couldn't get; that was worth seeing.

"Protector Anna," said a sudden voice coming from behind. "Paige."

I turned around only to see King Warren, who had just been surrounded by a crowd a short while ago. Paige greeted the king with a smile and I unwillingly did the same. He was too quick to approach us and was the last person I was hoping to talk to tonight.

"I hope you're having fun. These balls can be quite boring."

A louder voice played over the king's soft voice. "You should have learned how to have an actual fun one after the hundred and twenty-sixth time, Warren!"

Lord Theon was standing right behind him. He came over with long steps and gave me a look before putting his hand on his cousin's shoulder. "You should've seen my hundred and fifty-eighth birthday."

Then he turned to his cousin again, "You still don't understand what a real party looks like."

I smiled while Paige giggled. The healer girl eyed both noblemen and asked, "Aren't you going to ask me for a dance, Lord Theon?"

The lord extended his hand impishly and dragged Paige to the dance floor after murmuring something to her. King Warren stood next to me, where he could watch them. I wanted to tell Paige not to go and leave me alone with him, but it was too late.

I giggled as I looked behind them but the king didn't join me. Silence settled in between us. Then, as if he was disturbed by it, he was the first to talk.

"I never had the chance to explain myself after our meeting at the infirmary last time," he said. I kept my eyes focused on the guests. It had been weeks, I thought. But it was also the first time we were alone.

"It's because I'm a stranger, right?" I asked curiously. "Was that why you were eavesdropping on my conversation with Paige? To find out something about me?"

"Because I knew nothing about you. And I should know everything, for the safety of my kingdom."

"Are you planning on keeping me in check, King Warren?" I asked mockingly as I turned to face him. "Would you like that? To know my past or my weaknesses so that you can keep me under control just like you do the others?"

The king grimaced as if he had not liked my choice of words. He paused for a second, and while waiting for an answer, I saw his gaze trail over me. Paige was right, the gold-colored dress was beautiful and I felt powerful in it. I straightened my back and welcomed his gaze.

"I'm just trying to know you better," he finally said as his pitch-black eyes found my eyes again. "A king should always take interest in his people."

"Do you mean only the people in the capital?"

I realized that he really didn't have a clue what I was talking about when he knit his eyebrows. I continued. "You are talking about your people but when was the last time you left the capital?"

The king looked away at my words. "It's been many years since I've left Ardria."

I wasn't surprised, yet disappointed. The people of the capital had many privileges already. But what about my realm? What about the rest of us?

We continued to stand side by side in silence. For a while, I watched the people notice the king and bow, even though we were in a corner. And to me, they just shot a short glance. Finally, the king spoke once again.

"You look . . . *well.*"

"Because I am behaving the way you want?" I asked with a sarcastic tone. But I knew I did. And that was what he wanted from me. Act like a Protector who had been living in the palace. Not to be an outsider.

"*Because,*" I heard him say before annoyingly taking a deep breath. "You look beautiful and you are actually enjoying yourself just like them." He pointed out the group of nobles on the other side of the room.

I glared at him. "Is that a compliment? If so, that was terrible."

King Warren's hand went back to his neck and he cleared his throat. "Only the truth."

"You can't buy me with nice words or expensive gifts, Your Majesty," I said as I pointed out the silk dress I was wearing. "If that is all for keeping me under control, it won't work."

He shrugged. "At least you can't tell me you didn't like it."

I wanted to erase the arrogant expression on his face. "You act spoiled," I said, very annoyed. "All those rumors were indeed true."

"So bold," I heard him murmur. But his expression grew bigger; the king was smiling now. "That is exactly what I am. I am a king and today is my birthday."

His attention turned back to me then. "So, would you like to dance with me?"

I first looked at his extended hand and then his face. I softly cleared my throat. His words had hurt me more than I would have thought, but he could never understand that. I took a big step toward him as the hem of my silk dress flowed behind me and the cut opened, revealing the right side of my leg. I didn't know who had chosen this dress for me, but it was a bold choice.

I stopped right in front of him. His dark eyes found mine and his hand fell back. As I leaned over, his lips parted with surprise.

"Another thing you need to teach me during my stay at the palace." I looked directly at his dark eyes. "Please allow me to remind you, since you haven't been out of the capital for such a long time. The people living in the Seven Realms, at least most of us, don't know the dance nobles do at the palace because we don't have any time to waste on that. And that includes my village, too."

Reality had hit me in the face once again with the fact that he expected me to know the dance of the nobles. Besides, even if I could dance with him, I wouldn't want to attract anyone's gaze. This was the first time I had managed to blend in. I intended to keep it that way.

It took longer than I had expected for the king to understand what I meant. His lips formed a straight line as he locked his gaze with mine. His smile faded. I took a step back. With the distance I put between us, he let out a breath.

"If you'll excuse me, Your Majesty," I said, and bowed before walking away. My shoulder brushed his as I passed and I held my breath.

I didn't want to hear what he had to say, and the ballroom felt very small at that moment. I walked through the doors where guards stood by, and just as I turned into the glamorous hallways of the palace, a shadow next to the wall jumped in front of me.

"Leaving so soon?" Lady Bria's green eyes turned to me as her smile broadened. "Warren likes impressive balls." Then she turned to the ballroom and said, "A true king, isn't he?"

I smiled as I thought about the crowd inside and the exaggerated décor. "I'm sure Lord Theon had something to do with the planning."

What was she doing here? I hadn't seen her walk out because my gaze had been fixed on Paige so I could forget about the king by my side. We remained silent for a while and I couldn't help but examine her. It was obvious that she was much more striking than any of the guests inside. She was the center of attention.

"I thought you'd be in the ballroom," I said as she turned her green eyes back to me. I still had no idea why she was standing in front of me.

She shook her head slowly. "Why? Is it too strange that I wanted to be alone?"

*Yes*, I thought to myself. I was sure that someone as beautiful, glamorous, and noble as her would not want to leave the side of the other lords and ladies.

"I just thought that you wouldn't want to leave King Warren alone on his birthday."

I was sure there was no mistake in what Paige had told me about her and the king. I had seen the way the king had looked at her when she walked in. But apparently, despite all the gossip she had learned from the servants in the palace, there were things that even the healer girl didn't know.

Lady Bria's expression was as cold as ice and then she knit her thin eyebrows. "I thought you were keeping him company," she said as she pointed out the ballroom. "You looked like you were enjoying yourself."

I blushed at what she meant. Of course, she saw; everyone saw how close I was standing next to him. But that wasn't what I was trying to do at all.

"I was always around him ever since our childhood. I guess I can understand why people would think that way."

Even though I had just learned about everything from Paige, I looked away as if I was the one who had spread all the rumors. Lady Bria noticed how uncomfortable I felt and smiled.

"I am not anyone's shadow."

Despite the smile on her face, I noticed the change in her tone. Her eyes were fixed on a point behind me so I cleared my throat to draw them back onto myself.

"I'd better leave," I said.

Her lips formed a straight line. "But I guess the other Protectors will continue to enjoy the celebration."

The other Protectors weren't so much different from the nobles of the palace. They were from the Seven Realms, but they definitely weren't acting like it. Enjoying the ball and acting like nobles looked so natural on them.

I murmured, "I guess so."

I turned around and let my steps lead me outside, but I could still feel her gaze fixed on my back.

•

I passed through the marble pillars and looked around the temple that was barely lit in the darkness. The soft light of the moon helped me find the stairs as I climbed them slowly. I was moving timidly, trying to make as little noise as possible. When I reached the throne at the top of the stairs, instead of sitting, my fingertips traced the smooth surface of it. The throne had the clearest view of the gate of Aerlion that shone over the capital. I raised my gaze and looked at the sky through the pillars without taking my hand off the throne.

"Aren't you going to sit down?"

I flinched. A Phoenix, whom I recognized by his blue cape, was standing in the shadow of one of the pillars with his arms crossed. Our eyes met and he moved forward as his sharp features became visible. I stared into the familiar green eyes. I had moved a few steps away from the throne in the meantime.

"I didn't mean to . . ."

He was standing right in front of me now. He was wearing his usual blue cape, covering a part of the silver armor that shone under the moonlight.

"Hunter," I said slowly. I remembered Balfour calling him by this name, and that we had not left a good impression on each other during our first encounter.

The Phoenix shrugged his shoulders as I walked around the throne and closer to him. I took a glance behind and said, "That wasn't what I was trying to do."

He ignored me and walked along. I came down the stairs quickly as I said, "Please wait."

I put my hand on his shoulder and he suddenly stopped. His back was tensed and I quickly removed my touch from him. When he turned to look at me over his shoulder, he looked disgusted by the contact. I took a step back but didn't tear my gaze from his *green* eyes.

"You," I whispered, surprised. His gaze, trailing my hand, found my face again. I remembered the same green eyes looking at me. "You were the one who found me on the day I went to the city."

Yet he looked unfazed. He didn't say a word.

"Thank you for bringing me back."

Hunter rolled his eyes and looked away. "Whatever."

Then he started walking again. I let my hands down to both sides and slowly exhaled. I was not going to give up.

"I'm trying to talk to you."

"I heard you. And what do you expect me to say?"

"A simple 'you're welcome' would be enough."

I picked up speed to keep up with his long steps, and he continued to walk faster trying to leave me behind.

"Look, I didn't come here on purpose to fill Protector Breccan's place. I mean . . . that *is* why I am here. But not today . . . What I'm trying to say is that I just wanted to get away from the ball and I . . ."

My words were left halfway when he stopped abruptly. "Protector Anna," he said, emphasizing my name. His tone was quite harsh. "I was in the city when I felt your magic because of your *accident.* I was the closest Phoenix to the bar who could interfere before you actually harmed someone else. I don't expect an explanation. Now, if you excuse me, I don't have any more time to waste here. I need to go back to my post."

"Post?"

He crossed his arms but did not walk away.

"The gates and their surroundings are completely under the watch of the Protectors and their Phoenixes. The palace never takes any responsibility." He narrowed his eyes as he looked at my body, which was wrapped in silk. "Besides, none of us could dress up and join the nobles. We are not invited to the ball."

I could imagine that this had to do with the uprising of the Phoenixes. During the reign of the previous king and queen, the Phoenixes attached to the kingdom had revolted but after their unsuccessful uprising, they had all been given under the command of the Protector of their realm and all their ties to the king were cut. I could somewhat understand King Warren's anger at them, but it was cruel to punish those without fault.

When Hunter began moving forward once more, I wasted no time going after him. I saw the annoyed expression in his green eyes when he suddenly turned to me.

"Now what?" he asked.

I shouldn't have come here; it was a mistake. But whatever the case, they were Aerlion's guards and they were under *my* command. And it bothered me to know that none of them could stand the sight of me.

"You don't like me, do you?" I said, thinking of the Phoenixes that hadn't seen any harm in watching me with their steely gazes ever since I met them.

Hunter looked at me confused, "What?"

"You heard me."

The Phoenix quietly let out his breath as his gaze became softer. His shoulders relaxed when he said, "It's not what you think . . . Most of the Phoenixes are sold to the kingdom, leaving everything behind, when they show any trace of magic. It was the same for me, too. We were poor and when my family saw the magic I had, I was sent here for a fistful of gold."

He fixed his gaze at a point far away, as if he was trying not to look at me. "King Warren had just taken the throne when I arrived, and because of the things that had happened, I joined Breccan's army with the other newcomers. We were all scared. But Breccan approached us gently. He trained each of us himself, without asking for Commander Balfour's help, and he gave us a family. It's quite odd not having him around. And now, *you* are where he was supposed to be."

I could not tell if his tone was condescending or angry, but I thought I should feel lucky that he told me this without showing any hatred for the first time.

"How did he die?" I asked.

"Everyone blessed with the Goddess's power takes their magic from the tree. The power given to us returns to it when we die. Every magical being in each realm is connected and we can feel that bond. That day, we all felt the same thing; a feeling that we couldn't describe. I could feel it in all my bones, as if one of the links of the chain had snapped."

"So, you don't know how he died?"

Hunter scowled at my words. "*How*? He died of old age, of course. He had long passed four hundred years. Even *we* have a limit."

His angry tone was evidence that he didn't want to talk anymore. I remained silent. Hunter looked at me one last time and turned around. I kept staring at his figure moving away. As I continued to think, the only thing occupying my mind was the same old face that had invaded my dreams. If that old man was Protector Breccan, could he be trying to tell me something? What about Lord Cyril—would this prove him right? I continued to stare at the point where the Phoenix had disappeared as I remembered the fearful scream of the old man when he slid through the dragon's claws.

A voice inside me was saying something different about his death.

# CHAPTER 14

The footsteps rising from the other side of the marble doors echoed along the palace as the servants were running around, bringing gold or crystal ornaments and velvet cloths from all over the capital.

Balfour, who had been pacing behind me ever since I sat down, had gathered the heavy books from the shelves of the palace library that was full of thousands of old books. I looked at the pile that he had left in front of me. The smell of dust immediately filled my lungs. The commander turned his gaze back to the pile of books on the wooden table as I pushed forward another history book that was lying open in front of me.

"These aren't helpful," I said in disapproval. "I need to learn magic with practice. Not by reading books."

Balfour's thick eyebrows rose as he shook his head. "You can try all you want; if the inside of your head is empty, you won't survive for a minute. There are battles and strategies that you need to learn, and yet you also didn't have much improvement in your skills. The books will be your greatest friends to help you reach knowledge."

"Or . . ." I said as I roughly pushed back the wooden chair I was sitting in and rose. The shrill squeak echoed in the big and abandoned library. I raised one hand and then turned my palm to the high ceiling. I was able to make a slight white light shine, using the powers that I was still trying to control with the training. "I could go out to the training field and practice more."

Balfour seemed to find my confidence too exaggerated. He began stroking his beard with one hand. I left him behind and dove into the big shelves.

The library, which was full of books that had been collected since the first years of the kingdom and protected by magic, had been closed for us to work. This way, I had been able to express all my objections without trying to be silent, and the old commander's reprimands had echoed inside freely during the day.

I touched the polished shelves. Balfour continued to watch me for quite a while, his expression giving no clue of what he was thinking. "Could your impatience be because of tonight? Because you're nervous?" he asked.

"No, no. I'm not nervous at all."

But I didn't sound so convincing. I shrugged my shoulders and walked over to the wide window. I leaned my hip on the windowsill. I could hear Balfour's approaching steps.

"But you should be. It is not every day that a Protector becomes official with a grand ceremony. Besides, the public is also invited to see you there. There will be hundreds of people watching you."

I exhaled slowly and closed my eyes. "Thanks for reminding me," I murmured. It was as if his words had further clarified the flurry of the people working in panic outside.

The Protector of Aerlion had to take her rightful place with an official ceremony. It was mostly for the public, a way to show people how strong and loyal Protectors are toward the king and the kingdom; but also, an actual oath was needed. And for that very reason, without asking me, King Warren had sent a guard to inform me that a ceremony would be held today at sunset and that my duty would be officially announced in the Seven Realms after the celebrations. But I didn't feel ready at all.

"I thought I had to complete my training to become an actual Protector," I said as I continued to look outside. At the end of the palace courtyard, I could see the high platform where the palace guards waited. The doors would be opened when the sun started to come down, and the people would swarm inside to see the new Protector for the first time.

"That's right," Balfour said. He crossed his arms, but he kept his eyes on the great library in the opposite direction. "But the situation has changed . . . The rumors about the Old Ones returning are growing. The people need to know that you're ready."

"Despite the fact that I'm not ready?"

He lowered his gaze. "You have changed."

I rolled my eyes all too obviously and grunted, "Why does everyone keep telling me that?"

The commander ignored my words, "If you hadn't been the right person for this, your body couldn't bear the training. You continue to gain strength. Besides, you've started using your magic, too."

"What if I screw up?"

"You probably will."

My eyes grew wide as I turned to him at his words. Balfour curved his lips.

"When Darrell first came here, he almost burned the living quarters of his temple. And he had been raised as a Phoenix since childhood, like all others."

I smiled just like him while trying to imagine what had happened.

"Thalia got angry during a council meeting and she injured some of the members—unintentionally, of course. And Sam refused to take part in the training because he didn't want to harm anyone. He was a very young Phoenix then. People said that it was a mistake to choose a 'coward' like him."

"I'm scared," I said as I wrapped my arms around myself. "I'm not like them . . . I can't even protect myself, let alone others. I can't stand up to the things I saw in Belwald."

Even a dead Dralein had been enough to terrify me. I tried not to show my fear, biting my lips as I thought about the time it came running at me in my dream.

Balfour fidgeted in his place. He brought his hands over his chest, saying, "Dark times are coming. Even *I* don't know what this really means. There'll be great chaos, more unrest than at the time of the first Protectors. And even if you have no idea, you'll be one of those who face the battle at the front line."

Balfour's words didn't suppress my uneasiness; on the contrary, I was more nervous now. Although I knew that these were exactly the words that I didn't want to hear, he was right. I couldn't be eased by lies; I had to face the reality in all its bitterness.

"What happened during the time of the first Protectors?" I asked curiously. I took my gaze off the big courtyard where the preparations continued and turned to him.

I watched him walk back to the bookshelves without a word and reach to one of the higher shelves to pick up a few thick books. Then we both returned to the table where I had been studying.

"The era of the first kingdom," he said as he laid down a dark blue book that looked very old with its worn-out corners. He opened its thick cover. I skimmed over the writing and skipped the first few pages. The first thing that caught my eye was the crystals in seven different colors.

"I feel like I've seen these before," I said, puzzled, as I traced over the symbols with my finger.

I could feel Balfour's gaze on me. I didn't know much about the crystals, and it was the first time I had seen a book about them. But then, I suddenly remembered the nightmare I had had a few days before. I recalled the colorful lights reflecting from the shield; the dark figure standing behind me was holding all of them in its hand.

"The crystals that the Goddess presented to the Protectors," Balfour said while tracing the symbols with his index finger. Then he stopped on the yellow one. "This is Aerlion's."

I touched the drawing of the yellow crystal. I could feel the paint under my fingers. On the next page, there was a drawing that looked like a shadow. As I examined the drawing of the hulky man in black, I saw that the drawing was completely in dark colors, like a Dralein. Not a single feature of his face was visible.

"That is Rogue," said Balfour with his sharp eyes focused on the book. I remembered the commotion at the council after what happened in Belwald. In an attempt to silence the crowd, Lord Cyril had reminded them of this name.

"The First King in the history of the kingdom. King Rogue Montborne, the Master of Darkness."

*The First King* . . . the ancestor of King Warren. I leaned forward to examine the drawing and Balfour moved to the side to give me more space.

"The crystals were given to the first Protectors by the Goddess herself. For a while, they brought peace to the Seven Realms. But King Rogue thought the magic could be used for completely different purposes, so he stole them and ruled the dark magic; he created what we call the Old Ones."

*The Old Ones* . . . As I thought of the Dralein, I remembered how scary the black creature was. I exhaled with fear.

"There had always been darkness," Balfour explained slowly. "Back then, the creatures were few and not as dangerous as they became later. People would still hunt them though, just like they hunted dragons."

My eyes widened and I lifted my chin. "Dragons?"

He nodded. "Oh, of course. Not the Protector's dragons, but the rest were wild. One by one, they were slaughtered. The eighth, and last, dragon was killed by King Alastair's order, I believe. So, only seven of them were left."

I couldn't believe it. There were more dragons in the realms once. There were traces of magic *everywhere*.

"The creatures, the dragons... they were all magical beings."

The commander loudly sighed. "Rogue's intentions were evil and one by one, he took all seven crystals. People say the dragons were too powerful for him, but the creatures were an easy target. What Rogue did was to change their nature. With the crystals, he controlled them and created a new kind of dark magic, the Old Ones...The first Protectors fought him to take the crystals back. They destroyed him by using them. When Rogue was defeated, the darkness the Old Ones needed faded and in time, they became extinct. After the war, the first Protectors hid the crystals around the Seven Realms to make sure they couldn't be found. Even today, no one knows where they are."

After examining the dark figure of the First King for a while, I picked up the book and turned the pages. There were so many things I didn't know about the capital and the realms. The stranger at the bar was right, then. The crystals were so powerful that they could be used for anything, but that was also the reason why the first Protectors had put an end to it.

"Can I take this book?"

"Of course," Balfour said with a smile. "But you'd better not lose it. This book, like many of the others, is from King Warren's private collection. They are all a few centuries old."

I couldn't imagine King Warren doing anything other than sitting at his throne while grumbling, but Balfour's words caused me to examine the shelves lined between the stone pillars all over the library. There were thousands of books here; the king couldn't possibly have read them all, could he?

I tried to pull the wooden chair to continue studying but Balfour prevented me by pulling the chair from the other end. "Enough studying for today," he said with a broad smile. "We can continue some other time."

My hand holding the chair relaxed and I smiled back, pressing the book tightly to my chest. I began walking to the big double-winged door of the library while Balfour began collecting the books I had left behind. I knocked a couple of times and the guards standing outside pulled the heavy handles of the door to let me out. I hurried away from the library, unable to stop thinking about whether Balfour and I could continue our lessons the same way from today on.

I saw the servants rushing outside. I knew one of them would grab me at first sight and take me to my room to prepare, but I didn't feel ready yet. While passing by the wide window in the hallway, I was caught by a sudden urge to go outside. I turned in the opposite direction and walked into the hallway that led to the garden. The servants had nothing to do in the area at the back of the palace; they had planned to gather thousands of people at the glorious front side of the magnificent palace. I smiled with this thought as I held the book tight and began walking down the stairs. I was right. I could hear the birds chirping and there was no sign of anyone. I walked outside, raised my head, and inhaled the clean air. Despite the gray clouds, something inside me said that they wouldn't cancel the ceremony even if it rained.

I walked among the trees and reached the stone path. I looked at the great forest that began behind the hill further ahead. The side of the palace that didn't overlook the city was much more beautiful. But Balfour never left my side to make sure that I completed my daily training, making it impossible for me to wander around the palace on my own. I happily closed my eyes. I didn't notice the footsteps approaching. When I opened my eyes again, I saw that I was standing across from King Warren. We both stopped walking at the same time.

He greeted me with his head and said, "Protector Anna."

I bowed gently. "Your Highness."

I watched him as he walked slowly toward me. I was sure to get a scolding. Instead, he surprised me with a smile.

"Would you like to walk with me for while?"

"Rather not," I said without thinking. As his eyebrows rose at my answer, I quickly added, "I mean, it would be better if I went back to my room."

I didn't know if he believed my lie but he smiled understandingly, and I let out a sigh of relief.

"Just for a short while," he insisted. "You look thoughtful. Perhaps walking in the garden could help to ease your mind."

Even if I didn't want to walk with him, I knew that kings and nobles didn't actually *ask*. I nodded in response. "Very well."

I tried to keep up with his pace while keeping a distance, still holding on tightly to the book. His eyes moved to my hands, and then to my face. Even if he had realized that it was one of his books, he didn't say anything. He guided us toward the glass greenhouse behind the palace, hidden among thick trees. While walking, all I could think of was that I was in trouble. Otherwise, there was no reason for the king to bring me here.

Neither of us initiated conversation. I looked at his face in curiosity. The king really was handsome and he could have been a nice couple with Lady Bria. There wouldn't be a better couple in all of the Seven Realms.

"I want to ask something," I murmured when I realized that he wouldn't start the conversation. King Warren nodded without turning to me and I went on.

"I was told that the Old Ones were extinct. And now everyone says that the dark days have returned. Does this have something to do with the crystals? Do you think someone could have found them and used their power?"

Even after clearing his throat loudly, it was obvious that the king was trying to look away from me. He looked annoyed. "You know too much for someone who arrived at the palace only weeks ago."

"I thought I was supposed to complete my training as quickly as possible. Otherwise, why would there be a ceremony for me today?"

"I was wondering when you would ask," he murmured as he turned to me. "I want all Protectors to be ready, including you . . . Honestly, I don't know what exactly we are up against. And that's what worries me."

"So could there be another Rogue incident?" I asked as I looked at the book I was carrying.

In the throne room, I had noticed how everyone's face had changed with Lord Cyril's words. And similarly, King Warren stopped walking with what I said. His gaze shifted to the thick book in my hand.

"I should warn Balfour not to tell you everything."

I turned to him with narrowed eyes. I had to lift my head because of his height. "Why? Is there something you don't want me to know?"

He exhaled harshly and combed through his dark hair with his hand.

"Let's say that I trust the Protectors as much as I trust everyone else."

"I thought they *served* you." Then I immediately corrected myself silently. *We…* I thought. I was one of them now.

"But you also serve others," said King Warren. "That is your job, to be a bridge between. I can't trust anyone unless that person devotes himself completely to me. This includes the Protectors."

*So, he trusts no one*, I thought. He sounded arrogant but I wasn't surprised.

I didn't continue when King Warren started walking again. "Are you afraid?" I asked.

He turned to me when he realized I was not following. There was an expression on his face that I couldn't describe. "Everyone is afraid of something. I just prefer to do everything in my power to continue my reign. You can't blame me for being cautious."

I asked another question before he had a chance to turn away. "What about us?" I said as I straightened my back. "Are you also scared of the Protectors? For them to turn their backs on you just like the Phoenixes did?"

His lips became a straight line and I saw that he had tensed. There was a thin line and I felt like I had just crossed that. I shouldn't have said anything about the Phoenixes. I shouldn't have mentioned them, and what they did to his parents. But something in me was too desperate to know the answer.

His chest stopped heaving and for a second, I thought he was holding himself. I wouldn't be surprised if he said something rude; at least this time he would be right. Instead, he tilted his head and looked at me.

"Not from you." His voice was softer than I expected and he didn't look angry at all. But then he suddenly turned away. "But you carry more power than the Phoenixes. Thus, it makes you more dangerous."

"The Protectors are not a threat to your throne," I insisted.

He shook his head in response. "History repeats itself. Did you know that it was a Protector who started everything during the time of Rogue? That was how Rogue got hold of the crystals."

A *Protector*? Rogue Montborne was the First King and he had lived thousands of years before King Warren and his ancestors. Yet, he was evil. Balfour had just told me how he had become a threat after getting possession of the crystals. He had stood up to the Protectors and he had had to be stopped. But I couldn't even imagine that one of us would betray the others and work with the enemy.

"The problem with you Protectors is that you don't know your limits. Just like the Phoenixes, your magic may be used for good but it also bears a threat."

"But the crystals are still hidden, right?" I asked. What the stranger at the bar had mentioned about the king and the crystals sounded more meaningful now. "So, you don't need to fear us. We don't even know where the crystals are."

He didn't say anything and I didn't go on. There was an expression on his face to which I couldn't give any meaning. He kept looking at me for a while without moving. I began speaking to put an end to the silence that had come in between us.

"Why did you bring me here?" I asked quickly. I wanted to leave. The garden didn't feel as peaceful as I thought it would.

The king smiled. "Just to talk," he said as he took a step toward me. "I'm only trying to get to know the stranger that has taken a step inside the palace walls."

"Well, have you been able to learn anything about me, then?" I asked, raising my chin and staring at his dark eyes, causing an unpleasant smile to form on his face.

"Not quite yet."

We stared at each other in silence. He didn't turn away and I didn't move; his body was still close to mine and the gap between us could end with only a single step that either one of us could take.

I broke the tension. I slowly turned my back to him and hurried to the exit of the greenhouse. I suddenly noticed that I hadn't bowed to him but I couldn't care less about courtesy right now. I rushed back to the palace and left him behind.

# CHAPTER 15

The sun was about to disappear behind the mountains that surrounded the capital. The sky was painted in different shades of red, and darkness approached with each passing minute. I raised my head and turned to Balfour, who was standing right behind me. He gave me a slight nod when our eyes met and I let out my breath. Then, I began to walk.

The golden armor I was wearing felt heavier with each step I took. I tried to stand tall under the crushing feeling while coming down the stairs one by one. My hands found the stone walls that came up to my waist as I looked from the top of the rampart to the crowd gathered below. I watched the human flood that extended from the palace's great gates to the city, their words blending into each other, making it impossible to understand a single thing.

"Too crowded," I murmured.

"And they're all here to see you."

Hundreds of people were trying to squeeze into the wide courtyard, and the majority of the crowd had overflowed behind the ramparts surrounding the palace.

The buzzing increased when I appeared at the top of the stairs. As I walked down, I could feel the eyes on me. I had to remind myself that this was only a show for the people, but I couldn't help myself from enjoying it. They were all here to see *me*.

I passed the stone bridge that connected the two watchtowers and entered the inner part of the palace, only to notice that the crowd in the yard was no different from the one outside. The iron doors under the ramparts were left open under the watch of a group of guards. I looked at the platform in the middle of the courtyard that sat on four thick wooden feet. The royal guards were lined up around the platform, with their faces turned to the crowd. Noises rose from the people, and some started chanting.

My lips trembled against my will, and an almost-sincere smile formed on my face. I came down the stairs one by one and started taking firm steps toward the platform. Balfour was right behind me. The royal guards waiting at the end of the stairs surrounded me without breaking their formation and we began walking forward with matching steps.

A few people extended their hands to reach out to me but they were taken out of my sight by the guards who moved in between us. We reached the platform. The council members were lined up on the opposite side of the Protectors. Balfour left me with the guards and went to stand with the other commanders. He stood in the front row, closest to the platform.

On top of the two-story platform was a wide area that could hold at least five people, and right at the center was a big, iron throne. My eyes met those of its owner. The canopy over King Warren's throne was covered with red velvet curtains and his dark-colored clothes seemed to disappear into them. Yet the golden crown that was adorned with precious stones had been brought into the forefront with all the red in the background surrounding him.

That crown could feed hundreds . . . no, *thousands* of people. But neither the king nor any of the nobles would give up their luxuries. The words of the stranger at the bar were ringing in my ears. Was a different future possible? Could I use the crystals to free the people from their misery?

*And you can be a family again*, hissed a voice inside me. I dreamed of this although I knew that it would mean rubbing salt on wounds I had deep down. The pain reminded me that a better future was possible.

The king rose and took a few steps away from his throne. I watched him as he turned his dark eyes to me. I couldn't take my gaze away from his crown; it was fascinating. I wondered if that had been his intention. Was it not the king's purpose to threaten his enemies, to show that he was still strong and invincible? Especially when his enemies were so close by. Just a few hours ago, he had told me that he never trusted anyone completely. This meant that everyone around posed a threat to him.

I turned to the council members with this thought, knowing that King Warren was watching me. Lady Bria's dazzling smile broadened when I looked at her. It seemed as if Lord Cheng could cut through the wooden platform with his tough gaze on the floor. He wasn't looking at me; he was tense, but not so much that would cause a problem. Today wasn't one of those days when he objected to everything.

I saw the Phoenixes waiting on the other side of the area. Lord Cyril, who was standing in front of them, caught my attention. He had left his place at the council to his brother years ago so, he wasn't standing with them on the platform, but he didn't seem to complain about his position either. When our eyes met, his words rushed to my mind. He had told me to pay attention to my dreams, but I had no idea how they could keep me alive.

The guards slowed down as I walked on the first step of the wide platform. Then I stepped on the next one, then the one after that . . . I swiftly passed by the council members and the Protectors.

Protectors Leon and Thalia seemed much more serious than they had been in the ballroom, standing far away from each other. My eyes met Darrell's and a smile formed on the face of the Protector of Demos. The same happened with Protector Ramona. She had another expression on her face as she nodded: pride. Perhaps she saw a piece of herself in me. I had an ordinary past like her and I had been able to come this far. Whatever the reason, this boosted my courage. Protector Sam never took his eyes off me, and it was the same with Protector Edmond. The old man kept looking at me without blinking; this time, I didn't see any signs of mockery in his gaze.

I reached the top where King Warren was waiting. I remembered the instructions Balfour had given me for what to do during the ceremony. So, I knelt before the king.

A young Phoenix standing on the other side of the area raised a sword and began moving toward me but she was stopped by another Phoenix—Hunter. He slowly took the sword from the woman's hand and began approaching. He stopped in front of the platform, bowed down, and handed the sword to the king. His green eyes pierced me as he nodded.

King Warren took the sword from him as my eyes met the bright steel. The crimson colors of the sky slowly gave way to the darkness. I fixed my gaze on his leather boots. It reminded me of Selection Day; it also took place during the sunset.

"Rise, Protector."

I fixed my gaze on his dark eyes and stood up. King Warren held the sword horizontally with two hands and extended it to me. In the meantime, I was trying not to think about our conversation a few hours earlier.

"Each weapon you will carry represents your duty, your strength, and your will. You will serve the Seven Realms with each sword you hold, and you will ensure that none of your people will bleed. The only blood on your sword shall be that of your enemies."

I looked at the crowd. There were too many people watching. Even though the ceremony was not over yet and I wasn't officially a Protector, I still felt crushed under their expectations. My shoulders had shrugged as if affirming this thought. But no, I couldn't do that in front of all these people. I would not yield.

I stood straight as if trying to shoulder all the responsibilities, and looked at King Warren again. He truly looked invincible under that noble appearance, and maybe he actually was. I reminded myself that I could never be like him, but I didn't need to be, anyway. I wasn't a noble and I wasn't cruel. I was going to be different, *better*.

"Swear an oath that you will care for the people of Aerlion until your last breath, that you will devote your life to them."

I took a deep breath. "I swear to guard over my realm, to protect and serve to my people until the day I die."

These words were just a few of those that Balfour had made me memorize. The words coming out of my mouth felt like lies to my ears but my tone was determined and strong. I went on.

"I shall use the powers bestowed upon me by the Goddess Vitae and I shall never surrender to the darkness." By now, I was shouting. "As a Protector, I will remain loyal to the kingdom until my last breath."

King Warren examined my face before turning to the crowd. I knew that he was measuring my words. I had not missed a chance to rebel against him before and I reminded myself that nothing had changed. My people were suffering. The people of Aerlion were ready to give up on each other just to be able to feed themselves, and King Warren wasn't so different from the other nobles. One thing was clear, I thought: they were my enemy, all of them. Especially the king. And I was never going to forget what I, and my people, had been through.

"I consecrate you with the might and power bestowed upon me by the Goddess, Protector Anna of Aerlion."

The king extended the sword to me. "The new Guardian of the Light."

I took the sword, and as Balfour had taught me, I used my newly developing powers to surround the sword with the bright light spreading from my hands. My magic glowed in the courtyard. The crowd cheered.

As I held the sword with hesitation, I wondered what future days would bring. My only purpose in the village had been to survive, and the most dangerous thing I had done had been stealing from others for my family. I was a good thief; I moved quickly and with agility, and I was never caught. But I had never been a warrior.

The other Protectors waiting at the lower deck of the platform came over to complete the ceremony. When the six of them climbed the stairs and stood by me, we all went down on one knee in front of King Warren.

"Long live the king!"

The words said by the Protectors were repeated first by the Phoenixes, then the council members, and finally by hundreds of people. The inner court of the glamorous royal palace echoed with our words. I raised my head while still on one knee and looked at King Warren. Our eyes met. I stared into his face, and the king's thick eyebrows were knit together thoughtfully. Yet neither of us looked away.

Just at that moment, an ear-piercing voice rose from the crowd. I flinched, left breathless with it. My heart started pounding with fear.

When the people moved to the side, I saw the black figure among the crowd. I let out my breath hastily. Protector Ramona was the first to take action. She swung her sword as she ordered the royal guards around us. "Evacuate the courtyard!"

I stood up, as did everyone else. Sounds of drawing swords were heard and a group of guards began running toward the Dralein. Some of them had surrounded King Warren, although I was sure that he was able to protect himself.

People were scattered around the yard, screaming. I stared at the black figures when the crowd was swept to the side. It was only then that I realized the palace was surrounded by many of the Old Ones.

The Phoenixes moved and took their place next to their Protectors. I noticed Hunter's group in the front. I held my sword tightly with my shaking hands. When everyone with a weapon lunged forward, including all the other Protectors and King Warren, I took a hesitant step to do the same. But Hunter put his hand on my shoulder to stop me.

"You are not good at close combat yet," he said quickly. "Try this."

He gave me the bow that was on his back, together with the quiver full of arrows. I put the sword back in its scabbard, remembering clearly that I had unintentionally thrown an arrow at Darrell. *This wasn't the best choice of weapon for me either*, I thought. But my heart was pounding with fear and I was too tense to object to him.

"Don't get too close to those things, and stay with us."

I snatched the bow from his hand. I took a shaky breath as soon as my fingers touched the carved wood. Hunter looked at me one last time before running to the yard. There were two Phoenixes left to protect me. I chose to stand on the stairs of the platform and quickly placed an arrow on the bow.

I grimaced as I saw the Dralein up ahead. I examined the black, crooked figure of it, but something else distracted me. I looked at the dark, purple-colored figure between two royal guards in the middle of the yard. My eyes flew open in horror.

"What is that thing?" I yelled out to the Phoenix standing under the platform.

The woman's eyes turned to me for a moment with her bow ready in her hand. "Murgroth, the creatures of the underground."

It was a huge creature covered with dark purple skin, which seemed to be thick and cracked. It wasn't as tall as a Dralein and it had a much rounder figure. The creature looked around with its yellow eyes and roared thunderously as it swung one of its fists.

I pulled the string and aimed at it. The arrow flew and struck its thick skin, but it hadn't even felt it. Now I realized why the other archers had gone after the Dralein; the Murgroths' skin was too thick to be pierced by arrows.

"If you ever want to use your powers," said one of the Phoenixes that were staying with me, "this is exactly the right time."

I looked at the yard. I knew that Phoenixes also had magical powers, but their magic wasn't strong like ours. That was the reason why they preferred weapons instead. I hung the bow on my back and raised my hands. But I had never tried this before, at least not under such conditions.

"Focus," I murmured between my gritted teeth. "Focus, you can do this."

I closed my eyes tightly despite the cries coming from all around the platform, hoping that the Phoenixes would continue protecting me against any sudden attack. I felt the wooden floor tremble under my feet as my breathing slowed down. I opened my eyes slightly with a sharp feeling moving from my hands to my spine. I swung my hands toward the Murgroth. The bright light coming out of my palms shone and the creature turned into dust in seconds. Some of the Phoenixes turned to me in shock. My eyes met Hunter's. His lips curved upward and he swung his sword down onto the Dralein in front of him.

I looked at where the Old One had been standing. My knees were already trembling. I brought my hand to my chest and reached for the bow on my back. There was no way I could use my powers once more. I was so exhausted that it felt impossible to do it again.

I climbed back up the stairs and knelt down. Perhaps I couldn't use my powers, but I could still fight. I noticed a Dralein closing in on one of the guards protecting King Warren so I quickly reached for the quiver and loosed an arrow. My hands were still shaking so, the arrow missed its target and stuck in the creature's arm. It hissed and fixed its dark eyes on me before starting to run toward me.

"Damn it!" I said, breathing in panic.

I jumped down from the platform and tried to put some distance between us. But it was still coming after me. I gulped with fear and tried to take an arrow from the quiver. But this was impossible, I couldn't even hit a standing target.

I let go of the bow and drew my sword but I noticed that the Dralein wasn't chasing me anymore; it was after someone else. I followed the direction it was headed and saw a little boy sitting at the far end of the yard with his knees pulled to himself. His wet eyes were fixed on a woman lying on the ground. She wasn't moving, and the boy hadn't even noticed the creature coming at him.

"No!" I cried in fear.

I began running toward the boy as I kept on tumbling and my feet kept sliding on the ground. But I didn't slow down. When I got close to the boy, I slid on my knees and tried to pull the boy by his arm. He took his gaze off the corpse on the ground and looked behind my shoulder. His eyes opened wide but he was frozen in shock.

I held the sword tight in my hand and got in front of the boy. The Dralein stopped right in front of me. It roared, raising its hand-like claws to the sky. I stabbed my sword into its torso but it didn't even stumble. I drew back together with the boy as it swung one of its claws, and I used my body as a shield between the creature and the boy. I wrapped my arms around him with a protective instinct and kept him behind me at all costs.

I didn't feel the sharp pain. The grunting behind me ceased as I relaxed my hands around the boy and turned in hesitation. King Warren was right next to us.

His angry gaze met mine again for a second before turning back to the creature lying on the ground. He looked furious, but still checked on me with a worried expression. I didn't want to admit but I felt relieved as I continued to watch him take a few steps toward us.

"Are you okay?" King Warren asked. "Are you wounded?"

I shook my head but I was lost for words. His dark eyes searched over me as if trying to find an open wound or any blood dripping. His jaw relaxed when he saw that I was okay. He saved *my* life, I thought.

The little boy let go of his sobs and began crying out loud as the guards gathered around. One of them held the boy in his arms to take him to the infirmary together with the other wounded, but the boy's eyes never left the woman lying on the ground. The guards hurried the boy away as if they could make him see less of this chaos.

I tried not to look down and see the corpse lying at my feet. I knew that if I saw her, I could never take her face out of my mind. I turned my gaze from the boy to the king. The boy's painful cries echoed in the yard until he was gone.

King Warren seemed as shaken as I was. He took a few hesitant steps toward me. His scowl loosened when I asked, "What'll happen to him? What about the others?"

I brought my trembling hands together at my back so they wouldn't be seen. King Warren didn't care. He shook his head angrily. "I'll take care of it."

He bent down and took the sword, my sword, out of the creature's lifeless body. It was smeared with blood.

I closed my eyes. Maybe I couldn't prevent myself from hearing the sound of it, but I could at least not see the sight. King Warren wiped my sword on his arm and gave it back to me. I held it with shaking hands and put it on the ground. He said nothing. He took his dark eyes away from me and looked down as he turned the creature's head with the tip of his boot.

"What are you doing . . ."

But the words stuck in my throat. I looked at the thing on the ground in shock. Even though the same black figure was there, the creature's face wasn't what it was supposed to be. Its face was like ours . . . it belonged to a *human*. The dark feathers were slowly changing and its whole face was returning to its original shape. The face belonged to a man, an actual human.

"Lost people," said King Warren as he looked at the corpse. "The rumors were true." He raised his head. "People are getting lost in all the Seven Realms and they are being turned into the Old Ones."

I gulped harshly to suppress the nausea rising from my throat.

I remembered the first animal I had killed, how the knife in my clumsy hand had found the animal's hide and how the sharp tip dug into its flesh. I had waited by its side until the life completely left its eyes. The sight of the blood flowing out of its body when I pulled away the knife hadn't left my mind for quite a long time. And that had been the first and last time. Stealing from people and selling what I'd taken was easier than hunting. Yet at the time, I had reminded myself that there were no other options than killing that animal. I was just trying to help my family survive.

And now I had a purpose again. When I jumped in front of the creature to save the little boy, I had thought that it would be easier compared to that time. After all, that thing wasn't even an animal. But I was wrong. I stared at the face the king had turned with his boot. It was not a creature. It was a person. And I had killed him.

"They can't control their bodies in any way. They aren't aware of what they're doing."

"Why didn't you tell me?" I asked, unable to take my gaze off the man lying there.

My hands were covered with blood but I didn't even know whose blood it was. When I looked down at my hands, I saw fingernail marks on my palm, and it was only then that I noticed the pain. I didn't even notice Protector Ramona bend over and put her hand on my shoulder.

*Lost people*, he had said, and that this was happening in all seven realms. Why had I not been told? All this time, I had been thinking that the incident was limited to Belwald. Now, this? People were turning into actual monsters and I had no idea.

"You weren't ready."

I inhaled with rage. "You don't have any other choice right now but to trust me, do you?"

The king didn't take his eyes away from me. I relaxed my fist and turned my gaze from him to the ground. "How can they turn a human?"

"They use the crystals."

His words startled me. I raised my eyebrows and I knelt down to examine the human-creature, or whatever was left of it. I was right. Even though the king had refrained from giving me an answer today, I had made a correct assumption. "I thought the crystals were hidden. Their location is unknown . . . the first Protectors made sure of it."

The king nodded in distress. I wanted him to protest, to say something, but he just crossed his arms. "Apparently someone has found them."

One by one, the other Protectors began gathering around us. I heard Protector Edmond murmur, staring at the ground with his eyes shadowed by anger. His voice was cold and tired, but his eyes shone like flames.

"Something inside me says this was not a real attack; we handled it *too easily.*"

With Protector Edmond's words, I tried to move the thought of the dozens of people that were killed or injured away from my mind. *I wouldn't have called that easy.*

The eyes of Belwald's old Protector took turns looking at us one by one and finally stopped on me. He continued, "And I think this is just the beginning for the Seven Realms."

•

The sky was dark over the glass greenhouse. Although I had wrapped myself tightly in my cape, the cold had found a way to get in through my clothes. It was almost as if the weather was aware of what had happened after the ceremony yesterday, and it had cast a dark sky over Ardria ever since.

I found my way with the help of the stone steps that continued along with the flowers and plants that were as tall as I was. I was too lost in my thoughts to notice the approaching footsteps. I slowly turned my head to see King Warren looking at me from the other side of the path. Of course, he was here.

"What are you doing here?" I asked, my voice showing how shaken I was. The king seemed to notice.

I hadn't taken part in any of the meetings that continued since yesterday. Everyone had seen how much I had fallen apart after the ceremony and no one came after me. But the king of the Seven Realms didn't have such an option.

"I needed some time to think." He approached me. "I think I knew you'd become as attached to this place as I am after I brought you here." I looked at him over my shoulder as he continued. "I come here any time I want to be left alone. It's . . . peaceful."

I looked around, and without a word, I immediately headed to the exit of the greenhouse on the other side. But the king stopped me before I could brush past him.

"You don't have to leave. The greenhouse is big enough for both of us."

I slowly turned around, making sure to keep the distance between us.

"I assume we shouldn't expect to see you among us for a while." He had bent over at the red roses planted at the corner and he wasn't looking at me. But I realized that this was the end of the silence I had been trying to keep.

"No one came looking for me. From what I can see, you don't need me anyway."

The king looked at me over his shoulder. "Would you prefer that I send a guard after you and drag you into the throne room?" He sounded serious, but I could see his lips trembling with the effort not to smile.

I gritted my teeth and turned my back to him, continuing to ignore him. But the king didn't let me. His steps followed mine, one step after another as if we were kids playing a game.

"Is everything just a game to you?" I suddenly asked.

I watched him lean over and tear a leaf from behind my head. I stared at his hand as the long-dried leaf crumbled between his fingers.

He was standing too close to me and I could feel his breath on my neck. If he bent over, his nose would touch my cheek and I had a feeling he was doing this on purpose. His pitch-black eyes wandered over my skin, trailing an invisible line from my eyes to my parted lips.

"I should tell the gardener to come here more often."

I moved to the side, away from him and the plant behind. I never should have come here. I hadn't known he would be here; I just wanted to be alone.

"How are you feeling?" he asked me then. There was no sarcasm in his tone this time.

I smiled. "How does the kingdom want me to feel? After all, I have to obey orders of all kinds, right? Perhaps it would be easier for the both of us if you would tell me what I should do."

"You can believe the gossip as much as you want, but I am not as heartless as one would assume." The king stopped walking and crossed his arms as he stared at me. "So, how do *you* want to feel?"

I looked away. "As if it mattered."

"You can shout or cry if you want. You can mourn. In fact, I wouldn't care less even if you threw up in front of me."

We continued to stare at each other in silence. I was the first to break.

"I killed a man," I said, hating the bitter taste of the words coming out of my mouth.

His lips formed a straight line. When I started to look away, I saw him hesitantly extend his hand toward me. I thought he was going to touch me, but a shadow of emotion appeared on his face and before I looked back, his hand fell back.

"That thing wasn't human," he whispered. "Not anymore, at least. We can't reverse the effect of the crystals."

I quickly shook my head. "What if we could?"

He paused before answering. "We don't know if such a thing is even possible. We had to make immediate decisions and we didn't have any time to lose."

"You didn't hesitate to kill it," I said. "We could have chained it."

"And then what? What were we supposed to do with a monster living in the dungeons?"

"I don't know but—"

"It was going to kill *you*," he said, suddenly cutting into my words. "You and the child. You were between them, *shielding* the boy. So no, *I didn't hesitate.*"

I stared at my hands. It was as if I could still see the blood soaked deep into my fingernails, *my blood*. Because I was just a coward.

"When was your first kill?" I asked without looking at him. There could be no other explanation for his cold attitude during the ceremony. He wasn't a stranger to the feelings I was having right now.

"That day . . . when they attacked me and my family." He looked like he was in so much pain as he continued to talk. "Four people, four *Phoenixes*. I was able to catch up with a group of them before the royal guards took me to a safe place, and unlike you, I was completely aware of what I was facing."

I could see that remembering the old times hurt him. He raised his eyes from the stone floor of the greenhouse and looked at me, causing me to fight myself so I wouldn't look away immediately. At that moment, as I looked into King Warren's pitch-black eyes, I thought that this was the first time I didn't feel as if I was looking into the void. I could clearly read his feelings, and the sorrow in his eyes was obvious.

"The blood that has been spilled belongs to all of us," he said finally. "So don't try to bear the brunt by yourself, not even for a moment."

# CHAPTER 16

I leaned forward to look at the guests at the long dinner table. The palace's great dining room, which was used for special occasions only, was now filled with Protectors, council members, and commanders. I turned to look at King Warren, who was sitting close to me at the head of the table. He was eating without looking up, trying not to meet eyes with anyone. Lately, it had become difficult to see him wandering around the palace—which I wasn't complaining about—and anyone could tell how tired he was by simply looking at his face.

I held the silver fork tightly in my hand and looked down at the plate in front of me. The table was full of food, and the servants had immediately filled my plate before I could make up my mind. The palace cook had prepared the best food I had ever tasted, but I had no appetite. It hadn't been long since the attack. Yet we could still come together and act as if nothing had happened. King Warren had said that my official start as a Protector was something worth celebrating, but deep inside, I was sure that the conversation at the greenhouse had caused him to speed up his plans for this dinner. So here we were, acting as if nothing had happened. Celebrating was the thing nobles did best anyway. Yet it felt so wrong.

My eyes met with King Warren's. He raised the wineglass in front of him. I forced myself to look elsewhere, hoping that he would take his eyes off me.

I looked at Hunter over my shoulder. Two Phoenixes from each Protector's army had been called to guard during the dinner. Since Hunter was the next senior soldier among Aerlion's Phoenixes—after Balfour and me—he had been called, and there was another Phoenix next to him whose name I didn't know, but I had spoken with him a few times. They had been standing guard close to the wall behind me but they weren't allowed to talk or join us. This was cruel, and I was sure that was King Warren's purpose. His eyebrows knit every time he turned to look at the group of Phoenixes lined up next to the wall. There were fourteen of them in the room.

I took a long sip from the wineglass in front of me. The forced conversations among the guests had lasted until dinner was served, and no one said a word afterward. I could hear some murmuring now and then, but that didn't last long either. I didn't think that these people, who already had to see each other every single day, were too keen to get together again at the end of it.

"Tell me, Protector Anna," said someone, and I raised my head to look at Lord Conrad, the council member of the Tendros family. "What kind of a place is Aerlion? Tell us about it."

My eyes caught a glimpse of Darrell as all eyes turned to me. As I remembered our conversation before, I forced myself to smile.

"It's completely covered with forests," I said while smiling back at him. "I spent my childhood in the forest, but not so far away as to attract the wild animals. I have only seen Belwald so far but I can tell you that Aerlion isn't that cold."

Protector Edmond smiled and made a joke about how cold his realm could get. This seemed to somewhat soften the atmosphere. I was surprised by how the old Protector was acting less grumpy than usual.

I went on. "The people don't go into the forest but sometimes animals come from the meadows to the village. We enjoy all the seasons. Most of the villagers are either farmers or merchants."

Since I had never been out of the village before, I had no idea of what the other places in my realm were like. But no one said a word if they even noticed this small detail.

Lord Conrad kept the conversation going. "Sounds like a nice place for hunting," he said with a laugh before gulping down the remainder of the wine in his glass. A servant appeared behind him with a decanter before the glass was put back on the table.

"Absolutely ideal for this time of the year." Lord Theon's gaze turned to Lord Cyril, who was sitting next to him. "The hunting equipment of the Ironlash family is definitely the best I've seen in the entire kingdom. What do you say, old man, are you too rusty for this?"

Surprisingly, a smile appeared on Lord Cyril's face. Lord Theon's smugness seemed to humor him. I knew that there were strengthened ties between them because of King Warren's parents but I could never guess that they could be so comfortable with each other, considering that their families were once enemies.

"Everyone knows that there is no worse hunter than my brother in the entire kingdom." Lord Raymond turned to look at Protector Edmond sitting across from him. "After Edmond, of course."

Protector Edmond pursed his lips as he mockingly looked around the table. "I'll take Darrell along if we're going hunting. I've never seen a better tracker. The kid smells the animals before you idiots can see them."

My eyes opened even wider but laughter rose in the room with Protector Edmond's words. I looked at King Warren once again and saw he too had a smile on his face. He seemed to enjoy the dinner for the first time since it started.

"Are the people of Aerlion good hunters then?"

Lord Cheng's words cut the laughter like a sharp knife as I turned to him unwillingly. His face carried the same sarcasm as his voice. No trace of sincerity. I looked at the almost empty glass in his hand and realized that he was slightly drunk.

"No," I said challengingly. I straightened my back and turned to completely face him.

He smiled. "So, what are you good at?"

The atmosphere was slowly resuming its tense state once again. Lord Raymond turned to Lord Cheng with knit eyebrows but I jumped in before him. "Healing."

"Is it because you have this innate healing ability, of which we are unaware?" He laughed, but as usual, no one joined.

"You'd be surprised how diseases spread when you don't have the money to pay for even the smallest of treatments. We don't have a natural ability, but most of us know what needs to be done to keep people alive with minimal means."

Lord Cheng didn't seem impressed by my words. He waved his hand and brought the wine to his lips once again, causing the golden chains around his wrist to clink. "Of course. Some sacrifices have to be made."

"People *die* because of the sacrifices they make," I said between my teeth. "This is not a choice."

I saw my father's face before my eyes and I could hardly stop myself from jumping to the other side of the table. Many people died, including those in my village, because of how illnesses spread easier than words in Aerlion, and it took us longer to pull ourselves together since we were the poorest of all the realms.

"People die every day."

I hit the table with both hands, shaking everything on it. "And they all suffer. They too have people that they value and need to care for. Do you think you're the only ones that deserve to live just because you're rich?"

I heard someone exhale loudly. Darrell was unsuccessful in swallowing the bite in his mouth and he would probably have suffocated if the servant hadn't brought him some water. In response, Lord Cheng took a big slice of meat from his plate and started chewing.

"Of course not. But everyone plays the role they are given."

The room was covered in silence. When I finally began to speak, I heard Protector Ramona hold her breath next to me. But still, everyone at the table probably knew that I wouldn't be able to stop myself from answering. I never hesitated toward the king before—why would I stop myself for him?

"One day," I said, trying to keep a calm tone, "one day when you lie in your bed with silk linings and call the best healer money can buy, you'll remember all of this."

Protector Thalia turned her eyes to me but I kept going. "One day, your table will be full of food enough to feed an army, but you will not be able to eat any of it. You will start to get old and ill."

Lord Cheng had never looked so uneasy before, trying to understand the point I was trying to make.

"Death will come upon you. And at that moment, look well into the eyes of the healer because he could be your only chance. And if that healer turns out to be from Aerlion, remember my words well. You will see him as your savior; but for him, you will be another nobleman who wallows in money and who is full of himself. And on that day, you may have to beg for your life to the person who can't take care of his family because of the taxes, and who knows what it means to starve . . . You are going to regret this, but it will be too late . . . But as you said, people die every day, right?"

Lord Cheng suddenly threw his glass to the floor. The sound of hundreds of splintering pieces of crystal glass echoed in the room. The servants in the dining hall immediately began running over to gather the broken pieces but he didn't seem to care. He tried to stand up but King Warren raised his hand.

"Enough."

The council member had to obey him.

As the silence settled in, the king's gaze suddenly found mine. "What do you suggest?"

Attention turned away from Lord Cheng to back at me. I looked at the king. I didn't know what to say or what he meant until I realized how assertive my raging words had been. I had stood up to Lord Cheng but it wasn't only the noble families that protected this awful order, it was also King Warren. And unintentionally, I made the comment directly to him.

"I . . . I . . ." I took a deep breath. Silence filled the room. When Lord Cheng made a sound and the king looked disappointed when I didn't answer, I quickly added, "I want you to give away my next five months' salary to the villages of Aerlion." I spoke without thinking. I wasn't even sure if I was allowed to do such a thing but that was the first thing that came to my mind.

The kingdom was paying me enough already and at the same time, sending some money to my family as a fee for my service. I had thought that I would save the amount I was given, but if I was going to live in the palace for the rest of my life—which meant quite a long time—I wouldn't need a single penny anyway. Everyone knew how much the Protectors were getting paid.

The king wiped his mouth with the napkin in front of him and said, "Well, now I remember why we don't have such dinners very often, even if they're just a formality."

He pushed his chair back and stood up. He hadn't neglected to look at Lord Cheng. The king grimaced as he said, "I don't remember the last time there was so much noise in this room."

The council member realized that he wasn't going to get the apology he was expecting. King Warren turned to me once again as Lord Cheng's face turned red with both alcohol and rage.

"The money belongs to you. You are free to do whatever you want with it. Lord Cheng can take care of the arrangements in the morning when he is sober enough."

The slight smile on the king's face was the last thing I had been expecting to see. When he left the dining hall, Lord Raymond and Lord Cyril also stood up to leave. Lord Theon winked at me before following them out.

Balfour, who was at the other end of the table, was trying to hide it but I could see his smile as well, and his gaze that was focused somewhere behind me said that Hunter was no different. I knew money wouldn't be enough. No matter how much it was, it would end someday. Besides, I could only send money to a small group of people. But I was happy. It was a small step but yet, it was progress. And it could be enough for some change.

Despite being stabbed by Lord Cheng's angry gaze, I smiled too.

I thought I had made a friend in the palace. Just as Protector Thalia had said, the king could indeed be the most powerful ally in the palace.

# CHAPTER 17

The sword in my hand swung to the other side of the area when I fell to the ground. My muscles ached as I hit the floor for the tenth time. I turned to the green eyes watching me and didn't waste any time jumping back to my feet.

"Again," I said as I reached for the sword once more. The Phoenix grimaced as I gritted my teeth with the pain that struck me in the ribs when I bent over.

"No."

But I didn't care. I held the sword with both hands and pointed it at Hunter challengingly. "Come on! Again. Charge!"

Hunter looked at my face and turned away. But then suddenly, he attacked. I was too slow to defend back. My sword slid from my hand with his sudden charge. I lunged forward to grab it but my feet got tangled and I fell to my knees. I heard the giggling of a few Phoenixes practicing at the other side of the yard, but I didn't turn to look at them. Hunter walked over to me and extended his hand.

"You're still holding your sword wrong," he said in admonishment. He moved to my side as I got up. He extended his own sword forward in a way that both of us could see. Then he took my hand and made me hold the hilt below his own.

"That's better," I heard him mumble. He covered my hands with his own and swung the sword gently to the side. "There, see? You can move your wrist much easier now."

I nodded slowly. Just when I thought he would let me go, he looked at me tauntingly and a crooked smile formed on his lips. He suddenly hit the back of my knee and I had hardly enough time to move away. I heard his laugh as I stumbled.

"Nice. Now, guard up."

I did what he said just the way he showed me. Before long, Hunter lunged at me once again. This time, I blocked him. I moved around quickly, made a turn, and hit him in the back with the hilt of the sword. My movement had been much more agile this time. Hunter took a few steps forward; he was barely able to stop himself from falling. I was smiling when he looked at me over his shoulder. The other Phoenixes had begun gathering around us to watch our fight.

Hunter began walking backward but I could see his lips curving. When I attacked once more, he moved at the last instant, preventing the hit aimed at his shoulder.

"Are you trying to injure me?" he asked mockingly. I giggled in response.

Our swords clashed once again. At that moment, I thought I was as strong as he was. I knew that the Phoenix had been training for years but I had been able to show progress without receiving the same long-term training. I was *strong*.

Hunter suddenly drew a full circle in the air with his sword and mine flew from my hand. He pointed the sharp tip of his sword at my throat. "Surrender?" he asked with one brow raised.

I was still trying to catch my breath. I raised my hands while my chest heaved and watched the Phoenix draw back. This was my chance. I jumped at him and took the sword from his hand. He was caught off guard. I mirrored him.

"Never."

The other Phoenixes began to laugh. I heard a few of them whistle while clapping. I smiled, thinking that I had been able to impress them, and threw the sword back to the Phoenix. Then I let myself fall to the ground and closed my eyes.

I had stopped training with Balfour after the ceremony but I was doing my best to make good use of the time I spent with the Phoenixes. The old commander had told me that Hunter could teach me how to fight. After all, he was his best soldier. Even though the Phoenix wasn't too fond of the idea at first, he had gotten used to me in time.

I opened my eyes when Hunter threw a towel at me. I laughed and took the cloth off my face before sitting up. He was grinning. His blond hair was wet with sweat and some strands had stuck to his forehead. I looked at him, thinking that he had a nice smile. This expression on his face was better than the times he used to look at me with a furious gaze.

I tugged at the collar of my shirt and tried to let the cold air in through the loose fabric. It was soaked in sweat. "Thanks for taking care of me," I said to him as I stood up.

Hunter only shrugged. "Frankly, I was expecting much worse after what Commander Balfour had told us. You've been proving him wrong."

I grimaced. "He likes to exaggerate."

A crooked smile spread on his face. "Indeed, he does."

I knew Protector Breccan used to carry out the daily tasks; he was responsible for his Phoenixes' training. Balfour was taking care of the other duties at the palace, conducting regular visits to Aerlion and doing all the paperwork. And now, after weeks, Balfour had started his duties once again. After the ceremony, I had begun seeing him less. But it was enough for me to know that he was somewhere in the palace and that he would come whenever I asked for his help.

I hung the sword back at my waist and wiped my neck with the towel as I dragged myself toward the temple.

The area where the main gate was consisted of a big temple and a small training field built next to each other for the Protector and the Phoenixes. The throne inside the temple was surrounded by high columns, and it overlooked the gate. At the mountain foot, there was a cave for Deegan. The temple had only a few stories and it was mostly used as an armory. The premises continued down around the mountain. The sleeping quarters of the Phoenixes were at the backside.

Everything had been considered to make sure they didn't set foot into the palace. The same was valid for me, too. I had emptied my room at the palace after the ceremony and I had moved in here. Now I could understand why I didn't see the Protectors that much during my stay at the palace. The system was created to keep the Protectors away, just as the Phoenixes. The commanders were the ones that spent the most time inside the palace.

I entered the temple. The Phoenixes' sleeping quarters were on the path to my room. The hallway opened to the left for them but I moved to the end of the hall to go to my chamber. I moved toward my new room and extended my hand. But then I paused. The double-winged door was ajar. I cautiously pushed the door. It opened with a squeak. My hand went still on the hilt of my sword as I looked inside.

The double bed was still as I had left in the morning—the gates were quite far from the palace and servants were here much less. The big armchair in front of the fireplace was full of books stacked on top of one another. On the shelves next to the fireplace were antiquities, which I had not spared any time to examine. I looked around, thinking how normal everything was in the room, but then my eyes found the shadow in front of the wide window. I flinched, surprised that I hadn't noticed it until now.

"Nice place," said the stranger without looking at me. From where he stood, he had a clear view of the gate and the rest of the capital. "It can't be compared to your room at the palace, of course."

I held the hilt tight and took a cautious step toward him. The stranger finally made a move to turn to me. When I noticed his gray eyes, my shoulders relaxed with sudden relief.

"You shouldn't be here," I said as I crossed my arms and looked at the stranger whom I had met at the bar in the city a few weeks ago.

The man tilted his head to the side, causing his curly black hair to fall onto his high cheekbones. In the bright daylight, his face looked more stunning. "I lived in the palace for a long time. The palace has many entrances, but only a few sentry posts. It's easy to get in without being seen."

I shuffled uneasily when the man placed a smile on his attractive face. "What are you doing here?" I asked, this time with a curious tone.

He eyed me slowly from head to toe and then began walking away from the window toward the bookshelf. He stopped in front of the shelves and began examining the books. Seeing him in my chamber was odd, but my heart started beating faster.

"I came to see my only friend at the palace," he murmured. Then he grimaced and looked back at the books. "There's nothing of quality here."

"I guess they are more careful with what they have after someone tried to reveal the secrets of the kingdom."

A smile formed on his lips and his gray eyes found mine. "Are you coming from training?"

I hold my breath as I imagined how bad I smelled. "The Phoenixes are helping me." When he looked at the sword on my belt, I grinned. "I am now able to swing it without cutting myself."

But he didn't laugh. His gray eyes found mine. "You shouldn't let people make you feel bad about yourself. You're improving, even if slower than they expected."

He put the book back on one of the shelves. All I did was look at him with surprised eyes. I changed the topic.

"Do you come to the palace often since King Warren fired you?"

His eyes moved to the window where I left the curtains half-open to see the city view. "It had been years since I set foot here. But I came for you."

I tried not to sound too excited. "Me? Why?"

He shrugged. "I was bored."

For someone who was likely to be in his midtwenties, he looked more mature. But at the same time, when he shrugged, he reminded me of a teenager. His dark curls were touching his forehead and shadowing his pale skin. I watched him as his hands gently touched his curls and pushed them away.

"Well, I am glad to see you," I said as I took a step toward him.

He tilted his head. "Really?"

"We didn't finish our conversation."

I pointed at the balcony. I didn't want a servant or a Phoenix passing by to realize that I wasn't alone. He followed me without hesitation. I leaned on the rails as the warm air licked my face.

"The king is exactly like you described him."

His eyes narrowed. "I said a lot about him."

"I learned something," I said, trying not to reveal a lot. I knew I couldn't tell him about the Old Ones' return, at least not yet. I didn't know if he'd heard of the attack, although almost everyone at the capital knew it. But I wasn't going to bring up the topic first. "Something that the king, Protectors, and even my commander were trying to keep secret."

"I see," he only murmured.

King Warren had said someone was using the crystals to change people into the Old Ones. This meant someone had found them. I remembered the Dralein—the *man*—that I killed. King Warren was sure that we couldn't help them and maybe he was right. But if someone was able to find the crystals, why would it be hard for any of us? We could still help the rest of the people.

"You said the crystals were powerful. I was told they were used for evil, but at some point, their magic was bringing goodness to the people."

He nodded, showing me that he was listening.

"I—I believe in the crystals," I said. "I believe they can be used for good, just like you said . . . I want to find the crystal of Aerlion. You said only Protectors could find them. Would I be enough?"

"You want to find the crystals?" he asked, looking surprised.

"I *need* the crystals," I insisted. "You are the only person who would talk to me about them. I can't have this conversation with anyone else in the palace."

When he remained silent, I saw the doubt shadowing his face. I continued, "They all are scared. But I'm not. People of my realm are suffering and . . ." The man's face, lying on the courtyard, appeared in front of my eyes.

The stranger turned his gray eyes to the forest. The palace looked so tiny from where we stood.

"Why do you want to find the crystals, really?" he asked softly. "I don't believe this. No Protector before cared for his people. All they do is to act like spoiled nobles."

"You don't know anything about me," I said in one breath. "You don't know how much I suffered."

But he still didn't look convinced. I looked away.

"I lost someone," I finally said. "Someone who died way before his time. And if the kingdom actually cared for people like me for even a second, it wouldn't have happened. And now, with the crystals, I have a chance to change what happened."

I shut up, knowing that I would burst into tears if I told him more.

"One would be enough," he finally murmured as he exhaled loudly. "But you can't do it. They are hidden."

"I don't think they are anymore," I thought about the ceremony. "With my magic and your knowledge, we can find them *together*."

Sarah had always wanted us to be a family; she was too young when our family was broken up. I could do this for her, for us. We could be together again, and then I could use the crystals to end the poverty in the Seven Realms, which the king was unable to rule properly. There was no way that the Protectors wouldn't help me once they found out what I planned. Even though they had left their homes a long time ago, no one could forget where one came from.

"No, we can't find them," he said, and coughed harshly with his hand over his lips. He shook his head and went on, "Believe me, there's nothing I wouldn't do to find the crystals."

My eyes moved to his palm as he coughed and I noticed the blood dripping from between his fingers. I looked at him in worry as he took out a handkerchief from his pocket to wipe his hand.

"You . . ."

"I'm sick," he said after clearing his throat. I could see the blood on his teeth as he spoke. "And there's no cure for it. I don't have enough time."

"No," I whispered with worry and shook my head. "No . . . no, you can't be sick."

He leaned his weight on the rails and it seemed he was barely able to stand up. I hadn't noticed the trembling of his body until then. He was breathing heavily. He was *really* sick.

"That's why I'm here at the palace, I am looking for a cure. But I can't ask this of you."

"But you'll die!" I said quickly. "You're still too young. No! I– I . . . There must be a cure!"

I saw the sorrow in his gray eyes. When my father died, it was so sudden. He wasn't even old. It wasn't fair for him to die, but such was life. And now, I felt like I was living it all over again.

"We both need their magic," I insisted. "The first Protectors used them for a long time. I can use them for people of my realm, for myself, for *you*. That's why I was chosen, to keep the balance in the realms."

But in response, he shook his head. "I'm already about to die, but if you get caught, you'll be punished severely."

I looked at his trembling body; he seemed to be in a lot of pain. His gray eyes narrowed and his hand went through his dark curls.

"Do you remember what we talked about? The things I told you about the crystals?" he asked.

"Every single word."

"A single crystal… Everything is possible with its power. I could heal and you could bring back the person you mentioned." He laughed. "But you can't find it without being caught. You don't know what kind of danger you are getting yourself into."

"I can do it," I said determinedly. I knew I could. "I want to help you, *please*. I can't let someone else die in front of my eyes. I hate to feel this helpless… I won't give up without trying, even if it is impossible."

"That was exactly what Warren had said to me," I heard him murmur. "*Impossible*. But you are a Protector, connected to the crystals and the Goddess herself. I don't think I can show you the way for this— you are the only person who could find the crystal of your own realm. If you follow your instincts, it shall call you."

As I nodded with the idea of returning to Aerlion and looking for the crystal, I thought of my family that I had left behind. The king didn't allow me to leave Ardria and they couldn't come to the capital. But if I could somehow get there, I could see them *and* look for the crystal at the same time.

A part of me was worried for my mother and my sister. I had written to them a few times but I had received no answer. Were they all right? Was the money sent to them by the kingdom enough? Did Sarah have enough paint to draw? I was so curious to know the answers to all of this.

"The other Protectors could help," I said to him. "Imagine if we all find the crystals." Or the rest of them, in that case. If someone was really using them the create the Old Ones, I didn't know which or how many of them were still left hidden.

He inhaled with a loud grunt and shook his head. "But they wouldn't help *me*. Who do you think are the people that hide the truth in the first place? They're all the same. They would do anything to keep the crystals hidden. The rest don't care for their realms anymore. The capital changed them long ago."

Maybe he was right. When we were in Belwald, Protector Sam said the same thing to me. The Protectors were acting like a bunch of nobles, spending their time at the palace and sending their Phoenixes for any unrest among the people. They had stopped caring a long time ago.

"It was enough for an ordinary person like me to be fired, but you're a Protector. The magic you possess could become a threat for them, even more than you think."

I thought of being caught. Could he be right? Would they really see me as a threat? I didn't know them too well. yet I was bothered by the thought of them siding against me. I was one of them. Yet I knew what the king would think. He had said it himself; we were all a threat to him. If he knew what I intended to do, he wouldn't hesitate.

"Fine, only us then. I won't tell anyone. I can find my own realm's crystal." I sounded so sure, even if I had no idea how to do that.

A vague smile formed on his face.

"I'd been to some of the realms some years ago," he said as he turned his gray eyes to the forest stretching out in front of us. "And believe me, the poverty is the same everywhere. People are dying. They have nothing but… you can help them. You are not like the other Protectors, you actually want change."

He moved over and stood right in front of me. "We can try. We can bring a new order together, but only if you take the risk of taking on everyone for the sake of a new future."

"Tell me your name," I said as I turned to him. If we were to be together in this, I needed to know more about him.

He drew back, nodded with a smile, and extended his hand.

"My name is Audamar, once a researcher of the kingdom and a friend of King Warren," he said as he raised his hand a bit more for me to shake it. "You and I could change the future of the Seven Realms. Give me a chance."

Despite his warmness, his hands were so cold. When his skin touched mine, I tried not to think of anything else, but the uneasy feeling inside me did nothing other than create one unpleasant thought after another. I was aware of everything I was risking, but I would do this for the people. I could save them from poverty. I could save him. And I was going to start with my own family.

"Anna," I said slightly smiling. "Protector of Aerlion."

Audamar looked straight at my face with his gray eyes. I couldn't help but stare at his pale skin. Now I knew why he had looked so sickly before.

"For the sake of the Seven Realms," I said.

He nodded in response. "And for the future we'll create."

# CHAPTER 18

I continued to walk along the wide halls of the palace without knowing where I was headed. As I passed, I saw some of the servants stop and greet me before walking away and disappearing into the shadows. I was all by myself now. There were no torches placed around. The only light was the moonlight, coming in through the wide windows on the side.

I gave up on looking for a familiar face; there was no one here. I turned around to find my way back to the temple but a giant door across the hall caught my attention.

The door was made of marble. I moved over to look at the engravings on it. As I came closer, my palms ached with an odd feeling. I knew what that was. It was magic, but this time, much stronger. Whatever was inside, it drew me toward it.

I put my ear to the door to hear the humming echoing on the other side. I raised my hand to press it against the door, and pushed it in without too much force. Despite how heavy it looked, the giant door opened easily. The light coming from inside fell on my face.

The first thing I noticed was the floor, beginning from the entrance of the room and ending somewhere ahead, shattered in pieces on the ground. The stairs that began where the broken marble ended were going down into a wide hole, and the stairs were covered with grass. The light was coming directly out of the hole.

I noticed the tree branches extending out from the wide hole into the room. It was quite deep inside and the tree was enormous. I looked at the buds on its long branches and then I saw the pink leaves on the ground; they had completely covered the ground.

I went down the stairs. The tree was as tall as the bell towers outside of the palace gates. I raised my head to see that the ceiling was in the shape of a dome. And the roof of the room was made of glass. The moonlight came directly to the point I was standing at, allowing me to see that this place was much bigger than the throne room. I walked around it and stopped in front of the stairs. Then I heard footsteps from the other side.

King Warren was walking over to me. His hands were clasped behind his back and his dark eyes were fixed on the giant tree. He stood right next to me. I hadn't noticed him earlier, but apparently, he had seen me as soon as I walked in.

"So, this is the magical tree of the Goddess," I said as I thought about how this was the first time I had come here. I couldn't take my eyes off the Vitae.

I closed my eyes when King Warren asked, "Do you feel it?"

"Yes," I said without a second thought and placed one of the fallen leaves into my palm. "The magic is so strong here."

I brought my hands together, causing my palms to tingle again. Before long, the leaf began flying with a bright light. I was stronger now, gaining more control over my magic with each passing day.

"These leaves were given during the Selection," I said when I realized they looked the same.

The king nodded. "The tree blossoms only during sunrise and sunset; that is why Selection takes place in the evening. The leaves change color when the tree blossoms; it's something about the magic." He bent over just as I had, and took one of the leaves from the ground. "Then they fade quickly and turn to dust before the new leaves sprout out."

When he took a step back, his gaze found the paper I had folded in my pocket. "Were you looking for something?"

"Ah, yes." I took out the paper. "I was looking for Balfour, actually. A Phoenix brought me this." I turned the page toward him. "You cannot increase the taxes. People don't have any more money to give to the kingdom."

A muscle in his jaw popped. "I was advised to—"

I cut into his words. "The council members have no idea about the hunger in the Seven Realms. Whatever they advised, they were wrong."

The king still didn't look convinced.

"Please," I begged.

With that, he closed his eyes.

"As much as you think I'm deciding everything by myself, I still need to talk to the council members. But I'll make sure they all reconsider."

I exhaled with relief. "Thank you," I said, and I meant it.

A genuine smile formed on his lips. "Are you happy here?" he asked suddenly.

I was surprised, but he looked quite serious. I only shrugged. "After all, I'm not a prisoner here. I live in a luxury that I thought I could never have, and I never have to worry about starving again."

I closed my mouth. I thought they had been silly things to say to the king. Every word coming out of my mouth was true but he could never understand me; all King Warren could do was look at me in pity. And that was exactly what I was doing to myself.

I looked away and cleared my throat. "I have more than I could imagine."

"But are you *happy*?" insisted the king.

What was I supposed to say? Exactly how honest could I be in front of him? I looked away.

"No," I murmured softly. I felt guilty. "I like the palace, I do. But I don't know if I'm actually happy."

King Warren tossed the leaf he was holding back to the ground and it disappeared into the other hundreds of leaves. "You must miss your family."

I nodded.

"Tell me about them," he said as he turned his dark eyes to the tree in front of us.

I laughed in response. "There's nothing to tell. They're as ordinary as any other family."

I thought he already knew a lot about me. Still, it felt odd to talk about them to a stranger, even if he was the king.

King Warren smiled too, but it was bitter this time. "If my family were alive, I could find a lot of words to describe them, but *ordinary* would not be one of them."

I saw his face; he was in pain and I didn't have any words to help him ease it. I remained silent. The king cleared his throat, causing me to look back at him. His knit eyebrows hadn't relaxed even a little bit.

"I owe you for what happened at dinner," he said. His face finally loosened up when I stared at him, confused. "For driving Cheng crazy. In return, I'd like to do something that would make you happy."

My lips curved upward as I continued to look at him. After what had happened to his family, saying that the king hated Lord Cheng would be an understatement. He was a king and if he wanted to keep the noble families by his side, he had to remain objective, no matter what. But I didn't have such obligations.

"Despite everything that happened at the ceremony, you are an actual Protector now," he said, causing me to remember all those events. I shivered. "There is no reason for you not to leave the palace. You proved yourself when you fought so fearlessly and saved that little boy's life. . . If you want, you may visit your home."

The words that I had been waiting to hear for weeks had now come out of the king's mouth. My shock was indescribable. I smiled. I was *free* now.

With the thought of being able to see my mother and my little sister, I took a shaky breath. I wanted to laugh but then I saw his face. Unlike me, the king didn't have a family to visit.

"Thank you, King Warren," I said as I turned to the dark eyes watching me.

One side of his lips curved up. "Make sure you find your way back to the capital." I heard him breathe mockingly. "If you don't want an army after you."

I sighed. "You won't get rid of me that easily."

"I believe that."

As the silence took over, I slowly turned to him. "Maybe," I said, "maybe . . . you could come with me? I could show you my realm."

It was hard to read his expression but for a second, I thought he was really thinking about it. He smiled. "It's been so long since I set foot outside of the palace."

"Haven't you ever thought of visiting the villages outside the capital?"

Audamar had told me that the king didn't have the slightest idea of the poverty in the Seven Realms. Although I knew deep inside that he was right, I still wanted an answer from the king. Why? Despite everything, why did he turn his back on his people? Exactly how long had it been? He couldn't actually be unaware of what was going on outside.

The king shook his head coldly. I couldn't understand what he was thinking. "No," he only said.

I was disappointed, but I didn't know why I had put so much faith in him in the first place anyway. He had no interest in his people. Audamar had been right all along.

I realized that the conversation was over with his answer. I looked at the king one last time and hurried up the stairs so I wouldn't spend any more time in there with him. I headed outside.

I should have known. Even the slightest feeling I had for him disappeared in only seconds.

•

When I returned to my room, I found Audamar on the balcony. Every single time when he secretly entered the palace, he would find his way to my room in the temple. After a while, I realized that this was how I would meet with him without getting caught. It was easy for him to enter the palace. He would sometimes spend the day in here with me and we never once got caught.

I opened the door and stepped onto the marble balcony.

"A nice day for the capital," he said as he leaned over to see the city farther ahead. His gray eyes scanned the scenery lying in front of us.

"I have good news," I said quickly. I smiled. "The king let me leave the palace."

His brows rose with surprise. "You're going to Aerlion?"

"I am."

He lowered his gaze to his hands holding the rails. "I was born in the capital. I heard that Aerlion was a nice place . . . And now, the people there are due for a better future with the help of the crystal."

"Have you never been to Aerlion?" I asked as I rested my elbows on the rails.

"No, but I used to know someone who was born there a long time ago. Someone important to me."

I looked at him with curiosity but kept quiet.

"When are you leaving?" he asked after a while when he turned his gaze to the gray clouds above.

"Tomorrow, I think. I need to arrange a few things with Balfour first."

Audamar drew back. He took his hands from the rails and brought them to his chest. At that moment, my eyes caught a glimpse of the bulge in his shirt pocket. *Again.* It was just as the day we had met at the bar; his fingers always seemed to find that spot. Whatever it was he carried there, it was always with him.

"Good," he murmured with a nod. "Very good."

I nodded. "I'll find the crystal, no matter what."

"I owe everything to you." His lips slightly curled up. "Thank you, Anna."

My eyes shifted to him in curiosity and watched him move to the door. He stopped to look back over his shoulder once more before leaving and I saw the faint smile on his face as he disappeared into the shadows of the hallway.

# CHAPTER 19

Deegan's skin was shining under the sunlight as he descended to the meadow below us. The big dragon opened his wide wings to the sides and landed softly on the ground. I slid down and jumped onto the wild weed. I knelt by the dragon, put my hand on his body, and pressed him down with my hand. "Wait here," I said to him.

I stepped back when Deegan rose up quickly to walk over. "No," I repeated, louder this time. "Stay here."

I wasn't sure if he would listen to me but as I continued to walk, I looked back over my shoulder to see Deegan standing where I left him. His bright red eyes were fixed on me but he didn't move.

I passed through the pine needles that scratched my face and walked between the wooden houses to arrive at the tiny village square. Stalls were set up and the merchants were shouting at the top of their lungs to sell the goods that they had brought from other villages to people who were too poor to spend money on anything. I saw people carrying buckets to fill them before the wells dried up and a few people who had climbed up to their roofs to patch up their old houses. Everything here was the same.

I smiled when I saw the familiar house at the end of the road and I hurried up the steps. I raised my hand to knock on the door but I paused as excitement filled me. I grabbed the door handle and pushed it in slowly. As always, it was unlocked.

The first thing that drew my attention was how tidy the inside was. I had been used to the mess during all the years I had lived here, but now the little hut was unexpectedly spotless. The air flowing in from the half-open and repaired windows had taken away the dusty smell. The bowls that my mother used to store different herbs were lined up on the counter and I could see that new drawings had been added to the wall during the time I was away.

I walked over to the wall and traced my index finger over the ink marks on the wrinkled papers. I could see that it was no longer a problem to buy new paints for Sarah. They were able to afford it, and I thought that in only a few weeks, the wall across from the kitchen counter would be filled with pictures. The king had kept his word; my family was well. This could be the only thing for which I could truly be grateful to him.

I opened the top drawer, where my little sister kept her paints and inks, and I left the last of the coins I had in my pocket. I didn't need them; I knew I would find more when I returned to my room.

I turned around at the rattling sound of the door opening and saw my mother looking at me with eyes wide open. Her shoulders relaxed when her hazel eyes met mine, and she immediately threw down the wooden stick she was holding so tightly.

"Anna," she said with her arms open at her sides as she walked over to me. She embraced me tightly. I took my eyes from the stick on the floor and shut them as I wrapped my arms around her. But I could feel something wasn't right.

"It's been days . . . no, weeks."

I let her draw back and hold my hands to drag me to the old couch with worn-out fabric. The couch's springs squeaked when I sat, and she looked at me worriedly as she took her place next to me.

"Tell me everything. How are you? Are you all right? Are they taking good care of you there?" Then she swiftly waved her hand. "Ah, of course they're treating you well! You're a Protector. You live in the palace."

She put one hand on my cheek and leaned forward. I put my hand over hers on my cheek and brought it down.

"I'm fine," I said as I turned to her. "What about you? I saw the changes in the house. If you let her, the whole house will be full to the brim with Sarah's pictures."

A smile spread over my face but she didn't join me. I looked around. "Where's Sarah?" I asked. "I want to see her before I return."

My mother's face tensed. As fear began to settle in me, I held my breath. "Mom, where is she?"

My mother leaned over and pressed her lips onto my forehead before looking at me with worried eyes. "I sent her to a friend of mine in one of the villages far away. She's staying there with her and her daughters."

I wasn't happy with what I had heard. My shoulders drooped with disappointment. Sarah would always visit my mother's friends, and she would spend a few days with them. But it was different this time; I could see it.

"Is everything all right?"

My mother's eyes narrowed anxiously and the worried smile on her face faded. I took her hands and placed them on my lap as I continued to hold them tightly. "Mom, what's wrong? Tell me."

"The lost people . . ." she said as if she was suffocating with those words. "It's all messed up, just like the other six realms. People are so scared."

I flinched with what she said. The lost people . . . I could see how scared she was.

Our conversation was interrupted by the bell chimes. I looked out the window when I heard voices rising in the village square, and then I saw the gathering crowd. Some were carrying flags with them, dragging them along the village. The symbol on the cloth caught my attention— a bow against a dagger. But I had no idea what that meant.

I jumped up and walked to the door but my mother held me by my wrist to slow me down.

"Anna, listen to me. You have to leave."

I turned to her with questioning eyes. I could still hear the crowd outside. "What's going on?"

"People have started to revolt; they're talking about a rebellion. It's not just our village or even just Aerlion. There's a group that is gathering people to take the king off the throne . . . at least that's what I heard."

Her hazel eyes alternated between me and the crowd she saw through the window. She looked at me as if she was worried that someone could see me. "There's a rumor about an attack that happened at the capital. I'm not sure what it is but some say they saw the creatures there. Everyone's scared. They are sick of the kingdom, and when it comes to our lives, people don't believe that the kingdom would protect us."

I turned back to see the crowd once more. We were left to starve here a long time ago. One by one, we lost a lot of good people. And the kingdom never once helped.

"People don't want the king to rule the Seven Realms anymore," she continued. "Especially during these times. They're going to try to take over."

I didn't know what to say. I was trying to be careful of what I told her. Yet she seemed to know more than I thought. Something was off. My mother was very faithful to the kingdom, but I'd never heard her talk about the Old Ones before. Even I didn't know anything about them before I went to the capital. How could my mother, who was just a simple healer in my tiny village, already know so much?

My mother shook her head. "When I left for the other village to help, they let me examine the bodies. Those marks I saw couldn't be caused by an animal. I had never seen such big claws before."

I knew how easily word could spread. But the last thing I wanted was for my mother to be involved in this. I was hoping that she and Sarah would be safe, far away from everything that was happening.

I quickly opened the door and went out. I walked to the square to blend into the crowd but my mother held me tightly once again and dragged me away behind a small house. "They can't see you! You're from the kingdom, Anna. They can't know that a Protector is here."

I wanted to tell her that the situation was actually the opposite. The king didn't trust the Protectors and we weren't so different from the Phoenixes in his eyes. But the people didn't know that. Once, I was one of them. But now I was a threat just like the king. I wanted to scream.

"What about you?" I asked. "They know I am your daughter. You're not safe here. Come with me to Ardria."

I looked at her worriedly but she shook her head. "We're fine. Sarah is far away and I can take care of myself."

She then put her hands back on my cheek and forced me to look into her eyes. "Visit us more often, but just not now . . . Right now, you should stay in the capital. Don't come to Aerlion any time soon, Anna. Don't put yourself in danger. I know you'll find us when everything is over."

Then she reached for my hands. "I'm sorry for forcing you into the Selections. I want to think that the kingdom is the safest place for you but the latest rumors are terrifying me."

She looked at me for a while, as if she was trying to memorize my face. My chest ached as she suddenly wrapped her arms around my neck. "I'm so proud of you, and I know Sarah thinks the same. I never could have thought this would happen, but I want to believe that you were chosen for a reason, Anna. Everything is messed up and if you ask me, the Goddess chose you because she knew this would happen."

She drew back and I felt as if I had fallen into a void when I lost her firm grip on my neck.

"Now, go," she whispered. "Take care."

"Mom . . . I . . ."

"Go," she said, harsher this time.

"I'll find you," I whispered one more time before I turned away. "I promise."

I looked at her for the last time before diving into the forest. I wanted to believe that I was doing the right thing, but I was scared for them. I was scared for *myself.*

I kept running until the sight of my mother and the village disappeared. I was breathless when I reached the meadow. I put my hands on my knees to rest and looked at the dark figure a bit farther away. Deegan was still where I had left him. I was surprised that such a big creature as he hadn't been spotted by anyone. As I approached, the dragon's big red eyes turned away from me. He was sniffing the air when he started to growl. I hurried over and put my hands on his skin to calm the dragon down.

"Deegan," I said. The dragon only looked at me for a short moment and then began moving uneasily. I called out to him several times but then he rose and spread his big wings. My eyes grew with surprise; he wasn't listening to me.

I jumped onto his back before he took off. His feet left the ground the instant I landed on his back. I held on tight and forced myself to climb higher. I tugged at the reins to make him stop but Deegan didn't obey. The dragon flew away from the village and toward places that I had never been to before. I knew that the dragon had more experience in Aerlion, which he had gained during the time he spent with other Protectors before me. I just hoped we could safely make it back to the capital.

We flew over valleys and forests for hours before Deegan started descending. I realized we were very far from the village as the sun was almost about to set behind the hills. Before long, we landed on one of the hills. Deegan looked around in a flurry and it seemed as if he could fly away any minute. I looked at him with expectation and waited for the dragon to do something, anything.

I turned my head when the dragon's sharp red eyes got fixed on a point. Deegan was looking at the dark pile of leaves as if he could see behind the dense trees. I moved away from him and walked around the giant dragon toward the trees.

"Wait here," I said.

I left him behind and plunged into the woods. The big leaves tickled my face as I walked by and I pushed the last tree branch out of my way. I was greeted by a valley on the other side. The clouds were hiding the peak of twin mountains covered with lush green grass. And there was a river flowing on the plains where the surface began to rise.

I held my breath at the fascinating scenery and swung around to see it better. But I knew that the dragon didn't bring me here for this. Deegan must have felt something, but I wasn't sure what the problem was. At that moment, I thought that maybe he could have sensed one of the Old Ones. Maybe that was why he had brought me here. Protector Breccan could have tracked and hunted them, but I was definitely not planning to do so. I was going to run away from here the moment I saw one of them.

I took a step back and stopped abruptly with a feeling inside my chest. A ringing began to spread throughout the valley. I narrowed my eyes and swiveled around as the sound became louder. Was this what Deegan was feeling?

I could feel the magic now. I followed it and my steps slowly headed toward the river. I got into the freezing water. I dipped my fingertips. The shallow water came up to the top of my knees. I scanned the surface and then turned my eyes to the clear water.

I immediately noticed the shining yellow object in between the large stones in the water. I reached for it with one hand, then quickly pushed the stones away and dug into the river bottom. My eyes flew open when I finally felt the smooth surface at the tip of my fingers. I turned my palm upward.

"It can't be," I said as I breathed out. My eyes grew wide and I leaned over. "The crystal of Aerlion," I said to myself, unable to take my eyes away from the stone.

The crystal looked exactly like the ones drawn in the book that Balfour had given me to read. And *I had found it.* I breathed heavily while

I squeezed the crystal in my hand to make sure it was real. It had been *too* easy, much easier than I thought.

Many things were going through my mind at that moment but I knew what I had to do. A teardrop glided from my eye and fell into the cold water. I closed my eyes tightly and pressed my shaking hands firmly onto the crystal in my palm.

I wasn't going to regret it.

"We'll be a family again," I whispered. "I promise."

# CHAPTER 20

I passed through the dark streets of the capital where the sunlight didn't reach. I had pulled the hood of my cape down to my nose to cover my face and picked up my pace. I was holding a piece of paper that was scribbled in very nice handwriting. I was hoping to get to the address written on it as soon as possible.

The feeling that gnawed at me with each step grew as I walked along. On the way back to the palace, I had to remind myself that I had done something good; both for my family and for the suffering people of Aerlion.

Finally, as it said on the paper, I turned into the dead alley when I saw the small red house on the corner. The man hidden in his black cape greeted me in front of the dark and dirty stone wall that stretched out along the street. His gray eyes turned to me when he heard my footsteps.

"Did you really find it?" he said, excitement filling his voice.

Since I didn't know when I would be able to see him, I had left a note for Audamar in my room, saying that I had found the crystal of my realm. I had thought that he would come to the temple and wait for me there. But instead, I found another note that had been left on my desk. A piece of paper that indicated the time and place where we would meet. It was almost impossible for the other Protectors and Phoenixes not to feel the magic of the crystal, but luckily, I hadn't seen the old commander or any of the Protectors during the short time after my return. And I had done my best to avoid the Phoenixes as well. Audamar had been quick to respond.

"Yes," I said as I looked into his wide-open eyes. "I did."

He stared into my empty hands in curiosity, looking extremely impatient. "Where is it? Didn't you bring it?"

He looked different, I thought, more agitated than before. I kept staring at his face in confusion. His attitude seemed to have changed since the last time I had seen him. He was no longer that sick man in need. He was standing across from me impatiently as he waved his hands.

He was really desperate for the crystal's magic, I thought. And his time was running out.

"I . . ."

"Anna," said Audamar as he took a step toward me. "Help me. I need it to heal, *please*."

Now he was standing right in front of me. As I stared into his gray eyes, his fingertips found my cheeks. His skin was cold but the touch was gentle.

"Think of all the people we could help. *Together* we can correct the mistakes King Warren and his ancestors made." His fingers brushed my jaw when he begged once again. "Help me."

My hand went to my pocket and I felt the weight of the yellow crystal. Audamar watched me carefully but didn't move. He had seen my hesitation. His gray eyes quickly moved away from the place where the crystal was and fixed them on my face again.

"Think of what we can do with that," he continued. "The thing that you want the most. You can do anything you want; the crystal will help you."

Then he raised his index finger to the sky and said, "With only a single crystal."

*The thing I want the most* . . . My hand moved slowly in my pocket and it slid over the smooth fabric as I brought out the crystal. He *could* help me. He *could* give me what I wanted; make my family whole again . . . and it was enough for me to use a single crystal for this.

Audamar's eyes shone when I placed the crystal in his hands. I was so focused on his words that I hadn't even noticed the smile spreading through his face.

"When will I see you again?" I asked as I watched him. How much time did he need to heal? Would the crystal actually work?

"Tomorrow," he promised as he put the crystal into his pocket. He took a step and closed the distance between us. He held my hands then. His fingers were wrapped around mine when I heard him whisper. "Tomorrow, I'll come for you."

•

I pushed the wooden door and dashed inside. I sat on the big bed. I had been freed of the crystal's weight after the long walk I had taken into the city, but I had been lost in thoughts afterward, while I kept walking for hours. It was weird that no one had come looking for me but I hadn't really cared at the moment.

I lay down on the wide bed and raised my hands, trying to visualize the yellow crystal that I had held only a few hours ago. The crystal of Aerlion, the only key to my salvation . . . I threw the thick cape and jacket onto one of the armchairs. I rolled up the sleeves of the white shirt I was wearing and forced myself to stand up.

I heard shouting coming from the other side of the door as I was looking at the books on the bookshelf that I hadn't had the time to read ever since I'd arrived here. I moved away from the wall and went over to the window. The doors swung open.

Four royal guards turned their gaze on me, causing me to take another step back. I could see the curious servants and the Phoenixes standing behind the door, watching us, but I couldn't take my eyes off the guards.

"What do you think you are doing?" I said in rage. "You can't come in like this! Get out!"

The guard in the front took a step toward me. I realized he wasn't talking to me as he turned his head and made a signal. "Take her."

With his command, the guards moved. I hurried backward, trying to keep them away from me. "I order you to stop!"

But they caught me by my arms and pushed me down on my knees. I was forced to bend over with the pressure on my back. I could hear the whispers in the hallway but I didn't raise my head to meet their eyes.

"I didn't do anything!" I shouted. "Let me go!"

I couldn't free myself from the guards no matter how much I tried. An experienced Protector would have escaped them easily but I couldn't even use my powers when I needed them the most. I opened and closed my palms a few times but nothing happened, I couldn't reach out to my magic. I saw a weak light growing in my palm but as one of the guards held me tightly around my wrist, it quickly disappeared.

"Hurry up!"

They continued to support me until they saw me standing firmly on my feet. Then I was dragged behind as they began walking.

•

We approached the glamorous doors of the throne room, but even then, the guards' grip on me didn't loosen even a bit. I stumbled a few times, trying to keep up with their pace. Finally, the guards let me go and I fell to my knees. My hands burned when they found the marble floor and I gritted my teeth in pain.

No one talked, but from the sounds of breathing, I could tell that it was crowded inside. I tried to get up on my feet but my arms were aching after the firm grip of the guards. I raised my head and turned my eyes to the person sitting across from me on the throne.

"Explain this to me," I said as I barely kept my voice steady. My eyes were beginning to fill with tears. "Now!"

King Warren looked more serious than he had ever been. I was used to his harsh, cold, or rude expressions during previous encounters, but this time I was the target of his fury. His knit eyebrows never loosened during the whole time he stared at me with his cold gaze. But he didn't speak. He wasn't the same man from the greenhouse that walked with me. A feeling spread over my body; *fear* . . . did they know?

Everyone had taken their place in the throne room. The council members were on one side, and across from them, on the king's left, were the Protectors. My eyes searched for Balfour as I gazed through the commanders standing behind the Protectors, and I found him standing alone at the end of the line. His eyes were fixed on the floor, not looking anywhere else.

I turned to the king again and saw a familiar face that appeared behind the throne: Hunter. As soon as our eyes met, the Phoenix tore his gaze away.

"Tell me once more what Protector Anna did, Phoenix."

The king looked quite calm but I could feel the coldness in his tone. I had always thought that the king couldn't stand being next to a Phoenix after what had happened to his family; I couldn't understand the scene I was looking at.

Hunter's green eyes slowly turned to me as he said, "I saw the note. A stranger was coming out of her room and I found the note when I went inside. I followed the man and saw them talk. She had the yellow crystal, the crystal of Aerlion . . . I knew what it was; I felt its magic . . . And she gave it to him."

I heard whispers coming from the nobles behind us but a single look from the king was enough to silence them. It was clear that the nobles didn't want to miss any part of the action going on before them. They continued to watch us as they pushed each other to see better.

The king's eyes turned to me once again. "You can't even imagine how serious an accusation this is. This is why you are here, Protector Anna. Now answer." He walked down the stairs in front of the throne and stood right in front of me. "You found the crystal of Aerlion, the source of magic for the realm you swore to protect and one of its symbols, and you gave it to someone else. Did you betray us or not?"

The king's voice suppressed the sound of the flames heard from the wavering of the torches on the wall. Even though my hands were not tied and I could stand up, I remained on my knees. The king bent over impatiently and lowered his head. "Did you turn your back on your people? Is this true? Say something."

I gritted my teeth. I thought that I could have escaped Hunter's accusations if I wanted to; there was no proof at all. But I didn't do that. I turned my eyes to Hunter, despite the king who was standing in front of me, and the Phoenix averted his eyes from me at the same speed. I had thought that we could get along; he had helped me during the time I spent at the temple after the ceremony; but he still had turned to the king whom he despised. He hadn't even given me a chance to explain myself. His betrayal hurt more than I had expected.

"I did."

Shocked murmurs filled the room. The whispers were louder than ever now; I thought King Warren would have to work harder to silence them this time.

King Warren took a step back in surprise, with an expression on his face that I could never have imagined: disappointment. It was the same for the other Protectors. The council members looked around and waited for a response from the king. My gaze met with Balfour's for the first time. I took advantage of the chaos I had created and began shouting.

"We could create a new balance with the crystals!" I cried as I turned to the gazes watching me. I jumped up and the king moved back while the guards suddenly built a wall of flesh with their bodies between me and him.

"You don't even know what's going on in your own realms!" I said and looked at the Protectors. "People are poor and hungry. They die of diseases that could be cured but the only group that the kingdom tries to save is the nobles! The crystals can be used to help people; they are gifts given to the Seven Realms. Together we can put an end to this!"

I was speaking someone else's words, words that I had memorized after hearing them many times. But wasn't Audamar right though?

"The Old Ones have appeared once again. We can reverse the situation with the crystals' magic and we can stop the kidnappings, the deaths!"

The expression on King Warren's face was full of more shock than hatred. I noticed that my words did not affect him. Perhaps the king really was heartless and maybe his cold personality prevented him from seeing the warmth in other people.

"You gave Aerlion's crystal to someone else. To a stranger! This could be a trap. You've turned your back to everything you swore to protect."

A deep silence sank into the room. King Warren was breathing hard with rage, his hands on his head. He went on that way until his dark eyes turned to me once again. I thought of telling him that Audamar wasn't a stranger, that he was his friend once. But I could imagine that this could make the king even more furious.

"Those crystals needed to remain hidden. The first Protectors risked their lives for this."

"I felt its power," I said. "It was calling *me*. Tell me, how many Protectors could sense their magic before me? I am chosen for a reason! The Old Ones returned and maybe that is why I am here, so I can stop whoever is behind this!"

From the corner of my eye, I saw the Protectors exchanging a look. I had my answer then. None. I was the only Protector who has been successful in finding one. I wanted to believe that this was for something. This was why I was chosen, to make a difference.

King Warren quickly turned his eyes away and said, "Before you, none of the Protectors were searching for the crystals."

Then he shook his head. "There's only one punishment for this . . . I'm sorry . . . but I can't allow what happened centuries ago to repeat itself."

I looked at the nobles in the room. None of the Protectors were looking at me now. Protector Edmond was shaking his head rapidly side to side, and Ramona was covering her mouth with her hands. I turned to Balfour to make him look at me, but I saw that he had turned his gaze back at the floor. There was an expression of mourning on his face.

The king passed the guards and approached me with careful steps. "You once told me that you wanted to be *stronger*," he whispered. "Tell me, do you think power was worth the price?"

I shook my head as I recalled the conversation we'd had with him and his cousin Lord Theon in the courtyard.

"I'm not doing this for myself," I said.

*A lie.* Even though I wanted to help the people and Audamar, I knew that I never would have tried to find the crystal if it wasn't for my own good. I had a dream and I was ready to burn down the world for it.

With a single cue from the king, the guards standing around us grabbed my arms. As they dragged me away, I cried from the top of my lungs, "You'll see it! You'll soon see what the crystals can do!"

All my efforts to reach the king were stopped by the guards. They dragged me out of the throne room as my cries echoed in the palace. Until we turned the corner, my gaze never left the king's.

# CHAPTER 21

I woke up to the sound of approaching footsteps. I sat up next to the stone wall I had been leaning on and crawled on my hands to the bars of the filthy dungeon. I brought my hands to my hair and pushed it away from my eyes before looking at the leather boots of the person standing before me on the other side of my cell. Even though I had a hard time recognizing him under the dim light of the single torch, I moved over to him on my knees as soon as our eyes met.

"King Warren," I said as I grabbed the bars. "Just let me explain!"

I reached forward through the gap between the bars and tried to hold on to the king's clothes, causing one of the guards behind him to lunge forward. The king stopped him.

"It's not what you think. I gave the crystal away, but I didn't betray anyone. We can use them. Together . . ."

"They had to remain hidden." The king's voice was void of emotion. "You put everyone in danger without even a second thought. You don't realize how dangerous the crystals could be, do you?"

"You are scared of something you have never even seen," I said in a hiss. "Just because someone once used them for evil, it doesn't mean it will happen again!"

He didn't look impressed with what I said.

"This is your fault as much as it is the Protectors' or nobles'!" I continued. "You are a coward for hiding behind the palace walls. You have no idea how much people suffer."

The piece of cloth I held slipped away from my hand when he took a step back. The king looked away. "Perhaps . . . But I know how much they will suffer once the crystal is used."

He shook his head. "I can't let the past repeat itself. They might be used for evil as much as they can for good, and it's a risk I am not willing to

162

take. You knew the crystals had to remain hidden . . . I too made an oath to this kingdom, and I will protect the Seven Realms, no matter what."

He turned his gaze elsewhere. "We are still looking for your friend but we couldn't find anyone matching his description. Wherever he's gone, it should make you happy to know that he's disappeared with the crystal."

I looked at his dark eyes. "Are you going to kill me?" I asked with a shaky breath. "Won't you even put me on a trial?"

The only thing the king did was turn his head away. "A trial won't change your sentence."

He looked like he wanted to leave, but something made him stay longer. I watched him as he took a deep breath and then approached the bars once again.

"Why?" he asked suddenly. "You could have had a future here. You could have had *everything* you've ever wanted."

"I couldn't turn my back on my people," I whispered. "I am one of them and the time I spent at the palace will never change that. You knew this."

King Warren closed his eyes and I watched him raise his hand. Four men from the group of guards waiting behind him came to the front upon his signal and I saw a shining key in the hand of one of them. I walked back in panic and pressed my back against the wall. The key turned twice inside the lock.

"Please! Wait!"

I was suddenly lifted. They dragged me out of the cell despite all my struggling; perhaps for the first time since I was brought here, I wanted to remain behind the bars.

King Warren didn't even raise his head as I passed by. We left him behind and headed toward the narrow stairway. We were walking quite fast through the narrow hall that looked like a tunnel. It was so dark inside. The only thing I could feel was the tight grip on my wrists. It felt odd to be treated like a criminal. But wasn't that exactly what I was in their eyes?

The guards once assigned to protect me were now taking me to my death. I lowered my head. The soles of my leather boots were dragging along the marble floor as we moved on. We slowed down and I heard another door open. We arrived at a dark room after a heavy squeak. One of the guards held my arms and put heavy handcuffs on my wrists. My body began to tremble with fear and I did my best not to fall down. I looked around the room as my eyes got used to the darkness. There was nothing on the hay-covered floor but chains lying around. The guards standing before me controlled the handcuffs and made sure they were tight enough. Just then, I noticed the shouting coming from the outside.

"What's going on?" I asked the guard standing on my other side. I breathed in fear. "Where am I?"

I looked around for a way to escape, only to notice the group of guards standing in front of the door behind me. I had no chance. When I noticed the latched door at the other end of the room, I ran at it with all my might, despite the heavy handcuffs pulling me down. The door opened slightly and the noise became louder. I realized that the guards behind me hadn't moved to stop me.

The iron door moved out of the way completely and I blinked. Now I knew what the sounds were about; I could never escape from here. They had taken me out of the dungeon and brought me to another cell, and this one was much bigger.

I looked at the iron bars around the wide oval area and at the guards standing behind them. I saw the crowd behind the bars. People around the throne where King Warren sat completely surrounded the area, and all eyes turned on me when I stepped out.

I had been brought to an arena.

I stumbled backward and the royal guard standing behind me closed the latched door, leaving me out there on my own.

"Silence!"

The buzzing of the crowd died down as a familiar voice was heard in the arena. I looked at Lord Cyril's face through the crowd. I felt relieved to see a familiar face but his sharp gaze didn't look friendly at all. As soon as our eyes met, I knew he wasn't going to help me.

"We are here because of the betrayal of the Protector of Aerlion. King Warren will determine her sentence."

The expression on the people's faces told me that they already knew what it was. Apparently, the news had spread everywhere and to everyone. So, did my family know, too?

I filled my lungs with a timid breath, which might well be one of my last. The king's hands were on both sides of the engraved wooden throne that was less glamorous than the one in the throne room, and he was looking down. He closed his eyes tightly. I watched him raise his right hand. The chanting from the crowd grew louder.

I kept my eyes on him stubbornly. The king looked around before turning in my direction for a brief moment, but he quickly tore his gaze away. I looked at the empty space next to the throne. The council members had taken their places at his other side, but none of the Protectors were there.

The sliding door, through which I had come in, opened creakily and I walked to the other side of the arena. One of the royal guards had returned, holding a leaf in his hand. As soon as I saw the color of the leaf, I realized that it was from the Vitae.

I walked backward until my back hit the wire fence of the arena. The people behind the bars stuck their hands in and pushed me forward, causing me to fall to my knees. The guard was walking toward me. I crawled backward on my hands and the chains on my arms stuck onto the pieces of rock under my feet. I tried to get free but I was too late. I saw the glass bottle in his hand when the guard pulled the chains and lifted me. It was poison.

I waved my cuffed hands and made a light shine brightly to illuminate the entire place. As the people covered their faces with their hands and cried out, I knew I could still defeat them as long as I had my magic. But suddenly someone grabbed my arm and I fell. The rocks on the ground pricked my skin.

I felt the firm grip of the guards on me. Then they forced the glass bottle to my lips. I gulped harshly with the bitter taste. The magic shining in my palm slowly disappeared, and my body relaxed in the blink of an eye. I tried to use my powers again but nothing happened when I raised my hand. No matter what I did, I couldn't make the light shine again.

One of the guards harshly placed the leaf from the Vitae in my palm. I couldn't find the strength to oppose him. He pulled my chains when I tried to open my palms and made my hands clasp together. A sharp pain struck my arm from my wrists to my elbows. I felt too tired even to remain upright, and I thought that this must be the effect of the poison.

I saw Lord Cyril walk in. I forgot about the pain when I saw him and my eyes grew wide with fear. The leaf seemed to be glued to my palms. I fought to get rid of it but the guard pulled the chain roughly and prevented me from opening my hands. Lord Cyril stood right in front of me.

I raised my hands and narrowed my eyes as I begged him. "Please. Let me explain."

Lord Cyril had stood up to everyone when I had first arrived here, saying that he believed in me. But now it made me sick to see him do what he was told, like King Warren's puppet.

Lord Cyril closed his eyes and began murmuring as he leaned over and pressed his thumb strongly on my forehead. The guard next to me pulled the chains tighter and made it impossible for me to move away. The arena had fallen into silence. I could feel everyone's gaze on me, including King Warren, but I couldn't move at all.

The familiar tingling spread from my fingertips all over my body and I noticed the weak light coming through my hands. I couldn't control it. Lord Cyril continued his words and the magic became more evident with every word he said. The pressure of his thumb increased and my body began burning, causing me to let out a cry. Everything began to blur with the tears that filled my eyes with the pain. I tried to close my palms to keep the magic but it began to flow through my fingers like drops of water. I felt weaker as the light died down. I screamed with the pain.

It felt as if a part of me had been cut out; a part that had never really belonged to me. I no longer felt the magic in me. I was a human again.

The guard let me go when Lord Cyril was done. I fell on my hands and tried to catch my breath. I dug my fingers into the soil as I heard the same footsteps walking away. I knew I couldn't catch up with Lord Cyril. I raised my hand, hoping that the bright light would come out from my palm and reach him. But nothing happened.

The crowd cheered loudly. Some of them held the bars and began shaking them in excitement. They enjoyed watching this.

"The accused is now ready for trial."

When Lord Cyril's cavernous voice was heard in the big arena once again, the guard tried to hold my arms and get me on my feet. I couldn't resist. The cheering roared once again. I shut my eyes tight and lowered my head.

"Sarah," I whispered as I gritted my teeth not to cry. My dirty blonde hair had fallen over my forehead, preventing people from seeing the tears filling my eyes. "Mom . . . I'm sorry."

The arena fell into silence again when the king rose from his throne. He roughly cleared his throat; apparently, he had more to say. But before he could start, a horrifying sound filled the crowded arena. The people started looking around to see what was happening, and the sound became louder. *A roar.*

Some faces were already filled with horror. The ground began shaking fiercely before anyone could move, and a bright light surrounded the entire area. People scattered around with the explosion.

I became free of the guard's grip and fell backward, hitting my back on the wall. I could feel the pain spreading. I forced myself to crawl as much as the handcuffs allowed me. There was dust everywhere. When the ringing in my ears ended, I heard the screams. My hand automatically went to my waist, only to realize that I was unarmed. My powers had gone, too. I could protect no one.

I turned to the hulky figure with thick purple skin roaring in the middle of the arena; a Murgroth. The people on the other side of the iron bars, which were bent with the explosion, started running in fear. Screams rose. I looked at the chaos around me. I saw the tall, black figures among the flood of people as the Dralein began attacking every moving thing around them.

I brushed pieces of stones off myself and held the bent bars to stand up. A sharp pain stuck in my back and my ribs at the same time. The iron bars surrounding the arena were broken at places, leaving me a space big enough to walk out.

I saw the Murgroth that had been roaring in the middle of the arena move toward King Warren, and I instantly knew this was my chance. One of the Dralein let out shrieking sounds as it stretched its long body and began throwing rocks at the crowd. One of them came toward me.

Someone suddenly pressed me down from my shoulders and I instantly found myself on the floor. I was saved at the last minute. I stood up to see the owner of the hand on my shoulder.

"You!" I yelled as I lunged at Hunter, but my cuffed hands hindered my movements.

The Phoenix grabbed my hand in the air. He waved the key he took from his pocket. I paused as he looked at me.

"I'm sorry."

His quick hands were on my wrists. I realized that I wanted to cry as I looked at him; I wanted to shout and ask why he had gone to the king first. I had almost been killed. A shiver ran down my spine.

He placed the key into the lock and turned it, causing the thick metal pieces to fall to the ground. I rubbed my aching wrists.

"Anna, look . . ." he said as he put his big hands on my cheeks and wiped a running tear with his thumb. I was so scared. I wasn't even aware that I was crying. I fixed my wet eyes on his green ones.

"I was going to die."

"What you did was wrong, okay? You shouldn't have given the crystal away. *No*, actually, you should have left it where it was hidden. You did something you shouldn't have, but I'm guilty too. I went straight to the king and betrayed you, my Protector . . . I would have never done this to Breccan."

"Why are you helping me?" I whispered. "You wanted me dead."

My lips trembled as I slowly realized the truth and I did my best to prevent more tears from running down my cheeks. It felt weird to say this, but the Old Ones' attack had saved my life, and now Hunter was giving me my freedom back.

"I couldn't let you die. Especially since you were caught because of me."

He lowered his hands and rubbed my wrists, gently but also in a rush. "This is an opportunity. Get the crystal back and prove yourself to the king . . . Don't make me regret this."

The royal guard who was responsible for me, and who had been thrown to the other end of the arena with the explosion, stood up with difficulty and looked around. Our eyes met. He had a duty and he had to carry it out, no matter what. I knew he would never let me go. The man began faltering toward me as he raised his sword from his waist. Hunter saw him, too. The Phoenix roughly pushed me back.

"Go!"

I began running. I got through the bars and blended into the crowd, but before that, I stopped one last time and looked at the arena where the king and the council members stood. They were standing behind the guards who were fighting the Old Ones that had surrounded them. King Warren was swinging his sword at the dark figures that lunged at him. The council members were standing together and some of them looked frightened. My gaze met Lord Cyril's dark eyes.

I expected him to come after me but Lord Cyril looked away as I walked out of the arena, completely ignoring me. As if he didn't see me. So I continued to run.

The arena was built at the far end of the city and it was connected to the dungeons of the palace from underground. I flew down the stairs that surrounded the high structure and dove into the crowd of people running toward the city. The people, who had been chanting and watching me only a few minutes ago, didn't even give me a second look as I passed them. My hands turned into fists with the feeling of freedom. I was going to get out of here.

I began running toward the back streets of Ardria where the number of people became fewer. I moved through the ruined buildings and noticed that this part of the city had been deserted. I didn't slow down. I knew I couldn't go to one of the temples around the palace. The main gates were heavily guarded and the Phoenixes would come after me if they saw me. So would the Protectors. But there were other small gates somewhere in the city. I had to find one that led to Aerlion.

As I continued to run, the sound of someone else's footsteps blended into mine. I didn't have to look back over my shoulder to know that King Warren was coming after me.

I passed over the old stone bridge and arrived at the fountain in the square. My pace slowed down when I saw the person waiting for me in the middle of the street. The footsteps from behind me stopped, too. I turned to look at King Warren over my shoulder and saw that he was looking at the caped person standing in front of us, puzzled.

"Audamar," I said with relief when I saw him. He had come, just as he had promised. "We have to get out of here right now."

When King Warren heard the name, he turned to me in bewilderment.

"He . . . what have you done?" the king asked as he took a step back. There was something in his voice that I could call fear. My eyes paced back and forth between the two of them.

Audamar raised his hand from under his cape and I looked at the three colored objects in his hand; he had *three* crystals.

"Stupid girl."

Audamar suddenly closed his hand and a bright light appeared in his palm. The light found King Warren. I watched him fly backward with the magic, hitting his back on the fountain. Audamar's laughter was loud in the empty square.

The king gritted his teeth and brought his hand to his chest as he breathed heavily. He got up. His head was bleeding and his dark eyes were fixed on Audamar.

"You were supposed to be dead," the king said.

Audamar looked stronger than ever as the smile on his face broadened. He half-opened his palm and held the crystals high. I saw the yellow one in the middle.

"What's going on?" I asked, still confused.

With my words, he took his gray eyes away from the king. "They never wrote my name properly in the history books. You can't imagine how a single name could bring so much fear just because of some silly superstitious beliefs."

A painful moan came out of the king's lips as his fingers found the open wound on his head. His hand was soaked in blood.

"Allow me to introduce myself. My name is Rogue Audamar Montborne . . . the Master of the Darkness and the *First* King."

*Audamar* . . . I thought about how I hadn't thought of this before. It was an old and unusual name. And now, I knew why. He had been alive for thousands of years. My gaze turned to the yellow crystal shining in his hand and my eyes grew wide. It was all my fault.

Audamar began walking toward us, his hand still raised to his chest. When he opened the hood of his cape and revealed his face, I thought he didn't look the same as before. He looked more powerful with the crystals he had. He looked like a true king now. He was nothing like the man that I had met earlier. The person I had known was a complete deception.

He raised his hand and I was suddenly swung away. Audamar was standing right before the king now. He raised his empty hand and covered King Warren's face with it. The king began struggling but it was in vain. Warren was tall but Audamar was taller. He lifted the king as if his weight was nothing to him, maintaining his grip. I heard a painful cry as King Warren struggled to get free from the hand holding him. I saw the crystals in Audamar's other hand start to glow again.

Audamar's figure started to change. His short black curls became dark brown as his skin turned into a warmer tone, but his eyes remained gray. When he lifted his face, I saw King Warren's face on top of the body that belonged to the First King.

The First King's grip loosened and King Warren fell to the ground. His jaw and cheekbones were bruised from Audamar's tight grip. I hurried over to King Warren when Audamar walked away. The king wasn't in a condition to refuse my help. He was barely able to breathe as I held him, allowing him to lean his weight on me. I wrapped his arm over my shoulder and tried hard not to collapse under his weight. The First King turned around and walked over to the golden crown that King Warren had dropped. I couldn't look away from him. He looked so much like Warren that I had to turn and look at the person standing half-awake next to me.

I had to get away from here, as soon as possible. I could run but I knew couldn't leave King Warren behind, no matter what had happened...Audamar's back was turned to us, so I closed my eyes. I didn't know if it would work or not, but I was trying to reach out to Deegan. Though it would probably be in vain without my magic.

"You brought the creatures here with the crystals," I said as I turned my angry gaze at Audamar. "Was all this to get rid of King Warren?"

He glared at me over his shoulder but said nothing. He now looked intimidating.

"I trusted you. You made me believe that we could do all the things you said with the crystals. Was it all a lie?"

He smiled in response. "It wasn't a total lie when I said we could change the Seven Realms. It's just that the futures we desire are different."

"You fooled me," I said in rage.

"And you were fooled too easily."

He raised his hand and I drew back in fear. But instead of using the crystals, he pointed at the city behind us. "They were going to kill you but you were saved by my creatures. That was the reward for helping me; even for a second, don't forget that you are alive because of me."

I shook my head, even though I knew he was right. "So, now that you got what you wanted, what's next? The throne is yours now."

"*The throne?*" he spluttered. A furious expression passed through his face as he took a few steps in my direction. "Do you really think I did all this just for that stupid thing?"

He exhaled in rage and squeezed the three crystals in his hand. And with that, the small beam of light disappeared. "I want *everything* that was taken from me. All of it! The Seven Realms, my honor, my power . . ."

"Power? The crystals never belonged to you!"

I now knew why I shouldn't have believed the story Audamar had told me. Balfour was right. The First King had created chaos with the crystals and the first Protectors had hidden them. But I gave him the crystal of my realm on a silver platter.

One corner of his mouth curled up and he put the crystals back in his pocket. "I will paint my throne with the blood of my enemies . . . Then, I will build my *own* kingdom. It will be a victory that none of the kings after me has been able to accomplish."

His features tightened as he turned his eyes to the half-conscious King Warren who was leaning his head on my shoulder. "The weak will have no place in my kingdom, and those who oppose me will be destroyed."

He tilted his head and took a step toward us. I drew back in fear, dragging the half-awake King Warren with me. Audamar's face was unreadable as his gray eyes narrowed.

"You look just like her," I heard him murmur suddenly.

*Her?* I wanted to ask what he meant, who he meant? But there wasn't time.

I heard the heavy fluttering wings. The night-black dragon glided through the sky and I exhaled in relief. Audamar did something unexpected. He drew back.

Deegan landed on the square behind us and walked over to me. The dragon created a circle that contained the king and me inside. I pushed King Warren onto the dragon's back and then held on to him. Deegan spread his wide wings and took off. I leaned forward to make sure that neither King Warren nor I would fall off. When we were high enough, I looked down over my shoulder.

Audamar was looking at our indistinct figures. He had put on the golden crown King Warren had dropped. He watched us. Even though he had the crystals, he had done nothing to stop us. He didn't have to. I had fallen into his trap and I had given him what he wanted. He was done with King Warren and me.

He had the crystals of three realms. He had won.

# CHAPTER 22

I opened my eyes at the crackling of burning wood. I stood up with difficulty, and my gaze met that of King Warren, who was sitting at the other side of the weak flames. With fear, I suddenly crawled backward on my hands and put enough distance between us to protect myself. A cynical expression formed on the king's face before he turned his head away. He was wrapping his arm with a piece of cloth he had torn from his shirt. The red flames lit his face as he continued to wrap the cloth around his shoulder without saying a single word. I skimmed his skin and quickly turned my eyes away from his bare chest. His skin was full of bruises and cuts.

With the pain in my arm, I looked down. There was a cloth wrapped on my arm just like his and I realized that he was the one who had helped me. My eyes grew wide in surprise.

I saw the meadow we were lying on. Darkness had settled, and the moon and the stars in the dark blue sky illuminated everything. As I turned, I noticed Deegan on top of a hill, close behind us. His blood-red eyes were scanning the area, waiting on alert as if he was expecting something to happen.

"It's been a few hours since sunset."

King Warren was done bandaging the cuts. He put his shirt, which he had torn to use as a bandage, back on. Then he crossed his arms and began staring at the fire. I tried to read the expression on his face but it didn't reveal anything.

"Where are we?"

"Aerlion." He looked at Deegan. "He brought us the place he knows best."

I turned to the dragon once again. Deegan, as we turned to him, made a grumbling sound. Despite my numb legs, I forced myself to stand up. The king watched me.

"We can't stay here." I pointed around us. "Let's go to my house. I'm sure Deegan can find it again."

He gave me the worst look. "*Us?*"

I slowly let out a breath. "I know you don't trust me . . ." the king grumbled.

"But we have no other choice. We have to stay together."

King Warren lowered his eyes to the ground. I didn't know what or whom he was thinking about. Everything had happened so quickly and we had suddenly found ourselves in a completely different place. And the worst part was, it was my fault.

"I don't have to go anywhere with you."

"And I don't have to stay here," I said as I pointed at Deegan. "There is nothing here, and we both need a rest. You'll be left alone when I go away with him. Is that what you want, to fall prey to wild animals?"

He knit his eyebrows. "Considering that you almost got both of us killed, I can't really see the difference between those two."

My eyes narrowed. "Look," I said as I took a few steps toward him. I could feel the heat on my face, coming from the weak fire beneath. "You can do anything to me when we go back, okay? But you aren't a king right now and I don't think anyone will believe you after what Audamar did. So, until you get your throne back, we need to work together."

His puzzled gaze examined me for a while before he nodded slowly, but his face was still carrying a trace of anger. He stood up with difficulty as he brought his hand to his chest and breathed in pain. He was badly hurt.

King Warren pushed the soil with the tip of his boots to put out the already-weak fire. Then he passed by me in a hurry and walked to the dragon. I felt dizzy as I followed him. I stumbled. King Warren had to wrap his arm around me to prevent me from collapsing.

"The poison," he murmured. I felt his breath on my neck. "That was supposed to make you dizzy for a while. That way you would be unable to use your magic against us during the trial."

I pushed his hand away. He also drew back.

"Don't touch me," I said as I wrapped my arms around myself. I was completely unarmed.

King Warren watched my helplessness with joy. He seemed to be having fun despite the situation we were in.

"You need to trust people," he said mockingly.

I gave him the toughest look I could, still trying to maintain the distance between us. "*You* are telling me *that*?"

He shrugged. "I would have left you behind if I wanted you dead. If you don't trust me, don't fall asleep next to a stranger again."

"Maybe you just didn't want Deegan to attack you," I said. Because of our bond, I knew the dragon would protect me; at least I wanted to believe that.

He shook his head. "That also."

"So, you don't want to get rid of me anymore?"

I watched the king pause before answering. "It's still an option."

I walked over to him. I knew we had to work together if we wanted to survive. At least for now.

"I saved your life in Ardria, too," I reminded him, remembering how I didn't leave him with Audamar. "But this doesn't change anything."

"When we get back . . ."

I cut his words. "*If* we can get back."

I saw that he was struggling to keep quiet but he didn't reply. *Good.* I couldn't find the strength to argue with him any longer.

Warren climbed onto the dragon carefully because of his bruises. I could see him grit his teeth as he pulled himself up and held the reins. I did the same. I patted on the dragon's thick skin and Deegan stood on his feet. I envisioned my house and the dragon took off. Although I hadn't led him, I knew he was taking me in the right direction.

I turned my head, trying not to look at the king, and began watching the darkness that flowed beneath us.

•

We were both silent as we walked out of the giant trees where we had left Deegan and headed toward the hill with wooden huts on it. Darkness had settled long ago; the villagers were sound asleep. We tried to remain silent so as not to wake them up and passed by the houses before walking up the stairs of the familiar hut. The door was unlocked, as usual. I walked in and left enough space for King Warren to follow me inside.

I looked around in the dark. "Mom?" I called out. "It's me! I'm back."

My whisper was loud enough for her to hear me, but I didn't receive any answer.

"Do you live here?" asked King Warren as he looked around the small hut.

I turned to him over my shoulder. "What did you think, that villagers lived in mansions?"

"Of course not," he said but the expression on his face said otherwise.

I moved into the narrow hallway and left the king behind to examine the tiny old house. It was probably the first time he was witnessing the poverty in which people like me lived. I especially wanted him to see this, *all* of it. So, I let him wander around.

I went to the bedroom and pushed in the half-open door. I stuck my head inside but my mother's bed was empty. I looked inside in panic and hurried to the room next door. My rushed footsteps drew the king's attention.

"Mom?" I whispered.

I opened the door and looked inside the small room. But no, it was the same here. I couldn't find any sign of her. I ran into the kitchen. There was no one home. I breathed anxiously. I recalled her words the last time I saw her, and I hoped that she had gone to where Sarah was. But what if something happened to them? The royal guards could have gone after them after what happened at the capital.

King Warren looked at my panicked face. "The guards couldn't have come from the capital to find them in such a short time. Besides, I gave no such order."

I wanted to believe him. Audamar had let us go because he was done with us. I gave him the crystal of Aerlion and he took Warren's place; we weren't a threat to him anymore. But what if he changed his mind? What if the Old Ones came here? I searched for any clues inside the house but couldn't find anything.

I nodded slowly and went through the kitchen drawers to find the candles. They were next to Sarah's ink bottles and paints. I shot a glance at them and took a match in my hand, but the king stopped me.

"We can't put on a light; it'll be noticed."

I put the candles back on the counter gently. Then I left King Warren behind and half-opened the door of the room that was across from the kitchen. My hand was on the doorknob; I made no move to walk in. Everything was as I had left it. My bedroom was the same. It seemed to have remained as the sole proof of my life before being chosen as a Protector. I didn't want to ruin the only good thing left from my past. I exhaled with longing for the past, took a step back, and shut the door.

I found King Warren in front of the kitchen wall. He was looking at Sarah's drawings. He didn't tear his gaze away as I approached.

"Did you draw these?"

"My sister."

"She is talented."

I nodded. "I know."

I examined the traces of ink left on the paper. Then I looked away. No matter how much I thought, I never could have imagined seeing a stranger—especially the king—in my house. Him being here was . . . *awkward*. I guess my mother would have passed out with excitement if she had been here right now. She was one of the few people who blindly believed that the king was as holy as the Protectors were, if not more. Despite all the injustice and poverty we had suffered from, even before I was chosen, she still worshipped the kingdom.

"We should sleep," I murmured as King Warren nodded. We both headed to the hallway at the same time. When his elbow accidentally touched the bruise on my arm, I drew back, and my eyes widened with pain.

"Watch where you're going," I hissed. I pressed my palm onto my arm. Although my arm had been aching for hours, I hadn't realized how bad it was until the king bumped me.

He took a step toward me. I tried to move away but there was no place left for me to go as my back hit the wall.

"Let me take a look."

I grimaced with pain as I rolled up the sleeve of my torn and dirty clothes. His gaze shifted to the spot on my skin. It looked much worse than I had imagined.

He reached out his hand. I looked at him confused but he said nothing and just began sliding his index finger over my arm. I swallowed and began watching him without saying anything, still puzzled. His thumb brushed over my skin and he started massaging it.

"How much does it hurt?"

I gritted my teeth when his finger moved to the center of the bruise. I drew back as I flinched with the pain, and freed my arm from his grip. "I can handle it myself. I don't need your help."

But he didn't move away. He only sighed. "Let me help you. We are in no position to argue."

Then he moved his eyes away from the bruise on my arm and began looking around the small kitchen. "Where's the ointment?"

I pointed at the counter behind him and he reached it with a few long steps. He opened the jars on the counter one by one and smelled a few of them. Finally, he looked back at me over his shoulder and lifted the glass jar in his hand. I nodded. I lowered myself onto the stool in the corner slowly. I could see that King Warren was no different, but still, I watched him open the jar and dip his finger into the ointment after kneeling in front of me. His hands went back to my arm. He pulled my sleeve up and his fingers touched the bruise. I gritted my teeth as he spread the ointment over my skin. His touch was gentle and he was careful as his eyes looked me over.

I turned to his bandaged chest, which I could see under his torn shirt. "Your turn."

He first looked at me and then at the jar on the floor. "I'll do it myself."

"That's what I said, right?" I said, "I am a daughter of two healers. I know what I am doing. Promise."

I knew he was in pain; he was too worn out to protest. His hand slowly went to his shirt's hem and pulled it off over his head. I quickly looked away from his muscled body. King Warren turned his back to me and began taking off the bandages one by one. He was still on his knees.

I took the jar from the floor, leaned forward, and examined the king's back. I could see the scratch from his shoulder to his back. It didn't seem to be very deep but it was big enough to pain him. I dipped my fingers into the jar and brought them timidly to his back. In the meantime, I was constantly reminding myself that I was just returning his favor. He had taken care of me; he had not left me behind when I passed out, despite everything that had happened.

The sides of the bruise were already turning purple. He breathed painfully and leaned forward as soon as my fingers touched his back. His hands turned into fists with pain. I bent over and started blowing with my breath to ease the pain. His gaze found mine over his shoulder. With that, I drew back.

"It helps," I murmured quickly. I knew my cheeks were all red but when he turned away again, I was encouraged by the fact that he couldn't see my face. I was right behind him. I continued to spread the ointment gently over the wound. Then I moved on to his shoulder.

My hands had become sticky with the ointment. I screwed the cap on the jar and placed it on the counter next to us. We both remained still for a while as I sat on the stool and the king was right in front of me on his knees.

I finally cleared my throat loudly and stood up. He watched me as I walked by. I went through the drawers under the counter and took out clean bandages. I threw them at his face.

"Here," I said quickly, "You can do the rest by yourself."

The best thing about my mother being the village's healer was that we always had some medicine or supplies. This included the clean bandages that the king needed. We didn't have enough money to buy many things before I was chosen, but it was obvious that the king's allowance had been enough to make my family comfortable. He had indeed kept his word.

I walked out of the kitchen and I let myself down onto the squeaking sofa in the corner. I took my boots off by pushing them against each other. King Warren walked in before long. He hadn't put his shirt back on, but he had managed to dress his wound nicely with the clean bandages.

"You can take any room you want. The bedrooms are at the end of the hall," I said when our eyes met. "It's not a royal chamber but it will do."

I waited for him to hear the mockery in my voice but he didn't seem to notice. I pulled my knees to myself. The sofa wasn't comfortable and its springs squeaked with my move.

King Warren didn't say anything. I was expecting him to leave but he surprised me by moving over. He lay down on the old sofa that was slightly bigger than mine as he faced me once more. We stared at each other for a while. The thought of my mother and my sister was still bothering me as I moved and joined my hands under my head.

"What now?" I asked.

The king breathed through his nose and pulled his long legs to himself, just as I had. "I'm going to return to Ardria and reclaim my throne."

"It's just a throne," I murmured.

His narrowed gaze turned to me. "That throne is the symbol of everything my ancestors fought for over centuries. I will not give up so easily."

"Even if you need to die for it?" I asked. I had seen what Audamar did, how he called the Old Ones and how he threw us to the side with only a finger.

King Warren averted his eyes and lay on his back with his arms under his head. His bare chest heaved as he breathed. I received no reply from him.

"How could this be possible? Rogue . . . how is he still alive? The First King lived centuries ago. He should have been dead."

"I am not sure." He exhaled loudly and closed his eyes for a moment. "And it wouldn't be stupid to think that he wants the remaining crystals."

I watched him with thoughtful eyes. I had hoped for him to have the answers I was looking for, but King Warren was as clueless as me. I knew that I was the one that had spent more time with the First King and the one that had believed in his promises. But it had all been a lie. Audamar wasn't a researcher, nor had he been kicked out of the palace by the king. They were all lies to make me feel sorry for and believe him. And I had fallen into his trap. I felt stupid. Maybe that was why he chose me in the first place.

"How was I able to call Deegan? I don't have powers anymore. He shouldn't have been able to find us."

King Warren continued to examine the ceiling. "The fact that your powers have been taken from you can't cut your ties with the dragon. That bond will remain. For that to be broken . . ."

I finished his words. "I need to die."

The king nodded and regarded me as I said, "I was going to be executed."

"That's how a new Protector is chosen. When a Protector completes his duty and dies, both the power and the bond with the dragon find life in the newly selected Protector... Your magic would try to keep you alive. That is why you were given a poison to numb you. So that you wouldn't resist."

I slowly extended my right hand. "My magic…" I murmured as I remembered how it was taken from me. "I lost it. What did Lord Cyril do to me?"

"The leaf is the same as the ones used during the Selections, from the Vitae. What Lord Cyril did was to become a bridge between you and the tree. There are some people in the Seven Realms who have magical powers like Cyril. They have a strong spiritual side."

He breathed painfully as he brought his hand to his chest. "Your power was taken from you by the Vitae, just as you were given them during the Selection Ceremony. The Goddess chose to take back what was given. So, the ritual was successful."

I couldn't think of Warren as a religious person, but apparently, the king was no different from everyone else. I laughed. "So, I was able to piss *her* off as well, huh?"

I had no idea of what had given me my Protector powers, but despite all the stories I had been told, I—contrary to the king and everyone else in the palace—didn't believe in a Goddess or anything else. If there was really a Goddess, She, who made me lose my powers so easily, would have intervened with the poverty and illnesses in the Seven Realms before dealing with me. No one could talk about a divine power trying to dispense justice while people survived by chance.

"What you did was unforgivable," continued the king. "You couldn't return to your duty. So, someone else from Aerlion had to be chosen in your place. A new Protector. That is why people were there— your execution would be an example."

"So, you wanted me dead."

The king turned harshly to me. His anger was reflected in his voice as he said, "*I* didn't want this. It's not my fault that you simply gave the crystal away. There are rules, and you'd taken an oath. You saw what the crystals can do and why they are dangerous."

I looked away when he pointed his dark eyes at me. I had a reason. It had been a risky choice but I had thought that it would be worth the reward. I was wrong.

"Why weren't the other Protectors there?" I asked as I remembered I hadn't seen them. They could have stopped me from running away but luck was on my side. "I would have thought they wouldn't want to miss *that*."

The king turned his gaze to the ceiling once again. "I thought it would be dishonorable for them to witness one of their own being punished."

"And would it really work?" I asked. "If I was executed?"

He nodded. "There is only one Protector in the history of the kingdom that has been executed." He looked at me. "The first Protector of Aerlion."

My eyes grew wide.

"She was the reason why Rogue took all the seven crystals; she gave her crystal to him. It is said that thousands of people died. In the history books, it is written that she surrendered. A new Protector was chosen after the war ended."

I couldn't believe it. The same mistake had been made in the past, as well. When the king saw my expression, he shook his head.

"I shouldn't be surprised. I guess it's in the blood of the Aerlion's Protectors to turn their backs on the kingdom."

I closed my eyes but didn't say anything. For a while, we were silent.

"Let's make a deal," I whispered but my voice was loud enough for him to hear me. His gaze found mine and I tried to keep my voice steady as his dark eyes continued watching me. "I'll try to keep you alive and you'll do the same."

I watched as his lips curled up, but there wasn't any humor on his face now. "I don't need you."

"Yes, you do. You need an ally and I am the only one around."

His eyes narrowed. "I am the king, I have allies."

"But Rogue is the one sitting on the throne now. There was a reason why he let us go—he doesn't see us as a threat. With the crystals' power, he has no limit."

I heard him inhale sharply. "I'll figure something out."

I turned to him. "Didn't you see what he did to you, to himself? His face changed! He looks just like you. You won't be able to convince anyone with him sitting on the throne and continuing to act like you."

Silence filled the small room. He knit his brows and an angry expression took over. His hand found his face and he harshly rubbed his chin. "And then what?" he asked finally. "You would be forgiven?"

I tried to keep my face still. "If we survive all of this, I'll . . . I'll surrender."

"And why should I believe you?" he asked, and I thought he had every reason not to.

"We need each other to survive. *I* need you." His expression was full of distrust but I didn't let him speak. "I can't do this by myself and neither can you. Let's help each other and then I'll agree."

He raised a brow. "To what?"

"To whatever you want."

"Fine," he said after a while which felt like forever. "We'll figure it out once this is all over, but we need each other . . . deal it is."

There was a huge knot in my stomach and as he spoke, it grew bigger. I hardly swallowed. "I don't have a plan . . . I don't care about the throne, but I know it can't be Audamar who rules the Seven Realms."

The darkness had returned with him. He had used the crystals to turn people into the Old Ones. People died because of him. He was a threat, and if he was after the rest of the crystals, he would soon become unstoppable.

"He'll kill anyone who stands between him and power," Warren spoke. "If we are in this together, we can't do this alone. We need more people."

I didn't have my powers and the king—and the nobles—never had magic; he could live for hundreds of years like the rest of us but other than that, he was as ordinary as other people. We couldn't do this alone.

We spoke no more. I was exhausted after everything we had been through and I was confused. I was paying the price for the chaos I had created, and it was my fault that the king was here with me. As silence waded in, sleep wrapped its arms around me. I curled farther into the sofa as I heard the king's voice.

"Something inside me says things will get worse. History books don't mention Rogue on purpose, but everyone knows how dangerous he once was."

My eyelids trembled as I set my gaze on the king lying on the sofa across from me. He continued to examine the ceiling carefully, and I knew his thoughts would keep him awake for a long time. I blinked as his figure became blurry. I let myself fall into sleep. His face was the last thing I saw before I closed my eyes.

# CHAPTER 23

We left my house behind with the first light of the day, not knowing for how long. I didn't even know if I could ever return there once this was all over, and it had been a strange feeling to be back at home without my family. We walked out of the village before anyone woke up, and we took Deegan to fly over the sylvan lands of Aerlion. We weren't sure where to go, or what to do. Even our next step was unclear.

"This place is fine," King Warren said as he pointed at a big oak tree. "Let's stop here."

After flying for a while, we decided that we were far enough from any villages and we landed where the king suggested. Deegan waited for us at where we left him. We knew we couldn't fly over the villages on a big dragon; people would notice. That was why we had gone farther into the thick woods of my realm.

I walked over to the spot King Warren was pointing and sat on one of the big rocks in front of the oak tree. The king took out the folded paper he had tucked into his pocket. He laid down the map of Aerlion, which we had found at my house, and he began pointing at it with a branch he took from the ground.

"We came from here," he said as he pointed at the spot marked with a cross. "This gate opens to one of the portals outside of the capital city. Deegan went through this gate to come to Aerlion when we escaped."

"So, we can't return there?"

"No." He shook his head. "Rogue might be done with us, but you are still a fugitive. He's probably sent the guards after us so people won't be suspicious. They know where we were last seen; that'll be the point where they'll start looking."

"There is another gate close to my village," I said as I remembered the one I'd used after being selected as the new Protector. The royal guards and Lord Cyril had used that one to bring me to Ardria for the first time.

185

"That is one of the closest to the palace. We would go directly to the gardens."

I stopped fidgeting with the piece of branch in my hand and threw it to the ground. "We don't have any weapons . . . Can't we use the main gate of Aerlion?" I asked. "If we go to the gate that goes to the temple, I could sneak in and get what we need. And then we would return."

But the king shook his head. "Too risky."

I breathed out loudly. "So, *what* is our plan? No one knows what's going on. Everyone thinks he is *you*, and I'm a fugitive. No one will believe . . ."

The king roughly put his hand over my lips and signaled me to be quiet. I quickly drew back. Then, he stood up and motioned me to follow him. When I heard a cracking, my hand immediately went to the big knife on my belt, the one I had taken from our kitchen drawer. King Warren had the other.

I walked behind him, stepping in his footsteps. The king was on full alert but there was no one around. Finally, my shoulders loosened. "Maybe you heard wrong."

I hung the knife back on my belt and hurried over to him. "We're wasting time here. Let's just go."

As soon as I took my final step, a net—big enough to hold the king and me inside—sprung from among the dry leaves. We were drawn up on a thick tree branch onto which the net was tied. My elbow struck King Warren on the jaw and a painful cry escaped from his lips. I thought I had just added another to his still unhealed bruises.

We were stuck. The king's knees were pressing against my back. I tried to move and get free of the net, but all it did was make the king grumble.

"Wasting time? Seriously? Can't you just watch where you're going?"

I ignored him and lowered my head to look down. We were about seven feet above the ground.

"We could easily get out of here if someone hadn't ordered my powers to be taken away."

I heard his growl. "I'm telling you for the last time. You brought it on yourself."

I stopped struggling and let myself on my back with a huff. King Warren moved to the side and tried to make room for the both of us, but he lost his balance and held on to the thick ropes of the net at the last moment. We were face-to-face now. I stared at him as his tense features relaxed. He didn't seem angry, but it couldn't be said that he was happy at being stuck here either. He gulped roughly as his dark eyes examined my face.

"You're too careless and clumsy," he said, emphasizing each word, "for a Protector."

I tried to shrug. "It could have been worse."

"What could be worse than swinging so high from the ground? We're caught in a trap."

My hand went to the knife I had placed in my belt just before getting caught in the net, but I saw that it was on the ground. I turned to him for help and saw that his knife had slid from his hand and fallen as well.

"Great," I murmured.

Just then, I heard a whistling coming behind the trees and quickly turned my head. A boy with curly red hair appeared. He seemed to be around my age, and he was wearing dark green clothes matching his green eyes. His whistling broke when he turned his freckled face to us, and he grimaced in complaint.

"You don't look like dinner."

He took a knife from his pocket and walked to the tree across from us. He cut the rope tied to the tree trunk without warning. As we fell, King Warren reached out to me. His fingers slipped through my hair and I felt his touch behind my head, shielding it against hitting the ground.

I suddenly found myself on the ground, on *him*. I quickly withdrew. The king was on his back, lying flat as he cried with pain. But he gently took his hand back and stood up. I did the same. He held his bandaged chest and I knew the fall hadn't helped the bruises under the fabric. I couldn't understand why he'd tried to protect me when he was hurt so badly, but as I could still feel his touch behind my head, a warm feeling filled my chest. My cheeks blushed and I quickly turned to the boy watching us.

The stranger turned his big green eyes to where we stood and examined us from head to toe. "You look awful."

The red-haired boy looked at King Warren's naked chest covered with bandages, and then he took his dark cape, which we both hadn't noticed because he had left it on one of the rocks nearby. He threw it at the king and asked, "What're you doing in the woods? You cost me one of my traps. It took me hours to do it."

"We're traveling," I said without thinking. "We were taking a shortcut through the forest to the next village on our way."

He lowered his head and looked at the plains behind us. "Where's your stuff?"

The king jumped in while I was trying to make up a lie. "It was stolen."

The red-haired boy's eyes narrowed. "Really?"

"Forget it. Let's just go."

King Warren turned around and began walking away. I was about to do the same when the boy jumped in front of us. "Okay, okay! Come with me. I can help you. I know a place you can stay."

King Warren looked back at me over his shoulder. I turned to the stranger in indecision. After all, we *did* need help. It wasn't an offer we could turn down.

The red-haired boy began walking in the other direction without waiting for us. I took a few quick steps to catch up with him and the king came over, too. We began following him hesitantly.

"Where are we going?"

The boy looked at us over his shoulder and answered the king's question. "The only place where people like me can go."

The king grumbled at this meaningless answer but he said no more. We followed the stranger through the forest and finally stopped in front of a big tree stump. I watched the boy carefully as he bent over and pushed the wild herbs around the log to the sides, revealing a hole big enough for us to fit.

The boy turned to us and said, "Welcome to my home. Come on; don't be shy!"

King Warren leaned to my ear. "This could be a trap," he whispered. "Do I need to remind you that you're a fugitive? We're both in danger."

I turned my gaze to the boy who was tugging at the herbs on the ground. "I don't think he'll harm us," I said and walked over to the hole before the king could answer.

It seemed to go about ten feet into the ground. I leaned forward to see better and noticed the iron ladder inside. I let one foot down and jumped down as I held on to the ladder. First the stranger, then the king followed me in. We began walking in the direction the boy pointed.

"What exactly is this place?" It was the king who asked. He was curious as he examined the torchlit tunnel.

The curly-haired boy raised his hand and began counting his fingers with each word. "The starving, the tax avoiders, people hiding from the kingdom, the elderly, people who want to live free . . . this is a shelter for all of us."

We could hear a buzzing sound as the light at the end of the tunnel became brighter. They had dug a big oval area in the earth. There were crooked wooden tables placed in the dusky area that was illuminated by a few torches. I examined the crowd that had gathered around the tables. It wasn't too big but it wasn't tiny, either. Other tunnels continued under the ground.

"Thomas!"

The red-haired boy suddenly turned. An old man was coming over to us. There was an angry expression in his brown eyes that were shadowed by his thick gray eyebrows. He raised his big hand when he came over and grabbed the boy by the nape.

"You idiot! You brought strangers here? What did I tell you about keeping this place secret?"

Despite the man's voice, the boy, Thomas, grinned and freed himself from the old man's grip. He pointed at us and said, "A half-naked guy covered with bandages and a girl in rags! I had to help them!"

The king straightened his back and covered his bare chest with the cape Thomas had given him. I was sure that the king of the Seven Realms had never heard someone talking about him like this.

The man brought his hand to his face and stroked his beard. Then he fixed his thoughtful eyes on us. "Come with me," he said and nodded. "I guess I could arrange something for you."

We walked into one of the tunnels on the other side of the clearing but Thomas stayed behind. Now it was just the three of us. The old man spoke. "Forget about him. He's a good boy but I can't say he's too bright. He's usually just a drag."

The man pushed in the latched metal door at the end of the tunnel and moved to the side so we could pass. I saw that there was nothing in the small room other than a wooden desk and chairs. It was too plain inside.

I sat on one of the chairs and the king sat next to me. I looked at the old man and asked, "Where are we?"

He put two glasses next to the water jug on the table. Then he sat in the chair across from us. He crossed his arms and leaned back. "In the shelter. It's a gathering place for the people who run from the pressure of the king, from his oppression and taxes, and who want a free life."

King Warren next to me only grimaced. My confusion was evident on my face. "But why?"

The old man's brown eyes slowly turned from Warren to me.

"There are those who say the previous king was very fair. I never saw him, of course. He lived years before I was born." He shook his head as he went on, "All the people in the capital are sorcerers. They age slowly because of something like dark magic, but people like us can't understand that."

I knew that magic was still a mystery for the people. You would go to the capital when you were chosen a Phoenix or a Protector, and you were expected to leave your previous life behind. This was enough to keep the people of the Seven Realms clueless. We were living separated from them. We were all magical beings with the powers given by the Goddess herself. We belonged to different worlds.

"His son took the throne when the previous king died. Just as you said, he's cold and strict. People say he has a heart of stone . . . He increased the taxes as soon as he took the throne. Guards were sent to all corners of the Seven Realms. The doors of the palace were shut for the people as they died of starvation. All the medicines and the cures for illness were kept in the palace to keep just the nobles alive . . . for the last hundred years, people have suffered enough. We are just a group who want justice."

I pointed at the door. "So, where do the supplies for all these people come from?"

The old man scratched his chin. "There's a lot of stuff that goes between or from the Seven Realms to the palace and the nobles in the capital. The people here are brave heroes who are ready to do anything in the name of goodness. I'm sure the kingdom doesn't even notice a few stolen boxes."

I remembered the crowd that had gathered in the village square on the day I had visited my mother. The people were revolting; that was what my mother had said. I wondered if any of those people were here. They could look harmless for the moment but there were many people who would want to take advantage of the situation if they found out that the Protector of their realm was announced a fugitive. People would use the chaos to create a distraction. They were just waiting for an opportunity.

I examined the old man. Another reason that was causing the people to panic was the missing people and the Old Ones attacking the villages, but he said nothing about that. Maybe he was just trying to be cautious about people whom he had just met. Or maybe he just hadn't heard anything yet.

The king's gaze was fixed on the other side of the wooden table and I could see he had made a fist in his lap. He was angry. I had already seen the expression on his face when he was compared to his murdered father. I put my hand over his, trying to support him. I didn't even know what I was thinking while doing so. Warren's hand relaxed as he looked back at me.

"So, what were you two lovebirds doing here?"

I quickly withdrew my hand and leaned back on my chair. I could feel my cheeks warming up. I didn't have to turn and look to see that the king was similar.

"No. We . . . I mean . . ."

"Did you run away from the chaos in the capital?"

I paused. He went on, "There was an attack during the execution of Aerlion's Protector. There were creatures just like the ones that had come on the day of her ceremony. She managed to escape in the confusion . . . word spreads fast."

Then he pointed at us, "You probably don't want to travel again before everything settles down. It's best to lay low for a while. Everyone's doing the same. I sent a few people to Orin last week, you know. We're not safe here either. The guards will probably search all over the place because this is her realm. I don't what she did, but I can say she really is in big trouble."

I heard King Warren's voice as he took my hand in his and raised it for the man to see. "Yes, it is just as you said. We were afraid of the cruel king's rage. The capital is not safe anymore."

My eyes grew wide when he held me, and I tried to free my hand without struggling too much. The king insisted on holding it for a while longer but then he loosened his grip and we moved away from each other. The old man didn't seem to notice any of this.

"Well, you don't have to be afraid anymore. My sources tell me that the king has gone to Demos. Everyone is talking about a feast. Ironic, isn't it? I mean the nobles, having fun while we starve?"

The king stopped swinging his leg nervously as he had been doing ever since we sat. There was a surprised expression on his face and he didn't even try to hide it.

The old man stretched and stood up as he held his belly. "People could create problems if I remain out of sight for too long. We need extra attention for the care of the elderly and the children. The more people to help, the better!"

He walked to the door, opened the latch, and turned to us. There was a sincere expression on his face this time. "You rest now. You can stay here for as long as you want. Our door is open to anyone in need."

Then he walked out. We heard his footsteps until he was far away. The king turned to me as soon as he left.

"Something's not right."

I turned to him. "Like what?"

"I never left the capital after I took the throne, for security reasons. After the uprising, the council members banned the royal family from leaving Ardria."

I fixed my eyes on the floor. "But Audamar is leaving." Then I suddenly looked at him. "Do you remember the colors of the crystals he had?"

He nodded. "Yellow, purple, and blue. Aerlion, Carran, and Odeir. He had Sam's and Ramona's crystals."

"But he doesn't have Darrell's."

The king and I jumped up at the same time and headed for the door. This was all the rest we were going to have; we needed to go.

We passed through the crowded area and turned into the tunnel from which we had entered, trying not to attract anyone's attention. We walked along and reached the metal ladder. But suddenly a shadow from the dark jumped in front of us and blocked our path. It was Thomas.

192

He looked at King Warren and said, "You're not from Aerlion. You sound different and you don't look like us."

It was common for people from Aerlion to have fair skin with either ginger or blond hair. With the king's sun-kissed skin, it was hard not to notice.

"I'm from the capital," the king defended himself, leaving me in the focus of the boy's eyes.

"Funny," he said. "I was in Ardria a month ago and I am pretty sure I saw you there, on the platform. Though you looked much different then."

He was talking about the ceremony. He pierced me with his green eyes as I tried to calculate the distance between us and the ladder. We couldn't lose any more time, even if that meant we had to get rid of him.

"What do you want?" I asked, but he ignored my question.

"Let me guess. Aerlion's *fugitive* Protector and the council member of Montborne."

I didn't know what to say as I stared at him. No matter what the old man had said, Thomas was cleverer than he thought. My eyes found King Warren. He was very close in his guess and he had already realized who I was. His guess on Warren had to be based on the fact that the *king* never left the capital; Audamar was still there. Besides, the boy hadn't seen the king on the platform through all the guards. But he could see Lord Theon, and Warren and his cousin looked pretty much alike.

"It's okay, I can help you," he said and shrugged. He then turned to the king. "Do I need to bow in front of a royal family member? Whatever . . . don't expect me to do such a thing."

I was confused. "We can't trust you. I'm a fugitive; how do I know this isn't a trap?"

Thomas shrugged again. "I'm not interested in the royal family or their politics. I don't care if you're a fugitive. Besides, if anyone asks, I'll tell them I'm loyal to my Protector. You are supposed to be our leader." He paused. "Or something like that."

When we didn't look convinced, he went on, "In addition, I know where the stolen goods come in and out of the realms, and the secret gates around the woods. I can get you anywhere without being seen. I know people everywhere."

"Don't expect us to believe that you are doing us a favor." The king took a step forward and crossed his arms. "What do you want in return?"

Thomas brought his hand to his collar and turned a thick necklace around so we could see. Its chain looked heavy, and at the tip, two pendants were swinging. One of them was a black, round stone and the other one was a golden medallion with a symbol engraved on it.

"I'm looking for someone important to me. I have some unanswered questions but no one knows where he is. I'm sure there isn't any information people in the capital can't get. I want you to help me."

Warren first looked at the engraving on the medallion and then at the boy's face. Thomas hadn't noticed it, but I could see the uneasiness in the king's face. What I didn't know was the reason.

We were both aware of the fact that we needed him, and the thing he wanted in return seemed to be a small price at the moment. I nodded and Thomas grinned as he tilted his head.

"So, where are we going?"

# CHAPTER 24

The trees were flowing under us as the sun behind the high mountains of Aerlion shone on Deegan. Thomas was sitting at the far end of the dragon's broad back and was looking around with his baffled eyes. I could hear him occasionally murmur to himself. He looked down to see how high we were, only to hold on and pull himself back up as he breathed with excitement.

"Are you sure we're close to the gate?"

King Warren let go of Deegan's reins—the dragon didn't really need him steering anyway—and looked back at Thomas over his shoulder. "We've been flying for hours and there are no gates here."

Thomas grinned as he looked at us. "I spent years smuggling things to other realms through the gates. Give me a little credit."

King Warren breathed slowly. I could see that he wasn't happy with what he heard. He faced forward again and placed his hands on Deegan's night-black scales. I thought about how he had known Deegan and the other dragons for a long time; he had been with them since he was born. This was the reason why the dragon was obeying the king's orders so easily.

"We're here."

We turned to where Thomas was pointing as he leaned over. A white light was shining in the middle of the woods. King Warren pulled on Deegan's reins just once and the dragon began to descend.

"There's no flat surface for Deegan to land."

Thomas shook his head as he said, "We don't have to stop. We'll directly pass through the gate."

The king and I turned to Thomas at the same time. I pointed at the thick, tall trees. "There's no way Deegan can pass without hitting the trees."

Thomas just smiled in response. He climbed over and sat next to King Warren. Then he took the reins. We moved directly into the gate as the dragon spread its wide wings and slowed down. To my surprise, Deegan obeyed Thomas's orders instead of protesting. The dragon hadn't even reacted, although the boy was a total stranger. I shut my eyes and held tightly.

I slowly opened my eyes with hot air brushing my face. We weren't descending anymore. I looked around and saw the endless desert beneath us. We had already left behind the gate, which was hidden in one of the sand dunes. Thomas turned to look back over his shoulder with a grin. King Warren and I turned to each other.

"Welcome to Demos," Thomas said.

The dragon continued to glide in the sky as I looked down and watched our shadow on the hot sand. The sun was shining at the top, making the parts of my skin which were left exposed under my torn and ragged clothes burn in its heat. The warm wind was lifting the sand. I looked around to see any signs of life but there were none. I remembered Darrell's words. Demos had only one main city and I couldn't wait to see it despite the situation we were in.

Next to me, King Warren seemed to be as impressed as I was. He had said that he hadn't left the capital since he had taken the throne and I could see that he didn't want to miss anything. His dark eyes became fixed on a point ahead. I followed his narrowed eyes and the city came into view behind the dunes.

The first word that came to my mind was *magic*. As we approached the city, I saw that the sand suddenly disappeared. The ground was coated with tall, green grass. Tall trees were rising toward the coast and they circled the city from the outside in an unnatural and magical way. Some walls of the two-story buildings were covered with glass and from the window's fringes to the stairs heading up, all was gold. The trunks of the trees shadowing the streets were covered with gold as well. It was just how Darrell had described. The city was shining with the combination of gold and glass, and it looked nothing like Aerlion.

Wide crystal bridges connected the houses to each and thick ivy wrapped around them. I could see the wide bay and the ships both next to the harbor and sailing in the endless sea. The water flowing from the sea had divided the city into two sides, and two larger crystal bridges connected the coasts. The horizon ahead looked endless.

I noticed the crowds in the narrow streets among the houses. The streets were full of stalls where different kinds of goods were sold. There was a high mountain quite far from the coast, and I could make out the gold-colored steps leading to the mountaintop. And on top of the mountain was a big palace made of the same gold color. Demos's glamorous main gate was shining right in front of the gold temple next to the palace.

To not attract any attention, Thomas landed Deegan before we got too close to the city. I went down as soon as we landed. Thomas came next to me with the cloth bag he had taken from the shelter. I put my hand on Deegan's head.

"Will he be safe here?"

"Deegan has been alive since the first Protectors," said King Warren. "The dragons are more experienced in survival than all of us; don't worry about him."

I drew back. I took one last look at the pitch-black dragon and began walking, but I still felt uneasy. The dragon didn't come after us. Instead, he let himself onto the hot soil and hid behind a dense group of thick trees before closing his eyes.

Thomas looked over his shoulder. "I helped you until here. But this doesn't look like a good plan. If the king is here, isn't it risky for you?"

I shot a glance at King Warren, but then I faced forward and continued to walk as I said, "The others should be here with the king. I need to talk to them."

Thomas just shrugged. "I hope I don't get into big trouble by helping you."

He didn't receive any answer from either of us, despite the implication in his tone. We hadn't told him the truth; we couldn't. The people didn't know why I was running; they had only heard, through the crowd in the capital, that I was guilty. Thomas wasn't a part of any of this and our relationship was built on mutual gain. He had brought us here. What I needed to do was to talk to Darrell, and make him warn the others. This way, we could defeat Audamar together and put an end to everything. In return, we would help Thomas find the person he was looking for.

"What about you?" Thomas said as he turned back once again to look at the king. "Why are you with her? Isn't the king your family—why did you betray him?"

I saw King Warren tighten his chin as his features strained. We had continued our roles based on Thomas's assumptions. He thought the king was a council member: Lord Theon. Only the nobles and the palace folk had seen King Warren's face, so Thomas couldn't know.

"I don't approve of the king's decisions. Protector Anna was *right*."

He looked at me toward the end of his sentence. The anger in his eyes told me enough.

Thomas pursed his lips and turned back to me. "He looks really angry right now."

I grinned involuntarily at the oddity of the situation. The king stubbornly turned to Thomas and said, "I am not angry," but his gritted teeth said otherwise.

We reached the city after walking for a while. Both sides of the roads were filled with stalls and the sellers' cries echoed all around. We shouldered people in the crowd as we walked through. I saw King Warren steal a silk cloth from one of the stalls and wrap it around his head. He didn't stand out; this was the way that the people of Demos protected themselves from the scorching sun.

We were trying to find our way in the flood of people when Thomas turned to us and said, "Are we going to the palace?"

"Yes."

The merchants we passed by were shouting out. I observed the stalls on both sides. "What are those?" I asked as I pointed at the pots.

"Salt," Thomas said. "The mines are on the other side of the mountain. They are used for trading."

The scent of the salt burned my lungs as I tried to move in the shadows of the red velvet cloths hung over the stalls next to the gold-colored walls. All the merchants had the same goods lined up; mineral gems, crystal accessories, and lots of salt.

Despite how glorious and rich the city was, I took a look at the people around me. They seemed better than the people of Aerlion but still carried the same trace of poverty. I saw people sitting on the floor with their heads down, and little children in their torn clothes looking at passersby. Not all the people of Demos were fortunate, and this was the proof. People in all the Seven Realms were suffering.

Thomas started talking again. "Entering the palace may not be so—"

The king suddenly held both of us on the shoulder and pulled us to the side. I leaned my back on the wall behind me. We were in a narrow street between the stalls and hiding in the shadows of the houses. I turned to look at where the king was pointing and we all drew back at once. The Phoenixes, easily spotted by their blue capes, were everywhere.

"Normally there are only the guards in the city," Thomas said in a whisper. "Apparently, the king is close by."

The buzzing began as soon as he finished his words. I bent over and followed Thomas, hiding behind the stacked crates at the side of one of the main streets. Before long, the guards walking in single file came into view. I held on to one of the crates and got up on my toes to see over the crowd of people lined up on both sides.

I saw the man sitting on the throne placed on the horse-drawn platform. I could hear King Warren exhale roughly as we looked at the person whose face was barely visible behind the tulle curtains that covered the four wooden pillars of the platform. The man sitting there looked exactly like King Warren.

I quickly moved to the front and blocked Thomas's view so that he wouldn't see Audamar's face. The carriage and the guards around it continued along the street without pause. Neither Audamar nor any of the Phoenixes had noticed us. We hurried away while people began talking among themselves with the excitement of seeing the king, who had left his palace for the first time after so many years.

"We have to get inside, now."

But Warren shook his head. I watched him peel off the paper that was hanging on the wall across the street. "This won't be so easy."

"What's that?" I asked as I snatched the paper from his hands. I examined the face of the girl on the paper.

I could hear Thomas laugh behind me, "That's an awful drawing."

I quickly crumpled up the paper and turned it into a ball before throwing it to the other side of the street. I could imagine that my *Wanted* signs were hanging all over Demos's crowded streets. I couldn't show my face. Anyone who had seen them could easily recognize me.

"They haven't put a reward on your head yet," I heard Thomas say, but I didn't turn to look at him. Instead, the king spoke.

"Show us the way."

"Fine," Thomas sighed. "Follow me."

I looked back at the king. He was still standing next to the crates. His dark eyes were once again turned to the point where Audamar and the crowd had disappeared. I moved over to him and put my hand on his shoulder.

He breathed dismally and said, "I'm coming."

We followed Thomas into a back alley. The stalls hadn't spread all the way here and the sounds of the merchants were left far behind. Thomas put his hands in his pockets and said, "Demos is connected through the underground, just like it is with the bridges outside. The tunnels go everywhere; including the palace."

Thomas pushed the broken glass door of one of the abandoned houses in the back streets of the city and walked in. We followed. He pushed aside the furniture in front of the wall in the small room of the ruined house. Then he pulled the piece of wood placed there to cover the wall. When the furniture in front of it was out of the way, I saw the big void in the wall and heard the buzzing from the inside. Thomas knew exactly where one of the tunnel entrances was. This meant that he could be more useful than we had thought.

The breeze coming through the tunnel raised the dust inside the house. I covered my face with my hands and we both followed Thomas down the stairs which were leading to the tunnels under the house.

"In the past, all the houses used to be connected under the ground, but now nobody goes down anymore due to security reasons."

The underground tunnels smelled of dampness. I could feel the cold through my bones, and no light could reach the tunnels. We were walking in puddles of dirty water. King Warren's voice echoed while I stepped in one of them and got wet.

"So, this is how you smuggle things. I can't believe you haven't been caught. The royal guards are quite meticulous."

Thomas grinned in a way that made the king narrow his eyes. "There are hundreds of tunnels here; it's almost impossible to get caught by them. Besides, I don't think the people of the kingdom would care even if they did catch us."

"Why?" I asked as the king began looking even more annoyed.

Thomas stretched his arms and said, "Hundreds of crates go to the palace every day. They wouldn't even bother for just a few . . . Besides, the guards aren't smart enough to follow our traces. I don't know why the king pays them. Even someone like me could last longer in the city!" Thomas shrugged under the king's steely gaze. "I don't say smuggling is right, but people like us have to find a way to survive."

His steps suddenly stopped and he leaned his back to the wall. He brought his finger to his lips and signaled us to be quiet. Just then, I noticed two guards coming toward us. They were walking under the light of the torch that one of them carried. I held my breath and moved further into the shadows.

"The king's come to Demos," one of them said through his breath. "Now we have to deal with that, as if we didn't have enough to do already! Overtime . . . and the kingdom doesn't even pay us for it!"

"What do you think about the king's sudden visit?" asked the other. He was bulkier. "It must be because of that other Protector. The one from Aerlion. She's run away and they're looking for her everywhere . . ."

He looked around in disgust when the other one remained silent. "Look at this place! I can't believe they sent us here when the Phoenixes are all around doing nothing."

We waited until the light from their torch disappeared. Then Thomas began walking again. We continued in the dark in the opposite direction of the guards and finally stopped in front of a wall. When Thomas touched the stones on the wall in a certain order, a passage opened up on top of us. He stood on his toes to look up and whispered, "No one's here!"

We supported ourselves on the juts in the wall and climbed up. When we lifted the cover at the top, we found ourselves in one of the large halls of the palace. The cover of the tunnel was tied to one of the square-shaped stones of the hall. I caught King Warren's extended hand and pulled myself up. I looked around the hall darkened with fully drawn long curtains. I noticed that the ornaments inside were covered with cloths.

"It's too empty."

"The Protectors mostly stay at the capital," said King Warren. "This palace is just symbolic and for the royal family. Not for the Protectors. It isn't used unless there is a celebration in Demos."

I looked around and said, "The *king* could be anywhere right now."

"We don't have much time." He turned to me. "You'll get caught as soon as someone spots you."

"I need to speak to Darrell first. He'll help me."

Thomas hurried to put the cover back in its place when we heard footsteps behind the big doors. We crouched behind one of the tall pillars so we wouldn't be seen.

"Don't be so sure that Darrell will help."

With the king's words, I turned to him. "He will," I insisted. "He's a nice guy and understanding. Unlike you, he'll listen."

Thomas raised his hand to tell us to be quiet and the big doors opened to the sides almost at the same time. From the sound of footsteps that came in, I realized that two people were walking swiftly toward us. One man was telling the other about how he'd heard something. I turned my gaze at the square stone as the footsteps came closer. The stone cover, which connected the hall and the passage, hadn't been placed properly.

I could feel that King Warren's hand went to the knife that Thomas had given him before we left the shelter. When the man came closer to a point that we could see him clearly, I noticed the long sword hanging from his waist under his blue cape. The king hesitated. The man knelt and opened the cover. He narrowed his eyes as he threw his head back and turned to the other man, whom I thought to be another Phoenix. But before he could turn all the way, his eyes caught a glimpse of us, and our eyes met. He had already drawn his sword when we stood up.

"Run!" shouted King Warren.

We ran along the gold-adorned hallway of Demos's palace, hearing the footsteps coming after us. Even though we outnumbered them, I knew we had no chance against the Phoenixes. The king probably thought the same, as he slowed down when we reached the spiral staircase.

He came over and whispered in a way that Thomas couldn't hear. "If Theon is here, I have to find him."

And I had to find Darrell, too. "Let's meet where we first entered the city!"

They went down while I climbed the stairs. As we had flown over, I had seen where the main gate and temple were. Darrell had to be there.

One of the Phoenixes was right behind me, and the possibility of running into Audamar was making my heart pound like crazy. The crystal of Demos was at risk and only its Protector could help. I had to find Darrell.

I turned left at the wide hallway and felt the hot air when I opened the door across that was lit by the scorching sun, as the curtains weren't drawn here. I could hear the seagulls from the seaside. The wide balcony I stood on overlooked the big city and the harbor where the boats and ships sailed in the shallow water. It was the end of the road. I took a step back on the balcony surrounded by tall and separated pillars.

My eyes widened at the touch of a sharp sword at my nape.

"Don't take another step," said the familiar voice as he pressed the sword deeper into my nape.

"Darrell," I whispered.

I quickly turned around and freed myself from his sword with a sudden movement.

Darrell looked the same. He was wearing silk shirt and fabric trousers. I looked at the black cape on his back and something settled in my chest. Once, I would have felt disgusted at the thought of being one of them, but I would give anything for it now.

"How dare you come here!"

My lips parted but his sword brushed my face before I could answer. I stumbled and evaded the strike as I reached for the dagger on his waist.

"Listen to me! You're in danger." When he swung his sword once more, I withdrew. "We all are! I need your help!"

He gritted his teeth and thrust his sword once again. I bent over and kicked him in the stomach. He held my foot with one hand and twisted it. I rolled down and my back hit the floor. My eyes grew wide with the pain.

"I'm going to hand you over to justice myself, and this time, I am going to make sure you get the punishment you deserve."

I threw myself to the side at the last moment as his sword struck the floor. I crawled away on my hands. "The crystals aren't safe!"

He made a snarling sound in response. I ran to the pillars at the end of the balcony and hid behind one of them. I heard him say, "Of course they aren't! It's your fault."

I remembered his warm attitude when we had first met. Now the young man across from me was someone completely different. My shoulders drooped in disappointment, knowing inwardly that he would never be able to trust me again. The king had been right.

Darrell suddenly appeared before me. I raised the dagger in my hand in an attempt to fend off his attack. But I didn't have my powers any longer and he was much stronger than I was. I came down to my knees when he pushed me down. I tried to kick him again. He stumbled backward but gave no reaction. I knew it hadn't hurt him.

"Listen to me! That isn't King Warren; he's Rogue! He's alive and he has the crystals of three realms! He's much stronger than you think and now he's after Demos's crystal!"

Darrell breathed in rage. But I had seen the expression in his eyes. It was full of doubt and he looked confused. He held the sword tight in his hand but this time, didn't charge.

"You know King Warren better than I do! Didn't you notice anything odd in him? Why would the king come to Demos after all these years?"

His eyes narrowed as I said, "You're a Protector! I know how I felt before my powers were taken. I know you can feel the same thing coming from him. He's not the king!"

All that time when Audamar had visited me in the palace, I was aware of the feeling coming from him. And now, I knew why. I had felt the magic of the other two crystals.

I cursed at my plan to be separated from the king and Thomas. I needed the king for the first time, but he wasn't around.

Darrell swung his sword angrily after I finished but it was weaker than I had expected. He was confused. At hearing footsteps in the hallway, I panicked.

"What about the Old Ones?" I shouted. "They appeared again! That is not a coincidence and you know it!"

There was a gap between the side of the final pillar and the ground. I could use the large rocks jutting out from the earth as steps and get down to the courtyard.

I turned my gaze at Darrell's dark eyes. "Please, Darrell," I said, staring at him. "The crystals aren't safe, and I wouldn't return if they were. I can prove this to you. Just give me one last chance."

Then without waiting for a response, I jumped over the handrails and took shelter under the balcony. I pulled my knees to my stomach to avoid falling. I was holding tightly onto the rock under me and my other hand was holding the dagger firmly.

"Protector Darrell," said someone, out of breath. I realized he was the Phoenix who had been following me before. His footsteps stopped and I understood that he was now standing next to Darrell. "Sir, there were intruders in the big hall at the first floor. Would you like me to ring the bells?"

But he received no reply from Darrell. *He's thinking*, I thought to myself.

"Alert all the guards."

I held my breath as my eyes grew wide. I knew whose voice that was. My pounding heart rang in my ears as the approaching footsteps echoed on the balcony.

"Your Majesty, you should return to your quarters. It's not safe here! They could be anywhere."

I fidgeted in my place, hoping they wouldn't come closer to the pillars and notice me.

"Ring the bells," repeated the voice.

"Yes, your Highness!"

Darrell was still quiet after the Phoenix hurried out of the balcony.

"I hadn't thought she'd have the guts to come here . . . stupid girl." His voice reeked of arrogance. I had never heard King Warren talk this way. "Did you see her, Darrell?"

The Phoenix had no idea who the intruders were, but Audamar knew. I wanted Darrell to notice this detail. I stuck my head through the gap between the balcony handrails and saw that Darrell was still standing where I had left him. He slowly turned his eyes to the false king standing across from him and said, "No, my king. There was no one here."

Audamar's gray eyes, which looked nothing like King Warren's, became smaller as one side of his lips curled upward.

"Bring her to me. I want Protector Anna and her *friend*."

Darrell hadn't understood his words and his eyebrows rose, different from before. But I knew very well who he was talking about. My eyes grew wide with fear. From the beginning, Audamar had known that we were here and that I wasn't acting alone. He knew Warren would come back for the throne.

Audamar turned around and began walking to the door. Darrell placed his sword back on his belt and went after him, but I saw him looking back one last time over his shoulder before he walked out.

I moved from where I was hiding when they left and held on to the rocks beneath. The bells rang out before long. I breathed in panic and began going down the mountain as quickly as I could.

# CHAPTER 25

The bells were still ringing as I lowered my head and blended into the crowd, walking back to where we had agreed to meet. King Warren and Thomas greeted me in one of the back alleys of the city. When I came close enough, the king was the first to move away from the wall he had been leaning on. He left the shadows and his face lit up under the warm sunlight.

"I couldn't find him," he said as he shook his head. "None of the council members were there."

Thomas groaned as his eyes found me. "You didn't have to alert the whole city! Now they know we are here."

"They already knew," I said. "The *king* knows we're here." King Warren's face tensed with my words. "He's known everything all this time; he must have assumed I'd be going after him. We need the help of the others."

King Warren whispered so that Thomas wouldn't hear. "Audamar looks just like me. Do you think they would believe us or the false king, who's been with them all this time? We stand no chance against him."

As we walked over to Thomas, the king spoke again. "And what about Darrell? Will he help?"

I crossed my arms and locked my gaze on the ground. "I don't know . . . My words seemed to cause some doubt in him, but we still can't be sure."

"Are we going to try again?" I turned to Thomas when he spoke.

"We have to," I said but I knew it would be harder this time to get into the palace.

Thomas brought his hand to his hair and separated the curly strands. He rolled his green eyes and said, "I feel like I've made a mistake by agreeing to help! We'll never get out of this place alive because of you two."

The sound of bells had ceased. I could imagine that the Phoenixes would soon come down to the city. "We have to find a place to stay. The guards will start patrolling any time now."

I turned to the king and asked, "What should we do with Deegan?"

"He'll be fine."

I thought of the dragon that was still waiting for us in the desert. I was bothered by the thought of leaving him alone there but the king was right; Deegan didn't need my help.

We began following Thomas to the line of trees on the outer line of the city. The number of gold-colored houses became fewer as we moved away from the city center and the shore. We finally entered one of the abandoned houses and climbed up the broken stairs. Thomas took the cloth bag from his bag and placed it on the floor. I coughed as he pushed away the pieces of stones on the floor.

"We don't have any money and things will get worse if I don't eat something soon!"

With Thomas's grunting, King Warren walked over to the boy. "Didn't you take any money before you left?"

Thomas crossed his arms and eyed the king from head to toe. "I hunt in the woods for food. I told you I was a smuggler. Do I look like I have any money? You can find almost anything in the shelter but money isn't one of them."

He took a step forward and waved his finger at the king. The king raised one eyebrow; I knew Thomas had been trying his patience during the past hours we spent together.

"Your family has money. The king is your cousin. How come . . ."

"We told you we fled from the capital."

I walked over and stepped between them as I pushed them in different directions, "Stop it! Both of you!"

Thomas stumbled but kept himself upright, whereas the king barely moved.

"I guess I'll have to take care of myself," said Thomas.

I turned to him and said, "You can't steal."

I paused then. It was ironic how I was the one saying those words now. Mother used to tell me the same before. Stealing was the only way to survive for me but she never liked it.

I put my hand into my pocket and took out some coins I had found before leaving my house. But I knew this amount wouldn't last long.

"Take this," said King Warren.

He slowly exhaled as his hand went to his pocket. I narrowed my eyes when I saw the thick chain shining in his hand. Thomas's eyes shone as he leaned over to take it from the king, but I quickly stepped in between. I had seen the unsure expression on his face. The king looked at me and I shook my head. I didn't need words to understand how important it was to him.

I heard Thomas exhale loudly. He grabbed the coins from my hand and said, "Fine! But I'm warning you; don't expect a lot with only this much." He walked to the stairs and stopped at the top to look at me over his shoulder. "You don't even know how expensive things are in Demos!"

Then he left. As he was going down the stairs, I could still hear him complain.

The king took a few steps back and put the chain back into his pocket. Then he knelt down and began cleaning the floor. I helped him. When we had cleared an area big enough for the three of us to fit, I went over to the window. I leaned my back against the wall and hung one leg out the opening. The king walked over while brushing his hands to clean the dust off them. He leaned forward and placed his palms on the windowsill. We both started to watch the city.

"Does that chain belong to your family?"

"It was my mother's."

The chain still looked brand new; there wasn't a single scratch on it. He was carrying it in his pocket, rather than wearing it around his neck. That was how he made sure that it was safe, I thought, or that it wasn't seen. I looked at him thoughtfully. Perhaps Warren was a Montborne, but he also carried Ironlash blood. One had to be stupid not to understand how much he valued his family.

I faced forward again and thought of my own. I hadn't been able to see my sister during my last visit. My mother had said it was for Sarah's safety, but I was still uneasy. And now they were both gone. Were they safe? Did Sarah miss home? How could I even be sure that Audamar or someone else would not go after them?

"My father was the village's healer," I said suddenly. I didn't even know why I wanted to tell him this, or if he wanted to listen to it or not. But the expression on his face while talking about his family had reminded me of mine.

"He didn't know how to heal others, but people were sick so he volunteered and learned everything about it."

I leaned my head on the wall and closed my eyes. "I would see another stranger with him every day. He wouldn't just heal the people of our village, but also people coming from all over Aerlion. He would help the poor for free, and the money he took from those in better conditions would never pay for his efforts. But he was happy. I remember how my mother worried, despite his happiness." I sighed. "One day, an old woman came. She was very ill and my father didn't know how to cure her. Her sickness was lethal and contagious."

The king didn't say a word while I spoke. I hadn't even noticed the wetness in my eyes until I paused for a breath. A single teardrop ran down my cheek and I wiped it with the back of my hand. I could feel King Warren's gaze on me as I went on, "The woman died and my father followed her soon afterward. Everyone in the village said that it was a miracle that no one else had been infected. But I wouldn't call that a miracle."

I parted my eyes and wrapped my arms around myself. Despite the heat, I felt cold. "Audamar said he could give me my father back. The only thing he needed for this was the crystals. And I believed him, *trusted* him. I never thought things would turn out this way."

I wasn't crying anymore. I pulled my leg to my chest as the warm breeze came through the window and tickled my skin. I heard the king slowly let out his breath.

"I would have done anything to see my family again. But not even the crystals, with their powerful magic, can bring the dead back."

King Warren leaned his back to the wall as I had done. Our eyes met. "I'm sorry for what happened. But now, whether you like it or not, we are together till the end of this."

I slowly let out the breath I had been holding. King Warren hadn't taken his dark eyes from me even for a second.

"Till the end," I whispered.

Someone cleared his throat loudly behind us. "Um . . . Sorry to interrupt but I could really use some help."

I turned my head to the voice and quickly came down. Thomas was standing before us. My eyes met his, two green eyes wide open with worry, before they shifted to the dagger pressed against his neck. I noticed the silhouette behind him. King Warren drew his knife and moved away from the windowsill.

The person who had pressed the dagger to Thomas's neck moved to the front. The Phoenix let go of Thomas and stood right in front of us. I held my breath when he turned his green eyes to me.

"Hello, Anna."

# CHAPTER 26

"Hunter," I said as my hand curled into fists. I reached for the knife King Warren was holding loosely and brought the sharp metal to my chest, looking carefully at the Phoenix standing before me.

Thomas rubbed his throat as if he was trying to get rid of the feeling of the dagger on his neck. He took a few steps back and alternately looked at both sides. He looked so confused.

"Protector Anna," Hunter said as he eyed me once again. Then he turned to the king next to me and moved his head vaguely as if he was bowing.

"King Warren, your—"

I interrupted him in a hurry. "We saw King Warren. He arrived in Demos today."

Hunter narrowed his eyes, looking confused, as I looked at Thomas. Then I turned to the king and said, "Lord Theon and I were able to enter the palace."

Hunter slowly turned to look at Thomas, who was now standing behind him. He was totally clueless and I was planning to do anything I could to keep it that way.

"I understand."

The king fixed his dark eyes on the Phoenix. "What are you doing here?"

All the eyes were on the king now. I knew he didn't like the Phoenixes because of what had happened to his family, but his shoulders had relaxed now that he saw a familiar face after everything that had happened. Hunter turned his green eyes to us once again.

"I came to help."

King Warren crossed his arms while a voice inside me said that I still had to be cautious with the Phoenix.

"Help?" Thomas's complaining tone interrupted. "You almost killed me!"

"I know what happened," Hunter said without paying any attention to him. "We were following you, the *king*, and everything else."

"We?"

"Balfour and I."

I was startled when I heard the old commander's name. I gave the knife back to King Warren and stepped forward. "Is he all right?"

Hunter nodded. "I took advantage of the chaos and followed you after you escaped. I had to make sure you were okay. I left the arena after the king left and I saw what happened, *everything* . . . and then I went to Balfour."

"Who else knows?" asked the king.

"Just the two of us. We were going to tell the others but the king is keeping a close eye on the council members and the Protectors."

We were on our own again, but we weren't alone. I was relieved to know that two other people were on our side and the burden on my shoulders seemed to lighten for a moment. But we still had a lot more to do.

"Where's Balfour?"

The Phoenix shook his head. "I don't know; we split when we got here. I realized you were in Demos by the sound of the bells. I've been looking around for hours to find you."

Then he crossed his arms. "So, what's the plan?"

"I tried talking to Darrell but it didn't work out. We have to go back to the palace and find someone to help us. But *he* knows we're close."

Hunter exhaled loudly and said, "We can't defeat him on our own."

Thomas took a few steps toward us with his knit eyebrows. He had waited for a moment before asking his question, trying to make sure he had understood correctly. "Are you talking about overthrowing the king?"

We all fell silent. I turned my uneasy gaze to Thomas and saw that King Warren was vaguely shaking his head. His eyes were on Hunter and he made him understand that we wouldn't be talking anymore. I broke the dead silence as Thomas continued to look at the three of us in turns.

"We should sleep." I turned to look at Thomas's empty hands. "We don't have anything to eat and it's already late."

Hunter nodded. He seemed to be relieved by the fact the topic had changed. "I'll take the first watch."

I turned my gaze at him and said, "I don't trust you."

He only shrugged. "I know, but I'm your best option."

I looked away in defeat. We all lay down in the area that we had opened up by pushing away the old stones and wood pieces. I shivered with the coldness of the floor. I could hardly keep myself from trembling, but we couldn't light a fire. I pulled my knees to my chest on the floor and placed my hands under my head to use them as a pillow. King Warren lay down at the other end of the room and turned his back to us. Thomas was immediately asleep. Hunter looked at us one last time.

I turned away from him as he walked over to the windowsill. He sat on the bulge in the wall and set his eyes on the town. No matter how much I wanted to deny it, I felt safe. I could finally sleep in peace after many days. My body relaxed with this thought and I closed my eyes.

•

I opened my eyes in fear only to see it was still dark and night.

I sat up straight and blinked as I looked around. I'd had a nightmare again, the *same* nightmare. I shook my head in an attempt to get rid of the thought of it. I thought how much I missed the medicine Paige and Gavin had prepared for me during my stay at the palace.

My eyes found Hunter then; he was still sitting in front of the windowsill in the same position. I stood up and walked over to the Phoenix, watching my steps under the moonlight as I carefully stepped through the pieces of broken glass.

"Couldn't sleep?" he asked as he finally turned his eyes away from the view of the city and studied me. I nodded and moved to his side, leaning my hip and shoulder to the wall. My eyes found the harbor through the houses.

"He was killed," I said in a dry voice that was no different from a whisper. "I see Protector Breccan in my dreams. I see him . . . getting killed, and he's warning me. Ever since I talked to you after the ball, I am sure of it."

My powers were gone but maybe, just as I was connected to Deegan, I still carried a bond with the past Protectors. I didn't know the reason, but I knew what I was seeing wasn't just dreams. They were warnings.

I crossed my arms. Demos had fallen prisoner to darkness after the sun went down and it was almost freezing out there. I closed my eyes for a brief moment and thought about my nightmare. It was always the same. That old and tired man would fall off the dragon and his cry would be the last thing I would hear before the bright light shone on the valley. He and Deegan were running from something in my nightmare; I was sure of that now. He *was* the previous Protector; I had guessed right all along.

"If Rogue is behind this . . ."

I interrupted him immediately. "I know he is." I brought my hands to my hair and breathed heavily as I roughly pulled at the dirty strands. It had been days since I had bathed and I knew he could smell it. "I'm not like Breccan. I'm not strong, and Audamar has three crystals now."

Hunter tossed his head back and looked at me, thinking. "Stopping him will be more difficult than one would think. We could lose everything."

"I don't have anything to lose. But if we don't stop him, the Seven Realms will have a lot to."

"What about your family?"

I exhaled sharply. "They won't be safe, just like everyone else." I pressed my hands on the windowsill and loosened my shoulders. "This is my fault. I have to fix it. But no matter how much I try not to admit it, I can't do this on my own."

I saw Hunter's lips curve indistinctly as he said, "You're not alone. Nobody said anything about doing this by yourself. I also became a fugitive when I saved you in the arena, remember? Everyone saw it."

"I know," I said as I looked into his green eyes. "And I'm sorry."

Hunter examined my face for a long while. Then he turned around. His green eyes were fixed on King Warren's back, and then he moved on to Thomas. I could hear him snore softly.

"Who's he?"

"An outlaw . . . just like us." The word had not bothered me, contrary to what I would think. I had accepted what I was. I turned my gaze to Hunter, who was still watching Thomas.

"Did you know that there's a group rebelling against the king? Thomas took us to their shelter when we first met him. It was full of people hiding from the king and the capital."

He nodded. "There was a rumor that began almost twenty years ago, but people will always find something to complain about. So the king didn't take it as a threat. But recently, I started to hear more about them than before . . . If they find out what happened, that the king's throne could be challenged by anyone, an uprising could start once more. You should be careful to whom you reveal the truth."

He turned to look at Thomas again. "Does he know *everything*?"

I shook my head. "I thought I would have to tell him about the crystals if I told him about the king. The crystals are still a myth for the people. They would do many things for their power if they realize that they aren't just a rumor. I couldn't risk that."

The Phoenix's gaze slowly shifted to the king on the floor. "And what about him?"

He was lying still, too motionless for someone asleep, and for a moment, I thought he was awake, listening to us. But we had been running without any rest; he was tired.

"It's my fault that he lost everything. Even if Audamar would have gotten hold of the crystals somehow, I sped up the process. But I don't know what *he* is thinking. I can't say I've learned a lot even though we've been together for three days."

"He trusts you."

I exhaled softly. "I'm not sure about that."

I thought about what had happened when I woke up in Aerlion after we fled from the palace. I had seen the rage in his eyes. I was the target of his fury. But that had disappeared lately. He was now completely focused on one purpose; he wanted his throne back.

"I've known the king for a long time. He wouldn't have stayed with you if he didn't trust you."

"He stayed with me," I whispered as I stood up and took my eyes off the king's broad shoulders, "because he needs me. Just like I need him."

Hunter didn't reply. My thoughts went back to the dream again. I remembered how Breccan couldn't hold on and fell from Deegan's back . . . Deegan . . .

My eyes opened wide. How had I forgotten about him? "Deegan is still in the desert."

Hunter just shrugged. "Believe me, that old dragon has gotten out of much more difficult situations than you would imagine. It takes a lot to kill a dragon."

*To kill . . .* that word raised an unpleasant feeling. Hunter was probably right, but I couldn't get rid of the worry that gnawed at me.

I leaned my back against the cold wall and turned my head to the Phoenix. Just then, something whizzed through the space between us and stuck to the dusty pieces of wood in front of the wall. I felt its warmth before I saw it. My eyes grew wide and I took a few steps back. I looked at the arrow stuck in the wood; it was aflame.

"Get up!"

King Warren jumped up from where he was lying while Thomas woke up slowly and blinked. He was rubbing his face as if trying to understand where the sudden heat was coming from. His eyes caught a glimpse of the flames that now covered the old wooden pieces we had swept aside. He jumped up in fear. Hunter caught Thomas's arm in a not-so-gentle manner and dragged him down the stairs. King Warren and I jumped down the last few stairs and landed on the first floor. Then we dashed into the back alley.

I heard Hunter's voice from the front. "They've surrounded the house. Go the other way!"

My chest was tightening with each step and my breathing was unsteady. My legs began to ache. I brought my hand to my chest and tried to catch my breath, but there was no time for this. I could hear the guards coming after us. King Warren, who had been a step behind, ran past me and grabbed my wrist so I could keep up with him. He was almost carrying all my weight, but he didn't slow down.

The sun hadn't risen yet and the people of Demos were still asleep. We moved through the empty stalls and King Warren knocked over one of the tables on the side. He picked it up with difficulty and swung it at the group following us. But there were more approaching from the top of the street we were running along.

"Hunter!"

The Phoenix heard me and we dove into another alley before the group caught up. All the houses we passed began to light up one by one with our cries. When the earth under our feet came to an end, our steps began making thumping sounds on the glass floor. We passed over one of the wide bridges that joined the two sides of the city and reached an opening. I looked around to see where we were. The harbor was behind us. And there was nowhere to go. We were trapped.

The guards that had been following formed a half-moon around us. Their swords were drawn and they seemed ready to attack at any moment. The king's hand on my wrist loosened and he checked his waist, but we had left the weapons at the house together with the cloth bag as we had left in such a rush.

"Any ideas?" I heard Thomas murmur, but none of us were in a condition to answer.

The guards took another step toward us and, at the same time, the surface beneath us began to shake. And with that, a dark cloud of fog surrounded us. We couldn't see anything anymore.

I could hear the voices of the guards. I tried to reach out to find King Warren, Hunter, or Thomas, but we were left in the dark. A hand suddenly grabbed my arm and began dragging me in the opposite direction of the guards. I cried out in fear and tried to free myself, but it didn't work. I stumbled when the surface under my feet changed. We began going down the stairs that had just appeared before us. We were going into the tunnels. I tried to free myself one more time but the hand on my arm didn't even loosen.

"Calm down. We're here to help."

The girl's tone was calm and soft. I hadn't even heard the footsteps until she spoke. There were many of them.

The fog disappeared when we entered the tunnels, and I saw King Warren running farther ahead. Hunter and Thomas were probably ahead of him. The hand on my wrist disappeared as I picked up speed. I turned to the girl who had helped me.

As soon as I saw her, I knew she was from Protector Thalia's realm, Orin. She had small, hooded eyes and, compared to the Protector, a more tanned complexion. But her features were similar to Thalia's. Her pitch-black silky hair was short. She seemed to be around my age. She smiled vaguely when our eyes met.

The group in front of me slowed down. A tall, hulky man with dark skin stepped to the front and rhythmically knocked on the stone walls of the tunnel. The wall opened up like a door with his command and everyone began to swarm inside. I followed them. The door closed behind us when we all got in. I looked around the secret room illuminated with many torches. It was quite crowded inside. As I examined the group wearing brown leather clothes, the people sitting on stacked crates stood up. I looked at the crates and sacks pushed to the side and thought that these musts be smuggled goods Thomas had talked about.

As if trying to confirm my assumptions, Thomas stepped forward and walked to the man at the front of the group. They laughed and embraced each other. "Caiden!"

I heard Thomas speak between his laughter. "It's so great to see you!"

Thomas moved away from the hulky man in the front, Caiden, and walked over to the black-haired girl who had taken me out of the fog. I had guessed right. We were in the smugglers' den in Demos.

Hunter began walking toward me and I moved over to King Warren's side. I didn't know the reason, but I didn't want him to face the crowd alone. I realized he was nervous when his back straightened up. He shot a short glance at me before turning his eyes to the crowd.

Thomas was still laughing. "How did you know I was in Demos?"

The girl stood next to him and ran her hand through Thomas's curly red hair. Even though there wasn't much age difference between them, she acted as if she was older.

"I noticed your hair from miles away. You couldn't have thought that you didn't stand out in the crowd."

Caiden, who appeared to be the leader of the group, came to the front and I turned slowly in his direction. He had dark eyes. His face was wide and he had a long torso. His black hair was cut short. His dark skin showed he was from here, from Demos. The brown leather clothes, which all of them wore, seemed to be too tight for his well-built body.

"You disappear for months and then bring us the most wanted person in the capital."

Although Caiden was talking to Thomas, his eyes had remained on me. Then he turned to Hunter and examined his cape. "A Phoenix who helps the fugitive and turns his back on the kingdom." And finally, his eyes rested on King Warren. Caiden knew who he was; he didn't need to say anything for me to understand that.

He breathed loudly as a grin appeared on his face, "And the mighty king of the Seven Realms."

Thomas turned to us, looking very confused, just as everyone else.

"What I don't understand is that the king is at the palace, here in Demos . . . My men watching him told me that he never left the palace."

Caiden slowly eyed the king. "A king who turned his back on his people, an exiled Protector, and a Phoenix who's switched sides." He grinned as if this was funny. "I could imagine that the other noble families would pay us handsomely if we turn them in."

"You can't do that," I said as I took a step forward. Caiden quickly turned his eyes to me and I went on, "You're just like us. *Fugitives.* You'd be putting yourself in danger. The capital won't have mercy on either of us."

I crossed my arms and tried to stand tall. I saw the effect my words had on the crowd. Murmurs rose. Even though I wasn't good with improvisation, it seemed as if I had attracted the attention of the others.

I continued. "The smugglers help those who rebel against the kingdom, isn't that right?"

I remembered the people in Aerlion and what my mother had said. They weren't alone. The smugglers helped many of the realms, and there was a reason why Thomas was in that shelter. They had spread all over the Seven Realms. Thomas could see them as a simple group of thieves that dispensed justice, or maybe he just didn't trust us enough to tell the truth. In either case, the group we were looking at was much more than that. People wanted an actual rebellion.

Caiden's lips curved and he narrowed his eyes. "The smugglers *are* the rebellion."

I could feel King Warren holding his breath. The three of us, at one time at least, had defended the capital and the authority of the kingdom. But we were vulnerable against these people and we were outnumbered.

"All the Seven Realms have heard that you've run from justice, Protector. But the real question is why they want you dead."

I knew Hunter and King Warren were looking at me, just as everyone else in the room. I was aware of the fact that I was about to do something really stupid. But it wouldn't be the first time. I continued to speak without a second thought.

"I gave the crystal of my realm to someone else."

Hunter exhaled in shock and Warren leaned to my ear. "What are you doing?" he asked through gritted teeth.

I ignored him. "And now the Master of Darkness has returned. The First King, Rogue Audamar Montborne, is still alive."

A mocking expression passed through Caiden's face, but I could see the curious glow in his eyes. "Are you talking about the bedtime story people tell the kids in the capital?"

"It's not a story, it's the truth. And the king your men are watching is none other than Rogue."

The black-haired girl stepped forward with her eyes fixed on me. "The First King lived thousands of years ago. How could he be alive?"

My lips parted for the answer but Hunter spoke first. "He is using the magic of the crystals he has, and he's after the rest. He took the king's place with their powers and he woke up the Old Ones once again."

The whispering within the crowd grew louder and someone else stepped forward. "The news of the creatures' attacks has spread all over the Seven Realms. They could be right, Caiden."

Someone else said, "Those things had gone extinct long ago, but now . . ."

"He didn't just simply wake them," I said while looking at Caiden. "Those missing people are being turned into Old Ones by the magic of the crystals. He's killed innocents."

Caiden turned his gaze back on us as he scratched his chin. "And exactly what do you expect us to do?"

"We need your help . . . you want to bring down the king, and so do we. We have a common enemy."

I was aware of the fact that their real problem was with the king standing next to me, but Audamar was a much bigger threat and I needed all the help I could find if we were to take him down.

Caiden's indecisive gaze told me that he was immersed in thought. I went on as he looked at the three of us in turn. "Rogue is a threat for all the Seven Realms. The dark magic is spreading because of him."

Caiden's sharp gaze suddenly turned to me. "How could *you* help us? The kingdom is already after you. I also know what happened before you fled the capital. *Everyone* knows. You don't have your powers anymore."

My shoulders drooped. Reality had hit me in the face harder than I thought. My powers had not always been a part of me, but losing them had caused wounds deeper than I would have expected. I felt useless without my magic. I raised my hands and looked at my palms, "I can't help," I said. "Not like this."

I needed someone, I thought. It had been Lord Cyril who brought me to the capital after the Selection Ceremony and who took my powers with the king's order. He could give them back just the same. I needed his help.

"You are smugglers because you think the system is not right. You try to protect the people. But if Rogue gets hold of the rest of the crystals, there'll be no one left to protect."

I could see the group behind Caiden nodding and looking at each other. The whispering ceased when Caiden took a step forward. "And then what?"

Even though I knew that my next words would make me nervous, I knew I had no other chance. My voice became coarse as I said, "We'll destroy the crystals." But I didn't really know how to do that.

Hunter turned to me but I didn't look back at him. If it was so dangerous to use the crystals, perhaps the Goddess's gifts should never have existed in the first place. "Rogue is not like the Protectors. If we destroy them, *all* of them, he'll lose his powers."

Caiden seemed to be considering my offer as he tilted his head. "I have a condition," he finally said.

He then turned to King Warren on my left. "You'll abdicate."

King Warren, who had remained still without joining in the conversation, flinched visibly. "What?"

"You heard me."

They both began staring at each other. There was nothing King Warren wouldn't do to get his throne back, and the only thing I was sure of was that he would never give up. That was what he had said to me once; that his throne represented the royal family and his ancestors. The throne meant *everything* to him.

Anyone could sit on the throne without a crown on his head, but it didn't matter how bright a person's crown was if he didn't have a throne. This included Warren.

When Caiden saw Warren's hesitation, he crossed his arms and took a step toward us. "Your people are in great danger and the only thing you care about is your throne. You don't deserve them."

His words were sharp enough to startle Warren. A shadow of feelings passed from his face but disappeared before I could even figure them out. After a heartbeat, I heard his voice.

"Deal."

Everyone in the room, including Hunter, was baffled by the king's answer, but I didn't react. Caiden was also looking at him carefully. He slowly extended his hand to the king as I fixed my gaze on Warren. His face was as blank as paper, but I thought I knew him enough to know what he was thinking.

The king would never give up his throne, even if he had to die for it.

King Warren stepped forward. They held each other's wrists and everyone's mood changed with the forming of the new alliance. The group of smugglers began making plans with determination as I continued to stare at King Warren's back.

Contrary to everyone else's opinion, I didn't think that this alliance would last long.

# CHAPTER 27

The smugglers' shelter was full of different types of weapons that were unknown to me. I didn't have the slightest idea of how they had gotten hold of all this, but my surprise grew bigger when I thought that most of the people in the capital didn't know anything about what was going on in the other realms. Caiden seemed to be the leader of the smugglers, or at least he was for the ones in Demos, and they were successful in building such connections.

I placed the sharp sword into its scabbard that was lying next to me. I then fixed it onto the leather belt that had been given to me.

We were still hiding at the shelter where they had brought us after the chaos at the city's harbor. The underground shelter was illuminated by torches, which had been placed on the walls in a regular order, and it was silent inside. I was waiting with King Warren at the end of the rectangular room, far from the other smugglers. No one had said anything when I began to go through the chests that were lined up on the side.

I hadn't even noticed how dirty my clothes had been until I took them off. A part of me wished that they would burn those. The leather clothes that the king, Hunter, Thomas, and I were given were the same as the ones worn by the smugglers. When I first saw the clothes that were too thick to be worn in Demos in the daylight, I realized that the smugglers' connections were not limited to here. I was right. They were spread over all the realms, and Caiden had already told us that they were connected to the rebellion.

After changing his clothes, the king had taken the chain from his pocket and wore it around his neck. He wasn't trying to hide his identity anymore; he looked less tense. My eyes caught a glimpse of the chain that had been left to him by his mother, and I saw the symbol of the Ironlash family engraved in the metal.

I looked back over my shoulder. Thomas's emerald-green eyes were fixed on where we were and as soon as our eyes met, he walked over. His face was red under the light of the many bright torches.

When he approached, I felt crushed under the feeling of guilt and I said, "I'm sorry for lying to you," before he could begin to talk. "But you would have asked questions if you knew who we were. And the crystals . . ."

*I couldn't reveal the truth about the crystals.* But now they all knew about them, and I knew that soon, word would spread all over the Seven Realms.

Thomas tilted his head. "I understand, really. It's okay."

He sat on the wooden chest right next to me and extended his legs forward. "What you did was very brave," he said as he crossed his arms. "Even if I found myself in the middle of it without knowing what I was getting into."

He looked at me and winked with a broad smile on his face. "But I liked you. So, I can forgive you two, even if I'm not so sure about the grumpy king."

King Warren exhaled with a sigh and fixed his dark eyes on him. Thomas made a face as if he was offended. "Would you have thrown me in the dungeons for this if we were at the palace?"

The king rolled his eyes. "Why are you here?"

Thomas only shrugged. "It looks like we're going to be together for a while. That's why I'm not angry with you. I came to say I'll give you a second chance."

The expression on the king's face turned mocking and he shot a short glance at me. It seemed as if he wasn't exactly sure whether Thomas was serious or not.

Thomas held the chain around his neck and waved it at us. "I brought you to Demos. I'm expecting you to hold your end of the deal."

He turned his green gaze at King Warren. "Since you're the king, you *can* help me. You're the most powerful person in the Seven Realms." He turned the medallion to us so we could see better. "I'm looking for the owner of this medallion. You've seen the engravings on it; I've been told that such a job could only be done in the capital."

Then he rubbed his index finger over it. "This is the royal family's symbol and I think it belongs to someone from your family. Noble families don't carry the symbol of another noble house."

225

My eyes grew wide and I quickly turned to King Warren, who answered without a blink. "If you are trying to say that you have some kind of connection to me . . ." he paused, took his eyes off the medallion, and fixed them on Thomas's green eyes, ". . . you're wrong."

I tried to look for a similarity between them. They had different hair color and eyes. The king was taller, and their features were completely different. If Thomas thought he was from the royal family, he had to be quite distantly related to King Warren.

Warren looked at the necklace again. "Where did you even get that?"

Thomas shrugged. "It was left to me."

I thought Warren wouldn't settle for this answer but Thomas tucked the medallion back under his collar when we saw Caiden walking over. The leader of the smugglers stopped in front of us and crossed his arms. Hunter appeared behind him. I hadn't seen him since he left us hours ago to discuss the new plan with Caiden.

"We won't be using the tunnels this time," Caiden said as he eyed the three of us. "The guards saw us going underground and they're holding every exit. They'll be waiting for us."

From his pocket, he took out a piece of paper he had folded. I leaned over to look and saw that it was a map that showed the palace, the gate, and the nearby temple.

"You shouldn't have that," said Warren with an annoyed tone. "Those maps are given to the guards only."

"And they show the patrolling points," added Caiden. He didn't look bothered. Caiden's fingers traced the map. "The main entrance," he said as if he had just had a brilliant idea. "My men will get in first and open the gates for you. That's where we'll enter."

Perhaps King Warren had never taken part in an actual battle or he hadn't ever left the capital after his family's death, but he wasn't happy with that plan.

"The main gates are adjacent to the ramparts that surround the entire palace. The walls are high and protected by armed guards."

Caiden seemed to be expecting this comment; his smile broadened with the king's objection. "That's why my men will go in first. They don't expect a direct attack. Also, don't forget a lot of them are looking for you in the city. The palace is less guarded than ever."

He picked the map from the ground and stood up. "The only thing you need to do is to find your cousin, if he's there of course, or the other council members." He turned to me then. "And you need to find the Protector of Demos."

I had noticed the insinuation in his tone. *Leave the planning to me.*

Warren furrowed his brow, but Caiden turned around and disappeared among the smugglers before he could protest.

"This should make you happy," I heard him say angrily.

I turned to him. "What?"

"People like him planning a rebellion and taking control of the realms. Wasn't this what you wanted?"

I could feel Thomas's gaze on us, watching the tension increase, but he was silent. Probably scared to feel the king's rage on him.

"When I gave the crystal away, I thought Rogue could actually help. We all suffer more than you think. So yes, I *am* happy to see them finally do something," I quickly added when King Warren shook his head angrily. "It looks like we are going to spend more time with *your* people, Your Highness. Maybe soon, you will realize how desperate we all are."

I got up and without knowing where I was headed, I went after Caiden where he had disappeared. As soon as I turned the corner, I faced the smuggler's leader. I took a step back as I looked at him. He stared at me with an unreadable expression, arms folded. There was an awkward silence between us.

Caiden suddenly said, "You don't belong there."

"Excuse me?"

"You don't belong to the palace."

I stiffened. "I am a Protector."

"But you know damn well what hunger means for people like us. You saw it all the time in your village."

I didn't say anything. I could guess why he started smuggling. That was the same reason why he was a part of the rebellion. They were sick of stealing and we all knew something had to change. What they were doing wasn't enough.

"What do you even know about my village?"

"More than you can imagine . . . I used to visit Aerlion a lot."

I shrugged. "So?"

There was something on his face that said he wasn't telling me the whole story. But Caiden just took a step back. "You may work with the king for now, but he doesn't understand you. You want change, to help people. This is why we all are here. Once this is over, you'll be welcome to join the smugglers."

He extended his arm to show his soldiers gathered inside the room. "You belong here with people like us."

A part of me said he wasn't so wrong. The rebellion was working for the people and that was what I wanted in the first place. Nobles had no idea how we lived and the king was one of them. But I had no reason to trust anyone, including Caiden and his soldiers.

"I thought you made an agreement with the king," I said without blinking.

Caiden's lips became a thin line. "Yes . . . for now."

"And what about after?"

He shook his head. "He is a noble, a king coming from the royal bloodline. Everything you see was made by his ancestors. It didn't start with him, and it won't end with him, either. You know that, right?"

I stared at him but the leader of the smugglers didn't say anything, only stayed still. I closed my eyes for a second and shook my head. Caiden slowly nodded. He glanced at me over his shoulder one more time before leaving.

The rebellion was everything I stood for. But this meant turning my back on King Warren, which I found very difficult lately. We had been together for only a couple of days and we definitely weren't friends. But a part of me still had hope for him.

I wanted to believe we could work things out, and the idea of betraying him was more disturbing than I thought. But despite everything, a voice inside me was telling me that the king was already waiting for that.

# CHAPTER 28

I stuck my head out from behind the house in which we were hiding from the patrols, and tried to remain hidden while I watched the high gates protected by more armed guards. We had waited until the sun was setting and gone back to the city as Caiden had planned. I went over the plan in my head once again as I drew back and looked at the others waiting for me. I was amazed by the number of people Caiden could gather in less than two days. He had divided us into groups of ten, and I was the leader of the group in front of me.

I had to find Darrell again, and while doing so, the smugglers in my group would be there to distract any guard or Phoenix that would try to get close to me. Another group was going to break into the palace and make way for us. The distraction they would create should be enough for me or the king to continue without getting caught.

We heard a whistle.

I saw shadows approaching the palace's tall walls and suddenly disappearing in the darkness. Thomas, who was hiding with the other group on the other side of the street, moved. He was quick. As I watched him approach the gates, steps as fast as a flash, I thought I had underestimated him before. He really looked like one of Caiden's smugglers. He was so sure of himself.

The high walls began at both sides of the main entrance, and they surrounded the palace and the hill that had Demos's gate. Guards were on watch in the stone balconies that were located regularly on the ramparts. And two of the guards were in front of the gates, on the ground. Thomas's group went directly to them.

The guards drew their swords but they were too slow. The smugglers attacked at once. I watch Thomas take both of them down by himself and while doing so, I was amazed at how quietly they acted.

The other guards were pushed down from the ramparts one by one. My eyes grew wide when I noticed the girl in brown leather clothes. Layla, the smuggler girl who had saved me the other day, had now taken the place of the guard that was thrown down. The first stage of the plan was done, but she was too late.

One of the guards had been able to run away. I watch him light a torch and signal the rest of the guards on the other balconies. When the coal-colored metal pit caught fire from his torch, all the other balconies began to light up, and before long, the entire rampart was shining in flames. That was when we heard the bells. I saw Layla's group behind the iron gates. They pulled onto the chains behind the bars and lifted the heavy gates for us to walk in.

I hurried in. The three groups met immediately inside. Layla had already come down from the tower before we could get in. She looked at me.

"Go," she said. "We'll take care of the rest."

I didn't wait for her to tell me twice before I started to run.

I looked around only to see the guards running at us from two different directions. The smugglers started coming after me and they charged at the guards before they could start following me.

I shot a quick glance at Layla for the last time. I heard the clashing sound of swords coming behind me as soon as I left but I didn't slow down. I rushed toward the stairs. I could hear footsteps coming after me; there were still a lot of them. I looked over my shoulder only to see the blue-caped group—the Phoenixes. There were four of them.

I turned to the path among thick trees when I reached the courtyard, with the thought of going around, and someone suddenly pulled me by the arm. I found myself on the ground before I knew what was going on. The Phoenixes ran past me and didn't notice me lying behind the bushes. I turned my eyes and saw the person standing up from where he lay. His black eyes were looking into mine.

"Darrell," I said as I stared at him. I crawled backward on my hands with fear but Demos's Protector raised his hands in surrender. As I hesitated, he signaled me to be quiet.

"I want to help," I heard him whisper back. "You were right from the beginning, Anna."

"How do I know this is not a trap?" I asked as I shook my head.

Darrell took a step toward me but I was quick enough to withdraw.

"He's not King Warren," he said as he also withdrew. "Something's off. He acts differently. I get this vibe from him . . . a feeling. I don't know how to explain but I'm the only one that can feel this, the Phoenixes didn't notice anything."

"And what about the council members?" I asked. Warren was somewhere in the palace, trying to find his cousin or Lord Raymond or Lord Cyril.

Darrell shook his head. "After your intrusion, the king sent them back to Ardria."

I slowly let out a breath. We had wasted time trying to find them and now they were gone. Audamar was being careful.

"Something is wrong and you know what. That is why you warned me. You know exactly what I am talking about."

"The crystals?" I said without tearing my gaze away. I wanted him to see the expression on my face, how serious and desperate I was for his help.

Demos's Protector nodded. "It's a strong but dark magic."

"He is using them to create this. The dark magic, the Old Ones. Everything is happening because of him."

"And there is more."

I narrowed my eyes at his words.

"For the past few days, all he does is to go to the gate. He started spending a lot of time in the library doing some research from ancient sources. Servants have been carrying thousands-of-years-old books to his chambers. He is always around, looking for something. No one seems to notice him disappear, but some things aren't right. I've known King Warren for years. The feeling I had around him is different since the attack at the palace."

I felt the panic in every part of my body. "Darrell. We have to find Demos's crystal, *now*."

But all he did was shake his head. "No one has seen the crystal since the first Protector of Demos hid it away. King Warren . . . no, whoever that is . . . how could he find it?"

I didn't answer him. "Where is he right now?"

"He's at the temple again," Darrell said as he pointed at the mountain rising behind the palace. The main gate of Demos was illuminating the dark sky. And behind it was Darrell's temple covered with gold-colored stones. "He went there hours ago and put guards at the door. He said he didn't want *anyone* going in."

"We have to go."

I had a bad feeling and something inside me said that Darrell was feeling it too. We couldn't wait any longer. We dashed out from where we were hiding, and I let him guide me as we ran along the entire yard. The Phoenixes were already gone. We climbed the stairs two at a time, and I noticed the same high walls rising on both sides.

"Stand back," Darrell said and I knelt a few steps back as he approached the guards. They couldn't see me at that angle. The guards drew their swords as soon as they heard the uninvited guest. But they resumed their normal stance when they realized it was Darrell. I held my breath.

One of them called out. "We cannot let you in, Protector Darrell. His Majesty doesn't want anyone inside."

Darrell looked calm; it was difficult to see he was acting. He shrugged convincingly and said, "It was the king who asked me to come. Now, if you'll excuse me, His Majesty is waiting for me."

The guards looked at each other, confused. Their eyebrows were knit as they were undecided on what to do. The guard standing at the back turned to Darrell and I tried to climb up a step to hear the conversation better. Just then, I lost my balance and leaned forward to hold on to the golden steps. A few small stones under my feet fell down. The noise caused them all to turn toward me. When both guards quickly pointed their swords in my direction, Darrell stepped in between. He raised his hands, making a bright light illuminating the stairs, and the guards fell backward. Demos's Protector turned to look at me over his shoulder.

"This will give us enough time."

I scrutinized the guards lying on the floor. "Are they dead?"

Darrell shook his head. "Of course not. They'll wake up in a short while."

Darrell had no difficulty pushing the heavy doors. We left the guards behind on the floor and ran into the temple. I held my breath as we climbed up the wide steps. As we approached, I started to feel the darkness more. The thought of facing Audamar was quite scary even if I had Darrell by my side. I took the dagger from my waist and held it tight in my hand. I knew I could still fight.

The face of the temple was open like the one in Aerlion, and its ceiling was standing on tall pillars. I looked, amazed, at the great one-story building. There were long mirrors inside and I could see our reflection as we walked past them. The yard of the gold-colored temple was full of trees, and the main gate that was farther ahead was blinking with a bright white light.

Darrell nudged me. I followed his gaze and found the person we were looking for. Audamar was standing right in front of the big gate with his back turned to us. He didn't move when we came but I could hear him let out a slow breath.

"I knew you'd come."

Darrell drew his sword. "Step back from the gate. The Master of Darkness, even with the crystals, doesn't stand a chance against Protectors. We are stronger than you, Rogue."

*Master of Darkness* . . . I recalled the conversation with Balfour before the ceremony. I had taken too much time on the page where Audamar's silhouette was drawn in one of the books from King Warren's private collection. I never could have guessed that I would one day actually meet the owner of that name.

Audamar turned to us slowly and smiled as if he enjoyed this name that was given to him by the people. He ignored Darrell's threat. "I see only *one* Protector."

I tried to hold the dagger tighter in my hand. Audamar noticed this and his gaze slowly shifted to me. Although he looked exactly like King Warren, his eyes were different. "You have no chance when I have four crystals."

I took a hesitant step toward him. "You have only three of them."

But something inside me said that we were too late. I heard Darrell's angry voice. "Only Protectors can find the crystals. We are connected to them. That's why you tricked Anna; you need us."

I shivered as the grin on Audamar's face broadened. "Do I?"

As his eyes turned to me, a smile spread over his face. "The fourth crystal is calling me."

Audamar quickly raised his hand and turned his back to us. I was expecting an attack but he ignored us completely and walked to the gate. Was he fleeing? I wanted to take a step forward and get close to him to prevent him from getting away, but then I saw that Audamar wasn't extending his hand into the gate but to the side. Instead of going in, he rested his long hands on the side that resembled a frame, as if the gate was something solid. I saw the surface of it begin to shake; a chiming surrounded the temple. Within seconds, the dark red crystal was shining in his palm.

"The first Protector of Demos must have thought the crystal's magic would blend in with the gates. I must say it wasn't such a clever place to hide it."

Audamar's gray eyes turned to me once again. "I let you go because I knew you wouldn't pose a threat to me. I still think so."

He turned his hand holding the red crystal, and I looked at the others that appeared next to the stone: yellow, purple, and blue. His fingers moved over the crystals and he closed his hand tightly. Before I could blink, my feet left the ground. Darrell and I fell backward at the same time. I cried in pain when my back hit the wall behind me. Then I heard the roars. *The Old Ones* . . . Audamar had called them to Demos.

Before I could stand up, Darrell had already jumped to his feet. He ran over to Audamar but when he raised his hand, Darrell suddenly froze in his place as if he was being held by invisible chains. With a single finger, he swung Darrell's body toward me. I stumbled backward as Demos's Protector raised his hand holding the sword. It shone in the light. I didn't have my powers anymore but my feet were intact. I began running.

"Damn it, I can't feel my body!" Darrell cried in pain but he never let go of the sword. He followed my every move. Audamar, using him, was trying to corner me. I threw myself on the ground and heard Darrell's voice, "Anna! Step aside!"

The sword hit the ground right in front of me. I saw Audamar moving toward the gate as I rolled on the ground. I tried to go after him but Darrell stepped in between and prevented that. At the same time, I heard footsteps from the other side of the courtyard. I quickly turned to look. As soon as King Warren arrived, his dark eyes immediately fixed on the First King.

It had been enough for me to look at him to understand what he was thinking. The king didn't take his sharp gaze away from Audamar even for a second; he was going to go after him. Before even thinking, I began running toward him. I jumped on him to prevent the king from following Audamar into the gate. I wrapped him tightly in my arms and we both fell to the ground. Almost simultaneously, the sword that Darrell had swung stuck onto the ground in front of us. As soon as Audamar disappeared through the gate, Darrell fell to his knees and breathed heavily. He hit his fist hard to the ground; Audamar no longer had control over him.

"What's your problem!" I yelled as I drew back. I was angry but the king was no different. His hands curled into fists and he breathed rapidly.

"Don't you think it's obvious?" he shouted. He had an expression on his face that made me want to slap him. "We should have gone after him. You let him get away!"

I turned my gaze to the king's angry face. "We had no chance against him! He had the crystals, *four* of them! He has Demos's crystal now!" Warren turned to the gate and I held him by the collar to make him look at me. "We couldn't stop him! Not like this! He's too strong for you to defeat on your own."

The king shook his head. He seemed calmer although he was still breathing heavily.

"He went back to Ardria," I said as I pointed at the gate behind us that led directly to the Demos's main gate at the royal palace. "The guards have probably sent a warning to the capital; they can be here any minute, and they will come from here. If you went after him, they could easily get you."

"I am their king," he protested back.

"But they don't know that," I said. "If you went after him, they would believe Rogue, not you."

Rogue was able to change his appearance completely. No one would believe Warren was actually the real king, and before he could explain himself, Audamar would make sure that he couldn't talk. He let go of us because he was powerful and we didn't pose a threat, but he also wouldn't let us ruin what he had been planning over the centuries.

Warren turned his gaze away as I continued softly. "I'm not letting you get yourself killed. *Never.* Do you hear me?"

With my words, Warren stopped trying to get rid of my touch and turned back to me. He looked at me then, actually looked. There was a puzzled expression on his face and he looked like he had just woken up from a deep sleep, very confused. We stared at each other for a while. Then, he lowered his dark eyes, his gaze finding my hands, which were still on his chest trying to hold him by his collar. I realized the small gap between our bodies. I quickly let him go and got up. From the corner of my eye, I could see Darrell on the other side of the yard. But he didn't even turn to us.

I extended my hand to him. After alternating his gaze between the gate and me, the king wrapped his big hand around mine and he stood up. I heard Darrell walk over with slow steps. I turned to the gate again.

No matter how much I didn't want to admit it, Rogue had become stronger than he ever was, and now he was becoming invincible.

# CHAPTER 29

The big wooden ship was swaying to both sides with the huge waves hitting as the smell of the sea burned my lungs. Next to me, Thomas was covering his mouth and making heaving sounds while the harsh air of Demos penetrated through the cape I wore. A grin formed on my face.

"You didn't look this miserable on Deegan," I said to him.

Thomas spoke through his gritted teeth. "Even your giant lizard goes smoother than this ship . . . It's definitely not the same thing!"

He covered his face with his hands and I stretched where I sat, ignoring him. After our unsuccessful attempt at stopping Audamar, Caiden had told us that we needed more support. The council members weren't there and we couldn't risk going back to Ardria. That was why we were going to Belwald, to find people that could help.

I noticed Darrell leaning his back on the handrails on the deck. He had fixed his thoughtful eyes on his hands, which he had clasped on his lap, and he looked very tense.

When Audamar had used the crystals to call the Old Ones to the city, the temple filled with royal guards and Phoenixes. We had to flee. Darrell was the one who helped us to escape from the palace, and with that, the news of his betrayal had spread. Everyone was talking about it, that he had become one of us—a *traitor*.

I pulled my knees to my chest and slowly let out my breath. We had to lay low after everything that had happened. That was why we had left Deegan and Qimra, Darrell's dragon, behind. The moment when Deegan spread his wide wings and disappeared in the sky passed before my eyes, I sighed. I was afraid that Audamar would find them but Darrell had just shrugged when I told him this.

When their riders weren't with them, the dragons went to mountains or caves where no one could reach, and they fell into a deep sleep until the bond with their Protector awakened them. No one else could trace their magic, even Rogue, so they'd be safe and far away, he had said. I knew he was worried too but that had given me some relief.

When the ship swayed with another wave, King Warren, who was sitting on my other side, took support from the deck wall. I raised my head and looked in the direction we were headed. I could see the bright gate rising above the water. Two tall bridges were connected to the gate at the end of the bay. We would have to get through the guards watching the bridge before being able to get to the realm waiting for us on the other side.

"Everyone down."

With Caiden's voice, we walked down the stairs as the ship approached the gate. I knelt down. When seen from the outside, our ship looked no different from a trading ship going to Belwald. But it actually carried plenty of fugitives, two traitor Protectors, and a dethroned king.

The ship stopped as two guards took a step on the deck and I heard the wooden floor above me creak with their heavy steps. I reached out to the dagger on my belt, just in case. But it didn't go as I thought. I heard the guards say a few words and then leave the ship at once. We started moving soon after. I released the breath I was holding and started climbing the steps without waiting for the others. The bright light coming from the gate grew bigger as we approached. As we left the guards patrolling on the bridge behind, the ship passed through the bright gate and left Demos. We were now in Belwald. With the snowflakes coming from the sky, I lifted my cold hands to my mouth. I could see the vapor coming from it.

King Warren came over with long steps. "Do you think this could be a trap?" he whispered as he leaned in to my ear so Caiden and his soldiers wouldn't hear.

I murmured, still watching the sea stretching before our eyes, "He wouldn't have helped us if it was a trap. They've been taking risks for us since the beginning."

Caiden had saved us from the guards and helped us get into Demos's palace. He was keeping his end of the bargain. I was hoping that our new alliance would last longer than the king anticipated.

"The more the risk, the greater the reward."

"You need to stop this." I turned to him. "If it wasn't for him, we would still be in Demos, hiding."

But the king shook his head. "I've been living for a long time and my experiences tell me the exact opposite. People will do anything for their gain." He turned his eyes to Caiden's group and grimaced. "Especially people like them."

Sometimes, I forgot how long he had been alive. *A hundred and twenty-seven years*, I thought. It was still so strange to me.

"Not everyone is the same," I said to him.

In response, he turned his gaze back at me. I drew back a couple of steps and put some distance between us. His gaze trailed over my face.

"I haven't seen any exceptions so far."

It was hard to ignore his tone. I knew he was talking about me. After all, I had told him why I had trusted Audamar so easily and why I had given him the crystal. It had been for my own benefit. But I didn't care what he thought of me. Until Rogue was defeated, we were together.

At the bay right across from the gate, there was a big harbor. But instead of approaching the dock, Caiden commanded the ship to turn toward the valley surrounded by a thick forest and snow-capped mountains. Before long, the harbor and the big village around it had been left far behind.

I moved over to Caiden and asked, "Where are we going now?" as I surveyed the shore with its high pine trees. I couldn't see anywhere where we could stop.

"I have an old friend who could help us. He was once a smuggler like me; we would work together then. We need him and his soldiers."

With Caiden's order, one of his men changed our course. Before long, I saw five people waiting for us on a smaller dock, built in a narrow bay covered with tall trees. It was hidden and there weren't any houses to be seen on the hills behind. As we approached, the ship shook and came to the dock. After his soldiers gripped the ropes thrown toward them and tied them to the small wooden port next to us, some of them started climbing up.

Caiden pointed at the forest with his index finger. There was someone else in the thick woods, walking slowly toward us. I narrowed my eyes and let out a breath full of relief.

"Balfour!" I cried out in excitement. I smiled as my eyes grew wide upon seeing my old mentor. I had never thought I could be so happy to see a familiar face.

I let one leg off the deck with the help of Caiden's men and I held on to the rope tightly, without worrying that the skin on my hands would peel, and I came down from the ship like the others. Balfour's smile grew as I approached him. I gave Aerlion's commander a big hug, not caring what he would think about it. Balfour's hands remained in the air for a while in bewilderment. Hunter and Darrell came over and watched us with big eyes and I could feel the king's gaze upon us, too. But finally, the old commander put his hands on my shoulders.

"It's good to see you, Anna."

"What are you doing here?" I asked as I drew back. His smile grew even bigger and he turned to Hunter. "Two days ago, I found out you were coming here and decided to meet you."

Then his eyes slowly found King Warren. Balfour greeted him with a head gesture. "Welcome to Belwald, Your Highness."

Darrell took a step forward and said, "He has four crystals," as if he felt the need to give an explanation for the topic that had brought all of us here. But Balfour already knew.

"And unfortunately, it will be much more difficult to stop the Master of Darkness."

"That's why we're here." Caiden had appeared behind us and crossed his arms with his eyes fixed on the commander. "In the name of the Seven Realms that shall be freed, my men will help. We will hold our end of the deal," he said while looking intensely at King Warren.

Balfour only nodded. "We'd better hurry then."

The group of smugglers began carrying the last stolen goods from the ship to land. Caiden was still insistent on doing some trading while we were in Belwald. I didn't wait for them and followed my old mentor. Caiden moved past us; he was showing the way.

"Where are we going?" Darrell asked as he lowered the hood of his long cape. There was no need to hide our faces here. I did the same.

"To Vincent. He's an old friend of mine. I've worked with him for years while trying to build this system in the realms."

I realized he was talking about the smuggling and all the illegal stuff being moved around. King Warren sighed and looked away; of course, he wasn't happy to hear this.

Caiden led the way to a terrain that became rockier as we went. The people following were probably having a hard time carrying the loads from the ship, but they never held us back nor were they ever far behind. When the stones under our feet gave way to big rocks, we stopped at a clearing. I leaned down and tried to catch my breath. When I bent over and opened my eyes, I saw that I was at the edge of a snowy cliff. I drew back in fear.

"Where are we?"

Caiden surveyed the deep cliff that had divided the land into two and began walking along the side. He looked so calm that he seemed unaware of the fact that he could fall down with a single wrong step. He pointed at the other side with his head and I noticed the long bridge up ahead, connecting the two sides of the cliff.

"Vincent's house is on the other side. We have to pass from here."

Thomas, who was climbing up breathlessly, seemed to have noticed the cliff only now, since he had been following at the back. He opened his eyes wide and looked at the old bridge. "You've got to be kidding me! We'll all find ourselves at the bottom as soon as we set foot there."

Hunter walked over calmly and touched the bridge's ropes. The ropes shook under his touch. He then stepped on the wooden surface and took a few steps away from the edge. "Well, I'm still here," he said as he looked back at Thomas over his shoulder. Then he continued to walk without waiting for us.

Darrell passed by as he tugged at his clothes, bringing the fabric close to his face. "I really can't believe this is how you lived for the past couple of days," he said. He let go of the fabric as if he was disgusted with its smell.

I smiled gently. Darrell had been trained to become a Phoenix since his childhood, and he had continued the duty after the death of the previous Protector of Demos many years ago. So he had always been in wealth, always been taken care of. It would take longer than I thought for him to adapt to this situation.

We crossed the narrow bridge in turns. I looked at the soldiers carrying the stuff from the ship, but they all managed to get across without any problems. The dense trees became sparse after a while but nothing else changed in the scenery. Just when I was sure that Caiden had brought us on the wrong path, we suddenly stopped. My eyes found the wooden hut in the woods. Caiden began walking in that direction and I realized we were at the right place. The smugglers' leader reached the big door and knocked. But no one answered.

Layla, who was at the front with Caiden, looked in through one of the windows and said, "There's no one here."

"Caiden?"

A heavyset man, who had messy and wavy golden hair that came down to his shoulders, and whose neck was unseen under his beard, was walking over to us with a log on his shoulder, seemingly unbothered by its weight. The other logs were being dragged along inside a net. A heartfelt smile formed on his face when he saw us, and he threw down the log before walking over. They were both smiling when the two old friends embraced each other.

"It's been years," Caiden said as he tried to see how much his friend had changed. "Retirement hasn't done you good."

Vincent's hand went to his bulging belly. I could imagine he once looked exactly like Caiden did, but there wasn't much left of that image now. He was at least ten years older than Caiden, but he still looked agile, even though he was probably at the end of his forties.

"I live a peaceful life here. And that was exactly what I needed after all that chaos."

Vincent then turned to the group that was watching them. He looked at Caiden's smugglers and then took turns looking at Hunter, Darrell, King Warren, and then me. His dark brown eyes took more time on me, and he knit his brows when our eyes met. Vincent suddenly turned away, but I could see there was something bothering him.

"I never would have thought that you'd come here after all these years to talk business." He looked more bored than offended. "It's been years since I've quit."

"I need your help, Vincent. The situation is more urgent than you think." Caiden looked at us and went on. "I know you can still reach out to your contacts when you want to, and believe me, we need them all."

Caiden then turned his eyes from the group to the hut.

"Perhaps we should talk inside."

Vincent began walking toward the hut and Caiden followed. Hunter, Darrell, and King Warren went after Caiden, but I stayed back.

Thomas and the others began settling down and I thought we would be spending the night here. I plunged into the thick forest. I walked among the dense pine trees and inhaled Belwald's fresh but ice-cold air. I sat down on the rocks at the edge of the cliff we had just passed, the wide valley under my feet.

Every realm had its own time and seasons, so it was weird to arrive in Belwald after leaving the heat of Demos. At the same time, I was amazed by the magic that ruled the Seven Realms.

When I turned my head, I saw Balfour among the pine trees. The old commander walked over and sat on one of the rocks next to me. He looked around the valley, and I knew he was thinking of how peaceful it was.

"It's been a long time, hasn't it?" He closed his eyes. "You have changed since the time you first arrived at the palace. It feels like it's been years. You grew up to be an actual Protector."

I smiled at the familiarity of the conversation. "I made a mistake and I have to pay for it."

Balfour examined me for quite some time. "When your enemy is cunning enough, he'll always find your weak spot. It was just a matter of time."

I wasn't sure if these words were meant to relieve me. I stared at him. "So why me?"

It was always better to blame someone else. But Audamar had chosen me, among all those people. Why was that?

"You were the newest. You didn't know anything and you learned slower than the others."

I opened my mouth to speak but he stopped me and went on, "But finally, you learned. You proved yourself and your courage to all of us. That was what Audamar hadn't taken into account."

"Yet my courage didn't change anything."

He opened his arms and stretched, reminding me of the times we practiced at the palace yard. It seemed like years ago. "It could. The fact that nothing has happened yet, doesn't mean it won't happen in the future."

I turned to the valley again. "I miss my old life . . . I don't even know where my mother and my sister are, and all can do is hope that they are safe."

He asked, "But?"

"But what?"

His face wrinkled when he smiled. "There is something that you've chosen not to say and to keep to yourself."

I held my hair over one shoulder. "*But* . . . this was inevitable. Audamar would have found a way, whether I had been chosen or not. He already had two crystals before me. So, no matter how much I miss my old, simple life, I'd rather be here than be an ordinary person who would just bear witness to all this. I sometimes feel that I could be useful."

The smile on his face grew wider. "Now you speak like a true Protector."

I looked at him. "This was exactly what you wanted to hear, wasn't it?"

He just shrugged like a child and crossed his arms. "Hunter and King Warren seem to have accepted you," he said, and changed the subject. "You need to remain together against your enemies. A king and a Phoenix could be your best allies in times of need."

I exhaled. "They had no other choice. Unintentionally or not, I started this and I have to end it. But everyone wants to be involved somehow and wants to put an end to it. We are all responsible now."

Balfour lowered his head. "Hunter saw Breccan as his father. He was very young when his family noticed that he had magic. They received money when Hunter was given to the kingdom to be raised as a Phoenix. This is the same for all the families. So, his family gave him to the kingdom without a second thought and he never saw them again."

"That's awful," I said as I shook my head. "Who would do that?"

"Everyone, if they don't have enough means to take care of an extra person in their family. They knew that he'd be safe among the Phoenixes and that he'd be well taken care of. Besides, he would have a future in the capital, something that they never could have provided him. It was hard; they gave up their child for his own future. But the money they gave ran out quickly and it didn't take long for the starvation in Aerlion to take them away. The same goes for all the Phoenixes."

I lowered my gaze. "So didn't he see them before they died?"

Balfour shook his head. "Just as everyone else at the capital who have been blessed by the Goddess with power and long life, the Phoenixes are expected to devote their whole life to their realms. He couldn't see them during his training; they died before he completed it and became a Phoenix."

The vague faces of my mother and sister appeared before my eyes, and I let out a breath full of longing. I, too, had been forbidden to leave the palace before the ceremony.

Balfour went on, "Breccan was his tutor, his mentor, and family. He was for most of them, but Hunter had a harder time accepting his death."

I remembered Hunter's hate-filled gaze. He hadn't liked me since day one, but now what happened had brought us together. Still, it was difficult to understand what he was thinking.

"What about King Warren?" I asked.

"King Warren . . ." Balfour sat up straight and went on. "He's just scared after what happened to his family. The previous king and queen were killed right before his eyes. His own people betrayed the royal family . . . King Warren used to be quite a joyful person before that; spoiled even. There wasn't a single thing he couldn't have as the only heir to the throne. And after that, he became obsessed with maintaining order and continuing his family's heritage. He's afraid to let his ancestors down. But deep inside, he's still an inexperienced prince, just as he was before he suddenly took the throne."

My eyes wandered along the high valley, dimly lit by the sun behind the dark clouds. Snowflakes were still falling. "I don't know if I can gain their trust," I said and pressed my heels on the rock under me as I pulled my knees in to myself. "But I'll try."

He looked at me. "I'm proud of you, Anna," Balfour said. "You've improved a lot. You may not have your powers anymore but don't forget that you didn't always have them in the first place. It's not the magic that defines you. You are what you are and that's the only thing you need to be."

I smiled and watched Balfour as he brought his hand to his neck. He took off the long silver chain he was wearing under his clothes and showed it to me. "This is a tradition for Aerlion's Protectors. Each generation passes it to the next one."

I took the chain from his hand. Oddly, I likened the craftsmanship of the chain to the one Thomas carried around his neck. The symbol at the end of the chain was almost identical to that one, and the same pitch-black stone hung at the tip of the chain.

"It belonged to Protector Breccan for years. I've worn it long enough, but I think it's time for it to return to its true owner."

I put the chain around my neck, still smiling. "Thank you," I said as I touched the pendant.

"We'd better go back."

Balfour got up and began walking slowly back to the hut, and I went after him. We followed our tracks on the path we had used a short while ago and returned to Vincent's house. I saw the crowd waiting there.

"What's going on?" I asked as I approached Layla at the back of the group of smugglers. She turned her dark eyes to me and said, "Vincent will provide as many soldiers and weapons as we need. We sent a few people to reach out to his contacts. They should be back tonight and we'll set off at dawn."

I heaved a sigh of relief and looked around the group that had begun talking about the preparations. Hunter, King Warren, and Darrell were talking to Caiden. When I turned to Vincent, who was standing alone behind them in front of the small hut, our eyes met and I noticed he had already been watching me. Even though his face was blank, he had a look in his eyes . . . something that I couldn't describe.

I held my breath and tried to get rid of the bad thoughts. I couldn't let anything ruin the moment. We had no other option; we had to win, and I was going to do everything I could to make sure of that.

# CHAPTER 30

It had been hours since the moon had risen in the dark sky and cast its fair light on the giant trees. I could hear owls hooting somewhere in the darkness, but other than that, there was dead silence.

I stopped turning over and got up. I walked over to the small crowd gathered around the fire. King Warren was leaning on one of the big rocks around the flames and the seat next to him was vacant. I knew Caiden's soldiers were avoiding him, but I didn't care.

"Couldn't sleep?" he asked when I sat next to him.

The flames illuminated his face and I could see the bags under his eyes. Despite Warren's distinguishing features, which cried out the fact that he was noble-born, he looked more tired each day. I shook my head and reached toward the fire to warm my hands. The leather clothes, which I had thought were too much for Demos, turned out to be too light for Belwald.

The king noticed it and he started to untie his cape to place it over my shoulders. I moved away.

"What are you doing?" I asked.

He raised an eyebrow. "Just trying to be polite."

"You'll be cold," I said as I pressed the cape back onto his chest.

"I'll be fine," he said and put the cape back onto my shoulders while I continued to protest.

Hunter, who was sitting at the other side of the fire with a few smugglers, suddenly turned to me. Our eyes met.

I held on to the cape and moved closer to the fire. "I'm sorry for yelling at you in Demos," I said slowly.

King Warren laughed at what I said. "I did the same, didn't I?" He tucked his fingers under his armpits and leaned forward, causing me to feel guilty for taking his cape.

"I thought you'd jump into the gate after him."

"That was my plan. If you hadn't stopped me, of course."

I smiled as I sniffled with the cold. "I'm not sorry for stopping you."

"Neither am I for listening." His smile faded away. "I don't even know what would have happened to me if I'd gone after him."

We were both whispering, just as the group around the sizzling fire was doing. The rest of us, although I couldn't understand how they could, were asleep despite the extreme cold. I pressed my back on the rough surface of the rock behind me.

I went on with a yawn, "You know, when we first met, Audamar told me he was a researcher for the kingdom and that he was your friend until you fired him."

Warren shook his head. "I've only heard the myths about the First King," he said. "Lord Cyril would have warned me if he knew he was back. He would have sensed his dark magic."

I was warmer now. I pulled my hands away from the fire but I wasn't complaining about the presence of the cape over my shoulders.

"I felt the presence of the other two crystals when I first met with Audamar . . . and I guess even I was aware of that dark feeling spreading from him. But I didn't know what it was, so I chose to ignore it."

Warren had listened to me in silence. Then, "If we were at the palace," he said with a tired smile on his face, "that wouldn't have been such a good plea on your part."

I smiled too despite everything we had been through in the throne room. "I guess I would have just made things worse."

He looked at me once more while I tried to cover my face with one hand and yawned.

"What do you see when you look at them?" I asked as I watched the crowd around the fire. "I see hope. Not just for us, but for all the Seven Realms."

"I only see a group of thieves." I looked at him in surprise. He was speaking in a harsh tone while staring at the bright flames. "When there is nothing left for them to steal, they will come for the crown on my head."

Although I wanted to say that his crown and his throne were already stolen by someone else, I held myself back. I knew the king would never give up. He wouldn't stop until he got back what was rightfully his, and I felt like there was no point in talking to him on this matter.

"Maybe Caiden will look good with a crown."

The king immediately turned his gaze to me and breathed a sigh of relief when he saw the expression on my face. My lips curved up.

"Relax," I said mockingly. "I know only two people in the Seven Realms who are obsessed with being a king."

If there was anyone more ambitious than Warren, it was Audamar. I couldn't decide which one of them desired it more.

"I didn't know people were suffering this much," King Warren suddenly said. I was surprised and quick to turn to him.

"What changed your mind?" I asked and pulled the cape toward my chin.

"People in Demos. Despite everything, I had a chance to take a look around. What I saw there didn't make me happy. There is more going on outside of the palace walls than what I was told."

He looked down at his hands. "After what happened, I suddenly became the king and took the throne. My parents were murdered in front of my eyes and even after the number of royal guards increased, I didn't feel safe living in the palace . . . My home became a grave to my family. I was so scared that someone would come after me as well, to finish the rest. The council members agreed to keep me in all the time for my own safety. So, I never left the capital after I sat on the throne. But what I didn't realize was how the palace slowly turned into a cage for me."

Even if everyone suspected Lord Cheng and the house of Barrington, there wasn't any proof that he was after the murder of the royal family. I wondered if Warren also thought the same thing. I knew he didn't like him but he had been forced to see him for years. Yet he was innocent until proven guilty.

"This isn't me . . . my dad adored his people and growing up, I wanted to become just like him. But as I stayed inside the palace, I stopped caring for the people as much as I used to. I paid thee nobles to take care of the problems and believed that everything was settled. I didn't know it was *this* bad."

The king's gaze turned to the bright flames in front of us. The colors were dancing on his skin. His eyes, usually dark as pitch-black night, were now illuminated by the fire and they were the warmest tone of brown. It reminded me of autumn in Aerlion and I couldn't help but remember how peaceful it felt during that season in the village. I turned away while pain spread over my chest. I missed home and my family more than I could ever think.

"You know what," he said slowly. His lips trembled, forming a slight smile on his face. But it didn't even reach his eyes. "I wish we had met before what happened to my parents." He looked at me with sadness in his eyes. "You would have liked me then."

Balfour had told me the king wasn't like this before. His personality completely changed after his parents' sudden death. He had no one to trust, even the ones that were closest to him. As I watched him, I couldn't help but feel sorry. He was alone and scared.

I smiled and this time, it was real. "I like you now," I said without thinking. His gaze suddenly found mine but all I did was shrug as sleep slowly took over me. I rubbed my eyes. "You are not so bad as you think."

"I can't say people would agree."

"Because they don't know you."

He started to play with his hands again. "And you think you do?"

I couldn't answer immediately. "I used to hate the kingdom," I said slowly after taking a deep breath. "For everything that was happening, I blamed you."

He was listening to me carefully. Although his eyes were on the burning flames, I knew his attention was fully on me.

"I only know some basic things about you but . . . I don't hate you anymore. From the outside, it looks like you don't care about others but I know that it is not the case. You want your throne back but the people of the Seven Realms are also one of the reasons. You care for them but if you had asked me this then, I would have told you the opposite."

I exhaled. I could feel the cold burning my lungs with each breath I took. "You are not the ruthless king people want to believe, Warren. You may also believe that, but that is not the truth. And one day, you will prove this to all of us."

His face was unreadable, but something changed in his eyes and his gaze never left mine. We stared at each other, not moving even an inch.

I yawned once again with the weight of sleepiness. With that, he drew back.

"You should sleep. Tomorrow will be a long day."

I looked over my shoulder at where I had been lying before coming by the fire. The last person had to put the fire out. We were in the depths of the wood and it was late for someone from a neighboring village to go out, but we couldn't take any risks. In any case, the group that included Hunter was still awake and their whispers that reached us said that they wouldn't be sleeping yet.

"I know," I murmured as I tried to find a comfortable position by pressing my back further onto the rock, but it was cold and very uncomfortable.

My body relaxed with the heat and my resisting eyes finally gave up. I involuntarily shifted my weight to the king as I felt very drowsy, and my head fell onto his shoulder. I felt the king's body stiffen; he began sitting still as a statue but I couldn't find the strength to move away.

King Warren finally let out his breath and I heard him whisper, "Sleep."

I leaned further onto him and he leaned forward to make sure that my head wouldn't slip down from his shoulder. I could imagine how uncomfortable he was, but still, he didn't move away. I fell into a peaceful sleep after so many days.

# CHAPTER 31

I woke up at dawn. A thick layer of snow was covering the high mountains as mist had fallen down on the valleys, drawing a curtain between everything around. The fire had gone out hours ago and Belwald's freezing cold had found a way to get under my clothes.

While I wrapped the long cloak around my shoulders, my footsteps left traces after me on the ground covered in snow.

The sun was rising over the hills but the rest of the smugglers had some time before they had to wake up with the first light of the day. I passed by Darrell and Hunter, who was still asleep on the other side of the camping area, and my eyes found a few of the smugglers guarding while the rest were sound asleep.

As I followed the tracks before me, I caught a glimpse of the smugglers' leader waiting on the other side. Caiden was watching the high mountains in front of us. I slowly approached him.

"Your men really take guarding seriously," I said to him as I observed the smugglers. They were watching me without moving, fully on guard, when I stopped next to Caiden. They were overly protective.

Caiden only nodded. "You can't expect any of them to fully trust you. *Yet.*"

When he extended his arm and signaled, they all continued walking at once. I was impressed.

"It would be nice to have someone ready to protect you at all costs," I murmured as I thought about my Phoenixes. As their Protector, they had served me— once—but I knew I would never have a relationship with them like Caiden's smugglers. They were like a big family.

"I would trust them with my life."

My eyes turned to the small hut next to the camping site. Caiden followed my gaze. "And do you also trust him?"

"I've known Vincent for years," he said, still looking at the hut. "He is like a brother to me."

Vincent, just like Caiden, was once a part of the smugglers. I had learned enough to understand that there were many groups stealing from the kingdom and helping the poor or selling goods in illegal ways. Although Vincent was older and had left that life a long time ago, he still had the connections we needed.

In a few hours, the smugglers Caiden had sent with Vincent leading would return, and they would bring information on where to find Vincent's contacts. We would start to gather people, one by one.

My eyes found King Warren sleeping as far away as possible from the group. Although we shared a common goal, we wanted different things. King Warren had made a promise but I knew he was only waiting for the right moment. The first thing he would do if we defeated Audamar would be to betray Caiden and his group. But our allies weren't stupid, either. I knew that Caiden could see beyond anything the king would plan for, but whatever ran through their minds, they both chose to wait.

Caiden's dark eyes suddenly turned to me.

"Your parents," he said while tilting his head and scratching his chin. "Were they born in Aerlion as well?"

With his sudden question, I looked at him. "I think so, yes."

"What about your father? Does he travel a lot?"

I tore my gaze away. "What is the point of this?"

"Do you remember anything from your childhood? About them?"

I only shrugged. I wasn't going to talk about my family with him. "Why are you interested in my family?"

Caiden looked away. "I just . . ."

Caiden's dark eyes narrowed. Whatever was on his mind, he suddenly stopped talking. I looked along the valley and my eyes caught a glimpse of the trees at the horizon. It all looked normal for a second. But then I saw the branches shaking on both sides. And I knew it wasn't the breeze that was moving them.

I heard Caiden exhaling with fear as he ran to the hut and opened its wooden door. But when his eyes slowly turned to me and shook his head, I took a step back. The hut was empty, and its owner was gone.

I turned back toward the other side of the dense trees. It wasn't the trees that were moving. Something was coming toward us as it destroyed everything in its way. "Wake up!" I cried as I took another step back in fear and shouted louder. "Get up!"

Some of the smugglers rose with my scream. But it was too late. The creatures jumped out from the shadows one by one. The Old Ones raised their claws and screams could be heard soon after.

The smugglers drew their weapons. Caiden swung his sword at one of the creatures and shouted, "Run!"

Even though his tone was angry, I could distinguish the traces of disappointment in it. I glanced over the small hut. From the ajar wooden door, I could see how empty it was. The hut looked dark and cold, and it looked like it had been left hours ago. The personal items were gone, too. I could only think of one thing. Vincent knew they were coming, but he still decided to leave without saying anything.

I picked up one of the swords and gritted my teeth as I swung it at the Dralein in front of me. This time, I didn't even care that the Old Ones were once human before the dark magic of Audamar. I had learned an important lesson today: never trust a thief.

"Draw back!" shouted Hunter. He was trying to prevent the loss of more soldiers. "Cross to the other side of the bridge!"

One of Caiden's soldiers fell with a blow from the Murgroth he was fighting, and he started rolling down the slope, leaving a trace of blood after him. I made a move to catch him but I was too late. The man's eyes opened wide when his hand slipped, and he let out a cry as he fell down. His voice echoed until his body hit the bottom of the cliff. Caiden cried out in fury and killed the creature in front of him.

"Hurry up!" he shouted, but we just couldn't reach the bridge, there were too many of them. Hunter killed some of the Old Ones and created a gap through which we could reach the bridge. He shouted, "Cross to the other side!"

The screams were echoing in the snow-covered valley. It was dawn, but it wasn't the sun that painted everything red. It was blood. And the creatures were everywhere.

I ran back to the group and turned over my shoulder to look at Balfour behind me. He had drawn his sword as well. At that moment, he looked more like an actual commander rather than a mentor . . . the Commander of Aerlion.

Balfour looked over to me and said, "Get out of here." He sounded tougher but more tired than I had expected.

I quickly shook my head and walked toward him. My hand went to his clothes to hold him and I felt something sticky on my hand. I turned my palm to myself and looked at the blood between my fingers. I breathed with fear. "Balfour, you're hurt!"

I could see the blood running down his groin. He seemed to be wounded by a Dralein's claw. When had that happened? My hands began shaking as I tried to pull him once again toward the bridge, but he didn't even move. I looked at his face and saw that he was smiling.

"It was an honor to serve you, Protector Anna."

I still couldn't understand what was going on. I grabbed his arm tight and pulled him to myself once again but Balfour took his gaze away from me and turned to the Old One in front of him. He began swinging his sword at it.

I felt a tight grip on my arm and before I knew what was happening, Darrell's muscular arms held my waist. He was much stronger than I was. He began dragging me to the bridge while I cried out and tried to get free from his grip. I tried to reach for Balfour but we kept moving farther away from him.

"Stop! Balfour's left behind!"

I began hitting Darrell's arm. Then I scratched my fingernails at his skin but still, he didn't even flinch.

"Stop, Darrell! Please!"

We were the last to cross the bridge. The Old Ones began running after us but Balfour stepped in front of them and cut the bridge's ropes with his sword. The gap in between was too much for them to reach across. As I watched him, I understood what he was doing.

Balfour was stuck with them on the other side. The Old Ones' attention turned to him at once.

Tears ran down my cheeks as I sobbed. I saw everything in a blur but I still couldn't take my eyes away from my old mentor. Balfour was still smiling when he slowly turned around to look at me for the very last time.

There was only one target left for the Old Ones to destroy.

I looked at Balfour until they all surrounded him. He didn't fight back. I let out another cry as a Dralein's claws came down.

Darrell's firm grip became tighter but he didn't slow down even a little bit. From his shaking body, I could tell that he was crying, too.

# CHAPTER 32

The bright flames of the campfire warmed my skin, and the heat was taking me under. There was nothing to be heard other than the crackling of wood burning.

My gaze was fixed on the flames in shades of red. Someone had left a cape that was surely stolen on my shoulders, but I couldn't remember when. My eyes had swollen after hours of crying. They hurt now. I knew that my voice sounded cracked but I wasn't talking at all, anyway. I had no strength for it; I was exhausted.

Caiden was walking back and forth on the other side of the fire. He was breathing rapidly.

"I lost most of my men," he said through gritted teeth. Then he fixed his wide eyes on the fire. "Vincent knew the creatures were coming; the hut was empty. He left us all behind and ran away!"

I remembered the crowd at the camp we had set in front of Vincent's house last night. There were only thirteen left from Caiden's group and almost all of them were injured. Sitting across from him, Layla examined Thomas's wounded arm and wrapped the bandage back on. There was a deep cut on his arm, but he was going to be fine.

"What are we going to do now?" I heard Darrell ask.

I felt his eyes focus on me but I didn't look back. I was sitting a bit behind the others. I didn't want to talk to them or be a part of any plan they would make. Darrell's question hung in the air for a while. Even Hunter, who usually took on such tasks and came up with new plans, was silent. I knew he cared for the old commander, just like he did Breccan. His sad green eyes explained everything.

"If the Old Ones specifically came after us, Rogue probably knows which realm we are in," said Layla, looking at Caiden and Darrell. "They followed our scent to find us."

Then they began discussions. What to do, what our next step should be, how to find Audamar . . . I didn't listen to any of it. I felt a movement next to me, and I saw from the corner of my eye that King Warren had sat beside me. But my gaze remained on the flames.

"I know what's going through your mind," whispered King Warren. The others couldn't hear us anyway since they were engaged in discussion. "You want revenge."

I looked away. I could feel the king's gaze upon me, waiting for me to respond. "Revenge isn't a solution. Believe me, after what happened to my family, I wanted to find those responsible for it and kill them all."

"And in the end, you kicked all the Phoenixes out of the palace," I said. Didn't he get his revenge after all? He killed or imprisoned some of them, anyway. I swallowed with the burning in my throat, and I noticed again how hoarse my voice was.

The king was the first one to get any reaction from me after what happened. He didn't look away even for a moment and said, "Yes, but I couldn't find the actual person responsible for it."

Despite the fact that almost everyone suspected Lord Cheng, there hadn't been enough evidence to accuse the council member. I remembered Paige's words.

"Rogue Audamar Montborne isn't someone you can just kill out of revenge," said the king.

"Thanks for the advice."

I rose and the whispers ceased as the cape fell from my shoulders to the ground. When I moved, the gazes of those around the fire turned to me for the first time after several hours. I left them behind and walked away from the camp toward the forest. But as I walked, the footsteps behind me began to catch up.

"Leave me alone," I said without turning back to look at him.

"No."

"I'll find the crystals before him if I have to, and I'll use their powers," I said as I hissed with rage. "I'll get my revenge! Is that what you wanted to hear? Are you happy now?" I paused and added, "Don't worry. Whatever your plan is, I won't screw it up. Okay? You will get your stupid crown back."

King Warren leaned his back on a tree and fixed his pitch-black eyes on me. "Do you know why the Protectors are the only ones in the Seven Realms to own dragons?"

A story? Did I really look like I was in the mood for some chitchat? I looked away and dug into the earth with my leather boots. My eyes were on the stars that were buried behind the gray clouds.

"There were other dragons, but my father hunted all of them until only seven were left. The Protectors were the symbol of power and of the kingdom, and my father didn't want any figures of authority other than them. He knew that the people would try to rise against him by using the dragons; it had been tried before. The dragons are so powerful that even one could bring a kingdom down. So, he hunted all of them, one by one. I was very young when the eighth remaining dragon was slaughtered. And finally, only seven were left. Seven powerful creatures that only the Protectors could own."

He lowered his gaze and walked over with slow steps. I hadn't looked at him or responded, but I hadn't moved away, either.

"What he did was unacceptable. He slaughtered them all because he wanted to, because he simply could. Many ideas rose from all the Seven Realms. The nobles were not happy with what he had done but he always had the final word. Everyone else had to obey him because my father was the king, the most powerful person in the realms."

He was standing beside me now. I involuntarily turned to him when he took a step and stopped in front of me. King Warren's dark eyes scanned all over me and my lips trembled. I had to stop myself from crying and my hands turned into fists. I felt fragile. The mask on my face could be shattered to pieces by a single touch.

"Rogue is the same. He has the crystals and there is no limit to what he can do. He holds the strings. The fact that he is on a dangerous path means that we can't stand up to him, not like this. We can never beat him on our own, without a plan… He doesn't see us as a threat but when he does, he will never concede to anyone's will but his own."

He let out a sigh and went on, "Because he is the king now. There is no limit to his powers and desires, and he wants everyone to comply."

I gritted my teeth and took a step away. "I'll find a way."

I began walking away with quick steps but King Warren followed me; he wouldn't give up. "That's not what Balfour would have wanted," he said, this time at a higher pitch. "You'll be disrespecting the death of all those people because of your desire for vengeance."

Despite my long and quick steps, King Warren caught up with me. "I know you feel guilty but you can't live with that burden."

"Don't tell me what to do," I said and took a step in the opposite direction.

But Warren came closer, took my arm, and leaned forward. "Balfour's death wasn't your fault."

I pushed his hand away from my arm. I wanted to shout out or cry, maybe both.

"He came to me," I screamed. My hand went to the chain around my neck and I tugged at it to make him see. "He gave me this! It belonged to Breccan and to the Protectors before him. He said he was proud of me! It was as if he was saying goodbye, as if he knew he wasn't going to make it out alive."

I didn't know when I started crying. My legs trembled while the tears blurred my vision. I brought my hands to my face and covered my eyes. King Warren reached over and stood next to me for a while, unsure of what to do. Then he slowly wrapped his arms around me. I exhaled with bewilderment but I didn't draw back, nor did he say anything. I knew I wasn't close with the king, but after the days we had spent together, our relationship had changed. I could at least see sides of him that other people couldn't. And now I just needed someone, and the king was ready to give me whatever I needed.

"I didn't realize it," I said in a shaky voice that wasn't much different from a whisper. I pressed my forehead on King Warren's shoulder. "I could have saved him. I could have stayed with him from the start and prevented everything . . . He may have said goodbye to me but I never had the chance to say it back."

"He was wounded," said King Warren after remaining silent for a while. The words came out of his mouth timidly, as if he was afraid of hurting me. "He drew the attention of the Old Ones on himself and gave us the time to run. You may see Balfour's actions as a simple sacrifice but he died as a hero."

My shoulders were still shaking but I raised my head. The king's grip loosened as he looked at me, and I took this opportunity to draw back. We were still standing close to each other but I no longer felt the king's touch on me.

I remembered my father. He had caught an illness while trying to save someone, and had died soon afterward. That was it. The reason wasn't really important after someone died; all there was left was to learn how to live with that awful feeling. I shut my eyes tightly and pushed those memories back to the furthest corner of my mind. I didn't want to remember any of it.

"Death is just death," I said. "There is nothing heroic about it."

I began walking back to the campsite. I couldn't hear King Warren's footsteps but it didn't really matter. I looked at the group around the fire and noticed two people at the side; they hadn't been there when I left. When the shorter one turned in my direction, I recognized her immediately: Paige. The man next to her talking to Caiden was her father, Gavin. He, too, turned to me.

"What's going on?" I asked as my gaze went between the healer and his daughter.

Caiden was the first to speak. "They're here to help," he said and, in the meantime, Gavin took the ring off his finger and put it in his palm. He then extended the ring toward me. On his ring, there was a shape: a bow against a dagger. People against the kingdom. It was the same symbol the group was carrying the day I had visited my realm.

I heard Hunter's voice. "Are you a part of the rebellion?"

I narrowed my eyes with his words and turned back to Gavin. I knew that the smugglers were rebels, but Gavin and Paige?

"I thought I had provided you everything you needed to live a safe and comfortable life by taking you into the palace."

King Warren approached the group. He looked angry, standing behind me. He came over with thunderous steps and riveted his glare on Gavin. "Is this how you repay me for my kindness?"

Despite his words, Gavin smiled gently. "You held out your hand when there was no one else and you took me in. I can't forget that. But this isn't about you, Your Majesty. It's about the broken system created by your ancestors."

I knew what he was talking about; the starving people, the poor dying of illness, and the nobles turning their back on them . . . These weren't issues only of the time of King Warren, but also of the time when other kings and queens had ruled. The people wanted change.

The king breathed out. "Lately, everyone has a problem with my ancestors and with the royal family." He crossed his arms and turned his head, making an effort not to look in their direction.

It was Caiden who spoke afterward. "What news do you bring from the capital?"

I thought Caiden and Gavin must have a long history. It was obvious that they at least knew each other.

Gavin put the ring back on his finger, "No one knows what happened to the real king, but people are afraid because of the reappearance of the Old Ones and the king is doing nothing about it. People are angry at the king's indifference and the number of people rising against the kingdom has increased. Rogue is after the crystals but there's something he hasn't considered: a rebellion. He doesn't care, but we can use this to our advantage."

I thought about how long Gavin had been in this. Had someone told him, or had he seen the change in the king because it was his job to follow his every move?

I saw Layla turn to Caiden, who nodded and said, "The foundations of the rebellion were planted almost twenty years ago by Vincent, Gavin, myself, and . . ." he paused and I saw him turn his gaze to me. But he quickly resumed his speech. " . . . by a group of people. But we never really took action. Instead, we tried to help the people as smugglers. But the passing years grew the anger in all of us." He turned to Gavin again. "Our numbers have increased. I can reach out to the other leaders of the rebellion again."

There were more. I had already realized that Caiden was a leader but there were more of them than I had thought. *The leaders of the rebellion* . . . a group that could inflame the rebels and bring together angry crowds, like the one I had seen in my village. My gaze shifted to Gavin again. Apparently, the healer had been in this for a long time.

I stepped forward. "King Warren won't be safe among the rebels. It's too dangerous."

I was filled with an instinct to protect him. Deep down, I knew that the king's safety was one of the least considered topics for everyone else. None of them cared about this while we were facing such a great enemy. But I did. King Warren had been the first one to stand by me since I had embarked on this journey, even if he didn't volunteer for this, and I owed him.

I could see that the king was surprised by my words, and I realized that he hadn't been expecting me to defend him. Or anyone to defend him, actually. It took a long time for him to take his eyes from me back to the group.

"Rogue is after the other crystals," Darrell said. "If we can't prevent him from finding them, the rebels won't matter at all." Then he turned to me and went on, "Only three are left. The crystals of Leon, Edmond, and Thalia."

I had been fooled by Audamar and I had given him the crystal of my realm. It had made him stronger, and he had found Demos's crystal, too. But there was something I couldn't understand. How had he found the first two? Or how had no one realized this for such a long time?

"We can do the same thing Rogue does," Hunter said as he slowly turned his thoughtful eyes at us. "We could go after the crystals."

"We can look for them while we're still in Belwald." Warren nodded and glanced at Darrell. "He has your crystals, but your connection with them is stronger than what Rogue could have. And Anna is the first Protector to find her realm's crystal after all the years they had been hidden. This must mean something."

But I wasn't so sure. The connection I had with magic was weaker since I had lost my powers. Maybe Darrell could find it, but I had no trust in myself. Besides, it could be hidden anywhere in the entire realm.

"What do you think, Anna?"

I looked into Darrell's dark eyes when he said my name. They were all sure of themselves, but I no longer had my magic. The fact that I used to be Aerlion's Protector once didn't mean I could be the same again.

I suddenly recalled Balfour's words. He had believed in me. Not in that Protector who didn't have proper control over the powers that she had, but in that girl who had grown stronger with her own will and effort. I wanted to honor his memory. I was who I was, and I hadn't needed the crystals to survive until now.

The last conversation I had with him came to my mind and I felt the pain in my chest once again. He had said that he was proud of me; I wanted to continue making him proud. I nodded determinedly.

"Fine, let's do this," I said. "Let's find the crystals."

# CHAPTER 33

Belwald's cold was freezing me to my bones.

I was walking slowly on the snow-covered streets of the village. The merchants' loud cries echoed along as I looked at the nets full of newly caught fish, lined up on the wooden stalls.

"Belwald is nicer than I remember," murmured King Warren, who was walking by my side.

I watched a smile form on his face. This was the first attempt at conversation after quite a while. King Warren had offered to look around this village, where we had come to spend the night together with Caiden's soldiers, but we had hardly said anything to one another after leaving them.

I turned my eyes to the wooden huts with frosted roofs. All of the torches hanging on the poles spaced out on the side of the street were lit, but they didn't do much good against Belwald's cold weather, other than illuminating the streets. The thick layer of snow lay firmly on the ground. I pulled my cape down and Warren did the same. We were both taking a risk but we needed a break. I hadn't seen any wanted signs with my face on them yet, like the ones in Demos.

The king hadn't left the capital after what had happened to his family, until he was forced to run away with me. This village, located on one of the high slopes of the realm, was quite familiar and equally new to him.

"It's too cold," I whimpered as I held my cape with both hands.

I could see the people wearing woolen coats, in contrast with us, but we were both being very cautious with the money Caiden had given us. We had been warned multiple times to use the money only in case of emergency. We had to leave everything behind while fleeing from Vincent's place, and the remaining money was about to drain.

265

I smiled involuntarily when I saw him rub his trembling hands together to get warm. Warren was the wealthiest person in all the Seven Realms and a Protector was no poorer than any of the nobles. This made our situation even funnier.

"It snows only a few times each year in Aerlion," I murmured as I looked at the town square. "And the snowflakes melt as soon as they touch the ground. My sister always wanted to have a snowball fight but we couldn't try it even once. Despite that, it is always cold in the winter. It is similar to Ardria in that way."

"Maybe your sister would like the capital."

I slowed down, but the king didn't even seem to be aware of what he had just said. Sarah would have loved the capital, but even if I could make it back there, I didn't think that things could ever be the same. There was no place for me there, at least not anymore. Would they arrange my execution when everything was over; would I still be considered a criminal? Would the king remember that I promised him to surrender? Maybe I could join Caiden.

"Maybe," I murmured.

I didn't even know where my family was. I couldn't make plans for the future while I wasn't even sure of their safety. Besides, what did I think would happen? We were preparing for a war, and at this very moment, a happy ending didn't seem like a part of my future.

I followed the couple that passed by and walked hand-in-hand into one of the stores. Life seemed much simpler for the rest of the people in the Seven Realms. Most of them didn't even know what was going on.

"When did you first realize that you were in love with Lady Bria?" I asked curiously.

Warren turned to me, startled. I didn't even remember when we had come to be so open about our personal lives, but I hadn't thought about it before asking the question.

Instead of denying it, he asked, "Why do you want to know?"

I only shrugged. "Don't tell me you're not aware of the gossip in the palace."

He combed his dark hair with his hand and said, "I guess I've known ever since I was little. As a king-to-be, I was told to always follow the rules but Bria would do anything she could to break them. She was too bold and stubborn, and she never changed despite the passing years. She understood me. We were both raised under similar conditions, and talking to her made me feel I was alive. I would remember that I wasn't alone in that big old palace."

He let out a breath then. "But lately . . . I feel like something has changed," he added as he glanced at me.

The smile on his face slowly disappeared as I continued to walk in silence. I saw his face, a pair of dark eyes glowing with excitement. I thought I was jealous; not of Warren's feelings but the expression I saw on his face while talking about her. I knew I would never have someone to talk about me with the same feelings.

"The Lunavier family could help you," I said without looking at him. "Everything would be different if they knew the truth."

The first thought I had when I saw Bria Lunavier at the palace at the king's birthday was how perfect she was. In every way. I knew beauty was temporary but even the smiles she presented to those around her were exactly what was asked of her. Being born into one of the five leading noble families; she had been superior from birth. She was a council member, and she could be the queen of the Seven Realms someday. Despite what Paige had told me, and even despite the small talk we'd had with Bria, I couldn't imagine anyone else sitting next to Warren.

I narrowed my eyes when I felt surrounded by a feeling that was completely unfamiliar to me, and I breathed harshly. No matter how many times I told myself that I didn't care, for some reason I was bothered by knowing how well they matched.

I was so lost in thought that I didn't notice the Phoenix walking over from across the street. King Warren suddenly grabbed my arm and pushed me into one of the side streets. We both hid in the shadows with Warren standing in front of me. I rose on my toes and looked over his shoulder. I noticed the Phoenix's blue cape. He was one of Protector Edmond's soldiers, and he definitely shouldn't know that we were here.

We stood still until the Phoenix walked away. When I faced forward as he disappeared at the end of the street, I found myself within an inch of Warren's face.

"I wouldn't have imagined that my love life would distract you so much," he said with a grin.

His smile disappeared when I continued to stare at him. Our bodies were pressed into each other and I could feel his breath on my face. We kept staring at each other in silence until I pushed him away. He stumbled and roughly drew back.

"Let's go back to the inn," I said, meaning the place we had chosen to spend the night. I began walking without waiting for him. I could hear the sounds that the king made while following me on the snowy road.

Since we were moving with Caiden and his soldiers, we were still quite numerous despite all the smugglers who had died during the attack a few days ago. So, we had split into three groups so as not to draw any more attention. Darrell, Gavin, and Paige had joined the group led by Caiden, while Hunter, Warren, and I had remained with Layla, who was the next senior person in the party after Caiden. The rest were somewhere in the village. I wanted to take action as soon as possible, but Caiden and Layla had insisted that the smugglers had to rest. We needed some time after everything that had happened. But waiting felt more painful than ever while I burned with the desire of avenging Balfour's death.

I sped up when I saw the three-story inn at the end of the road. I pushed the door in, without even waiting for the king. I found Layla and the others chatting in the armchairs on the first floor. My body relaxed immediately with the heat radiating from the fireplace. I couldn't wait to warm my freezing hands. The innkeeper turned to us as soon as we walked in, and Hunter was the first in our group to notice us.

"What did I miss?" I asked as I walked over.

Layla had taken all the space on the sofa. She yawned as she stretched her legs that she had extended onto the wooden table.

"We're going to the castle tomorrow morning," she said. "We made a plan. The Phoenix, the king, and you will be in the group that goes in through the front. The rest will go in the back gates."

I looked around in panic, trying to make sure the other guests at the inn didn't hear us, but she seemed overly relaxed.

"How are we going to get in?" I asked as I crossed my arms. Whatever her plan was, it was probably easier said than done.

"Simple," she said and straightened up a bit while placing her hands behind her head. "Did you know that Rogue was throwing a feast for the nobles in Belwald tomorrow? There's going to be a party at the castle to celebrate his arrival."

I didn't know how we could even get inside the castle while it was so crowded. Perhaps we could take advantage of the commotion, but it also meant that security would be tighter. Protector Edmond could be at the capital with the others to provide security—after all, there were only five Protectors left now—but I knew that our job wouldn't be easy at all.

Hunter leaned forward when he saw the expression on my face. "This could be our only chance, Anna."

I was tired. I rubbed my eyes with my hand, murmuring, "Too risky." Then I turned to him and said, "But I trust you."

Hunter had already proven to us that he could be as good a leader as Caiden was. Besides, he had volunteered to lead. If he was sure it would work, then I would trust him.

After Layla's gaze alternated between Hunter and me, she shot a short glance around the inn and said, "There'll be a lot of carts going to the castle for the feast. Some of the stuff will be taken in during the early hours."

"And what are we bringing to the party?"

Layla's smile broadened. "The gifts. Who would have known that the new king likes to be pampered? Almost all of the lords and ladies in Belwald are sending their gifts to the castle."

Warren looked at her with knit eyebrows. "How did you find the cart?"

"We paid the cartman handsomely. He stopped asking questions the minute he saw the money. He seemed to be happy that someone would be doing his job for him, and frankly, he wasn't interested in the rest of the conversation after that."

It still felt as if we were wasting time. Even though there were just hours before the feast, I was sure that the servants at the castle were in a flurry because of the preparations. We could even get in right now and find out if Belwald's crystal was there or not.

Layla noticed the look on my face. "We all need some rest," she said as she looked at me. "We lost a lot of good men, and it took some time to make a new plan with so few of us. We deserve to have a break, even if just for one night."

Her gaze shifted to one of the guests at the far corner of the floor. A woman, who didn't seem to be much older than us, was sitting on a barstool. I silently watched as her gaze met with Layla's. The smile on the smuggler girl's face had broadened. She seemed completely distracted.

I sighed when she lost interest in the topic. Layla continued smiling at the women before finally catching my gaze, and shrugged before going on. "As I said, *I* deserve a break."

"Fine," I said as I rubbed the point on my shoulder that had been aching for days. If she wanted to rest, I could give her that for one night.

Layla began speaking again, "As you've also noticed, the inn is quite crowded today. That's why I had to make some arrangements." She paused. "I tried to separate the men and women but the rooms are too small for three people."

I took turns looking at Hunter, the smuggler boy next to him, and then at the girl sitting next to Layla. When I turned to Layla once again, she made a point of winking at me before her eyes shifted to the king next to me. I didn't like the expression on her face.

"*Your* room is on the top floor, at the end of the hall."

The king quickly looked away and brought his hand to his nape. His cheeks were the brightest color of red. I turned to look at the group once again. Layla was still grinning.

"I'm too tired for this," I said as I rolled my eyes. I wasn't bothered by having to share my room with the king, but I was irritated by the fact that she had done this on purpose.

Layla suddenly jumped up and gave me a key with a number written on it. Then she looked over her shoulder with a grin before heading to the stairs. "Have a good night then!"

As the others also headed for the stairs, I turned helplessly to the king. He cleared his throat, shyly scratched his neck, and followed them. I climbed the stairs slowly to the top floor and walked to the end of the hall. The squeaking sound filled the whole room as I pushed the door in. King Warren followed me inside. I looked around after lighting the candle on the small table at the side.

The room was indeed as small as Layla had said. I turned my gaze to the double bed in the middle of the small room, and King Warren cleared his throat loudly. "I'll sleep on the floor."

My whole body was aching and at that moment, the old bed looked very comfortable. I nodded slowly.

"Let me look at your wounds," I said, hoping that my voice wouldn't croak and that my cheeks wouldn't turn red.

We had been caught off guard when the Old Ones attacked, and I knew that the king's previous bruises had just begun healing. Even the cuts on my arms were still aching every once in a while.

He nodded as I moved over to him. Warren rolled the hem of his shirt up to his chest and I looked at his bandages that had become dirty over time. He pushed the fabric away and looked at the scar that had almost disappeared. I also leaned forward; it seemed better.

"I'll ask the innkeeper for new bandages," I said as I turned around, but he caught my wrist.

"No need, it's almost healed."

I first looked at his hand on my wrist and then at his face. I nodded and took a step back. The room was so small and there was nothing much to do in it. No matter how much I yearned for a clean bath, I knew I wasn't going to use the shared area downstairs.

I took off my cape. Then I slowly took off my jacket and the king's eyes locked on my shoulder. "When did that happen?" he asked, pointing at the scar behind my shoulder.

"Four years ago. Our roof was leaking and I climbed up to fix it."

I went on while smiling with the memory of that day; I could almost hear my mother's cries. It was the first few months after my father's death and I was the one who needed to help my family before the winter came. "I fell on the nails that I was supposed to drive into the roof. Two of them stuck into my shoulder." I grinned. "It's a good thing that my mother is the village healer."

His eyes grew wide when I rolled up my leather shirt and showed him the scar on my ribs. "I fell into the well while trying to take water from it. I can't say that I'm not clumsy."

"Yet you laugh about it."

I shrugged at his words and left the jacket on the chair at the side. "It was a long time ago. Didn't you ever hear that pain makes you stronger?"

I turned my back to him and started untying the braids in my hair.

"I did," I heard him murmur.

I glanced at him over my shoulder. He was sitting on the edge of the bed and the expression on his face made me freeze. I took a step toward him.

"I am sorry," I said, panic rising from my voice. "I didn't mean to."

He was thinking about his parents, I could see that. I cursed myself. It was his parents' death that had made him like this and turn his back on the Seven Realms. He had learned to never trust anyone. It was pain that made him grow cold.

"Not like it was your fault." He shrugged, but his attempt at looking unbothered was unsuccessful.

I carefully took another step toward him. I couldn't find the right words to say. I wanted to comfort him but I knew it wouldn't mean anything to him. I was a nobody. A complete stranger.

"I miss them," he said while focusing his eyes on the floor. After our short conversation in Demos, it was the second time he was opening up to me.

"I know," I said softly and without thinking, I knelt in front of him. His eyes found mine easily. Despite the weak light coming from the other side of the small room, his eyes were shining in the dark.

"I know," I repeated. My father's face appeared in front of my eyes. And then, Balfour's. I took a deep breath. "I know you do."

I forced myself to turn my head away. I rose, and so did he.

"Time doesn't heal, does it?"

"No, it doesn't," I said as I leaned against the wall. There was only four steps' distance between the wall and the bed. "That is a complete lie."

I knew he was also thinking that. Whatever the reason was, we both had lost people we cared about and we were more similar than I wanted to admit.

His lips twisted with the pain but he didn't say anything. He was just . . . looking at me and doing nothing. The same bitter smile on my face slowly disappeared. Suddenly, the air in the room was too thick.

"Your family is lucky to have you," he said finally. The left side of my chest ached with longing. He continued. "They will love Ardria and you—"

I took a sharp breath. "Don't."

King Warren stopped. "Don't what?"

"Make this harder than it already is."

He tilted his head.

"When all of this ends," I said and swallowed. "I will either be a prisoner or a fugitive again. There isn't a future for me in the capital anymore, not after what I did. And I will—"

He sharply cut off my words. "Do you still think so little of me?" He frowned when I said nothing. "After everything we have been through—"

"After everything *I* put you through," I corrected him.

He shook his head. "Can't you see it doesn't matter anymore? Nothing does. You . . ."

He stepped back and didn't continue speaking. His face . . . he looked so disappointed.

I crossed my arms. "You told me the first Protector of Aerlion was executed after the war. How am I any different?"

He knew I was right. That was the punishment for what I had done. It had happened before and I had made the same mistake. There was only one choice for me.

I cleared my throat and tore my gaze away from him. "I'll get something to drink," I murmured as I walked to the door. I headed downstairs without looking back at him.

I asked for water from the innkeeper who was behind the bar on the first floor. I idled around for a while before leaving the glass on the counter and heading for the stairs. I was hoping not to talk with the king again and I wished enough time had passed for him to fall asleep.

I took another step and saw the shadow that suddenly appeared before me. Hunter's eyebrows rose.

"Has His Majesty claimed the bed?" he asked in a mocking whisper. "I hope he hasn't asked you to fluff up his pillows before he went to sleep."

I raised my head and looked at him only to see the cruel smile on his face. Hunter had become colder than ever after what happened to Balfour. He sometimes amplified small problems and got into arguments during the past days, and that was the real problem. We were all out of patience. Maybe they were right; a rest would be good for all of us, even if for a single night.

Hunter saw the look on my face and the mockery on his face disappeared. "I'm sorry," he said. He took his hand out of his pocket and combed his blond hair with it. "Forget what I said; it wasn't even funny . . . I don't know why I said that."

But I did. I had cried quite a lot during the last couple of days, and talking to King Warren had calmed me down more than I would have expected. But Hunter had no one to talk to. He was walking around like a ticking bomb, going on with his harsh comments and waiting to explode.

"You know you can talk to me, right?" I asked as I looked into his green eyes. I meant it. Hunter had first lost Breccan, then Balfour. I was ready to do anything I could to make him feel better. After all, we were both being crushed under the same burden. In response, the Phoenix came a step down and closed the distance between us.

"I know," he said. But I realized that we were never going to have this conversation when he looked away.

I moved to the side to walk past him. "What I was trying to say"— I heard him suggest—"was that we could change the room arrangements if you like."

We were now side by side. I turned to look at him as my lips curved. "Do you want to share a room with the king?"

He shrugged but also grimaced with the thought. "You can go in with Layla and the other girl, and leave him on his own."

"The rooms seem too small for three people."

"I'll talk to the innkeeper," he said in earnest. "I'll find a way and get you rid of him. You don't have to put up with him anymore. You don't need each other to survive. We're together now."

I crossed my arms. "Do you trust Caiden and his soldiers?"

He shook his head, "Of course not."

"Then we still need each other to stay alive." I turned my back to him and began slowly climbing the stairs back. "Good night, Hunter," I added. I pushed the door in slowly when I returned to the room, trying not to make a sound. I saw Warren had fallen asleep on the bed. My shoulders drooped immediately.

"I would have the bed, huh?" I murmured silently, but when I realized how tired he was it seemed pointless to wake him up. Considering the broken bed I had slept on for many years, the cold floor didn't seem so bad.

I took my jacket, which I had left on the chair, and made it into a ball. I put it on the floor and spread my cape over it. I blew out the only candle in the room and lay down. I felt sleepy immediately. I tried to be quiet while yawning and then I turned away from the bed. The bed's legs hurt my back as soon as I did, and I realized why Layla had planned for only two people to sleep in each of the tiny rooms.

I barely heard the blanket being pushed as I dozed off. Even the creaking of the hardwood wasn't enough to fully wake me up.

Suddenly I was being lifted. I felt a big hand on the back of my knees and the other one curling up around my waist but before I could move, my back touched the mattress of the bed. I moved slightly with the weight of the thick fabric placed over me and parted my eyes. The king had already curled up on the floor and his back was turned to me.

As I fell back into sleep, I smiled softly. Warren was more than the heartless king known by the people of the Seven Realms, and he was proving it to me more each day.

# CHAPTER 34

I brought my arm to my forehead and tried to shield my face against the storm as I carefully stepped on the snow-covered ground, trying not to slip and fall. The cold went through the layers of fabric I had worn over one another. I looked at Hunter and Thomas walking a few steps in front of me; their silhouettes were blurry through the snow.

When we woke up in the morning, we faced the snowstorm that had taken Belwald under. Although the innkeeper warned us not to go outside, we had no time to waste. We had been walking for a few minutes now without seeing where we were headed, but we had left the village behind a while ago.

I stumbled when my foot hit a rock that was hidden beneath the snow. King Warren, who was walking behind me, held me tightly and prevented me from falling. My hood opened with the impact and my hair flew with the wind. He gave me one last look and his shoulder brushed mine as he followed the rest of the group.

Paige hurried over and took my arm. Her worried eyes searched the snowy land. "I feel like I'll freeze to death," she said and wrapped herself tightly in her cape.

I continued to walk as I took support from her so I wouldn't slip again. It felt as if a lot of time had passed since the time I had spent with Paige at the capital. And after everything I had recently found out about her and her father, she felt like a total stranger to me. She was part of the rebellion. But I was the same now, in a way.

"There." Caiden's voice was easily heard despite the wind.

I turned my eyes to the direction he was pointing and saw the horse cart waiting for us in front of a little hut. The cart was drawn by four white horses and there were big crates at the back. We hurried over to the owner and Layla gave the man a heavy-looking pouch. I knew they had already made a payment before, but apparently more money was needed to ensure his silence.

I went to the back of the cart and began opening the crates one by one. Just as Layla had said, they were full of shiny tableware, booze, and silk clothes.

We all climbed into the back of the cart while Layla and Caiden continued to talk to the man. Gavin, Paige, and five of Caiden's soldiers would wait for us at the hut here. They had to be sure that the driver didn't talk to anyone.

The big, stacked crates created a wall, allowing the middle to remain unseen from the outside. It was very dark inside. I sat myself on the cold wooden floor and tried to shrink as much as possible. Hunter took the reins, and the cart moved after a few seconds.

The buzzing of the wind hit the outer surface of the cart. The road was covered in snow and the storm was causing the cart to shake with each step the horses took. We slowed down after a short while and I didn't need to look outside to know that we had arrived at the castle. I shrank even further as I watched Caiden, Layla, and their soldiers get out of the cart.

"Belwald's castle," said Layla loudly.

I looked at the gray castle built on the mountain slope. The castle that stretched upward from the mountain foot was completely covered with snow. The gray walls were frozen and the tower, which was at the top, was connected to the castle with a wide bridge. The bright gate was partly blocked by the tower and it illuminated the valley from behind the thick clouds. I could see guards waiting with spears in their hands inside the black sentry boxes located on both sides of the castle's high iron gates.

Caiden pointed at both sides of the structure. "There are two doors, one on the east wing and the other on the west. There should be nothing to alert Protector Edmond while we are in the castle."

He used his index finger to point at the lower floors of the castle, which were below the entrance because of the slope and which stretched irregularly along the mountain foot. "The lower floors are used as cellars; one group will enter from there."

I turned my gaze toward the gate over the tower as he went on, "We have to make sure that the Protectors reach the gate."

This idea belonged to Caiden and Hunter. They had thought that being closer to the gate would help us better sense Belwald's crystal, and Darrell also agreed. The gates were where the magic was strongest in all the Seven Realms. So, we would start the search at the castle.

"Are you sure we won't be noticed?"

Layla turned to Thomas at his question. "Rogue's guests have already filled the castle. The rest of the Protectors are in Ardria, including the Protector of Belwald."

"You forget that Rogue uses the power of the crystals easily. He'll find us the moment he senses that something's wrong."

Caiden quickly shook his head. He turned his narrowed eyes to the castle and said, "You have to find Belwald's crystal. The crowd at the castle will be a great distraction."

My eyes found Hunter, who was standing a bit farther away and listening silently to the others. The uneasy expression on his face was unmistakable.

"It's true that we need Belwald's crystal," I said as I took a step forward. "Or any other crystals. We can't stop Audamar without them, and he's not an enemy that we can defeat easily."

I had witnessed his power; I had spent more time with him than the others had. Although it wasn't a long time, it had been enough for me to realize that Audamar could destroy anyone who crossed his path.

"We can't stay anywhere long enough to be noticed," Hunter reminded us and drew our attention to himself. "We have to leave before the sun sets, with or without the crystal."

With his words, the group started to move once again.

"Be careful," said Layla as she looked back one last time.

"What'll happen if Caiden's group gets caught?" I asked while watching the indistinctive silhouettes disappear into the storm.

Hunter turned to me. "We'll leave."

Darrell and I came eye to eye, but we both remained silent. It was true that running was probably the most logical thing to do, but how could we leave them behind? Yes, Caiden and the others were part of the rebellion but they had been with us since the start. They had agreed to help us.

"Edmond will come here if he senses that something isn't right." King Warren had to shout to be heard; the storm was stronger now. "If we want to defeat Rogue, our purpose must be staying alive, which also means fleeing."

I shook my head furiously. "We can never get the crystals before him if we run."

"Or if we die," said King Warren with a grimace.

We both turned to Hunter when he put his hand between us. "We're wasting our time," he warned us before going to the front to lead the horses again. "Let's go."

When he sat in the driver's seat, we returned to the back of the cart. There was only a short way to the castle and it was becoming more difficult to breathe with each turn of the wheels. Soon, the cart stopped abruptly. My gaze met Warren's. When I heard the approaching steps, I held my breath. One of the guards at the entrance walked around the cart and came to the back. I saw his shadow fall inside; he was standing on the other side of the crates. Darrell slowly raised his hand in case something went wrong.

"What are these?" asked the guard, raising his voice so Hunter could hear him from the driver's seat. Then he lifted the cover of one of the crates closest to himself. I crouched further down where I sat.

"Gifts from the nobles for the king's visit," replied Hunter. I realized he had a different accent now, and at that moment I was glad that he wasn't wearing his usual Phoenix clothes. No one could recognize him.

"Don't you think you're a little bit late?" The guard went on, "The king arrived this morning. You were supposed to be here before."

It was easier to cover our trace with the crowd inside, but still, I was nervous about Audamar's presence. I held on to the crates to keep my balance but my foot slipped and the heels of my boots made a screeching sound. The king and Darrell turned to me at the same instant while Thomas's eyes grew wide.

The guard, who was walking away from the cart, suddenly stopped. "What was that?"

A feeling of panic rushed through my body when King Warren's hand went to the dagger at his waist. But then I heard Hunter's voice calling out.

"Hurry up! I can't wait here all day. Do you want to be the one to explain to the nobles why the king's gifts were late?"

There was a moment of silence, until I heard the bolt of the heavy gates being pushed. A stupid grin formed on my face when the cart began moving slowly through the frozen gates. I leaned forward to look through the crates.

The castle was built with black stones and the high walls were covered with ice. I looked up as the cart continued along with the snow-covered courtyard. The main gate of Belwald was shining above the tower with all its glamour, and it was as if it prevented the cold air from entering through the walls of the castle. The cart stopped in front of the castle's back door.

We were late indeed, and no one was waiting here for us. People were in a rush with the king's arrival, and apparently, this had been enough for them to overlook some of the details.

Hunter jumped down to the empty yard and hit on the cart once. This was our signal; we went out one by one.

Darrell looked at me and said, "We'd better hide before the guards come to check the cart."

We hurried to the castle's back door, standing close to the wall and looking around with each step, trying to make sure that we weren't seen.

"We should split into two groups," Hunter said as he tried the doorknob; it was locked. Darrell moved to the front and waved his hand. A thumping sound was heard as a bright light shone. "Rogue is here and we have no time to waste. We have to find out if Belwald's crystal is in the castle or not."

The crystal of Demos had been hidden in the temple—that's why we would start looking for Belwald's at the temple here also.

Hunter looked at me and asked, "You can find the crystal without Darrell, right?"

I wanted to say *no* but I didn't have the strength to do that while they were all looking at me. I nodded to hide my doubt. Hunter quickly opened the door that Darrell had unlocked.

"The guests are probably at the feast in the grand hall."

"Do you think the council members are at the feast, too?" I asked.

The council members were also the heads of the most influential five families of Ardria. I had thought that they wouldn't travel so far away from the capital. Especially since Rogue was keeping an eye on them. That was why they hadn't been in Demos.

"The council members should follow the king's every step." It was King Warren who had replied. "They always accompanied us during my family's visits. We couldn't find them in Demos, but this is different. They should be here for the feast."

King Warren was looking at the long hallway in front of us, but I could see the doubt in his eyes. The fact that the council members were here meant that his cousin was here, too. During the first days when we were running, finding Lord Theon and telling him the truth had been a part of our plan. But things had changed now. I wasn't quite sure if the king's family could do any good since Audamar had become this strong.

"And what about the crystal?" I asked, changing the subject.

Darrell looked at me. "We don't know where the first Protector has hidden Belwald's crystal, but I can feel the magic of the gate already. If the crystal is at the castle, I should be able to sense it."

Hunter turned to me. "I'll go to the gate with Darrell. Anna, you and the king go to the Oblation Room."

I had no idea what he was talking about but it was too late to ask when he began running to the stairs and disappeared at the end of the hall with Darrell. King Warren held my wrist and forced me to turn in another direction. Under his touch, my skin burned.

"I know where he wants us to go," he only said.

The inside of the castle was as cold as the outside. The few torches in the hallway were only enough to illuminate the path, but not enough to provide any heat. The frozen windows were hidden behind pitch-black curtains, and the long carpet in the same color was absorbing the sound of our footsteps. I could hear the buzz coming from the end of the hallway, but we hadn't met any castle servants during the time we had been here.

"The feast," he reminded me in a single breath.

He led me down the stairs. It was getting colder inside as we moved away from the people where they gathered in the castle, and the light was getting dimmer. Despite the thick walls, the sound of the storm outside the castle was echoing in my ears.

"What is the Oblation Room?" I asked when King Warren slowed down. We were both walking at a normal pace now, as our quick breaths mixed into the silence.

"The oldest part of the castle. It is said that it was built by the first Protector of Belwald."

I followed him into another hallway where I suddenly felt the freezing cold. I looked ahead in bafflement. The castle's thick walls had ended, leaving in their place a path with thick pillars on the sides. On the wall to our left, there was a void in the space allocated for windows, and the valley behind the pillars was under my feet. We were standing at the edge of a cliff. I quickly moved away from it and over to the other side of the hallway.

King Warren continued toward the end of the hallway, where a wide door caught my attention. It was made of stone, as black as those of the castle. The door was quite big and it had engravings on it. He touched the smooth surface of the door. I walked to his side and put my hands on the stone door, just as he had done. It was ice-cold. We shifted our weights forward and pushed the door with all our strength. It was enough to push it gently for the door to open easily. I shot a glance at King Warren and dove into the dark room without waiting for him.

The first thing I noticed was the smell. The room smelled as if there was something rotten in it. I opened my eyes wide so they could get used to the dark.

"This was the place for the things that the first Protector presented to the Goddess: gifts, food, gold, animals, and even humans."

"Humans?"

Even though I couldn't see in the dark, I was pretty sure that the king was nodding. "They may have been Protectors, but they were just humans. The first people in the Realms, actually. Rituals used to be held here thousands of years ago. Rumor has it that the last thing that the Protector of Belwald sacrificed to the Goddess was himself."

I knew that Protectors vanished when they died, that they returned to the Vitae. Not a body or anything else would be left behind. The books I had read at the capital said that they turned into the dust of magic. But still, I was nauseous at the thought of all the animals and humans that had died here.

"That explains the smell," I murmured.

I grimaced with disgust and tried not to inhale it. "Is that why we're here?" I added. "If he gave his last breath in here . . ."

"He may have come here after the battle with Rogue. He could have hidden the crystal in this room before he died; it's a sacred place."

I didn't know how I could do this without seeing anything. I tried to focus and feel something, *anything*, but nothing happened.

"Look between the stones on the wall," Warren said. "It could be anywhere in the room. You should feel its magic if the crystal is here."

When he took a few steps farther into the room, the big stone door suddenly shut and the floor beneath us shook.

"I've been waiting for you."

I was startled by the sound that rose from the other side of the room. I looked around in panic but the only thing I heard in the pitch dark was approaching footsteps. The torches on the wall began lighting up one by one. I drew back from the flames.

The room was surrounded by high marble pillars and right in the middle was a statue of a woman. The face of the statue, which had been sculpted to the finest detail, was covered with another layer of stone that looked like a veil. As soon as I saw it, I realized that it represented the Goddess Vitae.

The shadow next to the statue caught my attention. My eyes met King Warren's, but I knew he wasn't the real king. A smile formed on Audamar's face. "This game has become overly bothersome . . . How about giving up, Anna, in the name of our old friendship?"

He came out from the shadows. His hand found the fur collar of his clothes. He had made his hair into a ponytail, and the rings on his fingers were eye-catching. Although his face was the same as Warren's, they were very different from each other.

"You'll never make it, Anna. That's not your destiny."

"I won't let you have the crystals."

He seemed amused by my words. He gave me a belittling look with his narrowed gray eyes. He sighed. "You're starting to get on my nerves."

Then he turned to the king, who was standing a few feet away from me. "Warren," he said, smiling again as if he had seen a long-lost friend. "So, you've decided to help Anna . . . what a shame. What would your family think if they saw you working with the enemy?"

King Warren's gritted teeth made it pretty clear that he wasn't happy with the mention of his family.

"You are weak. You're an embarrassment to the Montborne name. I find it hard to believe that we carry the same blood."

Audamar began circling slowly around the statue. I took a step back. Warren's eyes met mine as I gasped. He quickly came over and stood in front of me, between Audamar and me. His hand touched mine for a second before opening his arms and standing protectively.

"I must confess," Audamar continued. "I wasn't expecting you to come this far, or to even be able to get in here . . . You have surprised me." He paused for a brief moment. "You've made progress. You're gathering allies and you think you can really stop me . . . a bunch of fools. You can never defeat the Master of Darkness."

Warren cast a short glance at me and began walking. I did the same. Audamar's arrogant gaze was still on me so he hadn't noticed that the king was moving away from where I stood. I turned to Audamar as he continued to examine my face carefully. Then King Warren and I charged at the same time. I began running toward Audamar and King Warren threw his dagger at him. The sharp metal scratched Audamar's face and disappeared into the back of the room. His cheek bled.

The First King raised his hand from his fur coat and suddenly the crystals appeared in his hand. I looked at them carefully and saw that the crystals of Belwald, Orin, and Nadeer weren't in his hand. So, he hadn't found the remaining three yet.

Audamar was cornered. But I knew even a single crystal was enough to defeat us. His eyes alternated between the king and me before he suddenly turned his hand to Warren. A white light shone in the room.

King Warren screamed with pain. He brought his hand to his chest as I heard his weak breathing. He pressed his fingers on the left side of his chest so hard that I could see his knuckles turning white. He gritted his teeth. I was terrified. I tried to reach him, but Audamar swung his other hand and sent the king across the room.

"Warren!"

I left Audamar alone and hurried over to him. He was lying on the floor on the other side of the room.

"Anna." King Warren gasped with the pain. I held his arms tightly.

"Let this be my gift to you, Warren," said Audamar. He was watching us as he took a step back and took shelter under the shadow of the statue.

"I'll help you get your revenge and you'll be able to free yourself from the stain on our family name."

I couldn't understand what his words meant, but I didn't have to wait for the king to stand up to see that something was wrong with him. Suddenly, Warren pushed away my hand and rose. Audamar suddenly disappeared into the shadows. King Warren breathed in rage and looked around as if he was searching for something.

"King Warren?"

We heard a familiar voice at the entrance of the room. The king and I turned around simultaneously and saw Lord Cheng standing by the door. He was wearing a dark red coat, different from his usual black cape, and he had a furry hat on his head.

"I thought we were gathering at the ballroom . . . Why did you call me here?"

But he received no reply from the king. From the expression on Cheng's face, I realized that he had just arrived here. He hadn't seen the encounter with Audamar.

I looked at the half-open door and tried to figure out how Audamar had planned this. He had been able to open the door, which he had locked earlier, without even lifting a finger, just with the power of the crystals.

Warren fixed his dark eyes on the council member and kept staring at Cheng without a response. The lord looked around nervously.

"You shouldn't be here. This place is for the Protectors . . . Oh! What is that smell? How disgusting! Is this really the place they call sacred?"

He continued to grumble with a disgusted expression on his face as his gaze wandered around the room. He looked at the statues carved on the high walls and the ceiling and finally, as if he had just felt my presence, he turned his eyes on me. I stood farther behind the king.

"You!" Lord Cheng shouted. His eyes grew wide and he pointed a finger at me, saying, "She . . . she . . ." He turned in panic to the king, who was still staring at him. "I'll call Protector Edmond at once. King Warren! Get away from the traitor!"

He quickly turned around. My eyes grew wide in panic and King Warren's cold voice echoed in the room.

"Wait."

Lord Cheng stopped at the doorsill. He looked confused and it was obvious that he hadn't understood why the king had stopped him. "But . . ."

"I ordered you to stop."

I knit my eyebrows at the king's harsh tone. Lord Cheng equally recoiled. He obeyed the king's order and walked back into the room with careful steps. No one spoke for a while. The council member turned his eyes to me for a brief moment before quickly shifting his gaze back to King Warren, afraid to look anywhere else.

"Years ago," began Warren as he took a few steps forward and broke the silence, "you took my family away from me with the uprising you started. You killed them; you betrayed your king and the queen."

Despite the distance between us, I was able to see how Lord Cheng's face paled. He first looked around in panic, and then he took a step back as if he was about to run out of the room. King Warren suddenly stepped in front of him and drew the second dagger on his belt.

"I didn't say you could leave."

"Warren!" I shouted as I watched him in bewilderment. What was he doing?

"Did you really think that I wouldn't come back for this . . . that I wouldn't avenge my family and let you stain our name? The Montborne family had never been so humiliated before."

I froze with the words coming out of his lips because I knew that these words didn't belong to him. The king was repeating the same things Audamar had just said.

Every step Warren took was dangerous and Lord Cheng sensed it. He was hardly able to speak as he raised his shaky hands. "My king, please. I . . ."

But the only response he received from Warren was the dagger coming closer to his chest. The lord's whole body began to tremble. I knew King Warren wanted revenge but his words, his behavior . . . Something wasn't right. This person couldn't be the same person whom I had spent the last few days with.

Lord Cheng threw himself on the ground and put his forehead onto the back of his hands on the floor. "Please! It wasn't me! I swear I didn't do it!"

I knew it would be too late if I didn't do something immediately. I hurried over to the king and stepped between him and the council member before shoving him away.

"That's enough, Warren. We have to get out of here!"

But King Warren never even turned his eyes at me. I held his wrist tightly. All I wanted was to take the dagger away from him, but he easily got rid of my grip before I could do anything.

"Look at him!" I said angrily as I pointed at the council member on the ground. Cheng's shaking shoulders told me that he was scared. Lord Cheng was not a good man in many respects, but I could imagine that he had never been in such a situation before. Whatever he had done, he didn't deserve to be threatened with his life. And what really frightened me was the fact that Warren could still remain so cold.

"I'm not lying!" said Lord Cheng as he breathed in terror. His eyes were full of fear and tears. He looked at us for a moment but then he pressed his forehead back onto the floor. "I didn't do it! I swear! It wasn't me!"

King Warren gritted his teeth and continued to stare at the council member. I turned to Cheng. "Who was it?" I asked roughly. "Who started the uprising?"

The only thing we heard was Lord Cheng's trembling breaths. King Warren held the dagger tighter in his fist and ordered, "Speak!"

"Lunavier . . . Bartolomeo Lunavier."

The Lunavier family was one of the leading noble families of the council. It was also the family of Lady Bria, and the name that the lord mentioned belonged to Bria's father, who had passed away a few years ago.

The king stepped forward. "You're lying."

"It's true! He planned the uprising. All the family members . . ." Cheng sobbed. "Everyone! Bria was in on it, too!"

I had been told that the Lunavier family had always demanded independence. They didn't advocate for the system where people lived under the ruling of a single king. I knew that Lord Cheng couldn't be trusted, but when I thought about it, his words didn't sound so wrong.

"Shut up!"

But Lord Cheng continued. "He said that an inexperienced prince couldn't rule the kingdom if the king and the queen died! This way, they could leave the capital for good. He paid the Phoenixes . . . They promised me independence, too! But they all blamed me when the uprising failed!"

Warren lunged forward in rage but I jumped in between. I leaned my shoulder on his chest and tried to push him away with my hands. "Get out of here!" I shouted to Cheng.

Lord Cheng wasted no time in running. He rushed outside without even looking back. I had saved his life; he had evaded the king's rage but it wasn't important. I knew that Cheng would tell everyone that he had seen me in the castle. And I had no idea what he would do about his encounter with King Warren.

"Let me go!" Warren said through gritted teeth and turned his dark eyes to me for the first time since Lord Cheng had entered the room.

"No."

"Anna, let me go or . . ."

"Or what? Will you get rid of me first?"

I didn't know if my words had any effect on him but the king's resistance became weaker. Still, he was too strong for me.

"Let. Me. Go."

King Warren elbowed me in the stomach and I stumbled backward. There was nothing to stop him now. But when he turned around to go after the council member, he collapsed to the floor with the touch of a hand suddenly appearing on his forehead. There was someone in front of him. The dagger he had been holding slipped from his hand and slid away on the floor.

A familiar face greeted me.

"Lord Cyril?"

"Look at the mess you've made! I don't want such things in my castle! I missed the old, peaceful times here!"

I looked over his shoulder to see the owner of the grunting voice. My eyes met Protector Edmond's. He grimaced when he saw me and then looked at King Warren, who was lying in front of them.

"What's going on here?" I asked. Had Lord Cheng reached the others earlier than I had expected? Were Lord Cyril and Protector Edmond here to catch me?

"We came to help," said Cyril as he slowly turned to look at me. His words suddenly lifted the heavy weight off my shoulders. I took a deep breath.

"We found Deegan and Qimra . . . No, actually, they found us. They're really intelligent creatures."

Even though I had no idea what he was talking about, hearing Deegan's name made me understand that it was something good. He was okay. And if Deegan had reached out to them . . .

The old Protector's gaze turned once again to King Warren on the floor. His blank face became shadowed with his thoughts and he knit his thick eyebrows.

The old lord leaned over.

"I think I can help you."

# CHAPTER 35

I looked at his peaceful face, examining every inch of his skin. His tired expression seemed to be somewhat relaxed now. His chest heaved up with each deep breath he took while lying on the old bed. I sat on the small wooden stool. I watched the dim light coming from the candle placed on the wooden table next to me flicker as the door opened slowly.

"How is he?" Paige asked nervously, sticking her head through the gap. Her eyes were on the king.

"Fine . . . I guess. He hasn't woken yet."

Paige took small steps into the room and sat on the stool next to mine. She combed her hair with her fingers.

"We don't know what Rogue did to him." She sounded like she was trying to delay the bad news. "My father and I tried our best. Lord Cyril is looking for a solution."

When Warren woke up a few hours ago after leaving the castle, he was insistent on going after Cheng. Darrell and Hunter had to hold him as he tried to run again. So, Lord Cyril made Gavin prepare a strong potion that would put him to sleep.

I couldn't erase the memory of him shouting. Everyone agreed that this was better than having a raging and vengeful king around. But I disagreed. Whatever Audamar did to him, Warren was so furious and he couldn't think of anything other than revenge.

"The crystals' magic is very strong."

Paige nodded. "This is the reason why the crystals were hidden in different realms. They were made for the Protectors, not for mortals. And still, King Warren and even Rogue are still human . . . Rogue is very powerful, I don't even know how he resists the crystals." She sighed. "But I guess having crystals makes him powerful, that is why he is a great danger as long as he sits on the throne . . ."

I had no intention of interrupting her, but the words came out of my mouth automatically. I turned my head to the king lying motionless in the bed. "I'm sure that the problem is not just about Rogue, but more about the throne and any heirs to it."

I didn't continue. What could I tell her anyway? Ask why she was a part of the rebellion? Why she had joined the group that rebelled against King Warren? Why they didn't want a king or a throne? I knew I couldn't ask her any of this; otherwise, I would have to ask everyone else the same questions.

"My father has always been close with Caiden. I've known him for years and I've heard about Vincent many times. He has always been there whenever there was a problem in the kingdom, standing by the people. Taxes, drought, pandemics . . . They were part of the solution every time the kingdom neglected to intervene."

"So, do I have to thank them for that? We joined forces against a common enemy, but what will happen afterward? What do you think will happen if we win?"

I had witnessed King Warren telling Caiden that he would give up the throne, but we both knew that wasn't going to happen. He would rather die for that throne that his ancestors had fought for, and for which his family had died.

"I don't know," Paige said as her shoulders shrugged. She lowered her gaze. "Tell me, Anna," she asked, "if you're so against the rebellion, why did you give the crystal to Audamar in the first place?"

I heard her let out a breath slowly when I looked away. "You know why . . . You wanted to do something for the people. *This is why* you gave your money to the people of Aerlion. *This is why* you were full of hatred when you first set foot in the palace. You aren't so different from us and I think you already know that."

Wasn't that what Caiden had told me back in Demos? I didn't belong there, in the palace, with nobles and people who didn't care and would never care for us.

There was a knock on the door twice and then Thomas stepped in. He was wearing clean clothes; he'd gotten rid of the clothes that he had been wearing for the last few days. He seemed less tired and more adapted to the situation. I wasn't surprised; he had spent many years with the rebels.

"Protector Edmond is with the others, and so is Lord Cyril."

I nodded. There were three of us now. No matter how much I wanted to believe that this number was enough to take down Rogue, I knew that we still needed every single one of us. This was just the beginning.

Paige turned to him curiously and asked, "And what are they talking about?"

Thomas studied the sleeping king and then moved to the other side of the room. "I heard only a part of it, but they were talking about the council member helping Rogue."

"Bria?"

Lord Cheng had said that she had a part in the uprising against the royal family, that all her family did. If she was against the kingdom, that also meant her family was the reason why Warren's family were dead, why Warren was like this.

"That means treason."

I wanted to laugh at Paige's words, but I held myself back at the last moment. It was because of an enemy who had betrayed the king, that we were together with a group of people in a situation similar to ours. Could our situation become any more ironic?

"Is there any evidence?" I asked. "We need more than Lord Cheng's words."

Thomas shook his head. "Other than what he said, no. But it's possible that it's been her family all along."

I turned to the king again. King Warren's eyes were shut tightly and he was lying on his back. He was like a statue; he would have looked like a dead man if not for his heaving chest. His black hair, which he used to toss back with his hand every once in a while, had grown long over the days we spent running, and it had fallen over his forehead.

I involuntarily leaned forward to push back the locks from his face, but I quickly drew back when I saw Thomas and Paige watching me. I rose from where I sat and began walking around the small room. My shadow was dancing on the walls with each step.

"I'd better find my father," Paige murmured as she slowly rose to her feet. I saw her grab Thomas by the arm on her way to the door, but I didn't turn to them. I heard their footsteps blend into each other behind the door. They were walking slowly so as not to wake the king, but I didn't think that any kind of noise could do anything against Gavin's mixed potions. They were the best he could make.

We knew the crystals could be used for good and for evil, and Rogue was using them to turn people into the Old Ones. But Warren was still himself. There was nothing in the books about someone that the crystals were used on, yet remained human.

I gave up after walking around some more and sat at the edge of the bed. As I looked at him, I forgot what I was thinking. I courageously examined his features that I had found scary when we first met, and I thought the king, whom I once hated and from whom I once tried to run, was my only ally now. He had ordered my execution and I lost my powers, but I knew it was too late to hold a grudge against him. We had saved each other's lives many times.

My hand shyly went back to his face and I pushed away the lock of hair without touching his skin. He looked younger, more like a prince than a king, while his hair covered his face. I wasn't used to seeing him this way, so vulnerable. After what happened to his family, King Warren had always kept his guard up against everyone and everything. But now, the ice walls surrounding him had melted. Yet, I knew that it would be only a matter of seconds for him to build them up once he woke up. I was afraid of what or who I would face, after what Audamar had done to him.

"He hasn't woken up yet, huh?"

I turned around. Protector Edmond was leaning on the doorsill with his arms crossed. I hadn't even heard him come.

"Shouldn't you be asking Lord Cyril?"

He shrugged. "It's better than the effect of the crystals. A furious Warren is no good to anyone."

I got up from the edge of the bed and turned to Edmond once again. His narrowed eyes found mine before he turned around and walked away. I knew this was a sign for me to follow.

We needed a new shelter for everyone to gather, but we hadn't had enough time to find one. But things had changed with the arrival of Protector Edmond and Lord Cyril. It had taken only a few minutes for the old Protector to find a place where we could hide. This way, we had been able to get out of the castle without being noticed.

The shelter Edmond had found for us was underground, and it was only one of the hundreds that the Protectors once used. The fact that it was far from the castle also provided additional safety for us. One of the old mines of Belwald had been turned into a place where people could hide in case of emergency. But no one, other than the Protectors, knew of its existence. They mentioned that there were shelters all around the Seven Realms in case of need and they were used back in the times when the Old Ones and the dragons roamed freely.

Caiden's soldiers were around the metal tables at the center of the shelter, and they were eating loudly. I thought it was a good thing for us to be under the ground; I never could have thought that the few remaining soldiers could make such noise. I couldn't see Darrell, Hunter, or Lord Cyril, but I could guess that they were probably making plans in a more peaceful and less noisy part of the shelter.

I turned my head and saw the narrowed eyes of Protector Edmond, who was walking next to me.

"You don't like me, do you?" I asked suddenly, my arms crossed at my chest.

He grumbled, "This has nothing to do with personal feelings. I just think that what you did was a mistake. This includes you coming to the palace and being chosen as Protector."

"But the crystals . . ."

He interrupted me. "The crystals can be wrong, too."

This was the exact opposite of what I had heard from everyone else. I smiled wryly with the familiarity of this conversation.

"Why are you smiling?"

Protector Edmond's gruff voice made me fix my gaze on the floor. I let out a breath before talking. "Balfour was with me the last time I had such a conversation, and only a few hours later . . ."

I saw the anger disappear from Edmond's eyes. He looked serious as he faced forward. "Balfour was my friend."

"Do you know how it happened?"

How he died.

The old Protector nodded. "I was told he stayed back so you could escape . . . such an idiot."

He breathed through his nose, but he still had sadness on his face. I saw his lips slightly tremble but he was quick to hide it. He didn't want to show his feelings— or he was trying to hide them from me—but I saw the mourning in his eyes.

"Do you really think Bria is helping Audamar?" I asked, hoping to change the subject.

"Well, we now know Audamar is getting information from inside just like when the Old Ones attacked the palace during your ceremony—he knew exactly where and when to be . . . at your execution as well." He shook his head. "He already had the crystals of Sam and Ramona before you gave him Aerlion's. And now he also has Darrell's."

I nodded.

"Things have gotten complicated. We need more than Cheng's words for us to judge Bria and her family. Yet even if we do prove it, it may not change anything. Our priority has to be Rogue."

"If Audamar already had the two crystals before, why didn't the Protectors notice it? How could he have found the first crystal?"

Protector Edmond lowered his head and I saw that he was occupied with the same questions. The old Protector shook his head, saying, "I don't know."

"What'll happen when King Warren wakes up? If we tell him about Bria . . ."

I didn't go on; I could imagine the king's reaction. He would never believe us. I had seen what he had done at the castle; her betrayal had upset him more than I would have thought.

"How did you find us?" I asked.

"Cyril was the first to realize something was off with Warren. He came to me. Balfour was also with him; he was told the same thing by your Phoenix. Then, after what happened in Demos, Balfour left the capital to find you. I was very much against him doing this, but at the same time, I trusted his and Cyril's instincts. The king has been acting different lately but no one could tell exactly what the problem was, until I saw the crystals myself. I felt the presence of the crystals when Rogue first arrived in Belwald; it was so strong."

"And how did you understand he wasn't King Warren?"

"I didn't. Before he died, Balfour had contacted Cyril and told him. It was Cyril who explained everything, and I joined him without a second thought. He came to Belwald and we helped you escape from the castle."

The main reason for them to help us had been the old commander. He had saved our lives but I knew this wouldn't be enough. Unfortunately, his sacrifice had just helped keep us alive thus far.

"We need the help of the others," I heard Protector Edmond say in one breath. "Honestly, I'm not sure if the seven Protectors combined would be enough to beat Rogue . . . but, well . . . we'll try."

My eyes turned to Hunter, who had just entered the room, and I saw Darrell and Lord Cyril behind him. We came eye to eye with Lord Cyril. After the old lord looked at my face for a rather long time, he turned to the Protector who was standing right next to me. Edmond suddenly left me and began walking over to him. I headed toward Hunter.

"What's our plan?"

I saw Darrell looking at Hunter with a troubled expression on his face. "We're not sure, either."

I turned my gaze to Hunter. "What?"

"We don't know what Rogue's plan is, and there is no way we could go to Ardria when the other Protectors are at the palace."

"We could try to talk to them." I protested.

Darrell let out his breath softly as he combed through his hair with his fingers. "The crystals of Belwald, Nadeer, and Orin are still missing but we don't have the slightest idea of what he's planning to do next. We cannot just go there, and in others' eyes, we are traitors. Why would they even listen to us?"

I narrowed my eyes. "I made you listen to me, how is that any different?"

When they both opened their mouth to talk, I didn't let them. "We are wasting our time here. Let's just go to one of those realms, then. You, me, and Edmond can continue searching for the crystals."

"We're all torn up, Anna." Darrell insisted. "We take a bigger hit every time we attack Rogue and we have made no progress yet. We need to stop and make an actual plan."

I crossed my arms. "For how long?"

Neither of them answered my question. I turned around, displeased with the conversation, and left them behind as I headed to the tables with furious steps. I hurried over when I saw a vacant spot next to Layla. She turned to me as soon as I sat down.

She looked cautiously at my angry face, and then without a word, she offered me the piece of bread in her hand. I shook my head and watched her take a big bite from the moldy bread.

"This is the best we could find," she said as she let out a breath. "It'll be noticed if we steal anything from the villages nearby; probably the royal guards and Phoenixes are searching every inch of Belwald. I must say, the council member really made a big fuss."

I raised a brow. "Lord Cheng?"

Layla nodded. "He's telling everyone at the castle that he's seen you."

"And what about the things happened with the king?"

Layla put the bread back on the table and wiped her mouth with her sleeve. "I don't have the slightest idea; I can't say I heard anything about that."

That was really odd. I remembered how frightened he was when King Warren attacked him. But Audamar was still with them, posing as King Warren, so Cheng wouldn't do anything to put his life in danger. At least not now.

"Do you think he could have used the crystals on Lord Cheng as well? Just like he did on Warren?"

Layla shrugged. "Why not? The crystals are really powerful. Or maybe Cheng has been working for him the whole time. The nobles would do anything not to lose the power they hold."

She narrowed her eyes and began staring at the piece of bread she had just left on the table. "I hate useless soldiers who can't follow even the simplest orders."

I turned to her. "Which soldiers?"

She sighed. "I sent a few soldiers outside to bring some wood and to hunt. They still haven't returned . . . they are all useless. They probably couldn't find anything and ran away, afraid of what I'd do to them."

I looked at the smugglers sitting at the tables around us. I knew we had just arrived at this shelter and that we didn't have enough food to last for a long time, but apparently, we were much more unprepared. I had no idea what food she was expecting them to find in the forest in the cold of Belwald. Probably all the animals were hiding. Perhaps she was talking about stealing from the villages.

I pushed my chair back and said, "I'll go. I'll find them and come back as soon as possible."

Layla immediately jumped up to her feet and stepped in front of me. "Hold on," she said and blocked my path, preventing me from going any further. "Are you aware that you're still the most wanted fugitive in all the Seven Realms? What do you think will happen if someone sees you?"

"The shelter is deep in the woods, Layla. No one will notice me. There's no reason for anyone to be outside in this freezing cold."

She looked at me as if I had said something stupid. "Belwald is always covered in snow. Do you think people care for a couple of inches of it?"

I let out a breath; it would be more difficult than I thought to convince her. "I grew up in the woods. Believe me, I can find my way. I know how to hide if I see someone."

"Yes." she said. "Woods that are not covered in this much snow. It doesn't snow in Aerlion like this. You'll leave tracks behind."

I walked around her without waiting for her reply. She spoke again.

"Take someone with you."

I looked back at her over my shoulder. "Do you want to come with me?"

She grimaced. "No way, I hate the cold," she said and wrapped her arms around herself, pretending she was trembling.

I grinned. "Give me an hour. I'll be back with some food and your soldiers."

I heard Layla shout from behind, "Don't forget to bring some wood, too!"

I left the main hall and moved along another hallway. This underground shelter reminded me of the one Thomas had taken us to in Aerlion. It had the same low ceiling and the same narrow hallways. I wondered if that was also one of the shelters in Aerlion that was used by people before. I was told they were built in all the realms. When there were hundreds of them in each realm, it wouldn't be so hard for someone to discover one of them.

I held onto the ladder tightly and pulled myself up. Then I pushed the cover upward. It opened with a squeal and I was immediately struck with cold air. I brushed the snow off myself and put one leg up to the surface. I rolled out of the hole. I felt the snow-covered ground on my back and my hands began aching as soon as they met the cold. I closed the cover without wasting any more time and put some branches over it so it wouldn't be seen.

The forest was dead silent. I shivered and wrapped my arms around myself. My priority was feeding the hungry soldiers, so I began looking around with hopes of finding something edible. But the snow had covered everything.

Just in case, I reached for my belt but I paused when I felt nothing there. I hadn't brought any weapons with me. I looked back through the trees to the exit I had come out from, but I couldn't waste time by returning to the shelter.

"The soldiers first, then," I said to myself. I knew they carried weapons on them.

I went in the opposite direction of the shelter. I tried to inhale the fresh air but my lungs burned with the cold. I was still wearing the clothes that Caiden's soldiers wore. I tucked my hands under my armpits and exhaled my breath toward my chest, trying to feel the warm vapor on my face.

As I was looking down, the stains on the snow caught my attention. A few drops of red . . . *blood*. I raised my head and saw that the drops were turning into puddles of blood ahead. Three men were lying on the ground at the other edge of the tree line and there was blood everywhere.

I covered my mouth with my hand and opened my eyes wide. The torn leather clothes they wore told me that they were the soldiers Layla had talked about. But what had happened to them?

As I continued to look at the horrible scene in front of me, deciding whether to run away or approach them, an ear-piercing sound echoed throughout the woods. I didn't have to turn around to understand what the roar belonged to.

A Dralein suddenly appeared behind the trees and I saw blood dripping from its sharp claws. The creature raised its head and sniffed the air a couple of times. Then it fixed its big eyes on me.

I took a step back, then another one. I thought a sudden movement could cause it to lunge at me. The Dralein leaned forward once again and roared before starting to run in my direction. I didn't even realize when I took off; I had probably never run this fast in my life. But the creature was faster.

I ran through the thick forest and used my hand to take support from the trees and thrust myself forward. Laying low wasn't an option anymore; I forgot the number of times I screamed with fear. Having no one to help made the situation even worse. I was going to die here.

Instead of passing between trees, the Dralein just pushed them aside and I saw the pine trees come down one by one, just like dominoes. I managed to jump forward and save myself from being crushed under one of them.

The creature roared once again. I slipped on the snow and fell on my hands. It hurt more than I would have expected. My palms burned as I crawled for a few feet before standing up. The creature swung its arms at me from behind and its claws almost touched my back. Suddenly, my feet left the ground; the snow had prevented me from seeing the rock sticking out of the ground. I slid on my shoulder and rolled on the ground until I stopped when I hit my head on another rock.

I wanted to reach the aching spot to find the source of the pain that was spreading all over my body, but I had no time to waste. The Dralein suddenly stopped while my vision became blurred. It looked around for a while and sniffed the air again.

I saw a silhouette behind it. In seconds, the creature's body split into two with a sharp sword tearing it. I heard its ear-piercing cry for the last time. The Dralein fell down and its dark skin began to lighten as soon as its head hit the ground. Now its upper body belonged to a man. I was faced with one of the missing people.

The stranger began walking as she dragged the tip of her long sword through the snow, leaving a thin trace of blood behind. I looked at her face and my heart began pounding with fear.

"Protector Thalia," I said as I looked at her. My voice had come out more crooked than I had hoped, and the pain in my head wasn't helping at all. "What are you doing here?"

"Looking for you."

I tried to draw back when she suddenly pointed her blood-covered sword, which she had just used to split the Dralein in two, at me. But my head was spinning.

"Don't pretend like you don't know about the price King Warren put on your head."

"I . . ."

She interrupted before the words could even leave my lips. "Shut up."

Now her sword was just one foot away from my neck.

300

"Protector Anna," she said as she turned to me. "I have been ordered by King Warren to find you for the treason you have committed against the kingdom."

She stepped closer. No matter how much I tried to fix my gaze on her, I was about to collapse any minute. Her dark eyes never left mine and I heard her exhale angrily. Before she raised her hand and knocked me unconscious, I heard her last words ringing in my ears. Magic shone in the forest.

"I'm taking you back to the capital."

# CHAPTER 36

The first thing I felt when I parted my eyes was the pain.

I tried to let out a cry, but all that came out of my lips was a bitter grunt. The small stones on the surface where I sat were pricking my back and the numbness in my legs told me that I had been here for a while. I held the wall behind me and tried to sit up. It didn't take me long to realize where I was after seeing the narrow cell; Protector Thalia had done what she promised—she had brought me back to the palace.

As I felt another presence, I suddenly turned to the shadow standing behind the iron bars. My body ached all over when I tried to move away.

"When are you going to kill me?" I asked the man standing in the shadows who was wearing King Warren's face like a mask. But Audamar didn't answer.

I brought my hand slowly to the back of my head and rubbed the spot carefully. I remembered hitting my head on the rock before passing out; I could almost feel the blood that had dried on its way to my neck.

Audamar took a step toward the bars and I saw the crystals he was holding. Their colors were glittering and they illuminated the entire dungeon. I leaned my back on the wall again and thought about what he had done to Warren and the innocent people who had become the Old Ones. A quick death would be preferable to him using the crystals on me.

Audamar stopped one foot away from the bars. It was impossible to guess what he was thinking from his blank face. Then he did something I never would have expected; he extended the yellow crystal toward me. My eyes grew wide as I looked at the crystal of Aerlion that I had handed him a few weeks ago.

I sat up with difficulty and crawled on my hands to reach the bars of my cell. I had to hold on to the bars to be able to kneel. He didn't see me as a threat. I knew he didn't. I was hurt and didn't have my powers. I was helpless.

Now I was standing quite close to him but I still hesitated to take the crystal from his hand. I didn't know what he was after and the thought of this being a trap rang in my mind. My gaze shifted between him and the crystal.

"Go on, take it."

I reached for the crystal and sat back. The familiar tingling in my palm returned with the weight of the stone. I held the crystal tightly with both hands and closed my eyes.

The first thing that appeared before my eyes was my village. I was in front of our little hut in Aerlion. It was a sunny day, and even though I knew it wasn't real, I could feel the scorching heat touching my skin. I heard sounds of laughter from the back of the house and my eyes filled up with tears immediately. I took a few steps. I saw three people chasing each other and laughing, two little girls and a man. I looked at his young and healthy silhouette and held my breath. He was there. He was just as he had been before the illness had taken him away: full of life.

My gaze shifted to my little sister's youth, and then to my own, trying to keep up with them. I wanted to reach out and freeze that moment. If I could, I would always remain there, live the memory over and over again. But before I could even move, the weight on my hand disappeared and I quickly opened my eyes. Audamar had taken the crystal back.

"What did you see?" he asked. He was watching me carefully.

I looked at him with my narrowed gaze. "My family."

The disappointment on his face was all too evident. He thoughtfully lowered his gaze and took a step back.

"The crystals show the holder what they want the most, don't they?" I asked as I watched him.

But he wasn't looking at me anymore. He breathed out and began pacing in front of the cell. I knew how strong the crystals were; even one of them could provide limitless power to a person. I had seen my father; I had gone back to the past, even if only for a brief moment. The crystal had shown me what I wanted the most—to be a family again. Perhaps this was why Audamar was so enraged. Because every time he touched them, he saw the throne and the future he wanted to create. That had to be driving him crazy.

I continued to look at him carefully as I repeated my question one more time. "Why don't you kill me?"

The First King stopped walking. His gray eyes looked scary in the shadows, but something inside me said that he wasn't going to do anything. I kept crossing paths with him and causing trouble. Yet I was still here. He had let me go each time and I knew that this had nothing to do with the friendship we had built before I found out about his true identity. It didn't make any sense.

Audamar's gaze turned away from me and toward the colorful crystals in his palm. "Kill you? I need you. I'm not done with you yet."

"I don't understand," I said puzzledly. "You let me go each time. If you needed me, then why . . ."

Audamar lifted his shoulders to straighten the fur on his back. "Do you know that there have always been some Protectors who were stronger than the rest? Whose magic was more powerful?"

He tilted his head and his gaze searched my confused face. "They are called the LightBringers, special and rare Protectors who carry the same pure magic as the first Protectors. Over the centuries, there have been a few. But they all knew the past, and that is why even if they sensed their magic, none of them ever tried to find the crystals."

He took a step toward the bars. "But one day," he continued. "I felt the strong presence of Odeir's crystal. It was calling me. I followed the magic and saw Breccan, holding the crystal of Odeir."

I flinched at the name I heard and fixed my eyes on him. "Protector Breccan?" I asked with eyes open wide. All this time, I had thought I was the only Protector who had found a realm's crystal after centuries. But I guess we were all wrong.

"Breccan was one of them," he said. "He was like those Protectors, *different*. He knew he shouldn't even have tried, yet he couldn't resist the urge to follow the magic. He was able to find the crystal of Odeir. But when I found him, he wasn't going to give up . . . He knew who I was as soon as he saw me and I knew I couldn't take the risk and let him tell the others that I was alive." He lowered his head. "He fought until his last breath. But I had to stop him, it was the only way."

His shadow was dancing on the dungeon's walls. As he approached the cell once again, I saw that he was smiling. "I thought I had to wait another few centuries for a Protector like him to be chosen, but then *you* came. And I knew you would be much stronger than Breccan, than any of them. So, I waited."

I shook my head. "Why me?"

Audamar grinned. "Your *blood*. It wasn't hard to guess that you would be a LightBringer as well. You have no idea how strong your blood is . . . I knew you would be one of them, I could sense the magic you carry. I guess this is the second chance for your family to repay what was done in the past." He shook his head. "Fate . . . it works in strange ways."

I breathed in fear as I thought of Sarah and my mother. "My family?"

But Audamar ignored me. "I let you go because I needed you to come after me, to believe that you could actually stop me. It is true that the crystals are all connected, but they don't respond to me. I can use their magic, yet they were not created for humans in the first place. What I can do with them is . . . limited."

"Why are you telling me all this?" I asked. But I already knew the answer. I was the only one he could talk to because I wasn't going anywhere. I was trapped.

Audamar smiled. "Do you know why I waited for all these centuries, Anna? Why I didn't immediately go after the first Protectors and nobles who stole everything from me? After the war, they thought I was dead. I was wounded, and I wasn't healing fast enough. Then, my sister took the throne and became the queen. It took me centuries to regain my power after the war, but it worked. I used Carran's crystal to recover."

He went on joyfully when he saw the expression on my face.

"Yes, Carran's crystal was never hidden. I have had it all the time since the first war. The first Protectors had hidden the other six of them, but it would be yet another Protector to give them back to me. After all, why should I get my hands dirty when I could have someone else do the work for me?"

His hand gripped the iron bars. "When Breccan found Odeir's crystal, Carran's showed me the way. But when the crystals sense a Protector's magic, an ancient magic like the LightBringers carry, I cannot fully control them . . . So, all I needed was a Protector who I could deceive. The others were Phoenixes once, but you . . ."

He leaned over toward me. "You were different. You knew so well what injustice was that it was very easy for me to turn you against the kingdom. An outsider who hated the nobles, and who was desperate to do anything for her loved ones. I admire that, I do, yet you made everything so easy for me . . . I followed you. I wanted to approach on the day you were in the forest, but before I could do anything, Odeir's Protector found you."

I remembered how I had run away after learning the truth from Darrell. When I was following Protector Ramona toward her dragon Etha, I heard a movement coming from among the dense trees. And now, I knew why.

"The day we met at the bar I knew you could sense the two crystals I had on me. Their magic was responding to you. I knew I wasn't going to take any chances this time."

"But then how?" I asked. "If you cannot fully use them, how did you find Demos's crystal?"

"Me?" His lips curled up. "I was not the one who found it, Anna. It was you. I made you believe that I didn't see you as a threat, ignored you, because I knew you would return to stop me. I made you believe you could actually have a chance against me. No . . . no . . . *You,* the *LightBringer,* showed me the way to Demos's crystal. I only followed the magical bond that appeared when you showed up."

I wanted to cry and maybe shout, but all I did was to take a deep, painful breath. I finally knew the reason now. I had thought he no longer needed me when he let me go, but I was wrong.

I had woken up the magic in the places where I went, where he followed me. Just like Breccan had when he went to Odeir and found its crystal. Audamar had followed the magic Breccan brought out, because Protector Breccan was also a LightBringer.

Demos was an example of it. I found the crystal when I followed him to the palace, and the crystal showed itself to him because I was also at the gate then. When I left for my village for the first time, I was able to find Aerlion's crystal easily. Just like Breccan found Odeir's. That was why I was still alive. Now that Breccan was dead, he needed me.

Only three crystals were left, those of Belwald, Nadeer, and Orin. Audamar was now after Edmond's, Leon's, and Thalia's. Protector

Edmond was on our side but Thalia and Leon weren't aware of anything. Darrell and I were a couple of traitors in the eyes of the others, and although it was a secret for now, Edmond's choice would soon be revealed. I had no idea what Ramona and Sam thought, but I knew they wouldn't side with us while Audamar was still acting like Warren.

It could take days, weeks, even months for him—me—to find the three remaining crystals. He needed me and after that, there would be no reason for him to keep me alive. I thought of spending my remaining days in this dark cell.

I first thought of my duty, the one I had vowed to see through. Then I thought of my sister and my mother; it had been weeks since I had seen Sarah and I didn't even know where they were. Then the others rushed to my mind; Hunter, Darrell, Paige . . . Balfour, my old mentor who had sacrificed himself for all of us, and finally Warren.

Audamar thought I was so helpless, so completely harmless, that he hadn't even put chains on me. Knowing that I had let down the people I loved, that I would never see my friends again, made me want to scream.

"I always knew that Warren taking the throne would turn out to be in my favor. He has always been such a disappointment, even for someone from my sister's bloodline. My plan couldn't have been more flawless."

I was looking at him angrily, but at the same time, I was trying to hold back the tears filling my eyes. I was about to cry, not because of sadness or fear, but because of my anger at myself.

"You became a great duo with Warren. I owe everything to you two. My plan couldn't have gone so smoothly if you hadn't been so weak."

He sighed. "Goddess Vitae was cruel enough to put Aerlion's Protectors in my way, *twice*. But this time, it won't work. I did make a mistake once, with *Emily*, and I won't let it happen again. Breccan should be an example of it." A smile spread over his face. "I won, Anna, all thanks to you. And now, you will show me the way to the crystals of Orin, Nadeer, and Belwald. With you by my side, I will find the rest."

"Nothing's over yet. I'll *never* help you."

Audamar tilted his head. His gaze on me was so familiar that I couldn't help but flinch each time our eyes met. He reminded me of Warren so much.

"Why do you fight when you know who is going to win?" he said and took another step toward me. "Eventually, you'll lose everyone close to you. You can't defeat me."

"You're changing people into monsters," I said through my teeth. "You destroy everyone who crosses your path; innocent people, children . . . I will not sit back and watch this."

"I need an army," he said. He looked unbothered by my words. "I once used the creatures, changed their nature. It is a shame that they are extinct now . . . No, as I told you before. The crystals can't bring the dead back, just like they cannot be used to create something that doesn't exist anymore. So, my experiments on people are the only way for me to create them; changing humans' nature just like I did with the creatures of the darkness before."

I stood up without taking my eyes off him. I knew I couldn't reach him through the bars, yet I extended my arm toward him. Just then, the door opened noisily. I looked over his shoulder at the person who walked in. It was Lady Bria.

My stomach rumbled when I saw the food on the silver tray she was carrying, making me realize that I had been hungry for a very long time. I hadn't been able to keep track of time after Thalia had brought me back to the capital, but I hadn't had enough food during my time with Caiden's soldiers anyway, nor had I slept or rested enough.

My angry gaze turned to Lady Bria as Audamar spoke. "There's a council meeting I need to attend. I'll leave you two alone."

He gave us one last look and moved to the exit of the dungeon with slow steps. Bria left the tray in front of the bars as soon as he left. I couldn't take the tray in completely, but I was able to take the food off it piece by piece. I first took the cup of water and brought it quickly to my lips. The bitter taste in my throat was relieved for a brief moment. I kept the cup's cold surface on my lips as I turned my eyes to Bria and saw that she was watching me.

I had seen her only a few times and I still thought that she looked as beautiful as people described her to be. Her features, her long, wavy black hair that came down to her shoulders, and her ice-blue dress that looked expensive and revealed all the curves of her tall figure . . . But yet, I could never look at her the same way again. In a picture where everyone saw nobility, I saw nothing but an enemy.

"Traitor," I hissed. "Your family betrayed the kingdom, and so did you."

Bria crossed her arms. "No," she said as she tilted her head. "I've never chosen a side from the beginning. The Lunavier family doesn't take sides."

I put the now-empty cup on the floor. "You're helping Audamar! You have no idea what you've gotten yourself into!"

Audamar wanted to use the crystals for himself and to be invincible. He was going to change the Seven Realms and he had already begun doing so. The people that he turned into the Old Ones were an example of this.

"My family wants independence, and so do I. Do you know how it feels to be under the rule of someone for centuries? Having your every move watched? Our only difference from the Montborne family is that we weren't able to claim the throne at that time . . . I could have been royalty. I would be the ruler, not the ruled . . . the queen of the Seven Realms! But now, I can do nothing but live under the rule of a useless king as his council member."

"Do you really think Audamar will let you go when everything ends? He won't."

She narrowed her eyes and remained silent for a moment before answering. "Rogue swore an oath. After everything is done, my family and I will leave the capital and we'll never be a king's pawn again. We will become free after so many centuries and we will not serve anyone else."

"What about Warren?" I asked as I averted my gaze from her. It was already bothering me to talk about this. "He . . . he loves you."

Lady Bria took a step back. "He loves his *throne*. Warren will go down with his kingdom."

Even though Lady Bria didn't share Warren's feelings, she had known him for years; Paige had said that they grew up together. So how could she be so heartless? I recalled our conversation on the king's birthday. Bria had told me that she wasn't his shadow. Apparently, her intentions were clear from the beginning; it had just taken me too long to put the pieces together.

"The previous king and queen died because of your family," I said as I exhaled with rage. But in truth, even I was not sure of the reason for my anger. I was defending people whom I had never met, and moreover, I also used to be against the order they represented. But in any case, Bria and her family had committed a crime, a major one. I couldn't stand the fact that they would get away with it.

Bria breathed angrily. She kicked the tray on the floor and spread the food all over the stone surface, but I continued to stare at her face.

"This is the beginning of a new era," said Lady Bria as she crossed her arms again. Her cheeks were red with fury. "The Lunavier family has been belittled throughout history. We chose the Phoenixes for the uprising, making them believe they should be treated differently than just royal guards. They had magic, they were powerful and they could also lead just like the Protectors or the king."

She rolled her green eyes. "But they turned out to be a complete disappointment and our plan failed. And Cheng and his family were too afraid to take us on after the death of the king and queen when the Barrington family was blamed. You see, even then no one liked him . . . They remained silent against all accusations. Despite our failure, I was sure that no one knew of our involvement. We still had to put our plan aside for a while. We couldn't have people suspecting us. So, we waited."

She smiled. "Then Rogue came, making us an offer, an opportunity to change everything. He knew we were behind the uprising, and wanted our alliance as one of the most powerful noble families of Ardria. I immediately knew he could give my family what we wanted."

I looked at her. "Is Lord Cheng involved in this?"

What about the other noble families? The houses of Montborne and Ironlash would never betray Warren, but what about the Tendros family? Had Lord Conrad and his family already chosen a side?

"Cheng doesn't know what's going on yet, but he will learn soon. He will have to obey when Rogue reveals the truth." A cruel smile formed on her face, "Besides, I know he won't take the Montborne's side. He may not know what's happening right now, but during the uprising, he stayed silent. He saw what we could do. His family won't have any choice but to side with us."

Cheng was innocent indeed. I couldn't take my gaze off her as her eyes glowed with excitement. How could she smile while telling me all this?

"And you are now a part of this, whether you like it or not. You talk about treason, but what will it mean when you'll be the one to find the remaining crystals?"

"It doesn't matter. I'll never help him."

One side of her red lips curled up. "You will," she said and took a step toward me. "Rogue is following everyone and everything; there's nothing he doesn't know. There is *no limit* to his power. And if you want your little family to be safe, you *will* cooperate."

A sudden feeling of panic rushed over me as she spoke, and at that moment, I realized how truly scared I was. I didn't care what would happen to me and I didn't really care about letting the others down anymore, but my family . . .

"Where are they?" I hissed as I held on to the rusty bars of my cell. The bars shook under my grasp but I knew there was nothing I could do to get my freedom back. The iron bars wouldn't tear out no matter how hard I shook them.

Bria shrugged. "It won't take too long before he finds them. If you don't help, Rogue will send the Old Ones to the villages and continue hunting everyone down, one by one. Including them. The future of your mother and your sister depends completely on you."

She moved away and began walking to the dungeon's exit as she continued speaking louder, "You will go with him when Rogue starts looking for the next crystal."

And she left me alone in the dungeons.

# CHAPTER 37

The chiming of the bells was echoing in the dark city.

Hurried footsteps rose in the streets. The lights of the city were far away from where I was standing. I looked at the silhouette in a cape running through the dark streets in front of me. Even though I couldn't see everything from where I stood, I understood that I was in the back alleys of the capital. But something was different. As I looked at the low stone walls, the plain wooden huts, and old-style horse carts, it felt as if I had gone a few centuries back.

My legs began moving without my realizing it and I found myself following the caped stranger. She was running. I picked up speed to keep up with her but she never looked back at me despite the sound of my hurried footsteps. She hadn't noticed that she was being followed, because I was in a dream.

We arrived at another dark blind alley. The caped stranger turned in another direction as if she knew what she was looking for in the darkness, and someone else appeared ahead in the shadows. The stranger that I followed elegantly raised her hand and lowered her cape, letting her silver hair drop down to her shoulders.

I had seen her before; I narrowed my eyes and took a step toward her. I remembered the woman from the battlefield in my dream; the way her fearful eyes were looking at me as the shadow behind her was holding the seven crystals.

Her light blue eyes looked around worriedly as the bells continued to chime. "The other Protectors have realized that the crystal is missing," she said to the stranger.

Her hand went to the pocket of the trousers that she wore under her long cape and when she brought it back out, I saw the yellow crystal shining in her palm, the crystal of Aerlion. The woman extended her arm, presenting the stone to the stranger across from her. The man raised his head and his face, illuminated by the moonlight, came into sight. I saw his sharp, gray eyes.

"Audamar," said the woman, begging. "You are a lord and you'll take your father's place in the council one day. If anyone finds out that you have the crystal, you'll be sent to exile. We promised your father to keep the crystals safe—he won't like this. I don't understand why you want it."

My gaze shifted from the woman to Audamar. He looked quite young, even younger than King Warren. This young man with short dark hair and a sharp gaze was wearing all black, and his tall figure was hidden under layers of fabric. I knew that Audamar was one of Warren's ancestors. In fact, as I looked at him now, I couldn't help but think how much they looked alike. While I continued to examine him, Audamar snatched the crystal from the young woman's hand and held it tightly.

"I will not always remain a member of the council, Emily. I want more power."

The woman looked at him. I realized that this wasn't just a dream; it was a memory. I had gone back a few centuries at least. Audamar was the First King, and this meant that he hadn't taken the throne yet.

"It has been only a few years since the other noble families agreed to work with the house of Montborne, but there are already rumors about a betrayal. The people are not fully committed to the head family." He turned his gaze to the yellow crystal in his hand. "We are the strongest. We have the Goddess's gifts but it is only a matter of time before the others try to steal them. We are powerful, and powerful people are born to rule; not to manage the clans with a handful of family elders and collect taxes."

"Lord Chester would never . . ."

Audamar quickly interrupted the young woman. "My father is an old fool."

His lashing out caused Emily to step back. Audamar smiled gently and lowered his head. His words came out softer now. "There's a reason why the Goddess created the crystals; we are strong and we have to remain that way. But this isn't enough. My father took the crystals from the Protectors, yet he doesn't even use their powers."

He raised his arm to the sides and pointed at the space around him. "I will be the head of the family after my father's death, and that's when everything will change. There should be only one man to rule the Seven Realms, and I will be the one. Not noble clans or other family elders. Just me. A king."

The young woman's features became tense as he went on. "But who can say for how long I can keep my place in the family while my sister is trying to take my spot? I can't fail; I have to show everyone, Emily . . . I'll be the king of the Seven Realms."

"The Protectors do not serve under a king," said Emily quickly. "We exist to be a bridge between the people and the leading families. We represent equality."

I thought of the conversation I'd had with Warren at the greenhouse. Warren had said that he didn't trust the Protectors because we didn't work solely for the king, but also for the people. We were the bridge in between. Now, it was shocking for me to realize how similar Audamar and Warren's thoughts were.

It was a Protector who had given the crystal away and started the war centuries ago . . . that was what he had told me. It was Emily who had given this power to Audamar in the first place. I looked at the yellow crystal in Audamar's palm. Emily, the first Protector of Aerlion.

Audamar didn't listen to a single word she said. A broad smile formed on his face as he looked at his hand. "With this, I can destroy anyone and everything that stands in my way. Forever . . . a king that never dies."

Suddenly, fear filled her blue eyes. "You're talking about immortality."

Audamar put the crystal in his pocket and walked over to the woman. He put his hands on her smooth, snow-white cheeks. "Emily," he said softly. I saw his expression change. He was looking at her differently. If I hadn't known Audamar, I would have said it was love.

"We can do this together. You and I can rule the Seven Realms. Forever. Everything will change if we can get the other crystals."

But Emily took a step back. "I've already betrayed my Goddess by bringing you the crystal of my realm. And now you want me to betray my friends and my oath."

Audamar grimaced. "The Protectors aren't your friends. I'm the only one you need. We can create a new order together . . . just the two of us. Why can't you see that?"

Audamar held the woman's hand once again but she swung her arm and freed herself from his touch.

"I am the Protector of Aerlion." She inhaled with anger. "What you ask of me . . . I thought you wanted me to bring the crystal to help people . . . Each crystal was created for a Protector; no one is supposed to have all seven of them, you know that."

Then she quickly looked away. "Audamar, if you use the crystal for your personal gain, I will have to report it to Lord Chester and the others at the council."

"If you do that, everyone will find out about your treason. You brought me the crystal with your own hands."

The woman seemed hurt for a moment, as if she couldn't believe what Audamar was saying. "I don't know what your plans are but I will be forced to stop you if you go too far. Even if I have to throw myself in danger...This is my duty."

Audamar breathed angrily. "If you leave me, you can't be a part of the future I will create. Only an idiot would do that."

The woman quickly raised her hand and a white light shone through her fingers. Her other hand was on the hilt of the sword on her belt. "Give me the crystal back, Audamar," she said carefully. "If you return it now, I'll let you go and keep this between us."

Audamar seemed disappointed; he slowly shook his head. I began watching the two of them with curiosity and fear, not knowing what his next move would be. I wanted to shout and tell her to run, but Audamar quickly stuck his hand into his pocket, and as soon as his fingers touched the crystal, the young Protector reeled backward.

Emily was the Protector of Aerlion. I realized that although she had powers, she wasn't using them against him. But why? Was it because of her feelings for him?

She was leaning on her elbows now, trying to stand up, but Audamar swung his hand at her and she fell back down again.

"This is the first crystal I possess, but it won't be the last. I won't spare you if you cross my path again."

Protector Emily raised her hand and I looked at the light shining in her palm. But before she could do anything, Audamar pointed a finger at her and the young woman was thrust back down with a scream.

Audamar began walking, and before disappearing into the dark street I saw him looking back over his shoulder at the woman lying on the ground. His face still had traces of disappointment as he walked away.

•

The first thing I felt as I opened my eyes was the marble floor slipping from under me. I flinched at the weight on my wrists and I saw the guards walking in front of me while dragging me by heavy chains. I breathed in fear.

"Where are you taking me?" I asked as I tried to pull my arms toward myself.

But the guards didn't answer. I fought against their tugging and tried to keep my arms whole. One of the guards pulled my chains and I fell flat on my face. But they didn't even wait for me to get up. I was still trying to free myself and escape as they dragged me along. What was happening? Where were we going? Audamar had said that he needed me; didn't that mean they wouldn't harm me?

Although I knew it was in vain, I continued to struggle helplessly. After a while, I saw the big door at the end of the hallway. The feeling of panic rushed through me and I began pulling at the chains harder. The heavy door opened to both sides as we approached, and the guards let go of my chains after pushing me into the throne room. The chains were still rattling as I rolled on the floor.

I forced myself to stand up. The light from the burning torches in the throne room illuminated my face. The doors closed noisily behind us and it became silent as a grave. I forced myself to stand up once again, unaware of what I was going to face. I looked around and nervously let out a breath when I saw them. The Protectors were here.

I looked away from the four sets of eyes on me and turned to the shadow sitting at the throne. Audamar was watching me.

"Why am I here?" I asked, my voice filled with both anger and fear.

I realized he wasn't going to treat me the same way he did when we were alone. He didn't have that usual grin on his face. His personality was completely different now; the others were still part of his game and he wasn't going to reveal anything to them yet.

"Protector Anna. You've betrayed the kingdom and you turned your back on your people. We have been looking for you for days so that you can finally face the justice of the Goddess Vitae."

I had to admit that I saw none other than King Warren when he looked at me that way. He had the same upright stance.

"Why don't you tell them the truth?" I hissed angrily, "Tell them what you did! Who you really are!"

My answer seemed to amuse him. He raised an eyebrow and looked at me with a vague expression on his face that told me he was having fun. But it was so indistinct that I was the only one to notice it.

Suddenly the doors of the throne room opened and I turned to see the person walking in. Protector Edmond suddenly glided in through the tall doors. A feeling of hope sprouted inside me when I thought of the last time I had seen him at the shelter. But it went away as quickly as it had come. He couldn't save me. The fact that he was here meant that no one knew anything about him.

"I'm sorry, Warren," he said with distress that reflected in his tone. "I had a few things I had to take care of."

He walked quickly to where the other Protectors were standing, without even glancing in my direction. Audamar's lips slowly curled upward and his narrowed eyes watch Edmond take his place.

"You've completed your mission by bringing Protector Anna to the capital, Protector Thalia. You've brought the fugitive to justice."

I came eye to eye with Protector Edmond while my gaze shifted between Thalia and Audamar. He didn't even blink. Edmond turned his gaze away without the slightest reaction.

"When will Protector Anna's execution take place?"

I was startled by the question. I looked at Protector Leon, who was standing with the others. It had been a long time since I had gotten out of the cell where King Warren had put me the first time, and I found myself in the same situation once again; the same feeling of panic rushed to me.

Protector Leon looked at me with his pale eyes and went on, "A new Protector must be chosen for Aerlion immediately."

My powers had been taken from me but only one person could be chosen from Aerlion. They had to get rid of me so that a new person could be chosen to sustain the cycle of Protectors. I had to die.

Audamar looked thoughtful, trying to decide what to do with me. But I knew the answer. He needed me.

"We will keep her in the dungeons until we find the crystal of Aerlion," said Audamar as he turned to the others. I wanted to laugh at his words but only a bitter wheeze came out of my lips.

"The fact that the crystal is missing puts all the Seven Realms in danger. She's the only one who can tell us where it is."

I continued to look at him with unbelieving eyes. I wanted to say something about his lie, to cry out. I had to tell the Protectors and make them believe me, but I was frozen. I couldn't move.

"We've been looking for it everywhere," said Protector Sam as he took a step forward. "There's no sign of it. Whomever she gave the crystal to must have hidden it. Otherwise, rumors would have spread already. No one could resist using the Goddess's crystal and be quiet about it."

*He is not King Warren . . . Rogue . . . and he has them.* Many thoughts passed through my mind, but my body was frozen. I couldn't move, nor could I part my lips. My gaze shifted to Audamar as I stood motionlessly and our eyes met again. With that, the expression on his face changed. He was grinning now. When he made a fist with his hand at the side of the throne, I felt invisible hands on my throat. I gulped harshly and tried to breathe. My lungs ached for air. And I understood that he was using the crystals on me.

Audamar turned to look at Protector Leon again and his hand had loosened. I hungrily filled my lungs with a deep breath. None of the Protectors even looked at me, except one. Protector Edmond turned his worried eyes to me for the first time since he had walked in; he seemed to have felt something was wrong.

"Unfortunately," Audamar said as he suddenly stood up from his throne and began walking slowly down the marble steps. "Protector Anna won't be tried alone."

I turned to him immediately as I heard Protector Thalia's voice. "Darrell also . . ."

Audamar cut in. "I'm not talking about Protector Darrell."

When the doors of the throne room opened once again, I watched a dozen people rush in with their blue capes and silver armor. The Phoenixes were here. But from which Protector's army were they? What were they doing here?

I began looking at the incoming soldiers with the hope of seeing a familiar face. Then I saw the Protectors take a step back with a shocked expression. At the same time, I heard one of them draw his sword. The group of Phoenixes formed a small circle around the Protectors, and in the middle was Edmond.

No. I was still under Audamar's control but I tried to free myself and run over. My body felt heavy again. No one even looked at me when I lost my balance and fell onto the marble floor. The chains on my wrists felt heavier.

When Audamar made a fist with his other hand, the sword Edmond was holding slipped from his hand and fell onto the ground. The old Protector fell onto his knees. The Phoenixes around him put chains—similar to mine—on Edmond's wrists and Audamar's loud voice was heard.

"Protector Edmond," he said as he turned to the old man captured by his own soldiers. "I arrest you for working with Protector Anna and Protector Darrell. You turned your back on the kingdom and you shall stand trial for this."

Then he turned to one of the Phoenixes and said, "Take him out of here."

The Phoenixes used to be the symbol of independence against the kingdom. After what had happened to Warren's family, they had been given under the command of the Protectors and they no longer took orders directly from the king. They were still there, though. But now, they were obeying Audamar's orders, whom they thought to be the real king, against their own Protector. I was witnessing another victory of the Master of Darkness against us.

Protector Edmond was dragged out of the throne room the same way I had been brought in. I looked at him with eyes full of shock and fear, unable to turn my head elsewhere until he disappeared out of sight.

# CHAPTER 38

I looked through the rusty bars, feeling the cold wall on my back. The dirt between the stones on the ground had smeared my clothes and left me covered in dust. I closed my eyes. I didn't want to see any more of the tiny cell where I had spent my last couple of days. It didn't matter; I was never getting out of here. The thought of freedom seemed so far away.

"We'll die here," I said with a whisper. "We'll never get out."

Protector Edmond had been put in the same dungeon after the meeting at the throne room. I couldn't see his cell from where I was, but this didn't prevent me from hearing him. From the rattling of the chains on his wrists, I could tell that he was moving.

"He won't kill us," he said slowly. He sounded so tired. A few days ago, the Phoenixes had brought him the same poison I was given during my trial. It made him dizzy and unable to use his magic. "If he does, the cycle will continue and another Protector will be chosen. He'd rather keep us here than to have a new Protector to deal with."

A new Protector meant another enemy, another obstacle for him. It suited him to keep us alive while we were stuck here.

"For how long?" I asked as I leaned my head back and pushed deeper in between the stones of the wall.

"Protectors can live for centuries; who knows?"

His words left me breathless. Knowing that these tiny cells and dark dungeon would be the only thing I would see for years . . . no, I couldn't stay here.

"I talked to Bria," I said while gritting my teeth. "She mentioned my family. Audamar is after them."

I clenched my fists to stop myself from crying. My family was in danger because of me. I had only one option: help Audamar find the three remaining crystals. I knew my powers were long gone, but I still had my bond with the magic. That was how I was able to call Deegan. I still had my bond with him. I guessed that was also how I could find the rest of the crystals.

"So, the treason of the Lunavier family is true then?"

I nodded, even though he couldn't see me. "I have to help him. He said I could find the rest of them."

Edmond paused for a moment before answering. "You?"

"I don't know what to do. He should never have all seven crystals, but my family . . ."

I heard Edmond fill his lungs with a deep breath. "But is Rogue right?"

"There's something very close . . . a strange feeling, different from the other crystals. Ever since I found Aerlion's crystal, I am aware of the thing that has woken inside me, even though I don't have my powers anymore."

"How can that be possible? Without your powers—"

I cut into his words. "He said something about my family." I remembered what he said about my blood. I didn't even know what that meant. "He said I am a LightBringer, and so was Breccan. That is why I could lead him to the crystals."

"I thought it was only a legend," Edmond said slowly. "I didn't even know LightBringers were real. But it makes sense."

I let out a gentle breath, "And what about you? What did Audamar do to you at the throne room? You could've escaped him."

The answer took longer than I had expected. "If more than one crystal is used at the same time, they can even take a Protector under control . . . I had never felt that helpless before. I couldn't use my powers. I felt Rogue in my mind . . . the presence of the crystals was very intense."

I remembered what Audamar had done to Darrell in Demos. He had also used the crystals on him that day and controlled him.

I tossed my head back and began looking at the ceiling. The door opened. Someone walked in slowly. I looked at the entrance, fearing that it could be Audamar or Bria, but I saw that it was only a servant with food trays in his hands. The servant first went to Edmond's cell and put the tray in front of the bars. Then he came and slowly leaned over.

"We're going to get you out of here."

My eyes grew wide at sound of the familiar voice. I looked at the servant's face and found a pair of green eyes.

"Thomas," I said. But he didn't turn to look at me a second time.

"Protector Darrell is in the palace."

He picked up the tray of the previous meal as the door opened again, and this time, the person I saw at the doorsill was Protector Thalia. Seeing her made me forget that Thomas was still here with us in the dungeon.

As she walked over slowly, I continued to stare at her face. Thomas quickly got up with the trays in his hands and bowed in front of her before leaving. But she didn't seem to have noticed it.

She crossed her arms and took a few steps toward me, not neglecting to look back over her shoulder to shoot Protector Edmond a short glance.

"Why are you here?" I asked.

"King Warren wants to see you."

I laughed unwillingly when she addressed him by that name. I turned my head away and heard Protector Thalia's angry voice once again. "Don't think that we'll ever stop looking for Aerlion's crystal."

"He is not King Warren . . ." I said with rage, but I couldn't go on with my sentence. I paused. Whatever Audamar had done, I was still under its influence. My voice had stuck in my throat; I couldn't speak.

Protector Thalia narrowed her eyes, "Is that how you fooled Darrell; telling more of your lies?"

"You don't know anything." Protector Edmond's angry voice filled the dungeons. "None of you have any idea on how big a danger awaits the Seven Realms."

Thalia turned around and looked baffled at her old friend. "The Seven Realms are in danger because of her," she said as she pointed a finger at me. Then, in disappointment, she added, "I can't believe you've taken her side. I'd expect that from Darrell. But your betrayal . . . *never*."

Protector Thalia moved a finger and the lock of the cell's door opened. She immediately grabbed me by the collar of my shirt. I wanted to fight her, or maybe return to my cell. I was safer behind the iron bars. But Protector Thalia was extremely strong. As we walked to the exit, my eyes found Edmond behind the bars. I saw him shaking his head, but soon, he was out of my sight.

The royal guards were waiting for us at the dungeon's exit. As soon as we walked over to them, Thalia's grip on me loosened and the guards wasted no time in surrounding me. I was stuck between them.

There could be only one reason for Audamar to call me; his wait for the final crystals was over and he wanted to take action. I knew I had to stop him from having all the crystals, but the image of my family rushed to my mind and my eyes brimmed with tears. I didn't even have a choice.

"Listen to me," I said to Protector Thalia, who was walking in front of us. "You're in greater danger than you think. You all are! He's deceiving you. He's . . ."

The magic showed itself once again and the words couldn't leave my lips. I gritted my teeth.

"You all think that three Protectors have betrayed the kingdom! Do you think this is a coincidence? I may be new, but Darrell and Edmond have been here for centuries. Can't you just stop and think why they did that even for a second?"

Thalia spoke without turning to me. "Maybe you used the crystal on them. I don't know how you convinced them but you started all of this. And you'll be punished."

As I walked in the wide hallways of the palace under the company of the guards who had surrounded me and limited my every move, I couldn't help but think how much had changed during the last few weeks. This palace, where I had roamed aimlessly between the training sessions I received from Balfour, had now become the enemy's nest. And one of the Protectors that had sworn to serve the Seven Realms was delivering me to him. Protector Thalia was unaware of everything, just as the others were. On the other hand, the fact that I, the one who had started everything, couldn't do anything against Audamar brought the feeling of defeat deep into my bones.

Instead of heading for the stairs to the throne room, Protector Thalia turned into another hallway and the crowd of guards followed her.

"Where are we going?" I asked, but she ignored me.

All I could hear were the rhythmic footsteps. I looked at the guards on both sides, and I realized it was impossible for me to get away from them. We continued to walk along the palace hallways in silence, until the doors to the courtyard opened. It was Audamar who greeted us. He was standing alone in the middle of the yard, and as soon as we arrived, he turned to us with a smile on his face. I took a sharp breath when the guards stopped, and before long, I saw all of them walking to the other side of the courtyard. They were going to leave me alone with him.

I looked at Protector Thalia, who was still standing next to me; Audamar seemed not to have noticed her until now. He knit his eyebrows and said, "Leave me alone with her."

His tone was rude, more than I had ever heard from King Warren. Thalia was startled but she kept her eyes on Audamar.

"But—"

"I said, *leave.*"

She began walking after the royal guards, but she still had that confused expression on her face. Our eyes met as she passed by, but then she looked away.

Audamar turned to me after everyone left, his smile still intact. He took a step toward me and narrowed his gray eyes. I couldn't tell what was going through his mind, but I knew it was nothing good.

"You'll never find those crystals," I said as I continued to stare into his eyes. "We won't let you."

"Do you really think a bunch of fugitives can stop me? You saw what I did to Warren, and just a single crystal was enough for that."

"You didn't do anything to Warren," I said ragingly, but we all knew there was something wrong with him. He had been affected by the crystals' powers. My only fear was that this effect would continue after he woke up. *Had* he woken up? Was he conscious? I tried to calculate the number of days I had spent here as a prisoner but I didn't have the slightest clue.

"Perhaps not from the outside, but inside . . . I got into his mind and reached his deepest thoughts. Even *you* can't fix that."

I quickly shook my head. "You don't know him. You don't have the slightest idea of how strong he is."

His smile broadened as if my answer had amused him. "Warren is like me; I see my own youth in him. He's ready to rule, to control. The throne is not something easy to give up for a Montborne... You'll see that, just watch."

I looked around to realize that there was no one else in the courtyard, which was probably what Audamar had wanted.

"Wouldn't you like to know?" he asked suddenly. "Warren's deepest thoughts, *feelings?* Wouldn't you like to know everything in his mind about his family or the kingdom? His feelings for the Lunavier woman, or for *you?*"

"For *me?*" I tried to look angry but there was a slight curiosity in my voice and he noticed. His smile broadened.

"I must say I am impressed. For someone who hated the king so much, you were still able to get under his skin. He is so confused, thanks to you."

His words had caught me off guard. The unreadable mask on my face suddenly cracked as he turned back with a smile. He happily put his hand into the pocket of his jacket and took the crystals out in his palm. He then began making circles with his other hand. The surface under my feet began to shake and the enormous energy that I felt began spreading around. A new gate shone in the sky.

I knew that gates were scattered in different corners of the Seven Realms, but they were all in the same place since the beginning when they were created. But now, Audamar had created another one in a blink of an eye. I hadn't even thought this could be possible until I saw him do it. My gaze went between the shining circle and him.

"No one and nothing will come between me and the crystals."

But he was wrong. There would always be someone to stop him as long as the Protectors existed. Perhaps the others weren't aware of it right now, but something inside me said that Audamar wouldn't be able to keep his secret for much longer.

He suddenly turned his gray eyes at me. "Join me, Anna."

I was startled by his question and took a step away from him. "What?"

"I can teach you everything I know. Maybe your dream about your father can't come true, but it's not too late for the rest of your family. We can still change the Seven Realms."

I saw the shadows in his eyes as his lips curled intimidatingly. He had said that he needed me. He wanted my powers because I was different, stronger.

"You don't want to help the Seven Realms," I said as I angrily shook my head. "You want to rule it. You told me the future we desire is different."

"There has always been a ruler who reigned the realms." He didn't seem affected by my words. "The throne can never be left empty. I will rule the Seven Realms better than your little king. Warren is a taint on the Montborne family."

"People died because of you. The dark magic woke up when you laid hands on the crystals, and you turned people into creatures. All you want is power. You don't care about anyone else."

The chains on my wrists were still intact and I knew I could not get rid of them. Being stripped of my powers made me no different from an ordinary prisoner. I knew that I couldn't escape him; the only thing I could actually do was stall him. But I didn't know for how long I could continue to do that.

"You come from nobility, Audamar," I said in an attempt to distract him. "You became the king by betraying your family. The *First* King of the Seven Realms. You gained power by force. And then you turned your back on everyone."

Audamar didn't seem to be listening to me. He turned away, resolute, but I kept on without a pause. "You betrayed everyone. Your family, the kingdom, and *her* . . . *Emily*. You betrayed them all."

This time, I managed to draw his attention. He turned to me in rage. The crystals in his hand suddenly began to shine and I gasped for breath. I fell on my knees. The only thing preventing my face from hitting the surface was my hands, resisting the force on my back.

I gritted my teeth and tried to stand up but the pressure increased as I did. He was still standing in place without taking his angry gaze off me even for a moment.

I continued. "I made the same mistake that she did; I gave you the crystal of Aerlion for the second time."

He had begun visiting me, not while I was at the palace but after I moved to the temple after my ceremony. He was able to come in and out easily because the Phoenixes' powers weren't as strong as the Protectors', and I wasn't fully trained yet to sense the magic as others could. That was how he avoided the other Protectors. We were out of the palace borders when I found the crystal of Aerlion, so no one could sense the presence of the other two crystals on him and become suspicious. Not the Protectors nor the Phoenixes.

"But this doesn't mean that I won't do everything in my power to stop you. History will repeat itself and you will lose. And this time, I'll make sure you're truly defeated."

The pressure on me disappeared as soon as Audamar lowered his hand. He was still looking at me as he began to speak.

"These are pretentious words," he said, and went on, "I may appear to you as an ordinary opponent, an enemy that threatens the kingdom, but allow me to remind you of something, *Protector* Anna. *I* built this kingdom. *I* was the first to possess the crystals. *I* created a different kind of creature with the stones. *I* released the dark magic onto the Seven Realms. I've been living for thousands of years and I am the most powerful man alive."

His gaze shifted to the gate he had created. "You're going to help me, whether you want to or not. I'm not someone you can defeat just like that. I am invincible."

My knees began shaking when he raised his hand again. I took a step forward without my control and then I began gliding through the air in the courtyard toward him. Audamar was directing me by just moving his fingers and I was getting closer to the new gate. As I looked at the beam of light, I wondered where we were headed. Whose realm would we start from? Where was he dragging me? I tried to fight the magic back but he was too strong.

"Emily also didn't have a chance against me, but the other Protectors helped her. I was too inexperienced to realize how powerful the crystals actually were." He shook his head. "I won't repeat the same mistakes with you this time, Anna *Silverthorn*."

With the name coming out of his lips, I turned to him. "What did you say?"

But he only smiled and raised his hand. I felt the magic before actually seeing it.

I started tugging at the chains on my wrists, trying to free myself, when suddenly a bright light shone in the yard. It blinded us. My aching muscles suddenly loosened and I felt the magic lose its effect. I was no longer being dragged into the gate by invisible hands. I blinked and tried to look at what had distracted Audamar.

I saw the person that now stood between the First King and me.

"We felt it," said Protector Thalia without even looking at me. "The dark magic was summoned to the palace."

Her gaze was fixed on Audamar. As she slowly turned her eyes to the shining gate he had created, I realized that she had said *we*. I turned around, curious, and saw that Protectors Sam, Ramona, and Leon had encircled us.

"I don't know you, Protector Anna." I turned to look at Thalia's back as she went on. "But I know Edmond and Darrell. And I know they would never betray the kingdom."

She suddenly drew her sword from its scabbard and pointed the sharp weapon at Audamar. "You may look like King Warren but we all know you aren't him. I can feel the magic you possess, and the darkness you bring."

Audamar grinned as if he was having fun, but it was impossible to understand what he had in mind.

I flinched when Protector Thalia suddenly turned to me. My sharp gaze began shifting between her and Audamar. I was trying to figure out which side would strike first when Protector Thalia raised her sword. I opened my eyes wide with fear and the sharp metal suddenly found its way to the chains on my wrists. She shattered the chain with a strength far beyond that of an ordinary human.

Protector Thalia quickly turned back and pointed her sword at Audamar. She was looking at the enemy, and they were all trying to figure out his next move.

But Audamar was still smiling.

# CHAPTER 39

My gaze shifted to Audamar over Protector Thalia's shoulder as I waited for him to attack. The other Protectors were no different. Yet no one moved. I could feel the power spreading around us. The presence of Audamar and of the Protectors had brought together an enormous source of magic into a single place. And the magic emitting from the crystals was far from ignorable.

Audamar took a step forward. As he did, I saw the others gripping their weapons firmly.

"I was wondering when you would realize."

Audamar raised his palm toward the sky as I continued to look at the crystals shining in his hand. The other Protectors stared at his palm, bewildered, watching the crystals that they were seeing for the first time. They were the evidence that proved the legends right, and they were right before our eyes.

"Fall back!" I cried and turned to the others as I pulled Protector Thalia by her arm. "Run!"

When Audamar made a fist with his hand, the floor under us began to tremble. I let go of Thalia's arm. The Protectors stumbled away at the same time, trying to shake off the initial effect of the shock. It was Protector Sam who caught me and helped me to stay on my feet. I saw the dark creatures rushing into the courtyard from the gate that he'd created. Audamar was calling the Old Ones to the capital.

I heard Protector Leon murmur to himself, "What the hell is this?"

The number of creatures coming through the gate increased as if they were endless. I held Protector Sam by the collar of his cape and began pulling him. "We have to go!"

I saw the gray clouds gathering on top of the royal palace. The wind became stronger, silencing everything else other than its own buzzing.

"What's going on?" I turned to Protector Thalia standing a few feet away when I heard her voice. "How can he call the Old Ones? How does he have the crystals?"

But I didn't have any time to explain. A part of me was happy with the fact that they had realized I hadn't been lying, but the satisfaction soon disappeared with the fear and panic.

"There's no time to explain! We have to get out of here at once!"

"I'm not going anywhere!" Protector Leon stopped walking and pointed his sword at the creatures. "We can beat them. We're the Protectors!"

"But not him!" I said as I turned my gaze to Audamar once again. He was still standing in the middle of the courtyard. The crystals were between his hands and his eyes were shut. The storm seemed to be obeying him as it whirled around him, and the Old Ones' cries echoed in the courtyard.

"We can't beat the Master of Darkness!"

I noticed that I could talk freely now that Audamar's spell on me had been removed. There was no one left for him to deceive anymore. The Protectors flinched visibly with the words that came out of my mouth.

I heard Thalia's voice, "He . . ."

"Rogue! Rogue Audamar Montborne, the First King! And if we don't hurry up, we won't have enough time to run!"

I could see from the expressions on their faces that they were afraid. I looked at the Old Ones. Perhaps the Protectors could be enough to stop them, but the enemy with five of the Goddess's crystals was much stronger than we were.

"Anna!"

I turned my head to the familiar voice I heard and saw the crowd of soldiers approaching from the other end of the courtyard. Someone was running in the front and there were a few Phoenixes following him. The armored stranger took off his helmet as they came over.

"Darrell!" I said with the relief of being rescued.

I looked at the crowd of soldiers behind him and realized that Thomas had been telling the truth. Darrell had come to rescue us. And he had brought help.

The Protectors' gazes went to Darrell and I thought it was difficult to know what they were thinking. Protector Thalia knit her eyebrows and began examining her old friend, while Sam and Ramona's faces were unreadable. I looked around the wide courtyard again. The Old Ones had gathered around Audamar, taking him inside a big circle. He slowly opened his eyes as I watched him, and he turned in our direction. Although we were a large enough crowd to stand against him, I knew he didn't see us as a real threat.

"What will we do?" It was Protector Leon who asked.

"The Old Ones have covered the entrances. He'll send them after us if we run. We can't let him unleash them into the city."

Grunts began rising from the group of guards waiting behind Darrell. He raised his hands, and at his command, they all took out their weapons. My eyes met Audamar's once again. The smile came back to his face as I saw that the circle around him was getting wider with each passing minute.

Audamar also raised his hand. We all drew back, thinking that he would attack, but the Master of Darkness brought his hand to his face. I narrowed my eyes as he began pulling his skin with his thumb and index finger. He was slowly peeling off his face, making me look away in disgust.

When Audamar was finally done peeling the skin that had covered his face like a mask, he had returned to his usual self, the way he looked when I first met him. He didn't need to act like King Warren any longer. The Master of Darkness was back, and he was much stronger.

The same disgusted expression slowly disappeared from the soldiers' faces, and soon afterward fear clouded their eyes. The creatures around him started to move, roaring at the same time.

"Run!" I screamed once again.

But they were much faster than us. Hundreds of them began rushing toward us and soon they had surrounded the entire courtyard.

"Anna!"

Darrell threw the second sword on his belt to me. Not having my powers didn't mean I couldn't defend myself. An attack from one of the Old Ones would hardly have any effect on the Protectors, but it would be enough to knock me down. So I decided to take a few steps back and wait among the crowd. Protectors Sam and Thalia quickly ran at the herd of creatures and headed for the Master of Darkness standing next to the gate.

Both Protectors charged at the same time. Their moves were synchronized. Protector Sam held Thalia by the arm and swung her over to Audamar, who was barely able to stop her thrust at the last instant. He created a bright shield with the crystals in his hand. Audamar swung his other hand and this caused both Protectors to fly across the courtyard. But it didn't take them long to take their stand back. They raised their hands and the courtyard filled with light, but Audamar just clenched his fist and easily absorbed their magic.

A shadow appeared in front of me. There were two Dralein. I skidded on my knees to evade the claw of the bulkier one and stabbed the weapon's sharp tip into the creature's arm. But the Dralein seemed unaffected. It raised its arm with a roar and I saw the sword move with it. Before I could take it back, it slid on the floor and landed somewhere behind the creature. I rolled on the ground to weather its charge and the creature's claw hit the floor of the yard and shattered the stone into pieces.

I began running. I couldn't dare to look behind as I moved through the crowd of guards and creatures lunging at each other; the two Dralein were still chasing me. I turned around, causing the Old Ones to pause for a brief moment. I knelt down, skidding the final few feet to the sword. I grabbed it and turned around immediately. As soon as I turned, the sword stabbed the creature that was a few inches away from me. All I could think of, as I let out a cry, was how close the Dralein was. As I looked at its claw, which could have shredded my skin into pieces had it swung it a moment earlier, an arrow whizzed from the other side of the courtyard and sank into the creature's back. Two other arrows followed, hitting their mark.

The Dralein took a couple of steps back. I then held the sword tightly and pulled it out of the creature. It fell on its knees and tumbled to the ground. My gaze met Protector Leon's. He had saved me, but I had no time to enjoy the victory.

The second Dralein roared. The number of Old Ones was fewer, but the guards were also falling to the ground one by one. As I looked at the bodies piling up on the floor, I tried to calculate our losses. How many people had we lost today?

I could see that the Protectors were still trying to reach Audamar, and although the enemy was able to fend off their attacks, he seemed tired. It was satisfying to see that, after so many defeats against him, our attacks were finally doing some damage.

Painful cries blended into the roars, and a disgusting sound echoed in the courtyard every time that swords met flesh. Suddenly, the noise was suppressed with the strong flapping of wings. Before I could realize what was going on, the courtyard lit up with flames. The first thing I felt was the scorching heat; I had been caught off guard just like everyone else. I looked at the sky and saw the dragons gliding through the vapor from the bodies of creatures that had turned to ash. The Protectors' dragons had come to the rescue of their riders.

Etha, Protector Ramona's sky-blue dragon, was the first to touch the ground. The floor beneath our feet shook and the dragon's ear-piercing cry filled the courtyard. Protector Leon's giant, snow-white dragon, Nindos, turned the Dralein into ash with a single breath. Then, finally, all the dragons landed at the other end of the courtyard.

The timing couldn't be better. I turned around to continue fighting but then, I froze. I couldn't hear the battle anymore. It felt like time had slowed down, and the rhythmic sound of a pounding heart chimed in my ears.

The strength of the magic was making me feel a tightness in my chest. I knelt on my knees with the pressure and put my hands on the ground. I could feel the power; the power of a crystal, calling me. My heartbeat began pounding even faster.

I looked around in shock to see where the crystal could be, and my gaze focused on the gold-colored dragon on the other side of the courtyard. A pain struck my chest. I exhaled and turned my head.

I hoped he hadn't noticed *that* feeling. Although my bond with the crystals was stronger than his, Audamar was the holder of them. It was impossible for him not to feel it. And once again, I was leading him unwillingly.

The Master of Darkness was still fighting with the Protectors but he had also felt the magic surrounding the courtyard. Our gazes met and a smile appeared on his face.

"No!" I cried. My voice came out much louder than I had expected, and all the Protectors turned to me as my gaze shifted to the golden dragon.

"Thalia!"

My cry reached the Protector and she turned to me, but I wasn't looking at her. She followed my gaze.

"Ceissi!" she suddenly shouted.

In the blink of an eye, Audamar appeared in front of the dragons. Protector Thalia's golden dragon was standing at the far end of the group of them. The dragon breathed heavily as if she had realized something wasn't right. I looked at her bright skin; her golden scales had begun shining with the presence of the crystals.

Everything happened in a heartbeat.

Audamar reached out his hand toward the dragon and his bare hands pierced through the dragon's thick skin. I felt nauseous.

"No!" cried Protector Thalia and took a step toward her dragon. But Leon caught her immediately and didn't allow her to go any closer. It was too late. After struggling some more, Protector Thalia weakly fell on her knees but kept her wet eyes on her dragon.

Before long, we saw the white crystal shining in Audamar's blood-soaked hand. The crystal of Orin. It had been hidden inside the dragon by the first Protector of Orin.

Another painful cry came out of Thalia's lips. "Ceissi!"

The dragon slowly rolled over on the ground and its shining skin suddenly began to fall apart. Then it caught fire.

I froze when her cries, showing how much pain she was in, ceased. Ceissi shone once again among the flames. I looked at her giant body until it turned into dust and perished completely. As with all magical beings of the realms, the magic of the dragon also returned to the Tree of Life with death. Now the sky was covered with golden ashes.

Audamar's gray eyes narrowed and he raised the white crystal to the sky. Protector Thalia's cries were covered by Audamar's laughter. He had won; he now had the fifth crystal.

I turned my gaze from him to the gate he had created. When he moved, I realized he was planning to leave. Audamar looked at me for a last time. I knew that he still needed me for the last two crystals but I was at the far end of the courtyard. He gazed at the crowded group of Protectors and Phoenixes standing between us. Reaching me would be more difficult than he thought.

Protector Thalia was still on her knees. She let out a cry and raised her hand. The bright light emitting from her hand found Audamar, who hadn't been expecting the strike. He brought his hand to his chest when the light hit his body, and he took a few steps back. His angry gray eyes turned to her, and then back to me. I waited for him to come for me but instead, he turned to the gate. He was going to flee.

The others seemed to have fallen apart with the defeat but I knew we had no time to lose. I couldn't let him get away another time. I stood with rage and began running to the bright gate. I was trying to reach the other end of the courtyard before it was too late. I gritted my teeth and tried to force my legs to go faster. Audamar's victory had been so concrete that I saw people step back as he walked. Fear had swathed the entire yard. I pushed the people away and tried to open a path for myself as I leaped over the dead bodies on the floor.

The First King stuck his arm into the gate and its transparent surface rippled. I was almost there. He seemed to have heard my footsteps, but the euphoria of his victory caused him to notice too late. He turned to me over his shoulder and his expression changed at once. I saw the surprise on his face, but I didn't stop. I jumped on him and we both tumbled into the gate with my weight.

Audamar had been caught completely off guard. I wrapped my hands around his throat and everything around us turned into a blur. If he caught me, we would be getting out of here together and I would be his prisoner once again. That was why I wouldn't be captured; not again. I couldn't let him get away.

I tightened my grip on his neck and before he could shake off the surprise, I held his hand and forced him to loosen his tightly clenched fist. The crystals began scattering into the gate and I quickly tried to reach for one of them.

Audamar's eyes opened wide as the smooth surface of Carran's purple crystal touched the tip of my fingers. The crystal started to shine and a blinding purple light filled the gate.

My body trembled with the magic emitting from the crystals, and Audamar and I both reeled in different directions.

# CHAPTER 40

I could hear the roaring of thunder. I breathed the salty smell of the sea. I parted my eyes and noticed the endless shore that was shadowed by dark clouds. At the end of the beach was a dense forest.

I put my hands on the wet sand under me and sat up with difficulty. I looked around as I tried to guess for how long I had been lying unconscious on the beach. My whole body was burning and I could imagine that it was because of the crystals. They had backlashed, causing a great amount of magic to be released. I remembered the bright light at the gate as I stumbled a few times before finally being able to stand up.

I turned around after looking at the long beach and the giant forest that surrounded the entire bay. The sky was gray and it was quite cold. All my clothes were wet with salty water. I tried to get rid of the wet sand that was stuck to me before wrapping my arms around my shivering body. I had to find a way out of here, and more importantly, I had to find out in which realm I was in.

I noticed the big black figure on one of the rocks along the shore. He was almost indistinguishable, but as soon as I saw him, I began walking to the pitch-black dragon.

My ears began chiming, and I thought I saw the blinding bright light again. I didn't even know to which realm the gate had brought me. I inhaled dismally with the feeling of helplessness. That was the problem. All the gates in realms had only one exit and they were created a long time ago, but this one was created by Audamar, something that should have been impossible to do.

The old dragon had settled on the rock with his head buried in his wings. He slowly parted his eyes and looked at me when he heard my footsteps. But Deegan stood still. I slowly climbed on the rock he had settled on and knelt beside him. Finally, I raised my hand and placed it on the dragon's forehead. Deegan slowly closed his eyes. I hadn't seen him for weeks, but he had found me now, guarding me until I woke up. My fingers caressed his thick skin.

The fact that I no longer had my powers hadn't broken my bond with him. I blinked as I thought of what had happened to Protector Thalia's dragon. Audamar had killed it; a single blow had been enough to kill the thousands-of-years-old dragon. It scared me to even think that the same thing could happen to Deegan.

The giant dragon suddenly opened his red eyes and looked back. Just then, the vision of someone else's memory appeared before my eyes.

I first saw Protector Emily. How the first Protector of Aerlion got the crystal and held it for the first time, how she walked through a place that reminded me of a part of the capital, very familiar but also very different, and how she glided in the sky on Deegan's back.

Then, other faces appeared. Although I didn't know any of them, I realized they were Aerlion's Protectors in the past. And finally, I saw Protector Breccan. I had seen the old Protector many times in my dreams but now, he was standing right in front of me. I saw him walk in the wide hallways of the palace, training the Phoenixes and talking to Balfour . . . I felt sad with the vision of the old commander. I looked at him with longing but the images darted in and out, changing all the time.

At first, I didn't understand why I was seeing these. While watching short memories from hundreds of different lives, I realized that it was Deegan who was showing me all. The old dragon had probably served hundreds of Protectors and he had been with them since the beginning.

I opened my eyes again and stared at the dragon. His gaze narrowed.

"You were trying to warn me," I whispered in surprise. "From the start . . . you were the one who showed me all those memories."

The pitch-black dragon blew his warm breath at me as my hand slid over his skin.

I had seen Breccan in my dreams, and Emily on the battlefield and with Audamar; I had thought it was Breccan who showed me all that. I thought he was trying to reach me somehow. But in fact, it had been Deegan all along. The old dragon had been trying to warn me.

I lowered my head and held on tighter to him. But Deegan began to move. He sniffed the air and looked around. I remembered that I had been together with Audamar at the gate and this could mean that we might have been thrown to the same place.

Deegan continued to squirm and I quickly turned around. I was suddenly surrounded by an eerie feeling, the same as the one I had felt when I sensed the presence of the crystals. I looked around at the beach, in search of the First King or any of his creatures. But as I continued to scan the bay, I noticed the bright light emitting through the sand. Fear left its place for curiosity. I left Deegan behind and began walking. I bent over and picked up the crystal that had been buried under the sands. The purple stone stopped shining as soon as I held it, and I stared at my palm in bewilderment. I had the crystal of Carran, of Protector Sam. It had probably been thrown here with me after what happened at the gate.

A big smile formed on my face as I held the crystal tighter, trying to be sure of its existence. This could change everything.

I knew I had to get back as soon as possible. We needed a new plan and we had to be quick. I took a big step toward the dragon, but then thoughts rushed to my mind. I froze.

We needed to destroy the crystals so Audamar wouldn't use them. That was what we—I—had promised Caiden. But as I was holding it right now, I knew I didn't want to turn my back on the gifts of the Goddess and lose this opportunity. The crystals could still be used for good.

Audamar may have fooled me with promises never to be kept, but this didn't change the fact that the crystals could still work. There was hunger and poverty all around the realms, and people were dying. I could actually make a difference, which the capital had failed to do. I could change the Seven Realms.

I looked at the purple crystal in my palm and held my breath. I knew I couldn't trust anyone. They would destroy it. The crystals were a threat to us, but at the same time, they could be our greatest advantage in this war. If I could only take them back . . .

Something changed inside of me. I was suddenly captivated by a selfish feeling and I realized I wanted to hide the crystals from *everyone*. I wasn't going to share this; they wouldn't understand, anyway. None of them would.

I slowly put the crystal into my pocket. The dragon fidgeted as I walked back to him. I knew he could sense the crystal as he fixed his red eyes on me. I slowly caressed his head as if trying to comfort him.

"This will be our little secret, Deegan," I whispered. "Together, we'll change the Seven Realms."

# CHAPTER 41

I went through the narrow door of the shelter and reached the common area where Caiden's crowded group of soldiers had gathered. My hand automatically went to my pocket, hoping that no one would sense the crystal I was hiding. When the dimly lit corridor finally ended, I looked around in the hall where low murmurs could be heard. I saw Hunter standing next to one of the round wooden tables and talking to the soldiers there. I headed toward him but a sudden sigh from behind caused me to turn around. Paige's wide eyes were looking at me with huge relief.

"Anna!"

All eyes turned to me when the healer girl shouted my name, and the whispering stopped immediately. Paige came to me with quick steps, almost running, and embraced me tightly.

"You're okay!" she said and held me by my shoulders as she took a step back to look at my face. "You're alive! I can't believe it! We were so worried about you! Layla told us you'd gone to the forest but no one knew where you were. We thought you were caught. And then . . ."

Paige paused and examined my face. She then opened her eyes wide and ran her fingers through my hair. "Anna . . ."

"Paige, I'm fine. Really. You don't need to worry about me."

She pressed her lips together and covered her mouth with her hand, trying to be quiet.

Her voice had been heard by everyone, even those who hadn't been looking at us before. I could see a crowd slowly gathering around us. I saw a few familiar faces among the soldiers. As Caiden and Hunter walked over, everyone stepped to the side and made way for them. I noticed Lord Cyril following behind.

Hunter was the first to speak. "Are you all right?" His green eyes scanned me with worry but he was keeping distance between us. Yet I had seen his face; he looked worried. "Are you hurt?"

340

I shook my head and said, "There are things I need to tell you. A lot has happened. Protector Thalia caught me and I saw the Protectors at the palace. Bria is really working with Rogue . . . He was after Thalia's crystal and Protector Edmond is imprisoned at the castle. And, Thalia . . ."

"Slow down," Caiden interrupted me as he crossed his arms. "You've been gone for days."

He eyed me from head to toe. I could imagine how horrible I looked. Someone who had not showered or changed her clothes for days couldn't look nice, nor smell good either. And I was also carrying the scars of the battle.

"There's no time to rest." I remembered how Audamar found Thalia's crystal and quickly shook my head. My eyes searched for Darrell or Thomas inside. "We have to plan something *now.*"

"Where is she?"

I heard a familiar voice and when I turned around, I saw King Warren pushing the soldiers aside to make way. A strange feeling rose in my chest. The worried look on his face was definitely the last thing I was expecting. I kept my eyes on him and watched him walk over. He shouldered Hunter aside and stood between him and me. Warren ignored Hunter's gaze on his back. I was caught completely off guard when he suddenly held me in his arms.

The puzzled expression on my face became more evident and the crowd was no different. When I looked over his shoulder, I saw Hunter's gaze on us. Although everyone there was watching us, Warren didn't loosen his embrace even a little bit.

I shyly raised my arms and hugged him back, hesitantly. My cheeks blushed with all the people watching us, but I shut my eyes for a brief moment and tried to forget about everyone else. It was just him and I for that moment. I found a short-lasting peace in his arms.

I filled my lungs with a timid breath. Even in a crowd, it felt as if it was just us. I slowly parted my lips and said, "He took the fifth crystal. We lost, Warren."

I heard the king let out his breath. He pressed my head on his chest with one hand. "Nothing is over. Not yet."

I felt an urge to remain like this with him, in his arms, but I knew we couldn't. I slowly freed myself from his embrace. Warren looked at me and did the same thing Paige had done; ran his fingers through my blonde hair. I blinked as his fingertips brushed over my cheek. Where he touched burned.

He gently held a few locks of hair and said, "Your hair . . ." but he didn't go on.

I took another step away from him, hoping that this would be enough to put distance between us.

Hunter softly cleared his throat and drew the attention back to himself. I looked at him with gratitude. "Well, I think we'd better listen to the rest of the story now."

The crowd began to disperse slowly after his words. But I could still hear the whispers. As Hunter and Caiden turned around to head to the back rooms of our shelter, Warren looked at me. I turned away in embarrassment.

Hunter glanced at me over his shoulder. I tried to shake off the effects of the unexpected welcome I had received and hurried after him without wasting any more time. But as I walked away, I could still feel the king's gaze on my back.

•

Lord Cyril and I were silent as we walked side by side in the shelter's narrow hallway. The old lord hadn't made an attempt to say anything, and I had no idea how to start the conversation. He was too calm, and his calmness was getting on my nerves.

I slowly cleared my throat. "King Warren looks fine. It seems like whatever Audamar did to him with the crystal has lost its effect."

"Unfortunately," said Lord Cyril as he looked at me. The way he had begun his words caused an ache in my chest. "Since we don't know what Rogue has done to him, we can't treat him."

"You don't know? But the king looks like his usual self," I said.

"The magic is shaped by the thoughts of the crystal's owner and no one else can understand how they work. They are like unsolvable riddles. I tried everything I know but I couldn't enter his mind as Rogue did."

"So, does this mean he'll never go back to normal?"

I saw Lord Cyril eye at me. Then he cleared his throat loudly and waited for a moment before starting his words.

"Warren's anger is completely focused on revenge. What Rogue did with the crystals was to strengthen his emotions, *all* of them. He was burning with the desire for vengeance and rage even before, and Audamar knew he could use that."

Lord Cyril looked away. "Warren needed another emotion he could hold on to; something to clear his head and keep it elsewhere. Even if he can't be as before, he needs to forget his rage, focus on something else. I helped him find his way while you were away."

I stopped walking. "What you're trying to say is . . ."

"I directed his feelings to something else, to *someone*. You shouldn't have any questions on your mind after seeing how he treated you today."

Lord Cyril had just said that he had given King Warren another emotion to focus on, other than revenge and rage. Was he talking about *me*? I thought of my relationship with the king and I wanted to tell Lord Cyril that it wasn't what he thought it was, but Lord Cyril put his hand on my shoulder.

"Anna," he said and I flinched at his touch. I turned to his dark eyes. "It is very dangerous for Warren to go after Rogue. He can't stand up to him. You have to distract him away from those thoughts. Confuse him, make sure he is under control. Lie to him if you have to, but make sure you're playing your part right."

"I can't do such a thing," I protested, but the old lord hurried with his words.

"Love is a very strong emotion, even more than rage or vengeance. It would make him stay here rather than lose you. You're the only one here who can prevent him from going after Rogue."

"You don't understand. Warren and I . . ."

He cut my words. "I've known Warren since his birth. I know what I saw in his eyes and I am not talking about the dark magic Audamar used on him. Soon, you will notice that as well."

"You are mistaken," I said. "I cannot do anything to him to make him stay."

Lord Cyril's lips became a straight line. "He is angrier," he said slowly. I sensed the sadness in his voice and realized that he really was worried about him. "And he is taking his power from his rage."

I stopped walking. "What power?" I asked, confused.

I waited for an answer but Lord Cyril only shook his head and slowly drew back. He looked at me one last time before walking away and leaving me there behind.

# CHAPTER 42

I knocked on the door once, and without waiting for an answer, I took a step into the small room. My gaze immediately met with Warren's.

"Hey," I said slowly. "I wanted to see how you were doing."

"I feel better now. I guess I owe that to Lord Cyril."

But the old lord hadn't cured him. In fact, he had made things worse and I had found myself right in the middle of it. I kept quiet.

"What Audamar did to you . . ." I began and let out an angry breath.

"It was a gift."

I froze and turned to him as my eyes grew wide with shock. "What are you even talking about?"

"Rogue gave me a gift, Anna. A power to destroy my enemies."

"Warren," I said as I leaned over. I was worried, and his words proved how right I was. Something was seriously wrong, and it reminded me of the way he had spoken in the castle after Audamar used the crystals on him.

Warren turned his hand toward the ceiling, and a blood-chilling feeling covered me. I watched the shadows curling around his arm. I could feel the weak magic coming from him but it wasn't like anything I had seen before; it wasn't the magic the Protectors used. It was the opposite of what we had, and it felt just like the times when the Old Ones appeared. It was dark magic.

"I thought only the Goddess could give magic to people," I whispered in shock.

He only shrugged. "So did I."

Warren was smiling slightly as I looked back at his palm. It was the power Lord Cyril had been talking about. It made me worried. Rogue had plans for Warren, just like he did for all of us, and I knew he wouldn't just give powers to him. I had a bad feeling about it.

"Warren . . ." I began.

"Don't worry. I am not him. It's just . . . I feel more powerful now. And brave. I feel like I can do *anything*."

When Audamar had used the crystals, he had said exactly the same thing. *A gift*. I didn't know how powerful their effect could be but I was scared to test that. Warren was his enemy; what he did couldn't be good. The Master of Darkness knew we were with the rebellion; maybe that was his purpose. A king that bows to no one. Warren would never agree to work with the rebellion, and that was exactly what Audamar wanted: chaos. For Warren, I knew rebellion was a threat equal to Rogue. Or maybe greater.

"I wanted to thank you," I began slowly, but the king didn't turn to look at me this time. "No one knows the palace better than you do. I know you came up with a plan with Darrell. You saved me, Warren."

From the corner of my eye, I saw him nod. He murmured something but it was too low for me to hear. I looked inside the room for a while to linger around. Then I bit my lips and helplessly sat at the edge of the bed. I wanted to keep the conversation going but I didn't know what to say. I felt like the thing between us—whatever it was— had become worse than before.

The king turned to me when the bed sank with my weight. I fixed my gaze on the candle burning on the table. Its light wasn't enough for the tiny room but Warren was spending only a small amount of time here during his stay at the shelter anyway.

"I'm sorry for not being able to reach out to you earlier. We were waiting for the right time to attack."

I rubbed my wrists as if the chains were still there and let out a short breath.

"I thought I'd never make it out of there. I thought of the time I could spend in that cell; it could have been hundreds of years." I softly smiled before going on. "I used to fear time passing quickly because I didn't want to part with my family. But the only thing I could think of in the cell was death . . . and that means a long time for a Protector."

I tried to laugh but it was lacking joy, and Warren noticed this. I could feel his dark eyes on me as I continued. "Protector Edmond isn't a cellmate I could talk to about such things."

The expression on my face diminished when I thought of Edmond, whom I had last seen in the dungeons. Had he made it out? Had Darrell found him? I had returned to the shelter after Deegan found me, without even thinking about the others.

"But I was still hopeful," I continued. "I thought I was safe when Protector Edmond came; when Thomas told me Darrell had gotten the castle. I actually thought I could escape from Audamar."

"*Hope* . . ." I saw him smile. "No matter how magical we are, a part of us is still human."

"And that is the part Audamar can easily rip from me," I said as I watched the flames burn. "I'm scared to change. We lost many soldiers and I am scared to get used to that thought. I don't want to watch people die because of or for me."

"Those deaths won't mean anything," he said and the coldness in his voice made me shiver. But I knew he was right. "With each defeat, we are losing more."

And that was the exact reason why I needed to use the crystal . . .

"I was worried for you," he said and let out his breath. I quickly looked away.

"We've been together from the start, Anna. I could sacrifice everyone else but you aren't one of them. You were long gone when I woke up and I didn't know what to do. If I were there . . ." he raised his head and stared into my eyes. "I would have come for you, no matter what."

"I thought you trusted no one," I whispered. But then I saw how serious he was. He shook his head.

"I guess something has changed."

I kept on fidgeting with my hands on my lap. I had to try hard not to run away from this awkward conversation we were having. "I'm glad you're well, Warren," I said finally.

The expression on his face slowly changed. He looked like he wanted to say something, but instead, he just turned to me with indecisive eyes. We were too close. Our arms almost touched as we sat side by side on the bed.

One side of me regretted taking Lord Cyril's advice and confusing the king's mind by drawing his feelings elsewhere. That was what I was doing right now, wasn't it? Even though I wasn't sure what Warren was thinking; my heart was pounding nonsensically fast.

I needed to convince him to stay. Not focus on his anger, but to think about something else. *Someone* else.

I brushed through my hair with my fingers and Warren leaned forward. I tried to draw back. He held a few locks of hair on the right side and the golden locks slid through his fingers.

"Is there something wrong with my hair?" I asked. I was curious after Paige's reaction. The king raised his eyebrows and looked at my hair.

"Only a few silver strands."

"What?" I immediately held my hair and tried to see what he was talking about.

"A part of your hair has turned silver."

King Warren began looking around the room like he was searching for something. Finally, he handed me a mirror.

As he leaned over, I saw that his neck-length hair was short now. We hadn't had the time to take care of ourselves while on the run, and apparently, this had been one of the first things Warren had done after waking up. I thought of Audamar's curly hair. Maybe that was why Warren had cut his hair short; he wanted to look different from him.

I snatched the mirror from his hand and looked at my reflection. A few locks of hair on my right side had turned near-silver gray indeed, and that explained Paige and Warren's reaction.

The king crossed his arms, and I saw his lips curve upward. "It suits you."

I shook my head. "It must have happened at the gate."

I remembered how the crystals had scattered into the gate when I jumped in after Audamar, and how their magic had struck me. It wasn't going to be easy to forget the pain.

"You are brave," I heard him say.

I shook my head. "No, I'm not."

He ignored me. "You are. No one else could have jumped into the gate after the most feared man in the Seven Realms, especially not after Audamar defeated us once again. The others stayed back, but you didn't. You're different, Anna. That's why you'll be the one to save us."

I was quick to shake my head. "I'm not a leader."

"For now. But I know you'll become one; *everyone* does."

I wanted to protest and tell Warren that I wasn't the savior everyone was waiting for, but an uproar from the shelter caused this discussion to be left for another time.

I jumped at the loud voice that came from outside the quarters and we both drew back at the same time. My eyes turned to the door and I hurried out without waiting for Warren to follow.

The hallway was full of soldiers. I began pushing them aside to make way for myself in the direction where everyone else was headed. I could see the crowd gathered in a circle in the common area. After shoving the final two men from in front of me, I reached the front of the line and looked at the group of people ahead. Six pairs of eyes turned to me.

I first saw Protector Darrell. He was looking at me with a confident smile on his face. He nodded when our eyes met and turned to the others next to him. Protector Sam was looking around with questioning eyes, and Ramona was right next to him, barely able to stand upright. Protector Leon was on the other side, and Protector Thalia was standing tall next to him, despite her eyes being swollen with tears.

I walked over to them. Although there was only one reason why Darrell was with them, I still felt uneasy. After all, it had been the Protectors who had put me in that cell in the first place.

I felt Warren's presence by my side. He stood a few feet away and crossed his arms.

The Protectors looked at the king; I knew that they were frightened or confused after what had happened with Audamar. Lord Cyril walked over with slow steps and the crowd parted as he walked through. Lord Cyril confidently stepped to the other side of the king and placed his hand on his shoulder, putting an end to the questions on everyone's mind.

Finally, Protector Edmond came out from behind Darrell and took a few faltering steps toward us. I exhaled with the relief I felt when I saw that he was safe. Our eyes met, and the old Protector looked at me as he grinned.

# CHAPTER 43

The silhouettes gathered around the oval table were lit by the light from a single candle. I could feel the tension in the half-dark room. Eight pairs of eyes searched inside. The king took a step toward the table and we all turned to him. Warren slowly placed his palms on the table as we all waited impatiently for the words to come out of his lips.

"There's only two left," Warren said as he inhaled nervously. "Two crystals of the Goddess. If Rogue finds them, the Protectors will not be enough to stop him this time."

All eyes turned slowly to Protector Edmond and Leon, who were standing right across from me. Audamar wouldn't stop until he had Belwald's and Nadeer's crystals, and this meant that both Edmond and Leon were in danger.

Darrell suddenly turned to me with a worried expression on his face. "You're not safe either, Anna. Rogue still wants the crystals. You're his only connection with them; he'll come after you."

Protector Thalia was quick to respond. "And we'll be there to protect you," she said as she determinedly looked at me. I knew that a part of her was burning with vengeance and there was no hesitation in her voice. I forced myself not to look away when I thought that she had been advocating for my execution just a short while earlier.

I was more vulnerable than the other Protectors because I didn't have my powers. I knew Audamar would come after me, but I also had a secret that I kept to myself. Audamar was going to come after me either way because he wanted the crystal I had stolen from him. I hadn't said a single word to anyone about this. I was determined; I would use the crystals for the Seven Realms, and I wasn't about to share my victory with anyone. I couldn't trust them, not on this matter.

"The Protectors have served the Seven Realms and the kingdom for centuries. However, we are now at war and I don't need servants. I need warriors."

The memory of our conversation with Protector Sam in Belwald was still fresh. He had said that the Protectors, who had once been chosen to fight the dark magic, were now quite useless. We had become too lazy to leave the luxury of the palace. But things had to change now. After a very long time, the Seven Realms needed their Protectors once again.

A few murmurs of approval rose from the small group, and in contrast with the others, I turned to King Warren in silence.

"Protectors," said King Warren as he looked at each of us with his eyes that had become darker in the dim room. Then he added, "Guardians of the Seven Realms."

King Warren roughly put his hand on the table, "War is very close now. And the fate of the Seven Realms is in your hands."

He raised his gaze to mine only to realize I had already been looking at him. I nodded in determination, as did the others. The words that the king had said just a couple of hours ago were still ringing in my ears. He had said that I was the savior people were waiting for, that I would be the leader who would take down Audamar. I just couldn't believe that yet. Not after everything I'd done.

His words still felt meaningless. But as Warren continued to look at me without breaking eye contact, it felt as if we were alone again, despite all the people in the room. And under the king's determined gaze, I realized how much he believed in his words, and in me.

# PLAYLIST:

Aeralie Brighton – Unbroken

AURORA – A Dangerous Thing

AURORA – A Temporary High

BrunuhVille – Angel of War

BrunuhVille – The Last of His Name

Egzod, Maestro Chives & Neoni – Royalty

Ellery Bonham – Burning House (feat. Aaron Krause)

Generdyn – Chosen (feat. Svrcina)

Hidden Citizens – Hold On To Me (feat. Svrcina)

Hidden Citizens – I Follow (feat. Katie Herzig)

Hidden Citizens – Unstoppable (feat. Rånya)

Iliya Zaki – Glass Shard

Lauren Aquilina – King

Nadiiife – The Valley

Oh Wonder – Technicolour Beat

Oh Wonder – White Blood

Pim Stones – We Have It All

Rånya & Hidden Citizens – Strange Young World

SLO – Shut Out of Paradise

Tommee Profitt – Remembrance (feat. Fleurie)

Tommee Profitt – Tomorrow We Fight (feat. Svrcina)

Ursine Vulpine & Annaca – Without You (Extended)

Vera Blue – Fingertips

Zayde Wølf – Walk Through the Fire (feat. Ruelle)

# ACKNOWLEDGMENTS

Being a writer has always been my dream. I started writing my first story when I was eleven years old, and even though I never completed it, it made me realize how much I enjoyed storytelling.

For the past ten years, I dreamed of sharing my stories with readers. I started writing *The Seventh Protector* in 2018, without any plan to publish. But as I continued writing, I realized this was what I wanted to do. Now, as a twenty-one-year-old author, I am glad I made that decision.

This journey wasn't an easy one but it was fun, and it would've been impossible to do without all the support.

To my editor, Amie Norris. I wouldn't be able to publish this book without her. At first, self-publishing seemed really scary, but she was extremely prompt and professional, going beyond what I expected and I am so glad I had the opportunity to work with her. Amie helped me by not just editing the manuscript, but also guiding me during the whole process, focusing on every single detail, embracing the manuscript as if it was hers, showing me my mistakes, and coming up with suggestions every single time to make the final version better than the one before.

To the Ebook Launch team for this amazing cover. It couldn't be more perfect.

To my mother, for always encouraging me to continue writing even when I felt like giving up. She taught me how to fall in love with reading, and bought all the books I asked from her growing up. I owe my passion and love for literature to her.

To my twin sister, for listening my ideas and for her unwavering support.

To my family, my father and my grandparents, for their love.

And finally, to anyone who read or even thought about reading *The Seventh Protector*.

Thank you for making my dream come true.

Printed in the USA
CPSIA information can be obtained
at www.ICGtesting.com
CBHW071521050924
14051CB00011B/367